"Deftly weaving the threads *of her previous novels into a tapestry all*
its own, . . . part fantasy adventure, part dark fairytale, and all sharp
teeth as the latest of her bright, fierce heroines is forced to grapple with
the bonds of family, legacy, and love in order to save her world."
Genevieve Gornichec, author of *The Witch's Heart*
and *The Weaver and the Witch Queen*

"A rich and decadent world where mystery waits around every
bend, and darkness lurks just beneath the surface. Dark family
secrets abound in a perfect blend of Gothic and fairy-tale
fiction – Slatter knocks it out of the park once again."
A.C. Wise, author of *Wendy, Darling* and *Hooked*

"Angela Slatter continues to tantalise us with a further glimpse into
her intricate and thrilling world of interconnected tales. Another
beguiling tale from an author at the height of her powers."
Lucy Holland, author of *Sistersong* and *Song of the Huntress*

"A.G. Slatter has a unique gift for balancing light and dark in the
fairy-tale gothic. The result is a deliciously sinister fantasy world, with
vampire-slaying heroines to rival Buffy, witches who pay a bloody price
for their magic, and heiresses who uncover secrets lurking in their
family trees – but it's also a world so full of unexpected cosiness, warmth
and delight that every Halloween lover will want to curl up in it."
Ally Wilkes, author of *All the White Spaces* and *Where the Dead Wait*

"*The Crimson Road* delivers heart-pounding gothic adventure,
a glittering world of mystery and menace, and a formidable heroine."
Stephanie Feldman, author of *Saturnalia*

"I adored returning to Angela Slatter's Sourdough world. Violet's journey to
the mysterious Darklands revealed some delightfully familiar faces, as well as
some truly frightening new ones. A tale filled with adventure, danger, loyalty,
love and family secrets – readers will love sinking their teeth into this one!"
Kell Woods, author of *After the Forest* and *Upon a Starlit Tide*

Also from A.G. Slatter and Titan Books

ALL THE MURMURING BONES
THE PATH OF THORNS
THE BRIAR BOOK OF THE DEAD

THE CRIMSON ROAD

A.G. SLATTER

TITAN BOOKS

The Crimson Road
Print edition ISBN: 9781803364568
E-book edition ISBN: 9781803364575

Published by Titan Books
A division of Titan Publishing Group Ltd
144 Southwark Street, London SE1 0UP
www.titanbooks.com

First edition: February 2025
10 9 8 7 6 5 4 3 2 1

A CIP catalogue record for this title is available from the British Library.

Printed and bound by CPI Group (UK) Ltd,
Croydon CR0 4YY.

To my niece Meghan May, to paraphrase Gandalf:
A family, like a wizard, is never late, but always
arrives when we most need it. It's an absolute
privilege to have you in my life.

Up, up, up.

No, further north.

A little more north.

There!

You see?

That tiny part of the map? Not entirely snow and ice, but the summers are short and spring lasts no more'n a day or two. Nights are long and that's how they like it.

A little nation it is, barely a county but oh-so-significant. Dangerous. Some small towns, mostly villages set around the estates. A few cities – those that have managed to grow despite the nature of their overlords. Some know the value of carefully husbanding resources. Others are more… voracious.

Cities, yes. Like Caulder – or Calder, depending upon your origins and education – or The Spire or Fredegund's Ruin. Vibrant places, industrious and industrial. Then there's The Bowery and St Xenia by the Tower – neither of which you wish to see. Both are slaver cities, where human cattle are bought and sold, as serfs and food.

But the place that concerns you, Violet?

Here. It's barely marked – just that tiny x – faded now, this is an old map stuck in these pages. This is the spot.

Anchor-hold.

The Anchorhold.

Where, it's whispered, it all began.

Where it will all end.

[FROM THE JOURNAL NOTES OF HEDREK ZENNOR, GENTLEMAN OF ST SINWIN'S, WRITTEN TO HIS DAUGHTER AT THE HEIGHT OF HIS FINAL FEVER]

1

The pillow feels solid, weighty, like it can do damage.

My own hands, clawed around it, are age-spotted and thin. I think, *This can't be right*, then the thought leaves my mind and I'm back to the task, grip so tight I can feel each thread in the cambric pillowcase, every delicate structure in the feather stuffing. Standing, looming, my thighs pressed against the mattress, my talons descending.

The pillow over my father's face, obscuring his withered features, hollow cheeks and eyes, the greying stubble, the lips canyoned by desiccation, the hair still surprisingly thick and mostly honey-coloured. Some days I forget he was only nineteen when he sired me, hardly a man. Over forty now, but looking twenty years beyond that. And in this moment, this second, moving, moving more than he has these past weeks, surprisingly strong, the wriggles, the jerks, heels drumming the bed, nails tearing at me or trying to but unable to get past this fluffy, fluffy pillow. The noises, not quite loud enough for anyone to hear, not even Mrs Medway were she to traverse the corridor of the second floor of our house. I push down harder and harder, feel his struggles lessen,

9

become shudders then tremors, the muffled protests, dying away until there's no longer any indication of life.

A sense of relief shoots through me like fresh blood – and I wake with a start.

Still in the chair beside Father's sickbed, the distance between us several yards, the same as when I went to sleep. No disarrayed bedsheets. No pillow in my hands, hands that are nothing like those in the dream; these are white and plump, unblemished by anything except some few small scars where I've been careless with weapons in training. Breathing fast, heartbeat staccato. My neck and back are stiff from dozing upright, the book I was reading lies on the floor – was its hitting the polished wood what woke me? Perhaps not. Perhaps there was no sound at all.

I glance to the bed again, the hangings removed from its four-posted glory some days ago when my father shouted that they smothered him. It's bare but for the form lying in the middle of the mattress. Nothing out of place, no sign of a struggle.

But Hedrek Zennor no longer breathes.

* * *

My father's death came as a surprise only in the time it took to occur.

He'd been ill in varying degrees for years; indeed, I can barely remember a time when he wasn't ailing. His survival was the thing to make folk remark; they didn't know what burned inside of him. I did not help him along even though there were days I yearned to do so. Lady Death put her gentle hand on him with no aid from me. That I dreamed his death, my own responsibility for it, was mere coincidence. Yet I can't help but feel something's lodged in my bones, some coldness carried by the violence of my hatred for him, that I would dream of bringing his end.

Or perhaps it's merely the chill of the day, unseasonal for this part of spring. Or perhaps it's the heavy rain sweeping across the cemetery lawn down the slope that leads to the cliff, water cascading over the edge and into the misery-wracked sea. Most of the other mourners (quite the number but generally stickybeaks and look-sees) have given up, leaving immediately after the service in St Sinwin's cathedral. Only a small band of diehards remain: those of us with no choice and those who think they'll benefit from staying.

Despite the enormity of the Zennor fortune, my father has been laid to rest in a slim grey mausoleum where my mother has waited all these years. A simple final place. The cathedral is a magnificent thing, the entire wall behind the altar made of stained glass (a glory, a true wonder) but its uniqueness doesn't really allow for anyone to be buried in its walls lest the vibrations cause fractures. And the crypt beneath the flagstone floor is reserved for ecclesiastics. We've not been a rich family long enough to justify anything larger, although I'm sure Father would have had one built, had there been more years left to him; Hedrek Zennor, despite his illnesses, didn't think death would come for him quite yet. He had other matters on his mind. And I? I lack the inclination to raise a greater memorial than currently exists.

Bishop Walter looks like a wet, bald raptor, raindrops sluicing the few remaining hairs on his head down towards his collar. His purple silk robe, embroidered with gold and silver, studded with gems along the ermine collar, is soaked, a cat dropped in a well. Not a one of his attendants has an umbrella over him or themselves, either a dearth of planning or the belief that nothing should come between this last office and the Lord Above. Walter's voice, which is a deep baritone and rather fine for sermons and psalms, quavers with the cold.

'We commit the last remnants of Hedrek Zennor to this sacred earth. He will find himself in the Halls of the Lord and be welcomed by His mercy. Remember him in your prayers, and now you may all go in peace.'

Beside me Mrs Medway, more prepared than a legion of god-hounds, holds an umbrella above us both, a very large one, that keeps trying to catch the wind and fly away. My housekeeper is determined, though, and I'd not bet against her even in a contest with the elements. She's got her other hand around my arm; I know it's for comfort, but a voice in my head claims it's for ballast, to hold her down. Around us are gathered, in no particular order of favour or otherwise, Junius Quant (banker), Titus Pendergast (solicitor), Talwyn Enys (the Harbour Mistress), Jack Seven-Gates (my childhood friend, once a source of comfort), six bedraggled god-hounds, and three other men whose names I cannot recall but are likely to present themselves at some inopportune moment as potential future husbands. Women are not fool enough to stand in the rain on a day such as this, and I've no doubt several will pay visits at my home in the weeks to come. A groundskeeper, grizzled and impatient, awaits our departure.

Mr Pendergast raises his feathery grey eyebrows in my direction and I nod wearily. *Yes, yes, I know.* He moves off, sharing an umbrella with Quant; Talwyn pats my shoulder as she passes and my knees almost buckle with the heft of her hand; Walter and his protégés follow suit to make their way back towards the sprawling white-painted rectory that sits alongside the cathedral. I watch them all go, then return my attention to the mausoleum as the groundskeeper closes the burnished copper doors. I don't know what I'm expecting: an apology echoing out the narrowing gap, perhaps. From my father for his treatment of me, from my mother for leaving me with him.

Instead, there's Jack's voice, saying my name. 'Violet. Violet. Are you—'

I nod, dragging my gaze away from the now-closed doors, the groundsman putting the key in my gloved palm, and notice how very well-dressed Jack is. He's always loved clothes, but these seem even more elegant than usual, albeit standard grief-stricken black. 'Yes, Jack. I'm well enough.'

He grips my hand, looks at me sadly. 'I do have to go, Violet, Mother will—'

'Of course. Thank you for coming.' I sound so formal, try to fix that: 'Come by later, Jack? Tomorrow?'

'I'll try,' he says. 'I'm so sorry, Violet.'

I hope he'll succeed; I'd welcome the chance to chat or even sit in companionable silence. He turns away, hat held down over his auburn curls, charcoal umbrella flapping, and trudges to the lychgate of the churchyard, thence to the cobbled streets that will take him into town, back to his mansion, newly purchased to replace the one that burned down just gone two years ago.

'Well now, my girl. It's just us.' Mrs Medway squeezes my arm, speaks gently.

'Yes.' *Just us.* All the other staff dismissed, with excellent bonuses and references, not because they'd done anything wrong but because they were my father's choices. Mrs Medway said not to hurry about getting anyone because the beekie – the little hearth hobgoblin – would take care of things for the moment.

All the cleaning done as long as he's properly compensated with extra milk and bread left out each night and a glass of rum on holydays. I've never seen him (though gods know I would sneak down and try as a child until Mrs M caught me and told me if he's seen he'll depart and take all our luck with him – or worse, become destructive. My mother would tell me tales too, of how the only way to calm one down, perhaps keep him from leaving, was to give him whatever was in your pocket.). When there are new servants, he'll go back to just doing the small things, like stacking the firewood, collecting the cream off the milk, churning the butter, but he'll need to be told there are new folk coming, that there's no harm in it, no criticism or complaint. That they're here to help him.

As I think about the empty house I feel something lift from me. The weight of my father and the life he put me through. The constant study and training, the tests physical and mental, the sense that no matter what I did it was never good enough. Hedrek Zennor's gone, and I will have a life that I choose. I will refuse his plans, his wishes. And there's not a thing he can do about it.

Pulling the fob watch from my pocket to check the time – almost six – I sweep the bone orchard with one last stare. Then I turn my back on the mausoleum, and drag Mrs Medway along until she matches my stride. She'll be anxious to check on her birds in their dovecot, make sure they're settled before night proper closes in.

The light is fading as we leave the churchyard – a late funeral for Hedrek – and at first I don't see the figure at the gate. When I do, I think for a moment it's Jack or one of the others, doubled back, but it becomes quickly obvious that it's not. A man in a long, dirty cloak, face obscured by a scarf, but the knife in his hand very clear even in the dusk. He lunges at us – at me – and Mrs Medway knows what to do.

She steps away, gives me room to move. I bring my hand down and grab the man's wrist, pulling it and the knife past me, tightening my grip and digging into the pressure points. The man curses and drops the blade. Twisting, I try to knee him in the groin, but he jerks aside and I make contact with his thigh, which is effective enough. He grunts and staggers, then limp-runs out the gate. He rights himself and gives me one last look, calculated despite the harm I've done him, then spins to bolt away. I scoop up the dagger from the ground and throw it. It hits the target just as he's about to round a corner – there's a thud and a bleat. My aim's not as good as I'd like because it gets him high in the shoulder and he keeps going, disappears just as the sun drops. Perhaps he'll crawl off and die somewhere. I'm disinclined to go after him.

'Gods!' shouts Mrs Medway. 'Those thieves are bold. Can't a body bury their family without being attacked? That Constable's not earning his money – they're getting worse.'

'He didn't fight like a footpad, Mrs M. Fought like a soldier.'

'That sort return from wars and become thieves too. Not all are heroes.' She gives me a once-over, nods approvingly. 'Not a sweat broken, not a hair out of place. Your father would be proud, Miss Violet.'

Those aren't words I'm longing to hear from anyone, and I know they're untrue. Hedrek would somehow know that my knees are shaking beneath my plain ebony skirts, that the adrenaline's leaving me as fast as it arrived, and I'd like to be already collapsed in front of the fire with a glass of winter-lemon whiskey or buttered port rather than negotiating a path home beneath the dancing flames of the streetlights.

'That's as may be, but I've had enough for one day. When we get home, send a message to Mr Pendergast and tell him I'll not be attending at his practice this evening. He'll see me first thing in the morning, whether he likes it or not.'

Mrs Medway knows better than to contradict me, and she's got no love for my father's friends; nor for my father, but I think she stayed all those years because of me. She contents herself with saying, 'You showed him,' and I'm not sure if she means Titus Pendergast or the would-be robber. There is a satisfaction, in spite of everything, at having prevailed. Still and all, I'm cautious as a cat while we make our way from the cemetery, pausing at the mouths of alleys and avoiding unlit cut-throughs.

2

St Sinwin's is a sloping sort of town; built on a hillside that feeds down to the harbour, the entire place has a vague air of sliding into the sea. Locations like the port-city of Breakwater are flatter, the surrounding hills gentler. But we cling here nevertheless, a determined mix of fisherfolk, sailors, merchants, sea captains and the occasional 'retired' pirate (once they were all gone, hunted to near-extinction, but some hardy types are taking back to the old ways), families rich and poor, the god-hounds, thieves and bankers, doctors and lawyers, craftsfolk. It's pretty: buildings painted white and blue, the occasional pink, although those closer to the docks are faded, often in disrepair. Higher up, are the mansions of stone and imported exotic wood, a curve of them almost like a battlement in case of attack. Most of the cobbled streets wind back and forth to combat the worst effects of gravity – no one wants a goods cart or fine carriage careening off and collecting who-knows-how-many lives on its way.

The inhabitants are a canny lot, figuring out the shortest, smoothest ways to get wherever they're going – not lazy, no, but practical – and there's a brigade of muscular lads and lasses who carry palanquins up and down for those with coin to spare. There are five main 'spokes' that lead from the city gates above, all the way down to the maritime heart of our town; wooden benches are set at convenient rest points for visitors and the elderly. Lots along these major arteries are highly sought after for businesses wanting visibility. Running between the spokes is a network of thoroughfares of varying width, popularity and usage; mostly residential. I suspect it was all meant to form a tidy grid system, but urban planning seldom survives encounters with people's desires for bigger houses or smaller, combining structures to create warehouses, splitting others up for tenements, inserting gardens for contemplation and seduction, sinking wells and ornamental ponds.

Pendergast & Associates is roughly halfway up or halfway down, depending on your perspective, and has a clear view to the waters of the harbour, the ships moored there and all the busy little ants rushing hither and yon loading and unloading, clattering across the docks, swaying along gangways, swarming up rigging. It's a well-respected establishment, three solicitors, one of whom is Mr Pendergast's daughter, the other his son-in-law. The rooms are surprisingly light and airy, quite ruining the expectation that a legal office should be gloomy and dust-ridden. None of that means it's a pleasure to visit, and I've spent many hours of my life here learning about contracts and crime as part of my very specific educational curriculum as defined by Father. When Father came into his fortune some thirteen years ago and found himself in need of legal guidance, none of the fancier firms would take his business. Walter (a mere deacon then) referred him to Titus, who tends to any finances the now-bishop doesn't want known to the Church.

I've known Titus Pendergast, Esq., more than half my life and he and Walter were always kinder than my father, insistent but not cruel, or not excessively, so you'd think he might have had some inkling about my feelings, might have expected my reaction to his reading of the will. Yet Titus, who is now staring across his desk at me and saying, 'But, Violet, you must,' apparently did not.

'But I shan't. My father controlled me in life, he will not continue to do so in death.' It's all I can do not to grind my teeth.

'You really must, Violet.' He leans forward, elbows on the desktop, fingers clasping each other in a desperate steeple. 'This was the mission he set for you, for which he ensured you were trained. There's so much at stake. Your father was very determined.'

'My father was very determined, certainly. He was also manic and obsessive, driven by demons and haunted by phantoms. We're both aware, Titus, he was not well in his mind.' I lean forward in the uncomfortable leather seat, tap on the blotter pad with a sharp pink nail. 'There are Leech Lords, yes. But they are confined in the Darklands. They cannot get out. There is a border and it is *held*.'

He makes a gesture which says he concedes the point. 'But he intended—'

'Wasn't it enough? What he did to me? Haven't I suffered enough pain and anguish? Do you really think I am going to undertake a journey to the north, find the Anchorhold, find my brother – his corpse! – and then what?'

The sunlight from the window shines down on his silver fluff of hair and highlights the beads of sweat on his brow. I slump back into my chair.

'Violet, there is more than you—'

'I wish to know nothing more! I repeat, Titus: my father controlled my life. He's not going to continue to do so in death.'

'Violet, it is critical. There's too much at stake for you to be childish about—'

My voice thins to a stiletto blade: 'It's preposterous, what he wants. All his mad fancies trying to bind me from beyond the grave. And you should be ashamed to be helping!'

And he does hang his head.

'Then I believe we are done, Mr Pendergast.'

'But—'

I raise a finger.

'We. Are. Done.' I rise, rearrange my long black mourning skirts (embellished with jet beads), straighten the ladylike gloves, hang the beaded velvet reticule and silk fan at my wrist, adjust my ridiculously tiny silk hat, and give the solicitor a brief brittle smile. 'Please arrange for the transfer of the house title, of all his properties and all funds from his bank accounts into my own. I have let all the staff go except for Mrs Medway' – *I want to choose my own household* – 'so please ensure that Father's bequests to them are made as soon as possible. Do you wish to continue as my solicitor? If not, tell me now so I can make other arrangements.' Perhaps one of those fancy ones that rejected Hedrek all those years ago. A bluff, really, I don't want the trouble of it; thankfully, Titus nods. 'And thank you for your consideration, Mr Pendergast. I do appreciate your efficiency and kindness in these matters.'

I'm at the door when he says, 'It is a condition of your inheritance, Violet. If you do not travel north and fulfil your father's instructions…'

My fingers convulse on the brass doorknob, seeming to swallow the shine of it, as if all of the hope I felt last night now rests in the belly of a wolf.

'If you do not do this, Violet, everything will go to the Church.'

The moment feels endless, but I know it's no more than a second before I say, 'I'll not be held hostage to a dead man's demands.'

* * *

Out in the fresh air, I take a deep breath and lean against the stone wall. Titus's last words, that I have three days to decide, ring in my ears. The barely legible lines from Hedrek's journal (given to his solicitor for safekeeping a few days before his demise, I was told) appear across my vision, a palimpsest laid over the sight of the harbour and the blue, blue sky.

But the place that concerns you, Violet?

Here. It's barely marked – just that tiny x – faded now, this is an old map stuck in these pages. This is the spot.

Anchor-hold.

The Anchorhold.

Where, it's whispered, it all began.

Where it will all end.

And the yellowed piece of paper, ancient and thin as onion skin, the contour lines on it the muted blue of deep veins.

You will go north, Violet.

You will find the place where your brother resides.

You will destroy the Anchorhold and whatever moves within it.

And you will save your brother.

Save Tiberius.

Neither journal nor map did I take, nor were they offered. Perhaps Titus knows me well enough after all – given a chance I'd have touched them to a candleflame, sent them into the ether. *I have no need of money*, I tell myself, then amend, *I have no need of riches*.

I don't need the house or the real estate portfolio or the myriad business interests, nor all the gold and silver stacked in bank vaults. I don't need servants to dress me or clean or cook, to open doors and do my washing, and tell visitors that I'm not at home. I don't need the carriages or the horses. I *do* need *some* money to survive. To flee. To feed myself until I can get settled elsewhere. Quickly, I calculate how much is in my own accounts, how much jewellery I have that might be sold before the Church tries to claim it as well, arguing it was no gift from my father, merely a 'loan'.

To my left, the harbour and all its ships. The Harbour Mistress would put me on one, no doubt, a decent one with a captain who could be trusted to deliver me across the sea, to some foreign land where I could proceed to get lost. To my right, the route up the hill to Zennor House where Mrs Medway waits; I don't think I could live with myself if I left her in the lurch. And there's Freddie too. Who'd look out for her? It's not lost on me that I dreamed my father dead, but can't bear to leave these two behind.

I turn and head upwards, the heels of my boots clacking on the cobbles, my skirts hissing behind me as if some Medusa follows. At home there will be a warm bath, a comfortable dressing gown and the scandalous joy of bare feet. Mrs Medway to bring me hot buttered port and biscuits even though it's not yet lunchtime, and I can hide for the rest of the day, reading in front of the library fire with the fine mantlepiece carved from the bone of a whale and a mirror, once thought to be magic, above it. Forgetting the world and my losses, the burdens my father left me. Tomorrow, I will think of a way to get out of this ridiculous situation.

The slope of the hill is insistent but I'm strong – years of climbing up and down, and the training, always the training – my legs are sturdy. But I don't pass up the opportunity to take an alleyway to my left, a gentler incline, then another alley and another. Past the bakeries and coffeehouses, taverns and grocers, past the modistes and gentlemen's ateliers and jewellers, past the physiks and dentists and apothecaries, and all the houses in between, streetlamps hung zigzag to ensure a safe light when darkness falls. Far to the right I catch glimpses of the promontory where the cathedral sits, where goodbyes were said to my father, hymns sung a little off-key for that's the nature of a congregation.

Some passers-by recognise me, call out or nod sympathetically, condolences sincerely given. Others simply push past, either not caring or unaware of who I am. How long before Hedrek is gone from memory? Mine and others? Will he last, seemingly carved into the very air I breathe, inescapable? Or gone like a feather on the breath of the gods? Will I be able to let the memories go or will they remain as a bright aching wound?

Both Titus and Bishop Walter have told me over the years that my father loved me, but he was unable to show it. That my mother's death, the circumstances of it, had warped him out of true. And that was why I had to learn such strange things; not in a school where I might make friends other than Jack Seven-Gates, but with two old men whose offices were repurposed as classrooms. Law, mathematics and economics with Titus; religion and myth and magic with Walter. Not to mention learning to fight in a warehouse by the docks under the Harbour Mistress's watchful eye and, all too briefly, history and deportment and grooming in my stepmother's solar. And now… now…

. Shaking my head, I try to concentrate on the stones at my feet, but I can't stop Titus's reading of my father's words from resurfacing.

Go to the north. Go into the Darklands. Go to the Anchorhold. Destroy whatever resides there. Rescue your brother.

My brother who's been dead for thirteen years.

* * *

'They've already started.' Mrs Medway's tone is all *I-told-you-so* as she steps into the library.

Prematurely grey hair, smooth-skinned, sharp-eyed and sharper tongued, her mauve gown's covered by a pristine white apron that I've never seen dirtied. She places the silver tray on the coffee table beside me; port and cheese biscuits just out of the oven.

'Which "they" are we referring to?' I didn't share the details of my meeting with the solicitor; merely said that matters were 'in train'. No need to bother her sooner than I must.

'Your *suitors*. The flies flocking to a pile of fresh warm shite.'

'Am I the shite?' I ask, eyebrows flying upwards. 'As long as I'm fresh and warm, I suppose.'

'You know what I mean.' She dips a hand into her apron pocket and produces a stack of cards, generally uniform in size and quality of stock, but in varied hues and degrees of embossing, with the occasional flash of gold foil from the very rich or the very ambitious. 'Thirty this morning. Not that Seven-Gates lad, though.' She gives me a sidewise glance, which I ignore. 'And you only a day from burying your father. Hardly decent.'

'I see what you mean. Isn't there a mourning period in which they should be leaving me alone?' I take the cards from her, flick through them. *Thirty*. The prideful part of me thinks *Not bad for someone who didn't go to Mistress Tilwater's Academy or Lady Crompton's Finishing School, who didn't grow up in high society*. I suppose it doesn't matter when there's money to be had – when their parents realised just how much of a fortune Hedrek Zennor had left me. The cards: mostly men, some women, some of the finest families, some of the wealthiest, and those two groups don't necessarily cross. This one has breeding but no money. This one plenty of money, but even less pedigree than I – make no mistake, I'm the daughter of a first-generation merchant, barely out of the dirt.

'Yes. But it's that they're disguising their approaches as mourning visits to pay their respects that irks me.' She begins dusting the shelves in irritation, displacement activity. Not conducive to my quiet time.

'I could place a notice in *The Courier*? That I am not at home to uninvited guests for the next three months. Might help – the better-bred ones won't want to be seen being so gauche.'

'Doesn't mean they won't pounce on you in the streets,' she grumbles. 'Waste of money.'

'Then it's either remain indoors all that time or sneak out in disguise.' And in truth, neither of those ideas are completely awful. If the intrusions get truly insistent I can always pen a brief missive on a sheet of Zennor Enterprises stationery, a polite way of saying KEEP OUT. 'I'll leave it for the moment.'

The Courier began as nothing more than a list of tide times and weather predictions, ships due to dock and those to depart. It still prints those things but with the addition of births, deaths and marriages, announcements of social movements such as holiday destinations for the wealthy, notices of estate sales, sales of other sort, blanket apologies, accusations and occasional insults, calling out for duels, and notifications of availability or otherwise, a few columns of scandal, reports of crimes committed, those caught for it and their punishments. It carries, once a month, advertisements for Zennor Enterprises – notices of new incoming cargo, space for outgoing merchandise, destinations, calls for passengers, and the like. And now, perhaps, this notice of unavailability. Something new for them, I'm sure.

Penelope Medway nods, and departs. She recognises at last my need for quiet. We'll need to advertise at some point in *The Courier* for new servants but for the moment I'm enjoying how silent and slow the house is. Time to adjust to what my life is now without the constant vibrating presence of my father and his needs, his illness and anxieties and fears. Time to *feel* how I fit in this house now that it's mine. Now I'm alone.

This house – not the one I was born in, not the one we all began in, not the one where memories of my mother reside – is, was, Father's and mine alone. There was only ever he and I in this place purchased with the fortune given to him by the cloaked man almost thirteen years ago. It's one of the biggest in St Sinwin's, and for all it's called a townhouse, it's really a mansion, a stone structure at the top of the bowl of the harbour. All the furniture included in the asking price because we had nothing worth moving, and insufficient taste to know how to decorate such an abode. We learned – because money can buy you knowledge or the services of those who have it – and gradually replaced piece after piece so that everything's been made almost anew, like fresh skin cells replacing old. But the first things we owned were second-hand, belongings of the rich-poor old man who'd died here without issue.

Just Father and I in a home with multiple bedrooms and dining rooms, washrooms larger than the old cottage itself, a manicured garden out front, a stable and carriage house, several libraries (some disguised as studies or offices, even parlours) to which my father began to add a collection of strange and eldritch books. Father in those days, not so terrible, not what he'd become; still remembering that he'd loved me.

Now, in the biggest of the libraries, I return to my usual spot, the green brocade wingback to the right of the hearth. Putting my bare feet up on the hassock, I reach for the port. The dressing gown is warm, the flames toasty, and soon spring will reassert herself, I'm sure of it, yet I'm chill to the very core of me. I stare at the empty seat opposite. Raising my glass to the empty chair, I nod.

'I hate what you tried to make me, are *still* trying to make me.' Pause. 'I hate what you *made* me. But you're gone and I'll be my own creature yet.'

3

I'm thirteen and it's my sixth year of *this* life, so different from the old one.

The sixth year of running and jumping and swimming, of climbing trees and walls and surfaces with barely anything to grip, of learning to use knives and axes and bows and arrows and swords, garottes made of scarves and rosaries and rope and fine chains that otherwise look like jewellery. Of learning to fight boys and men far larger than I, of sparring with anyone Talwyn Enys saw fit to pit me against.

Of thumping one of the punching bags hanging from a beam in the warehouse over and over until, after enough crimson and skin have been offered up, my knuckles are tough and coarse and callused. Even in my dreams, I can smell the stink of sweat and dried blood, feel the heated air, the rough calico of the bag, the shudders that go through me with each blow, hear Talwyn shouting at the others, those who hope to join her Harbour Guard.

The cadence of those drills, the thud-thud-thud, became a song to me, a lullaby that would repeat in my head to send me to an exhausted sleep at night.

Thud-thud-thud.

Thud-thud-thud.

Thud-thud-thud.

Then the noise spills out of my sleep, into the bedroom, and I wake to a hammering somewhere in my house.

It takes a few moments before I realise it's a knocking on the front door, far more loudly than if they used the mermaid-shaped knocker. Wood against wood? Next, voices raised. Mrs Medway and one I'd hoped not to hear for some while, but chance would be a very fine thing. I push myself out of bed, slip my feet into the slippers on the rug, find the soft green velvet robe and throw it over my nightdress.

Shouts are issuing from the foyer as I pad down. My housekeeper, her back to me, is trying to close the door on our guest but he's managed to wedge a staff into the gap. They don't hear me approach, but when I step from the shadows of the unlit grand staircase, the bishop's eyes widen. For a second, he looks frightened, then his expression shifts to startled, and finally settles on angry. I don't know what he thinks he saw apart from a stocky irritated blonde. Mrs Medway glances over her shoulder, spots me, then shouts at the prince of the Church, 'There, you've done it.'

'Walter,' I say, 'you're here so soon? Or should I say so late? It is very late indeed for taking your crozier for a walk.'

I thought I might get a few days' respite, at least, but I'm willing to bet someone's been telling on me. The bishop's pitch carries as if he's addressing the congregation and needs to reach those sitting at the back.

'Titus Pendergast told me you're refusing the call.' Of course he did. Hedrek, Titus and Walter, the unbearable trinity of my life.

'Good news travels fast.' I pause for a moment, calculate the chances of just leaving Mrs Medway to deal with him, perhaps thrash him with his own staff. Not good – not because it's beyond Penelope Medway to administer such a beating, but because the consequences would be ones I don't feel like managing. 'Ah, let the bastard in.'

Behind him, peering from the night, the faces of two lesser god-hounds, his escort and looking too young to be out after dark. 'Mrs Medway, feed the lads, they're terribly thin.'

She rolls her eyes, but gestures for the youths to follow.

'Come along, Walter.'

'*Bishop* Walter.' His tone is sharp.

I don't reply, just lead him into the nearest parlour – small, decorated in reds, the artwork vaguely pornographic, nudity hidden by diaphanous drapes in the paintings, but the statuettes on tables and plinths have no such modesty, a veritable array of breasts, slits and cocks – the decorator Father hired insisted it was the height of good taste, that all folk of quality had such a room, and Hedrek didn't question it. I gesture to the scarlet velvet chaise; do not offer him a drink. My father would always host him in the big library, but that space is mine now and I'll not have it contaminated. Walter drops to the seat, studiously keeping his hazel eyes on me, not his surrounds. Beaky of head and ovoid of body, he looks a little like an outraged eagle on top of a large egg. In his sixties, skin florid and unhelped by his workaday purple robes (no silver or gold embroidery), he glares at me as if I'm a recalcitrant child.

Which, I supposed, is accurate.

'Violet Zennor, you have a duty to perform. An obligation.'

'Walter, all these years I obeyed my father without question, hoping obedience would lead to approval – that it might take me back to a time when I held his affection. When he cared for me as a parent. But that never happened, and this is all nothing but madness.'

'Hedrek had told you all these years—'

'Yes. He'd told me what I was meant to do. Go north. To the Anchorhold. But, Walter, he never mentioned my brother.'

'He planned to tell you and very soon because time is of the essence.' He shakes his head. 'Then he fell ill again, into that fever.'

'And he hardly spoke again. Four weeks and he barely spoke again.'

Walter scratches his hairless chin. 'Your father raised you to be the instrument of his penance.'

'I didn't get any say in it. I wasn't born simply to be a *thing*. An *implement*.'

The bishop looks surprised, as if slapped by a fish. 'You're his child. You will obey his wishes.'

'He's dead!'

'Your father's salvation lies in you. You are his atonement.'

'Once again: he's dead. I'm not. Don't I get a life of my own, Walter?'

'*Bishop* Walter.'

'My father made choices, *Walter*. Those were not mine.' I rise. 'And, *Bishop*, I will not go.'

Perhaps he sees something in my face – that peculiar obduracy that my father said rendered me "so mulish" he half-expected ears and a tail to grow – because Walter seems to physically deflate, a sagging purple balloon, all its air seeped out. It almost makes me pity him.

'You taught me about the Darklands and the Leech Lords. That there is the border and it is *held*, and has been for centuries by the Briar Witches. That the Leeches cannot cross it.' I shake my head. 'Whatever you fear – whatever madness you three old men shared – cannot come to pass. The Leech Lords are *bound*. Trapped. I'll not leave this life now it's become my own just to fulfil a dead man's fanciful wish.'

'Your brother's thirteenth birthday approaches. In three months—'

'My brother is dead! He was stillborn! It's the thirteenth anniversary of his death!' My voice is louder than I'd have wished. For a moment he looks set for one last try. 'I wouldn't if I were you, *Walter*. Now, please leave lest I put some of my training to good use – and be warned that the thought of applying my foot to your arse is a little too pleasing.'

The bishop rises. 'Just because we don't want to do things, Violet, doesn't mean we don't have to. And it doesn't mean that life will shift around us to accommodate our wishes.'

I lead him back to the foyer. His escorts are eating apricot tarts and sitting in the carver chairs by the door. Mrs M is nowhere to be seen, obviously having drawn the line at babysitting them. As Walter follows the god-hounds out, he takes one last shot: 'And just because nothing's happened yet, doesn't mean it never will. The time is coming.'

'Goodnight, Walter.'

'I'll return in the morning, when you've calmed down, are more reasonable.'

'Don't waste your time. My father was mad. There will be no missions, no journeys northward. I'm not going anywhere.'

32

'Miss Violet! Oh, Miss Violet?'

Despite my disguise – one of Father's old suits, a stout pair of boots and my long hair curled up under a tweed cap to keep any condolers away – the childish voice, high and clear, makes it obvious that at least one person's seen through me. I look around though I know she'll be invisible until she chooses otherwise. Urchin. Ragamuffin. Waif.

She appeared almost two years ago – keeping body and soul together with what she can beg, borrow and steal, sleeping in haylofts and attics, beneath bridges and by inn fires when someone forgets to remove her. I saw her the first day I left my bed after an illness, and I don't know why but she attached herself to me. The child's bright and clever and deserving of better than living rough. I've tried to talk Freddie into Zennor House, learning domestic skills from Mrs Medway, or going to the best of the orphanage-schools if she'd prefer, or undertaking an apprenticeship (to seamstress, butcher, baker, candlestick maker, whatever she pleases) – but she'll have none of it. I know she holes up in our stables on occasion and a basket of food is left there whenever she's noticed hanging around. But Freddie likes her freedom. She likes learning things, watching people and their doings, keeping track. I wonder, if she survives long enough, might she let me set her up in business, a private detective? Freddie's Investigatory Services. She'd never be out of work, making a mockery of my camouflage as she does.

'Hello, Freddie.'

And there she is, as if she's stepped from the air. It's just a trick, the child knows how to hide, how to blend. I suspect that someone once spelled her shoes and clothing or taught her how to make them silent and unseen; or she stole the knowledge, which helps no end with her thievery. *Skilled acquisition*, she calls it. Still and all, it keeps her safe from prying eyes, predatory ones; helps her slip beneath notice. A smudge of a child, small, maybe eight, bright blue-eyed, clever, mud-red hair and a covering of dirt on her skin and ragged attire. In autumn I'll have Mrs Medway leave a good coat in the stables – it'll keep Freddie warm, then she can hawk or barter it at the end of winter. A larger one will be supplied at the next change of season.

'Hello, Miss Violet.' There's a lengthy cut on her bare arm (the sleeve torn), still seeping ruby drops.

'What have you done to yourself, missy? Will you go to see Mrs Medway? She'll make sure that doesn't get infected...' I've found it's best to ask, make it seem like it's her idea, that she's doing you a favour rather than being told what to do.

'Someone was chasing me.' She shrugs, falls into step. 'Caught myself on a nail or thorn or something.'

'Well,' I say, biting back 'be careful' because that will just annoy her, make her disappear for days or weeks on end, depending on her mood, 'you know what you're about.'

We keep walking. After a few moments she says, 'Sorry about your da.'

Which is charitable of her because my father had no time for Freddie, nor urchins in general; no great giver of alms, Hedrek. Perhaps he didn't want to remember how close I was to being like her. Gods know he'd chase her out of the stable or the garden or from the kitchen door whenever he found her there.

'Thank you, Freddie.' It might be easier, now with him gone, to coax her into the household, keep her safe.

34

'Miss Violet?'

'Mmmm?'

'There's been a woman and a man around the inns. They dress like quality but talk like toughs. Asked about your father 'til they heard he'd died. Then they asked about you.'

'What did they want to know?' I flip two silver quarter-coins from the pocket of my suit jacket; they fly upwards and disappear even though I barely see her hands move.

'What you're like, your daily schedule.'

'What did you tell them?'

'That you were a sweet and timid thing who loved needlepoint and dogfights.'

'Is that how you got cut, Freddie? When you gave them lip?'

She shakes her head; might be telling the truth, might be lying to save her professional pride. 'I can find them, follow them…'

They might be amongst my father's legion of "researchers" who've found him books on esoteric topics over the years; or they might want to be. Some are far less erudite than others – better to call them "gatherers" or "harvesters". Hedrek always paid handsomely, even when the search wasn't dangerous.

'No,' I say. 'They can find me easily enough.'

She seems to deflate, lose interest. Freddie starts to drift away, just a step or two but I recognise it as the precursor to a disappearing act. Casually, so as not to seem needy, I say, 'Mrs Medway's made apricot tarts.'

She nods, then slips away, back up the hill towards Zennor House where I know she'll at least be fed and that cut attended to. I continue my descent towards the docks. The Harbour Mistress

35

sent a summons this morning; I can speak with the woman about ships and escape plans, killing two birds with one stone.

* * *

Talwyn Enys has been the Harbour Mistress longer than I've been alive, almost thirty years since she took up the post from her mother, who took it from her mother and so on. Not a hereditary position, but won through their sheer gift for organisation. St Sinwin's is the best administered port-town anywhere. Never an argument over berthing or traffic management, larger ships are piloted in with ease, loading and unloading of cargoes moves with the precision of clockwork. It doesn't hurt that Talwyn's well over six feet tall, muscled as a stevedore, swears a blue streak and isn't afraid to hit anyone causing her grief.

Her office is on the second storey of an old wood and tin building on the wharves. Knowing what I do about her precision and organisational abilities, it's always a shock to find that this room is a mess of mounds of ledgers and maps, pieces of paper, notes, permissions and licences, arrival and departure logs, tide times, and cargo manifests and passenger lists. Yet she can always put her meaty hand on whatever is required, within seconds. It's a gift. An astounding, confounding, unlikely gift.

Said office, when I step into it, looks even worse than usual, like an actual rummaging has taken place. The next thing I notice is a young man, his feet not touching the ground because the Harbour Mistress has him by the throat and is shaking him. He's making noises, none of which are actual words. She's shouting up into his bloodied face.

I raise my voice. 'Mistress Enys, not to interfere, but I think he needs to breathe.'

36

I'm smart enough to stay in the open doorway, poised for flight, just in case she doesn't find this helpful. Talwyn glares in confusion at me, eyes a little red, there's something of the bull about her, including her short black hair and brown skin. I remember not everyone's got Freddie's perceptiveness so I remove my hat, shake my hair. The fury fades and she gives a frustrated sort of snort, followed by several profanities, and releases her victim. He curls into a ball on the floor; had it been me, I'd have made a point of running. Possibly he fears if he tries to escape, she'll be after him, and Talwyn's land speed is surprising, her size deceiving. She leans down towards the lad, who's even younger than I'd thought, and hisses: 'Filthy fecking rat!'

'Ah,' I say as if it all makes sense, righting one of the chairs, and planting myself.

Talwyn stomps to the liquor cabinet – a wooden crate turned on its side – and pours a measure of something dark and syrupy. She lifts the bottle in my direction; I shake my head in turn. Far too early. Focus my attention on the lad: maybe sixteen, wispy mouse-brown hair, half-starved cheekbones, barely even peach fuzz on his cheeks.

'And you are?'

'Wilf.' He tries for defiant, but just squeaks as he rocks into a sitting position.

'And what have you done, Wilf?'

'Smuggling!' Talwyn growls from where she and her glass have taken up position behind the broad desk. But she stays there so she's calmed down enough to realise that honey might extract what vinegar cannot.

'Let's not set her off again, Wilf. You can speak to me now or I can leave you with Mistress Enys while I summon the Constable in a leisurely fashion. Your choice.' I cross my arms, then my ankles. All in all, a picture of nonchalance. For good measure, Talwyn gives another growl.

Wilf decides quickly. 'They telt me I could make extra money. That it's just dodging the customs duties and no one gets hurt.'

'Interesting.' I shoot a glance at the Harbour Mistress, who's prided herself on keeping smugglers out of St Sinwin's for the last ten years; the tales of that violent campaign, I'm assured, are still told in drinking establishments from here to Bellsholm and beyond. 'And who suggested this enterprising idea?'

'The first mate on my ship.'

'Which ship?'

'The *Fortitude*.'

'How many of the crew are involved?'

'Me, the captain's boy, eight others.'

'And what's the plan?'

'We hide the goods in a false hold, tonight we're to row them around to the Merrow's Cove Cave for handover.'

'To whom?'

'Dunno.'

I glare at him for a moment. 'Talwyn, give him another shake.'

She's surging out of her chair and he's squealing. 'I dunno, I dunno, I swear on my mother's soul I don't know anything else!'

And I believe it. If I were putting a smuggling operation together, I wouldn't share the details with someone like Wilf, either. There's a chance they're not even planning to pay him and his colleagues. A few drowned men mean extra coins in a larger purse. There might come a day when the lad's grateful for Talwyn catching him but that won't be for some time yet. I tap a finger against my chin, pondering.

'Wilf, if you know what's good for you, you'll keep your mouth shut. Act normal, load the ill-gotten gains and take it to the cave. Play us fair, and when all this is done, we'll look at a better life – an apprenticeship and a place to live. Or a new ship to crew?'

'I get seasick,' he whimpers. 'Don't want to do it no more.'

'Apprenticeship it is, then.'

'Thank you, Miss.'

'If you play us wrong? You won't have to worry about *her*.' I nod towards the mountain of muscle and ill-temper sprawled in the corner, then a flick of my right hand brings the concealed knife out of my sleeve. Another flick, and it's gone. The lad goes pale.

'Scarper,' grunts the Harbour Mistress and the boy's up and out like a shot, papers lifting in disarray at his flight. Talwyn gives me a calculating glance. 'Coming out tonight, then? And you so recently in mourning.'

Mistress Enys and I glare at each other for a few moments, until I say, 'All the fun of the fair. You had something to discuss? Or was it the redoubtable Wilf?'

'Gods, no. That was unexpected – found him trying to pick the lock on the door, contraband in his pockets.' She grabs a pile of papers, indistinguishable from the other piles of papers. '*This* is what I wanted to show you.'

I rise and cross the room. 'What am I looking at?'

'Passenger manifest for the *Siren's Song* which docked early this morning. It was an old O'Malley ship.'

The O'Malleys were the stuff of legend until they weren't, and became a cautionary tale of families that grow too big and bold. Of business ventures that overreach through greed and arrogance. For the longest time they grew and grew and grew – until

39

everything they had and everything they were began to wither and at last they disappeared from the face of the earth completely. There were tales, in some of Walter's lessons, about them and their bargains with the creatures that lived beneath the waves; some were stories brought back by the O'Malleys on their travels of monsters and magic from the deep. Now, only whispers and rumours and fragments remain and none of them are good. Until, until, until.

'And?'

'Over the page, right at the end.' Her tone's far more patient than I'd have expected after what she just did to Wilf. There's also a touch of patronising an idiot.

I flip through impatiently, scan down, down, down.

'Oh.' All thoughts of ships and escape leave my head.

4

Once upon a time, there was a little girl whose mother died. She and her father lived happily together until the father remarried...

Once upon a time, there were two children, a girl and a boy. Their mother died (or perhaps she did not) and their father married again (or perhaps he did not). Their stepmother (or perhaps their true mother) did not like them, and during a time of plague and famine suggested to the children's father that life would be easier without two extra mouths to feed. After all, they could always have more offspring...

Once upon a time, there was a girl whose mother died and her father took another wife with indecent haste. This woman had her own child and while the stepsiblings grew close, the other-mother could never find it in her heart to love the new daughter. She took it into her head to remove that child from the father's affections...

For all my parental misfortunes, none of these stories were mine, though I read them often enough in the books in Father's library, heard them in enough of Walter's discourses on lore and folk and fairy tales – because in such recountings lie grains of truth that can help one survive. I was, therefore, prepared for a wicked stepmother. They're a dime-a-dozen, after all, cut from the same cheap cloth, out to make a nest for themselves, to bear new children to displace those of a first marriage. All in the interests of their own security.

Yet when mine at last arrived, she was nothing like I'd been taught to expect.

Temperance married Hedrek when I was almost sixteen and cared for me as well as any blood mother. I adored her. For two years, things were better. She made Hedrek softer, if not kind, and gentled his focus on me. For a while, oh such a short while, my existence was not so regimented, the training not so harsh. Although no fool, she was kind rather than clever, and that was what I needed. Temperance taught me the ladies' graces that had been lacking in my father's curriculum, and Hedrek seemed to see the wisdom in this. No point having a daughter who couldn't be trusted around the finer elements of society – no point in having a child who looks and behaves like a ruffian when you want her to pass unremarked and unsuspected through the world. She taught me how to dress, to appreciate lovely clothes, how to use cosmetics and do my hair, the value of gems and precious metals and art; taught me manners and etiquette, which are the passports for a certain sort of existence. She and Mrs Medway became great friends, supports for each other – and if one could not sway Hedrek, the other might – and for a while at least life was better.

Two years. Two years before Hedrek became too much, his obsessions in ascent once more. When I was eighteen, Temperance Zennor took ship for parts unknown (at least to me) and left us all behind. While I knew she left because of my father (I'd not curse anyone to eternity with him) and she took great pains to explain that I was not the cause of her departure, there's still a tiny shard in my heart, something crafted of hurt and rage, resentment and love, which tells me otherwise.

Bursting through the door, all I can do is think what if she isn't *here*, if St Sinwin's was nothing more than a place to come ashore and she's already caught a carriage from the inn outside the city walls, is already on her way to somewhere else. And it doesn't matter that I'm a grown woman of twenty with blood on my hands, because we're all just little girls left alone in the forest when it comes to our missing mothers.

A panic I'm not accustomed to builds as I pelt from reception room to reception room, from parlour to library and back again, only to find them empty. All of them. Temperance has gone. She did not bother to visit even briefly. I try to compress the disappointment, slip it below that little shard of ache. I school my features to serenity, turn my feet towards the kitchen where there'll be the comfort of freshly baked cake if the universe has any mercy. Where Mrs Medway will listen as I tell her in a voice that tries not to quiver, that Temperance was so close for such a short time. No one else needs to know that my stepmother passed this way and could not be bothered to say hello.

Down the cold stone steps, along the grey-flagged corridor, past storage rooms made ridiculous by the single girl and one housekeeper living in this great house. Past the entrance to the wine cellar that stretches beneath the entire building where an army could slake its thirst. Past the pantries where Mrs Medway dries meat and fish, preserves fruit, stacks cheeses as if we might one day be under siege and in need; where the beekie hides during the day before sneaking out to do his chores unseen. Into the barrel-ceilinged kitchen lit by sconces, the hearth fire and the thin twin beams of sunlight that come from the sole window, over the sinks and terribly high, the only part of the kitchen that's above ground.

Temperance Zennor and Mrs Medway sit at the blackwood table, sipping coffee from delicate porcelain cups, ones so old that the glaze is crackled and a little yellow, the painted flowers strangely intense in such a setting as if blooming where they should not. Free hands joined, fingers tightly entwined, and all I can think is that Mrs M is holding onto my stepmother for me, keeping her here so she doesn't float away.

'Hello,' is all I manage and despite the defiant tone, I feel at long last the heat of tears, the fill and overflowing that I've resisted these past days. I've refused to cry for my father. But the sight of this woman, who was kind to me, undoes me entirely and I'm sobbing like a child as I fall into her arms.

* * *

My own mother, I had for the first seven years of my life (before my baby brother made his way into the world). Though my memories of her are often hazy, enough are clear for me to recall her with affection. She was kind and gentle, she smiled a lot even when sad. Her hair was crow's-wing black that shone as if stars nested there, skin as white as snow and lips red as crushed berries. Slender and sleek – nothing like muscular me – and during her pregnancy with Tiberius, she slept a lot, was sluggish when awake. A disease of her blood, my father would whisper when I asked why Mama was so tired. Back then, in the *before*, Hedrek was a loving father.

Vesper Zennor moved slowly around our tiny hovel down by the water, sometimes kept me fed, told me stories when she had

44

energy, tales of her home far to the north. I do remember a time when she wasn't so frail, when her laugh was a hearty thing, and she carried me up and down the streets of St Sinwin's as she went from market stall to market stall, seeking the very best bargains she could find, to make our pittance go further. Then she went away, up north to care for her own ailing mother, and when she returned home, Vesper Zennor was sick. I looked after her as well as I could, so Father could find work, pay our rent, put bread on the table; I, a tiny nurse, tottered about when Mother could not, making thin gruel and feeding it to her, spoonful by spoonful, as she grew swollen with my baby brother.

Memories of that home sit strange in my mind, only fragments are sharp and sometimes I think wherever there's a blank, I fill it in with parts of other places I've visited. The things I'm sure of, however, are the swarming darknesses, the corners without light (as if that light dimmed more each day my mother grew sicker). The tiny loft where I slept, suspended over the kitchen and sitting room, the rickety ladder that led down. The washroom barely more than a crack between walls. And my parents' sleeping space, an uncurtained alcove crowded out by no more than a rickety bed and a chest of drawers.

Sometimes I dream I wake up there again.

By the time Temperance arrived in St Sinwin's we were wealthy beyond our wildest dreams (all from that one awful transaction), but Father had long since ceased to be regarded as an eligible bachelor. Oh, there were some who still saw him as a challenge, or redeemable, but after one or two dinners at a fine restaurant or in a private home where some man or woman hoped to seduce him with their cooking, the hunter soon realised their prey was far stranger and ultimately more unsettling than they'd foreseen; his topics of conversation limited to the dangers in the darkness, very esoteric reading materials, and means of making money. I think Father still had enough vanity that he enjoyed being pursued but truly had no interest in another person. Not when he had his obsession, and a weapon to hone.

Temperance was another matter.

A tiny golden-haired doll of a woman, sepia porcelain in complexion, dark-eyed and wide-mouthed, frown lines in her forehead despite her youth (from thinking, she told me, never be afraid of such lines). Her father had been a pirate, but he'd devoted a tranche of his ill-gotten gains to her education (very different from mine). She had no taste for the sea but for books alone and opened a bookstore in St Sinwin's when she arrived. That's what had drawn my father in; his requests for esoterica fascinated her, and conversation quickly led to courtship which resulted in a wedding and some little span of bliss. Eventually Temperance realised his obsessions could no longer be dampened. That he would always be aimed, body and soul, at one thing, a secret he'd never share with her.

My stepmother offered me books to read, ones that did not relate to my father's curriculum, stories and tales, novels and essays about the entire world. Subjects that did not require my memorising, nor action. There were no knives hidden within the pages or spine of those tomes, nothing I was required to throw at a target and hit in the centre or my father would yell that I was dead, dead, *dead*! Is it any wonder I loved her so soon? She gave me hope of another life, and when she left, she made me swear I'd keep it alive, that little flame of belief and longing. Even though I thought her lost to me, I'd kept my word.

Now, she sits by my bedside in my room with its shades of green and black and strokes my hair to send me off to sleep as if I'm an infant. All the words between us today, catching up, dancing around recriminations, and why she's returned – perhaps Father sent for her when he sensed his end approaching. She did not arrive in time for him, but she's here for the daughter she never had.

'Will you stay?' I ask now, in a very small voice, knowing I'm a child mothers leave behind.

'As long as you need me to, Violet.' She smiles.

'The bookstore is still there,' I mumble sleepily. I don't say that I'd stolen the keys when I knew she was to leave, that I have snuck away each day for however long or short a time I could manage to be there, to breathe in the books, to read things that were no more than tales. To hide when I could. 'Perhaps you'll reopen it?'

'Perhaps. But for now, let us settle into this new life, yes?' She kisses my forehead as she used to do and I can believe for the slimmest sliver of time between breaths, between seconds, that nothing ever changed, that she never left, that she was my real mother – and that I've not been abandoned twice by women who should have loved me better. Who should not have left me alone with Hedrek Zennor. And I make myself forget, or pretend to, that there were many of my questions Tempe did not answer this day, that there are gaps in her story to be filled.

I nod and close my eyes, breathe evenly until it seems I slumber – and indeed I'm in that dozy state where I might slip beneath consciousness. There's the rush of air, the smoky sweetness as Temperance extinguishes the candle on my bedside table, strokes my hair one last time, then leaves.

I wait another few minutes before dragging myself up to proper wakefulness and throwing back the covers. Black trousers and sweater will help hide me, the soft fabrics will be easy to move in, a dark peacoat against the cold out on the water. A black knitted cap on my hair, boots slung over my shoulders to be put on when I'm safely down the trellis outside my window (it once bore roses until I realised how hard it was to manoeuvre past thorns). Outside, I make my way through the gardens, towards the stone wall between my home and the ruined Seven-Gates mansion, clamber over said wall, then exit through their gate. I promised Talwyn I'd help her tonight and don't feel like arguing my way past an overprotective Tempe and Mrs M. And there's something compulsive about doing what I want, even if it may be stupid and dangerous – at least it's what *I've* chosen.

Well away from home, I pick up the pace. The Harbour Mistress will be waiting with diminishing patience.

5

They can't cross water.

Not under their own steam. They must needs be carried –
moved *– by another. On the back of a servant, or in a carriage*
driven by another. Over a bridge or through the very waters
themselves, but this is too great a risk for most of them as one
must trust the bearer to be utterly surefooted and/or utterly
loyal and devoted to the survival of the creature in their care.
~~*They cannot ride a beast over a bridge or ford a water course*~~
~~*on their own – once again, they must be borne by another*~~
~~*person, mortal, not a beast of burden.*~~* †

I do not know why this is. My researches have born no fruit in
this direction.

The fact remains that the northern-most border of the
Darklands is surrounded by an ocean, unpredictably frozen,
and impassable by ship or sled, and where there may well be
dragons. Never has there been any tale or rumour of these
atrocities coming from that direction. All of this suggests that

The boat bobs in place, lulling me into a half-trance, taking my mind to thoughts of water. That piece of scholarship, strangely tangential, surfaces unbidden. My father's books and Walter's, my constant scholarship. I shake my head a little too violently, rocking the vessel and those in it. We're anchored, two longboats, just beyond the low headland on the far side of Merrow's Cove. Talwyn gives me a glance, as much curious as irked. I raise a hand in apology. We've been here almost an hour, waiting in silence.

On the headland itself, Savage, one of the Harbour Guard – Talwyn's small but beefy squad of young men and women who enforce order and collect information – is lying on his stomach, keeping watch. I wonder if he's as cold and regretful of his choices as I am.

50

Eventually, a warning hiss comes, and soon after the dip and splash of oars above that of the waves. Conversations and coughs and curses carrying, no sense of a stealthy approach. An assumption that the Harbour Mistress is complacent, believing her docks to be law-abiding, the fear of her ironclad. When the noises fade, and Savage scrambles carefully back into the craft, he holds up both hands, fingers wiggling – ten people.

Slowly, as quietly as possible, we round the rocks and glide towards the cave opening. The empty curve of the cove's sandy beach glows in the moonlight. I take a deep breath as we slip into the dark maw, everyone bracing their palms against the rough walls to keep the lifeboats from scraping, calling a warning. Those far ahead of us are nothing more than a trickle of lantern light. The tunnel seems to go on for far too long, as if we'll be trapped here forever under the weight of the earth with the hunger of the sea lurking beneath us; a rising tide would lift us, crush us to the roof. I clench my fists until the nails bite.

When we at last reach the exit, making sure our prey's grounded their vessels on a narrow shingle and disappeared into another tunnel, we paddle out into a large sea cave, towards the thin form waiting beside the boats. Torches dug into the sand glint dimly on Wilf's hair, turn his shadow monstrous large. Keeping watch while his comrades carry pilfered cargo deep into the honeycomb of the world.

When we beach, he gives us a tense glance.

'Anything we should know?' I ask quietly. He shakes his head, looking nervously at Talwyn, going even paler when he spots the gothic warhammer (it belonged to her mother) resting on her shoulder. 'Stay here, lad, we'll see you safe after this.'

The Harbour Guard are bristling with the weapons of their choice, and there are axes and short swords, cudgels and scimitars, a morning star and one truncated spear. My own dagger is cool against the skin of my forearm, safely in its sheath.

Talwyn clears her throat, her message clear: *Let's get this over with*.

We follow sets of footprints into the tunnel.

More torches show the way and the further we go, the firmer the sand becomes. To the left and right are rough doorways leading to chambers large and small, most of them filled with crates and sacks, chests and coffers, barrels and bolts of cloth. Whatever's been going on at the St Sinwin's docks appears to have been happening for some time. Talwyn's expression grows grimmer by the second. The faint sound of voices and footsteps grows fainter still. We speed up, round another bend and find ourselves in a circular space. A dead end. Too late do I realise there's no exit but the way we came. I open my mouth to give warning—

An explosion rips through the quiet and I'm thrown against a wall and into a dream of one of Hedrek's books.

They cannot move by sunlight.

Being dead – having died and returned – renders them creatures of the darkness. The night tells lies on their behalf, the glow of candles and fire giving bleached skin the illusion that something other than malice runs through their veins. That breath still animates them.

The truth can be revealed by day, which burns away the deceit of life they've created for themselves. Proper death, true death is almost instantaneous – do not touch them as they immolate for the flame sears like nothing in the natural world and you might well be taken down with the abomination. No water can put out such fire.

They maintain their existence by the drinking of blood, pure and simple. They do not need to kill the one from whom they drink, but there are those who prefer to do so, claiming murder amplifies the effect – or is simply more pleasurable. After death, the teeth elongate and taper to a sharp point, the eyes become fit for seeing in even the blackest of caverns; they can move silently, leap far distances so it seems they might be able to fly.

But they cannot bear the touch of light, nor the taste or smell of garlic (such plants were banned from the soil of the Darklands and believed eradicated hundreds of years ago), nor the application of the wood of the hawthorn tree, the briars of a wild or dog rose, nor (some whisper) the presence of a witch.

MISS AMELIA WATERSTONE,
NOTES ON LEECHES AND THEIR ILK

Something sharp is digging into my throat and I'm certain it's teeth – fangs – that somehow there's a Leech Lord come here, to a smugglers' cave by St Sinwin's. It doesn't matter that this makes no sense, I'm filled with fear and panic, my ears still ringing from the blast and my eyes gummed shut. *Quiet*, I think. *Just quiet your mind, slow your breathing. Are you hurt?*

There's no pain apart from in my neck; I wiggle the fingers of my right hand, tentatively touch the side of my throat. Find a splinter embedded in the flesh there. Not too big, nor too deep, but enough to hurt. It comes away easily enough, leaving a slow *slug* of blood creeping into the dip of my collarbone. Nothing feels broken. I'm half-sitting, leaning against… not rubble, but a tangle of bodies. Boots up near my face. Someone's torso across my thighs. I'm gentle when I shake my head to try and clear the ringing, in hopes I can hear someone else breathing or groaning – in short, being alive. Slowly, I sit straighter, feel other people's limbs slide off me.

An explosion.

I rub at my eyelids with the heels of my palms – not sure how useful that is when my hands are covered in dust and dirt. Still, it helps to dislodge the gum of grime until I can blink and blink and blink.

Details of my surroundings become clear, despite the fact there are no torches, nor anything on fire. But the bodies are visible. I look up.

The moon stares down at me.

The chamber's open to the sky, the walls reaching up twenty feet, ledges and gouges all up as if a giant corkscrew were used to make this hole. I wonder if this is what saved me – the fact the space wasn't sealed. Some of the force dissipating upwards.

I say, 'Talwyn,' or try to, end by coughing instead. When I finally stop, I try again. 'Talwyn?'

Nothing for long seconds. No noise or sign of life in this chamber to which there's no longer any entrance, but a wall of displaced rock. If it rains enough, I'll drown. Then, a groan, a few more. Tears threaten – the idea that I was alone with so many dead weighed on me more than I care to admit.

A roar and some swearing.

Talwyn.

'You're alive, I take it?' A hysterical note to my tone. 'They were expecting us. That little shit told, they lured us into this fine ambush, and we obliged like idiots.'

'I'll strangle him,' moans the Harbour Mistress.

This was an opportunity to dispose of not only Talwyn Enys but also her most trusted foot soldiers – what smuggler worth their salt could resist? Me? I'm irrelevant, caught in the crossfire; in the general run of things, I wouldn't have been here. Pure coincidence that she'd summoned me to her office, that I was bored and wilful, that I was unsettled by the unexpected arrival of my stepmother. That I thought some violence might help clear my mind.

'Is everyone alright?' I ask hopefully and begin shaking limbs as I find them, making sure they're still attached, trying to locate heads and check for pulses. The first two I try are not moving, rapidly cooling.

'Fenwick? Addison? Harrington? Savage? Woods? Lowell?'

Mumbles and moans and replies. In the end, there are four other survivors, but Harrington and Savage aren't amongst them.

'Can you climb?' Talwyn asks me. I stare upwards once again.

'Not my preferred sort of course, but yes, I think so. Be kind enough to break my fall if I drop, though.'

'Not likely. Get out and go for help.'

I take a good look around while I kick off my boots then tie them to my back belt loops, shrug off my jacket, and spy a heavy coil of rope on the splintered remains of two crates; the space must have also been a storage spot, and they'd been hasty in their clearing of it, anxious to lay the charges. I'm willing to bet they didn't expect anyone to be in a state to use whatever might remain. Tying one end around my waist, I shake my head. 'It was ham-fisted, this whole thing.'

'Are you sure you can do this?' asks the Harbour Mistress as she offers a boot up.

I nod again.

'And when we get out?'

'One problem at a time. I'd like to concentrate on not dying.' I check my own knots. 'Whoever did this thinks we're dead, which gives us the element of surprise.'

She nods and I put my foot in the cradle of her clasped hands. Talwyn gives me such a boost I almost fly and have to grab at one of the rocky ledges before I drop back down. The endeavour is painful and perilous, and my body reminds me that it's been a while since my last vertical climb. I've refused to exercise since before Hedrek's death – the moment he could no longer speak, could no longer order me about, I ceased.

More than once a hand or a foot slips and I'm left dangling by rapidly numbing fingers. Falling isn't an option and my fear of that keeps me going. I don't want to die, I don't want to be maimed, this is not where or how I want to end – not when I've so recently reclaimed my life from Hedrek's mad schemes.

After forever I drag myself over the rim of the pit and lie in the dirt and grass for long enough that the Harbour Mistress starts hissing that if I'm not dead, she's going to kill me. On my feet once more, I look around, recognise the spot. There's a copse of trees not far off and I choose a sturdy oak, knot the rope around the thick bole and call down, shaking the rope. 'Your turn,' I call, and slump to the grass again to put on my boots – and rest while I can.

According to the pocket-watch (a birthday gift from Tempe, engraved, and miraculously intact) it's almost 3 a.m. by the time the living regroup atop Shadwell's Point. A little longer still until breath has been caught, aching muscles stretched and a proper inventory of injuries conducted in the moonlight.

'Well?' I say at last. 'They think we're dead. Where will they be?'

'If it were me? I know where I'd go.'

6

We crouch in the shadows amongst crates and barrels and sacks; above us, Talwyn's office is bright as a ship at sea, lantern light spilling from the windows. Another hour or two and the place will be abuzz with the day's activity, but right now it's quiet enough for those with ill-will to break into the Harbour Mistress's stronghold. They'll be looking for records and trying to get into the safe for the gold and silver that passes through the Talwyn's hands, for any valuables that have been entrusted to her while folk undertake journeys from which they might not return. There are those who trust her more than they do banks and bankers, and I've never thought that a foolish idea.

There's a crash and the shattering of glass – laughter and profanity, presumably from those who broke the decanter and those who miss its contents respectively. Beside me Talwyn Enys gestures for the last of her squad to go around and secure the back stairs, to hold position until her signal. I pity anyone who gets in her way during the next cold hour.

When Fenwick, Addison, Woods and Lowell disappear into the last of the night, we make our way to the bottom of the steps that lead to the main door, as quiet as we can be. No one will be expecting us, but then again, they won't be expecting anyone, so any noises will likely lead to a frosty welcome. We wait, giving the others what feels sufficient time to get into position, then Talwyn nods and we make our way upwards, carefully sticking to the outer edges of the stairs where the planks are more firmly affixed, less frequently used, and creaks are less likely.

The door's already open, so we simply appear in the frame, take note of the figures in the office – eight, all men, which means two are missing, presumably reporting to someone, somewhere – in various positions around the space, rifling through the desk and drawers, cupboards and shelves. Papers are scattered across the floor and in one corner, three of them are huddled over the great black safe with its dials and locks, its maker's name emblazoned across the battered door. One of them is muttering about explosives, and I wonder how much they've got in stock, how much they know about it. Not experts, certainly, and the gods only know what might happen if they erred on the side of excess here. There might be nothing more of the harbour left than a boiling sea tossing about splinters.

'Evening, gentlemen.' Talwyn's voice rumbles across the room, deceptively calm, and all movement ceases. 'Let me know what you're looking for and I might be able to help.'

Before any of them can venture a reply or move a muscle, the Harbour Mistress wades in, swinging the warhammer, the flat side smashing into cheekbones and noses, the pointed side puncturing holes in heads on the backswing. She makes short work of them before they've had a chance to even move. Before *I've* even had a chance to step in and protect her flank. This night's work will ensure that Talwyn's red temper, already legendary, will be spoken of for years to come. Her remaining foot soldiers have poured through the back door, and stare at the proof of the Harbour Mistress's lack of need of rescue or aid.

Seven men lie dying, and the only survivor is Wilf, who she's caught up, one hand around his skinny throat, his feet once again not touching the floor.

'Who's in charge of this? Who ordered this? All those caves filled with all that stolen cargo, it's been going on for a *long* time.' Talwyn's shouting in his face. I wish I could say I didn't feel a sense of satisfaction, but her people died and the rest of us could have too because of this little rat's decision.

But I can also see from the fear in the youth's eyes that he's far more afraid of whoever employed him than he is of the woman with her meaty fists and bloodied weapon. He'd rather die than tell her anything.

'Talwyn,' I warn, 'let him g—'

But there's a sudden *snap* that says he's gone. I wish I could say she doesn't know her own strength. I wish I could feel something about his death; that I could throw recriminations at my old trainer, but I've too much blood on my own hands, from too young an age. There's a numbness in my soul that I fear will never lift.

* * *

The dawn's well and truly done by the time I get myself home. The Constable has been spoken with, his men sent to explore the cave system in Merrow's Cove, to find any stray smugglers that might remain there. To bring home the bodies we left behind. Talwyn's still righting her office aided by the remains of her Guard.

The need I felt earlier for violence is very much glutted, very much in abeyance at this moment. Hopefully it will remain so for some while. Tonight's experience tells me I must find other ways to use my time, to expend energy that's no longer directed to a daily regime that was never my choice. The fighting and exercising, the study of legends and whispers and nightmares captured on parchment and bound between covers. All the things that haunted Hedrek Zennor – and by extension, me – for the past thirteen years.

With all the nervous energy burned away, I find I'm both starving and exhausted. The starvation wins out. In my pocket is a sweetmeat wrapped in a kerchief – from Talwyn's supplies; the idea of it turned my stomach earlier and now it's insufficient. I tiptoe towards the kitchen. On the other side of the door that leads into the cavernous space, are noises. The clatter of dishes, the splash of water. Thinking Mrs Medway awake, I enter.

It's not Mrs Medway, not by a long shot, and her name dies on my lips. It's a wee wizened man with a green cap, brown shirt and red trousers, and he's standing on a tall stool beside the sink, doing our dishes from the day. There's a moment, perhaps, when I might have gone in time, but I'm exhausted and fuddled by the sight in front of me. Before I can even think to leave, the round head turns towards me, beard grey, eyes black like pieces of coal, the nose bulbous, and expression of building rage on his face.

The beekie.

All I can think of is Mrs Medway telling me all the luck of our house will flee with him, now he's been seen. Or worse, he'll get destructive and pull the building down around our ears – and don't we have enough trouble to deal with right now?

Then another voice from so long ago, my mother's: *Give him whatever's in your pocket. He won't care what it is – that it's personal is enough. Whatever's in your pocket.*

I reach into my right pocket, pull out the fabric-wrapped confection and hold it up.

The beekie's expression shifts to suspicion, then curiosity. I go to the blackwood table and put the offering there, don't unwrap it. Then I back away, saying, 'Thank you for all you do.'

When I'm in the doorway again (my appetite gone), the wee man climbs off his perch and swarms up the leg of the kitchen table. With his still-damp hands he plucks at the handkerchief, exposes the sweetmeat, picks it up, sniffs at it, takes a tentative bite. His face lights up and a squeak of delight comes from him.

I know better than to push my luck, and quickly leave.

I'm so tired I don't even bother to draw a bath or remove my clothes, just kick off my boots before tumbling atop the covers and falling into a very deep sleep, hoping it will be dreamless.

* * *

I'm seven and I'm in *that* house again.

The one against the city's eastern wall, only a street up from the part of the harbour where waste goes, where the water stinks at low tide, is only slightly less ripe at high. A tiny home we could sometimes barely pay for when work was thin on the ground for Father, when Mother was too ill to take in mending or to do the fine embroidery for one of the modiste boutiques far up the hill. When I didn't manage to steal fruit from the market stalls or eggs from Doctor Castiagne's chicken coop, or bread off the windowsill of the rich house in which Mrs Medway then worked. She'd become a friend of Mother's, would put sewing work her way when she could, would bake two loaves and leave one for me to hone my thief's skills.

I'm trying to wake up. This isn't a dream I want, but its grip is too strong.

Outside, it's afternoon, bruising into evening and my mother's been in labour most of the day, in their bed in that cramped room, her screams reduced to moans as her energy and will to live have drained away. I'm sitting atop the ladder that leads to my tiny loft platform, haunting like a cobweb because no one's noticed me, and no one had said I shouldn't. Mother's been like this for hours and it seemed as if each breath, each contraction, peeled away a layer of her life as Tiberius tried to make his way into the world. Little good it did him.

The doctor, when Father finally went for him, had refused to come knowing we couldn't pay. By the time Mrs Medway, having finished her work as a cook, arrived it was too late. My little brother had died almost as soon as he hit the air, and Mother followed him soon after, while I watched from above. Father sat helpless, his dead son in his hands.

Perhaps I sobbed, for Mrs Medway spied me and called me down, made me kiss Mother goodbye; the sensation of her rapidly cooling skin on my lips is the memory of an ice storm. Made me touch my little brother's sticky cheek. Then she sent me back up to my bed, for night had fallen by then, with instructions to be a good girl and go to sleep. No one had thought to feed me, but I wasn't hungry.

Yet I don't obey, but settle once more on the rough loft floor, staring down at the big room where half of my family lies cold, my father weeping and drinking some fearful rot-gut as Mrs Medway

63

prepares the dead for their last earthly journey. I'm watching still, though drowsing by then, when a knock comes.

The sun is hours away, yet a man waits on the doorstep. He's dressed in dove-grey trews, high boots with gold details, a black jacket beneath a long woollen cloak with flecks of rain on the shoulders. When he steps inside, he pulls the hood of his cloak back, shows the sleek black hair beneath. He's very tall, very handsome.

Hedrek lets him in, hears him say that he wishes to speak in private. Hedrek, by then very drunk, shoos Mrs Medway out with barely a thank you. At our scarred table, he pours two glasses of rum and the man offers a solemn toast to the lost.

The man leans closer to Father, talks in a low voice. He talks for a long time, glance flickering around the cramped space, as if assessing what he might offer, what might be considered, taken. Never once does he look up and find me. Finally, he takes a piece of thick paper from his coat pocket and slides it to my father. Hedrek, eyes glazed, puts a hand on the parchment, slowly pulling it towards him as if its heavy. Perhaps it's weighted down by what it represents. What it *buys*.

When the stranger leaves, sometime before dawn, he takes my little brother's body with him, wrapped in the cream woollen blanket that should have kept his poor crib warm, the very same one I'd had as a babe in arms. Hedrek continues to drink – and will do so for months, on and off depending on his level of grief.

Tiberius was dead for sure; I remember, I was there. A clear view I had, of my mother giving birth and expiring, expelling that little scrap of dead flesh – skin as white as snow, hair as black as ebony, beneath the blood that covered everything. He did not draw breath, or barely, so I cannot imagine what that man wanted with his tiny cadaver. My mother went into the earth alone, Tiberius was carried away (north, north, north), and in return we were suddenly, obscenely, ridiculously rich.

It's not a dream, not really, but a memory that repeats again and again, re-emerging whenever I think it's gone. It's a memory and not a dream, so it shouldn't change. It *should* be the same, a routine, a ritual, like the moves of a dance or a punishment.

But this night, for the first time ever, there is something new: the cloaked man with the golden pin on his collar turns as he hovers in the doorway, the bundle of my brother held tenderly against his chest. He turns, just his head, and his pale blue eyes find mine. His look says he's seen me. I have been *noted*. That I will not be forgotten. Except that never happened.

And when I wake, finally pulling myself from sleep with a cry on my lips, I'm drenched in sweat and shaking.

7

'I'm afraid, Violet, there's nothing to be done.'

Junius Quant does his best to get all his features in the right order for sympathy, but as it's an expression he doesn't use often the effort falls rather flat. Looks as though he's suppressing a burp.

'My father's death should not have led to a freezing of *my* accounts, Mr Quant.' The pleats in the bodice of my dress are very straight and I'm running my fingers along them to try and keep calm, concentrating on their sharpness. Coming here meant no disguise, meant dressing well and prosperously, reminding the banker of who I am. Apparently that doesn't matter. 'I don't understand how this has happened.'

'Ah, well. You'd have to speak to Mr Pendergast about the whys and wherefores. Red tape and legal jargon, all beyond me.' He shuffles the papers on his desktop, adjusts the angle of the banker's lamp with its green glass shade.

'Given your position, sir, I'd have thought you'd know considerably more about such things. Or no one, my father included, would trust you with their money.' I grind my teeth as I stare at him. I could have come here immediately after I met with

Titus, but I doubt it would have made any difference. I'm willing to bet Hedrek suspected I'd try and disobey so he primed his friends to make sure I was backed into a corner. No wonder Titus, when I'd sent a note asking for a little more time to consider, had been so willing – he knew I'd find no aid here.

'Violet—'

'*Miss Zennor.*'

He sits up straighter. 'Miss Zennor. Any funds you had originated with your father. Every penny can be traced to a transaction made by him. Now, never fear – all funds will eventually make their way to you, but there are "i"s to dot and "t"s to cross, and you know the law takes time. It will be a good month before Titus can appear before the Magistrate and petition for probate.'

'And how, Mr Quant, am I supposed to pay the bills of my house? Put food on the table for myself and my stepmother and my housekeeper?' My stepmother who has in no way been provided for by my father, despite the fact they've remained married.

He lifts a hand as if to ward off a tantrum. 'Violet, no one will allow you to starve! Titus will continue to pay Mrs Medway's salary, and all providers should present their accounts – duly signed by you or your representative – to Pendergast & Associates for prompt payment.' He smiles. 'See? It's all very simple.'

'I cannot tell you, *Junius*, how much I would like to castrate you.' The man was never part of Hedrek's inner circle, merely the keeper of his money; Quant must have suspected my father was doing something untoward, but he had a banker's conscience which seldom asks questions and is easily quelled by the *chink* of coin.

'Now, Vi—Miss Zennor, don't take on so. I'm more than happy to advance you a loan against your inheritance. Just name a figure and provided it's reasonable, you can walk out today with gold jingling in that pretty purse.'

I could hit him over the head with my pretty purse, which contains a set of knuckledusters and would make quite the dent in his skull. But I'd rather have money to hand, so I force a smile, ask for fifty gold coins of my own money. He shouts towards the closed door of his large office with its mahogany furnishings and thick carpets, and a flunkey appears in a second. Junius Quant makes his demand and the flunkey moves off with impressive speed. In just over a minute, I'm handed a leather pouch, which I put into my bag, making it even more of a weapon.

There are several jewellers in St Sinwin's; I can take the gifts my father gave me over the years, something shiny for each birthday and holyday. It won't be a fortune, but it will get me away. This afternoon I'll visit those jewellery stores, and tomorrow I'll ask Talwyn about departing ships, the goal I'd forgotten the other day when distracted by news of Tempe's arrival. Junius has risen, is levering me out of my chair as if he's a gentleman, avuncular, rather than trying to rush a problem out the door.

'Once again, Miss Zennor, my condolences on your loss.' Junius Quant, not a friend of my father's, not one of his conspirators, but an instrument of his will. 'And please don't hesitate to come and see me again should you need another advance.'

The smile I pin on my lips doesn't really go high enough to be convincing, I can feel it. He doesn't seem troubled, however, as he says, 'And perhaps, when you're feeling more social and your grief is less acute, you might agree to walking out with my youngest son, Jude?'

The older two are married already; none of them have any better personality than their father. I'm sure there are worse fates, but I cannot for the life of me recall what they are.

'Perhaps, Mr Quant. Perhaps. But my mourning will take some considerable time to reach its end. I'm sure you understand.' His gaze flicks to my dress – a deep purple, not really grief-stricken – but he's clever enough not to mention it as he almost pushes me out the door.

* * *

'I heard there was a ruckus down at the harbour last night. News of smugglers in Merrow's Cove, an explosion.' My stepmother's found my hiding spot, the rose alcove in the garden. 'All on the front page of *The Courier*.'

They must have done a rush job on that, rousing a reporter from their bed in the wee hours. I wonder who told? Probably Talwyn, eager to let folk know she's triumphed. Possibly the Constable, eager to let his superiors know he was all over the aftermath, handy with a metaphorical broom to take credit for someone else's blood, sweat and tears.

The roses are in early bloom, reds and whites, oranges and pinks, variegated yellow and purple, and my favourite mauve that looks a little like moonlight. They'll grow thicker in the coming weeks and a new gardener will be needed, but right now there's not enough to hide me. It's unfair to blame the blossoms: Temperance Zennor knows me of old. This was always a favoured hidey-hole. I shrug as if I had nothing to do with any ruckus, fracas or other incident. 'Really? Did you hear the blast?'

'No. We're too far away. Lives lost, they say.'

'Terribly sad.'

'It was reckless of you to go. Talwyn shouldn't have let you.' She pauses, about to sit, hovering as if uncertain of her welcome, then finally descends, settles beside me, her black-and-white-striped silken skirts frothing over my purple silk.

'Who said I was there?' I don't look at her. 'You were the one who taught me I should help my friends, and gods know I've got few enough of those.'

'The Harbour Guard don't need to enlist you—'

'The wonderful thing about Talwyn is that she knows better than to try and tell me what to do, which makes her a standout from most folk around me. All those old men, trying to make sure I *behave* according to their wishes.' On the bench next to me is the reticule, stuffed with the fifty gold coins and not much else. My visits to the jewellers, my tentative approaches as to whether they would view gems for a possible sale? Not a one of them would even discuss the idea. I sense the hand of the trinity there, forewarning anyone who might offer me aid; Titus, I suspect, it seems like his sort of influence with businesses. He's thought ahead, or my father did and his legal representative continues to enforce his will.

'You should have told me you were going out,' Tempe tries again, hands gripped in her lap, turning pale at their constriction. 'If you'd not returned I'd never have known—'

'And you've still not told me why *you* returned.'

'It was always my goal,' she says mildly. 'But how sad for me to do so only for you to risk death in an ill-considered venture.'

'I'm not a fragile flower, Tempe. Neither delicate nor breakable. And Talwyn taught me how to fight. I can take care of myself.' Admittedly last night's events did shake my faith in that idea, but I'll not tell my stepmother that. 'It was my own choice.

Do you understand why that's important? Do you understand why honesty's *critical*?'

She touches my hand. I don't react. Temperance sighs. 'I left St Sinwin's because your father asked me to find something.'

I turn to stone: she'd told me, all those years ago, that she was leaving because life with Hedrek was simply too much. I remind her of this, and she nods. 'That was certainly the case. But he'd asked me for one last consideration, one final favour in memory of whatever had been good between us. For your sake.' She's not looking at me but staring into the centre of one of the pink roses as if she can see something there.

'My father never did anything for my sake.'

'He *thought* he was. He believed it sincerely.' She raises a hand to ward off my reaction. 'Violet—'

'No, Tempe. Whatever affection he'd once held for me died quickly, as soon as my mother went into the ground.' I shake my head. 'What did he ask you for?'

My stepmother's silent for several moments, then hesitantly replies, 'A book.'

I shrug. 'Well, we've always had plenty of those.'

'This is a very specific book, Violet. Very rare. Your father always said there were no frivolous books in your home.'

'What book?' I'm surprised by how calm I sound. 'What book *specifically*?'

'A journal written by a scribe called Murcianus.'

There are myriad volumes of lore and myth by Murcianus on the library shelves, gold lettering on the spines. Walter had me memorise pages and pages of them. Why would this dusty scribe's diary be of interest? But I can't ask my stepmother for to do so would be to speak a secret I was sworn to keep, and the habit of concealment remains strong even though my father's gone. Even though he can no longer harm me, I still cannot force those words past my lips. Perhaps it's simply because it's a weight I've carried for so long, the idea of putting it down seems somehow… wrong. Almost blasphemous. Perhaps, when – if – I even speak it aloud, then I'll know I'm truly free. But for now, those words will not come. Besides, Tempe's never know the truth of Hedrek's plans.

'Hedrek wanted it for his collection. You know what he was like.'

I did. I do. If it was something Hedrek wanted it was mostly related to his obsession with the Darklands. But the Leech Lords barely featured in Murcianus' writings.

'Violet—'

'Did you find it? This journal?'

'Your father's information was that it had been carried across the sea as part of a princess's dowry to Edrick's Bastion. I followed its path, it took six months, and when I at last reached my destination? It was to discover the city had been set to the torch, the rulers strangled and thrown upon the pyre of their own palace. A librarian remained and told me, in return for an excessive price, that part of the collection had not burned. It had been sold off before the revolution, sent to another grand library, and he was adamant the journal survived. So, I set off once more.'

I take a sidewise look at my tiny stepmother. Temperance had never been adventurous or brave; what had driven her to be so intrepid? At Hedrek's request she'd turned treasure hunter. She was leaving him, but she still undertook this task at his asking. What had he done to inspire this devotion? Or how had he *compelled* her? 'And did you find it there?'

She shakes her head. 'The abbey – St Godgifu-by-the-Sea – to which I'd been directed lay in ruins, but an old nun, a relict who still wandered the dusty halls, swore she'd seen it once or twice, that the chests containing the royal library had been separated. One to a remote estate outside the city of Corentin's Forge held by an ex-princess of Lodellan and her ex-witch lover, the other to a tower house on an islet – Katarin's Fastness – in the middle of a lake that froze at the whim of its inhabitant. But she couldn't tell me which chest contained the journal. So, I travelled to both places. I found it in neither. The trail ran cold then, and I'd lost not only months but years. I began the trek home – much more direct this time since I knew where I was going.'

She looks away again and I wonder at the details of her journey, her trials and what scars it might have made in her soul and skin. Perhaps one day she'll tell me. Perhaps one day I'll ask. I think of telling her about my dream, of the pillow in my hand, of placing it over my father's face, of his breath being stopped. Perhaps not. 'Why did you go, Tempe? Why such a travail? What did Hedrek have over you?'

'There are secrets that aren't mine to share, Violet.'

He's gone and she's still protecting him. I rise. 'I have an engagement this evening. I'd best start getting ready.'

I don't need to do this yet. There're hours to go. But I don't want to hear anything else Temperance Zennor has to say on this or any other subject.

* * *

'I'm sorry it took me so long,' he says, 'but I thought an outing might help.'

Jack Seven-Gates, sitting beside me, looks resplendent. My ebony beaded gown is positively dowdy next to his evening suit, a fine brocade, its velvet lapels sewn with gems that look like stars each time he turns. A gold watch chain sparkles across the brilliant white shirt and the cummerbund is embroidered with gold thread. The cost of the overcoat and scarf he left in the cloakroom would feed a small village. The invitation to see a play arrived at lunch in the be-gloved hands of a well-bred footman who wouldn't leave without an immediate reply. I'd hoped that Jack would simply arrive on the doorstep unannounced, soon after the funeral, that we'd talk in the privacy of my home. However, this was the only option and, given my encounter with Tempe, I had no wish to remain in this evening.

'Well, it got me out of the house.' Which, to be honest, isn't necessarily a good thing: my excursions these past days have consisted of a funeral, an expedition that resulted in almost a dozen deaths, and unsuccessful visits to a solicitor, banker and several jewellers. Thus far this outing has been uneventful.

The Wave Theatre is a horseshoe-shaped structure by the shore, tiers of rough benches in the stalls with the quality of the seating becoming better the higher you go, the more you pay. The stage itself is built out in the harbour, the acoustics carefully designed so voices carry clearly without the performers having to shout. Tempe would take me there once a week to an opera or a play, outings very different to those with my real mother when she'd somehow scraped together the half-coppers needed for the cheapest of cheap seats. Those were silly skits I barely remember, a terrible ventriloquist, dancers in pretty dresses but with little actual grace, a baritone with rather a fine voice and

74

some romantic songs, but the one act I most definitely recall was the automaton.

In a robe of silver tissue, hair a fall of black curls, argent lines swirled up and down her arms and chest and neck as if she'd been tattooed most prettily. She did not move, was wheeled out onto the stage by a young lad, who wound a key in her back, then retreated to the wings as she began to sing in a language I didn't recognise, nor anyone else apparently. It was one of the most beautiful things I'd ever seen or heard, but my mother looked even more enchanted than I felt. The baritone reappeared and sang the last tune as a duet, staring at her in a way I now suspect to have been love. *Violet*, my mother had whispered, *I saw her once before, when I was young, when we lived in the northern climes and the troupe ventured there. I've never forgotten her and nor, I hope, will you.*

Tonight, however, there are no automatons. Just a play about ghosts, which may well be perfectly good, but I can neither concentrate on nor enjoy this rare outing. The exclusive gold velvet-lined balcony box gives a little privacy from the other theatregoers, yet we've caught attention and folk have been staring, whispering behind their hands. Jack seems unbothered, is watching the stage avidly, jumping in his seat whenever the phantom appears and delivers his dire threats, when the sound of manufactured thunder rumbles from the stage, when a duel is fought and won by the hero. He sighs when the heroine is soundly kissed by the good man who's loved her all along. It takes my entire store of patience not to fidget the whole way through.

When it's over, Jack turns to me with a broad grin that soon fades. 'I'm sorry, Violet. I thought this might take your mind off things, but—'

'It was a lovely thought, Jack. I'm just not really in the mood.' His company has not lifted me as I'd hoped it would; perhaps I thought it would feel like when we were children, but we're grown now and things change. I take a sip of champagne from the coupe on the crystal table between us; it's gone flat. 'Everything around me is in upheaval, it seems.'

'I *am* sorry about your father.' Jack leans forward, and I mirror him, thinking he'll touch his forehead to mine like we used to when we were small, when we hid in the garden from our fathers and their rages and demands. But he tilts his head and kisses me. Quickly, tentatively, inexpertly. I jerk back, almost falling off my seat.

'What are you doing?' I manage to keep my pitch to a hiss. But it still carries, and I can hear murmurs and gasps from the private boxes around us.

'I thought we might… now you're free… we could perhaps join our fortunes?'

'Our fortunes?? Why would you think that, Jack? Why? And now of all moments? Now?'

His face falls. 'I'm sorry, Violet. That was clumsy and crude.'

'You're too much like a brother to me!'

'I see.' His whole body seems to shut down, his key unwound, his strings cut.

76

8

We walk in silence, weaving back and forth through side streets, gradually rising. Every nerve in me wants to move faster, wants to jog, to have these agonising moments done with. I think about saying something, there's an apology on my lips, a stupid thing because none of this is my fault. In fact, the longer we're together, the more convinced I become that Jack's action was calculated.

That he kissed me in full sight of St Sinwin's finest society to put a claim on me.

It's just the sort of thing he would do. I've known him long enough to be aware of his habits, how territorial he is, how aware he is of status – how much his father's loss of the family fortune two years ago affected him. I've heard him, at his lowest, list his mortal enemies, those who snubbed him, how he'd get his revenge once he rebuilt said fortune – and I've seen him make good on most of those vows. I know him well, like an older brother. He's been my friend. A friend who's amused me and comforted me. A friend who's been closer than he might have been had I had other friends in my life. A friend who grew apart from me when his family lost everything. Or perhaps that's simply the nature of growing up, to grow apart.

Like most, he simply regarded Hedrek as an eccentric, overbearing father. My secrets I have kept for myself – only the trinity of Hedrek, Titus and Walter have known the truth. Talwyn knew only that she was bid to make a killer of me; Mrs Medway only that I must be patched up when I came home bleeding; Tempe only that I needed to learn feminine graces and to "pass" in high society. Three women who never asked questions. The truth of me, of what I've done, has never been shared with a friend because the scars Hedrek left on me from my seventh year were put there as a warning, an admonition to silence.

Finally, at the wooden gate in the high stone wall around Zennor House, Jack stops. Normally he would come in, have a nightcap, speak with my father man to man, cheer me with gossip – lift the atmosphere of my home with his light talk. But Hedrek is gone and Jack has made a hole in our friendship that I don't know how to fill – and don't know if I want to.

He gives me a curt bow, barely low enough to be considered polite, and turns on his heel, a neat pivot, and cuts into the night, disappearing quickly in his black attire, every line of him tensed, a child deprived of a toy to which he considers himself entitled. A tiny part of me thinks to call out, to summon him back with an apology I don't owe. The larger part of me is angry. *How dare he?* Never any sign of romantic intent in all these years, never a sign of interest in me beyond that of a sibling. Yet tonight, three days after I put my father in the ground, he thought to make a claim on me in front of all those fine folk, all those other potential suitors. *Look! See what I have? What I've put my mark on?*

He thought himself clever, to present as a friend, lull me into a false sense of security, to sneak under my guard. As if I would bargain away the freedom I have at last – all for a ring and a husband and the prison of marriage sanctified by the Church. As if, with liberty in sight I would chain myself to a husband, something the removal of which tends to require poisoned cakes or greased steps.

I close the gate behind me, lean against it, enjoying the sense of something solid when my world feels entirely unstable. I take deep breaths, trying to centre myself. Looking up at the house I'm struck by how few windows are lit. It's not terribly late and even though there's only the three of us living here, the beekie has taken on the (unseen) duty of lighting the lamps and candles of an evening, then snuffing them after we've gone to bed. I wonder if he's taken offence in spite of my offering, or if something else has happened.

I step through the front door into a dimly lit foyer, only one lamp flickering weakly there. I close the door quietly, tilt my head as if that act will allow for listening more intently. There should be voices – Temperance and Mrs M had immediately resumed their old habit of chatting by the fireside in the scarlet parlour after dinner, sipping lavender tokay and nibbling on sweet biscuits. But as I pass by on tiptoes that little parlour is empty and dark, even the fireplace unlit. I touch my fingers to the modest long sleeve on my right forearm, feel the reassuring shape of the knife and sheath beneath the fabric.

I continue along the corridor until I'm almost at the library.

The door is ajar and a low murmur trickles out. Through the gap a tense-looking Temperance is visible, sitting in a chair opposite Bishop Walter. The sight of the prelate is almost enough to burn away my caution with rising rage, to see him in my house, but I restrain myself from charging in. I force myself into habits of caution, note both are bound and gagged, then look at the mirror over the mantlepiece and spy three more figures.

Mrs Medway, separated from the other two, is tied to a chair in the middle of the room, a footstool in front of her as if for comfort; a white cloth is over her mouth and blood trickles from her forehead, a bruise already forming on one cheek. I've no doubt she gave them far more trouble than either Tempe or Walter. "Them" constitutes a man and a woman, dressed in black trews and frock coats. The man's seated at *my* desk, the woman leans against the nearest bookshelf, a tome in hand. If they don't already know I'm here, they're expecting me. They don't look like common thieves. Uncommon ones, perhaps. As I'm pausing, the man calls:

'Come in, Miss Zennor.'

Unhurriedly, I push the door further, step into the breach, holding my hands up to show them: *empty*.

'How kind of you to invite me into my own home.'

'We'll not keep you long,' says the woman, more softly, almost apologetically.

'Which one of you hit my housekeeper?'

They don't answer but the way the man's eyes dart away says it was him. I take them in: older than me, middling years, but with a hardness to their features and bodies – muscled beneath their clothing, somewhat like myself. Have they been trained from childhood? Who did not spare the rod? I've no doubt they were beaten. There are some few in the world who, having had terrible experiences, make a point of not meting them out to others in turn; I don't believe this pair are in that category. The woman might sound regretful, but that doesn't mean she'll hold back.

80

'Why have you broken into my home and assaulted my family?' It's irksome to include Walter in this, but it feels unavoidable, and somehow unforgivable not to. As if I would condemn him were I to deny his place in my life. If they think he has value to me, he might survive a little longer. Although surely they know he's a bishop, surely they'd not injure him needlessly. I notice, however, they chose to hurt Mrs M – I can't help but wonder if this was a choice made by her perceived lack of status. That Tempe and Walter remain otherwise untouched because they're "quality".

'We've no intent to harm your family, unless you refuse to play nicely.' A dagger – a copper-coloured blade, carved, what looks like a horn hilt – appears in the man's long fingers. He tosses it lightly hand to hand, a circus performer uttering threats.

'And what do you want from me?' I ask, as if I can't see the woman moving quickly towards me, thinking my attention is on her companion, who's drawing back the dagger.

'Only your death,' he says as he, still seated, releases the knife.

They know nothing about me, nothing about how I've been raised; they think me a lamb to the slaughter. I bodily heave the woman in front of me. The blade thuds into her back, and her eyes, so close to mine, widen; her last breath puffs out as if pushed. His aim was good, but I'm faster.

While he's still scrambling up from the chair, I'm airborne. No complicated flips or turns, for Talwyn taught me they're a waste of time and effort and slow you down, just a step onto the footstool Mrs M kicked towards me, a leap upwards, straightening my right arm with a jerk to release the knife strapped there, feel it slide into my palm, and as he half-rises, lifts his gaze to watch the arc of the swing, I slash his throat as my boots land on the desktop. He drops, gurgling. I take a few moments to watch him die, staining the carpet and the desk and the curtains with each arterial spurt, then move to free Mrs M. I wipe the blade on my skirt, slide it back into its sheath.

'Are there any more in the house?' I cut her bonds then those of Temperance and Walter. All three shake their heads.

'Just them. They knocked soon after you'd gone out, said they were among your father's researchers, here with an artefact and seeking payment.' Mrs M spits. More blood on the carpet, but she remains fearless. I wonder how the beekie will like cleaning *this* mess.

'Bishop Walter was visiting,' says Temperance, her eyes huge.

'Without your attendants, Walter?' I pretend shock.

'I thought you might be more reasonable if I came alone,' he grumbles.

Tempe asks: 'Violet, what did they want?'

'Common thieves, Tempe. How fortuitous, Walter, that you were here.'

'And a good thing I was, Violet Zennor. You want proof that your father was right?'

I close my eyes, exhausted. 'Walter, I must say that this feels most ungrateful when I've just saved you from being turned into a saintly corpse. Not even a "thank you, Violet"?'

He barely pauses for breath: 'They came from the Anchorhold – see those pins on their coats?'

'Perhaps we should discuss that in private.' I look meaningfully at Tempe and Mrs M, reminding him as he's so often reminded me that there are secrets to be preserved. 'Mrs Medway needs attention. Tempe, do you think you could attend to her? Are you strong enough?'

A flash of irritation from both my stepmother and housekeeper. I remember that the gentle Tempe who left us behind has been strengthened by her own vicissitudes and adventures, and Mrs Medway has always been stoic and discreet, never asking questions she knew weren't owed to her.

'I'm more than capable, Violet. I'm not some frail creature. We will send for the Constable,' she says sharply, but I note she wobbles as she stands. Mrs M is quickly by her side, supporting her, and together they leave, arms about each other's waists. Neither looks back; I wonder if it's anger or simply discretion. A strong will, to keep from looking back.

'They seek your death, Violet.'

'But I'm still standing, Walter, and they're making a mess on my very expensive silk rugs.'

He shakes his head and for the first time the bishop looks something other than angry or frustrated with me. He looks so terribly sad, as if he knows what I've been turned into by my father; as if he knows how he helped and that it cannot be undone. It might be this that makes me weaken.

'There are things your father did not tell you, Violet. Things he held back, but you need to know them. Whether you make this journey or not.'

Or it could be this acknowledgement of the fact that I might not do what I'd been bid. What I've been brought up to do. 'Speak your piece, Walter. This will be the last time I entertain you.'

'Violet, the Anchorhold knows of you *now*. For the longest time it did not. Your father did his best to keep you a secret, but something has happened. Something has warned it that you exist.'

'Walter—'

'*Bishop* Walter!' He stomps over to the bodies, pulls at the front of the man's buttoned jacket and the shirt beneath it, reefs the fabric back to expose the flesh beneath the left collarbone. He rolls the woman over, has to remove the knife to allow her to lie flat, then undresses her, careful to preserve her modesty – gods forbid he see a tit. He straightens, waves his hands in a *ta-dah!* motion.

Identical marks. Raised scars. The one on the woman pinker, newer; the man's white with age. Intricately entwined shapes that might be a serpent or a vine twisting into an elaborate letter "A". And on the inside of their coats, hidden from public view, are gold breastpins in an identical style. I recall Freddie and her news of a man and woman asking about me, how they looked like quality but spoke like toughs.

'You see? Not random scarring. Not birthmarks. Brands. The sigil of the Anchorhold.'

9

I pour two glasses of winter-plum brandy, knowing Walter's preference for it, and that my stock of port is on the low side. We'll both do better with some liquid fortification, loath though I am to prolong his visit. When we're sitting in the green brocade wingback chairs by the hearth, the fire fed and roaring, the bodies out of our line of sight, he throws back his drink, helps himself to more, then begins:

'This is the history of the Darklands and the Leech Lords who rule there, or at least what is known.

'Once, that tiny nub of land was *ordinary*, distinguished solely by its northern climes and harsh winters, the months on end when there was only night and people huddled in their homes, whether hovel or castle, and did not leave for fear of freezing to death or being lost forever in the blackness. There were, then, only two large towns, almost cities: Calder (or Caulder depending on your age or education), and The Spire. In between were scattered villages, the occasional manor and estate, isolated farms. Its name came from those long winters.

'It was quite ordinary. No greater dangers than those experienced elsewhere. Wolves who walked sometimes on two legs, those who remained on four; the former being more dangerous and less kind. Water creatures beauteous or otherwise, kelpies and merrows, nixies and mer, women who sang on rocks to lure the unwary beneath. Those that lived under the mountains, creatures with hollow backs and cows' tails, trolls who haunted the forest looking for food in the form of babies, leaving their own offspring in empty cradles. Ghosties and ghoulies and things that went bump in the night. Then, one day or another, somehow, something new was born, though no one seems to know how it happened.

'The Leeches came into being.' Walter clears his throat.

'They'd been human, once, but something changed; they were gripped by the urge to feed on others. On their blood mostly but some would eat the flesh of their victims, gnaw on their bones and suck them dry of marrow. An utter consumption in some cases, whatever a person was or seemed, their kindness or intellect, their charm, their possessions real or imagined. Their very *themness*.

'At first – the very first or so it's said – there were two, and only two. It remained thus for some time, just the Lord and Lady ruling Caulder and its surrounds. But even revenants multiply – whether because they wanted the company of their own kind or the control of longer-lived servants no one knows. But two by two by two they increased, not through any breeding one might recognise but through will mostly, occasionally by accident or so it's been said.' Walter shakes his head as if the act of mating, of breeding, is incomprehensible to one such as he – but the tales of clerics and their children had on housekeepers and whores are frequent, far-ranging and famed so his self-righteousness seems disingenuous.

'Eventually, the Lord and Lady realised that if this multiplication continued the place would be overrun. Others of their kind had struck out and created their own towns and cities and estates, set themselves up as nobles. A council was formed of the five oldest Leeches who used their age and power to gain ascendancy and establish a rule of law for all their kind in the Darklands. They devised coats of arms and emblems for those in their employ or possession; the worst of them made brands. Any Leeches who did not wish to be ruled in this way travelled south, to other lands; some remained and tried their luck at rebellion. Some won and established themselves in the hierarchy; some lost and their possessions went to the victor.'

Walter refills his glass yet again, but doesn't drink, instead stares into the fire. 'As you know from your studies, the predations of these monsters who'd left for newer climes were noticed and the Church drove them back or hunted them to extinction. There remained the risk of the Leeches regrouping, mounting a sustained push southward, but before that could happen the brilliant Archbishop Narcissus Marsh built a great gate at the pass to the Darklands, made it impenetrable.'

Here, I can't help but interrupt. 'He made a bargain with the Briar Witches, that they would hold the border by *their* magic. And they've held it for three hundred years without help from the Church. And there are two things forbidden in the Darklands: witches and god-hounds. Be honest, Walter, I know this history as well as you.'

The bishop grumbles, then carries on: 'Those Leeches who remained in the Darklands made accommodations. The clever ones bargained with the humans under their rule, ensured that their service had benefit. Folk were rewarded for their feudal labours, for paying the bleeding tithes, for sending their children into service in the houses of the Leech Lords, either domestic or military. Some houses are given to cruelty and excess, are known to hire bandits to kidnap travellers within the Darklands or beyond its border and deliver them to blood farms where they live very short lives indeed. There are Leeches who still hunt in the old ways, indiscriminately slaughtering, but the Council disciplines them, except those too strong to be vanquished. There were some human-led rebellions but for the most part people found the life acceptable, whether their Lords were fair or foul.'

'Mrs M's always said that people don't like change, even when it's for their benefit. They'll stay in terrible situations simply because it's familiar. It's the terrible they know.' I think about myself – might I have run before Hedrek's death? Made a new life? I refill my own glass and drink deeply. 'Where are you going with all this, Walter?'

'The point is that no new houses arose. Not for a long time, none that weren't approved of by the Council. Yet one hundred and fifty years ago word came of another stronghold. It wasn't new: had been existing for a very long time without anyone's knowledge, it seemed. A small joint force was sent to this place in the very far north of a region already very far north. That force, a mix of humans – day-runners – and Leeches – night-runners – didn't return. Not a single one.

'Another expedition was sent, a larger group this time, with the same result.

'A third incursion was being planned when an envoy arrived in Caulder during a Council meeting, bringing with them a message from the mysterious stronghold. The Council would cease and desist sending its soldiers into the northernmost territory and, if they left well enough alone, would be allowed to continue to exist. If they did not, the Anchorhold would make them regret their defiance.

'It was the first time anyone had heard this name.'

Anchorhold.

A dwelling place for a religious recluse. A place of tethering. Of grounding. A threshold. A space between life and death.

'The Council did not know if this Anchorhold was ruled by master or mistress, but they counted their losses – highly trained troops, completely disappeared – and weighed them carefully. They decided that obedience was in their own interests.

'And the Anchorhold went back to its obscurity as was its want. No one or no one connected to the Council ventured northward. The border remained intact.'

'Walter, it's growing late.'

'Patience, Violet Zennor. The peculiar life of the Darklands continued at its own pace. Folk were born and died one way or another, and now we come to your parents. Your father was a son of the west, raised in a village so tiny it didn't even have a name. Hedrek dreamed of bigger things and the way to those seemed to be to take to the roads. He apprenticed himself to a tinker, acted as a dogsbody while the man sold his goods. Hedrek travelled further than he'd ever thought to, and at last they entered the Darklands – which was where he and your mother met.'

That I did not know.

'They were determined to marry, which meant your mother's freedom had to be paid for. Your father gave all he had to the local Lord, who finally granted his permission. They left the Darklands, but your mother's mother, stepfather and brothers remained there.

Hedrek and Vesper had you. He was happy, had lost his urge to make a fortune.'

'I know. I remember the nights we went hungry,' I say sharply.

'Leeches and humans cannot breed – or generally nothing comes of it when they have congress. On a very rare occasion, however, there can be a pregnancy, and rarer still for that pregnancy to come to term and for a child to be born breathing. Your mother was such a rarity. Her mother was human, her father the Leech Lord.'

I think about my mother, how pale she was, how black her hair, how red her lips. How little I look like her.

'Children like you are also rare, second children rarer still. All might have been well had she not become pregnant again. Mostly, there is no further pregnancy, but… but Tiberius was a miracle.'

'But why would it be so different to me?'

'Because when the child of a Leech mates with a Leech, the result is catastrophic.'

'My father isn't—'

'But Tiberius's father was. Your mother's mother was ill, Vesper went home to nurse her in her last days. Conception happened there. A new Leech Lord ruled her old home, took a liking to her.'

'My mother—'

'It was not consensual.'

I feel sick, dizzy. I think of my father always calling Tiberius "your brother", never "my son". 'Walter—'

'Let me finish, Violet, I'm almost done.' The bishop looks very old all of a sudden. He was a younger man, when he taught me, I'm sure. When he and my father became friends. Surely? 'What happens with such a pregnancy, what few people know, is

90

that the foetus' – he pauses, swallows – 'eats the mother from the inside. Hollows her out – they're little parasites. That's why your mother grew so ill, why she was bedridden by the end. And the child never survives them.'

'I know, Walter, I was there. They both died and the cloaked man knocked upon our door and Hedrek sold my baby brother's body without a second thought.'

'I can't defend what he did. But he was grieving, his faith gone, no means to keep either of you, so when that man appeared, made his offer. Your father… he took it, and that money bought a new life.' Walter gestures to the richness of the library. 'When his grief had ebbed a little, he began to regret what he'd done, began to question why such an offer was made. It weighed on his soul, and he came, eventually, to me. Hedrek made his confession, mentioned your mother's heritage. I'd studied the Darklands in my youth, the history of the Church's battles with the Leech Lords, and the events your father described struck me as very strange. We began our research and eventually it was clear that he'd done something truly dreadful.'

'But Tiberius was *dead*.' I'm scouring my memory, trying to recall a time when Hedrek called Tiberius "my son", but there's only the phrase "your brother", for years and years.

'And even the dead may serve a purpose, their component parts repurposed. Vessels without souls can be filled in other ways.' He rubs his hands over his face, the bags under his eyes seemingly enlarged by the action. 'There is the prophecy, Violet. There's been the prophecy for a long time and such things cannot be ignored.'

'What prophecy? About me?' I scoff.

He matches my tone. 'Of course not. About Tiberius. I told you: your brother was a miracle, although a dark one. You're irrelevant except for the part your father chose for you to play. Nothing but a tool. Violet Zennor, an instrument to set things right.'

That hits like a slap to the face. I swallow. 'What's the prophecy, Walter?'

'In the city of the saint by the waters
From the evening song will come the lad
With the lad will come the crossing place
Thirteen summers will pass,
For the blood will come the lord
To break the border, the lord be free'

'That's rather ambiguous,' I observe.

'What do you want? Names in full? A personalised note?'

'Well, yes.' But I'm aware St Sinwin's is the only port-city named for a saint, that Sinwin was the saint of calm waters, and I'm even more aware that my mother's name, Vesper, means evening song. It's not perfect, but it's enough to disturb me. 'How did *you* know about it?'

'I began my career as a scribe in Lodellan's Ecclesiastic Archives, assigned to updating the codices of prophecies. A fascinating task, and I read everything I could. Some prophecies stayed with me, that was one of them. It was the main reason I pressed for a posting in St Sinwin's. I didn't know, of course, when it would come about, in my lifetime or not, but… it was a romantic notion.' He doesn't notice my eye-roll. 'Your father's confession, the details… I was meant to be here then. Now.'

'Walter—'

'If the border of the Darklands is open, the Leeches will flood the world. Your brother will be thirteen in three months.'

'Why now, Walter? Why try to kill me now?'

'Your father was very careful in keeping secret your lessons, what you were learning. Somehow word has filtered northwards.'

I think about Tempe and her travels, looking for that journal for so long, asking her questions in her open and honest way. About word of her search filtering back to other ears.

'And there have been rumours of ructions to the north, new leaderships in some cities of the Darklands or coups that leave no leadership at all. Things are changing.' Walter leans forward, pointing a shaking finger at me. 'Violet Zennor, you *must* do your duty.'

'Why *my* duty? Why can't you march an army of your brethren northwards, put the Leeches to the sword?'

'Because… because their numbers have grown. When first the Church hunted them, they were not so prolific – now, there are so many more inside the Darklands. They don't like us but they have no fear of us. It would be a massacre.'

The ringing of the brass bell at the front door interrupts any answer I might give. 'Walter, that will be the Constable. After you answer his questions, I suggest you leave.'

'There's more to tell—'

'I've had my fill of you for this evening, and I don't imagine any of my problems will disappear overnight.' I sigh, feeling defeat spread its oily fingers on me. 'I'll come to the cathedral tomorrow, Walter.'

The Constable appears in the doorway and I steel myself to remain calm. It'll be a while before I see my bed.

10

The widow's walk is the perfect hiding place. It's quiet up here, the sun hasn't yet grown too warm, the sea breeze is fresh and cool. The view across the rooftops is calming – until I look down to the harbour and the temptation of ships' masts and the open seas beyond. Tempe and Mrs Medway stopped calling for me about an hour ago; they don't know all my hiding places.

I can be on a ship on the evening tide and simply leave everything and everyone behind. Let someone else deal with the mess my father created. Yet the idea of Mrs Medway and Temperance and Freddie being left to fend for themselves holds me here. After I went to bed last night, there was very little sleep, turning everything Walter had said over and over in my mind. Considering that despite his claims he presented no actual evidence. Then I think about the man and the woman who'd come to kill me, about their branded chests, their breastpins – inner and outer marks, easy to lose an emblem, harder to remove a scar.

The Anchorhold.

The prophecy. My brother a dark miracle foretold. Me a

no-account creature, a convenient weapon for my father's use. If I flee, if everything Walter and my father feared comes to pass, how long might I hide? Who will stop the Anchorhold from doing whatever it wants? Who will stop it from using my baby brother for its own ends: Tiberius, who should be nothing more than brittle bones by now.

But what if he's not?

What if I run away and the Anchorhold succeeds?

What if the border is open to the Leech Lords, and the lands beyond become a feast for them?

What if they overrun us? This continent? How long before the Leeches also flow across the sea, carried on ships by their willing helpers? What if the whole world is overwhelmed?

Where might I hide then?

'Hello, Miss Violet.'

It doesn't matter that the voice is soft and sweet and piping childish – I'm sitting cross-legged on a high place, and it startles me enough that I jump and swear.

'Freddie! How'd you get up here?'

'Same way as you, I expect.'

'I used the stairs to the attic; you appear to have scaled the side of the house.'

She settles beside me, not touching, but near enough. Her child's face is tilted up like a flower following the sun, sweet and delicate and it reminds me of a loss, makes my heart hurt. I shake my head, shiver away the memory. I squint. There's a bruise on her left cheek, recent, shading towards purple-blue.

'Who hit you, Freddie?'

'A man. That man you killed.'

'Was it the one who'd been asking you about me?' She nods and I don't bother asking how she knows about the deaths – rumour and truth travel at different speeds, but both are always inconvenient, and the Constable doesn't know how to keep a secret. 'When?'

'Last night, before they came here – before the woman joined him – down by the Kelpie and Badger.' One of the less reputable drinking holes on the wharves. 'I was following, but he caught me. Thought I was just a pickpocket, yelled at me for trying to take his gold.' She extracts a black leather purse from her trouser pocket, offers it to me. The coins I shake into my palm are like nothing I've ever seen. One side scored deeply for breaking into smaller denominations, the other struck with the symbol of the Anchorhold, just as seared into the assassins' flesh. I try to return the purse, but Freddie shakes her head. 'He was rude, so I did take it.'

I think about how close she came to something worse; I think she realises it too as she goes on: 'Didn't even recognise me, did he? Might have been a problem if the woman had been with him the second time, she seemed sharper.'

'Well, neither of them will bother you now.' I think of the bodies on the slab in the mortuary. The Constable will have looked them over, his clerk enumerating the very few possessions found on them: knives and garrottes. The woman wore a ring in the shape of a snake; the top of its head could be opened to show a fine white powder inside a small well. Poison or a sleeping drug.

Freddie gives me a sideways glance. 'I know where they were staying.'

I take in her proud little face, the smug smile. 'Have you told the Constable?'

A look of scorn.

96

'Of course you didn't. Came to me first.' I smile. 'Good girl.'

'Wanna see?'

* * *

The house is firmly set in the poorer part, close to where the sewers let their contents out; near where I used to live as a child. The hovels on either side are empty, one missing its roof, the other its entire front wall, only the door remains incongruously upright in its frame. Down here, everyone minds their business, but choosing this place with no neighbours shows an abundance of caution, and not a small amount of reconnaissance. I'd assumed the cottage was also abandoned, but when I follow Freddie inside, step into the space that's kitchen and dining room and sitting room all at once, I'm hit by the odour of decay. I gag. There's a lantern on a rickety table and I fish the flint from my pocket, light it.

'In the cellar,' she says, pulling her shirt up to cover her nose and mouth; I mirror the action. I also realise she's already been in here, on her own, as if she hadn't learned a lesson from her close squeak with the man whose pocket she'd picked. The man who would have gleefully killed her and me and mine. Freddie stands back and watches as I hook my fingers into the iron ring of the trapdoor in the floor and heave it open. There's a set of stairs hardly more sturdy than a ladder and the stench, freed, is unholy. Several days they've lain here, perhaps a week. I don't go into the cellar – that's what Constables are for – but I can see three adults: a man, a woman and a youth. Presumably the family who'd had the misfortune to live here. Their home a coveted hideout. In the light of the raised lantern, we can see dried red lace frothed at their throats where they'd been cut.

'Did you know them?' I ask belatedly.

She shakes her head, and she seems untroubled. I wonder how many awful things she's seen in her short life. I've asked before, but she's never answered. I wonder, if Mother had survived, if Father had remained fine with his lowly status – might I have ended up anything like Freddie? An urchin on the docks, someone that could be easily disposed of? What would I have been like, uncushioned by wealth?

Feeling light-headed from trying to breathe shallowly, I drop the trapdoor back into place. There's another set of stairs leading up to a sleeping platform. I find nothing there, no bags, saddle or otherwise, no weapons, no records or map, books or instructions. They travelled very light, took what they needed when they came for me. It doesn't appear they were going to come back after having dealt with me, either.

The stink is still too strong and I almost slide down the steep steps to get outside. I double over and vomit on the cobbles, getting pitying looks from Freddie. When I'm upright again, it's a moment before I can speak. I'm desperate to wash my mouth out, but the well water in this part of town is notoriously foul, and definitely not the best of two bad choices.

'You alright, Miss Violet?'

Unlikely to be again, I think, but say instead: 'Freddie, off you go and fetch the Constable. Tell him I sent you, shout it if you must' – I'm aware how easily the man might dismiss an urchin – 'about what he'll find here.'

'And where will I tell him you've gone?' Sharp as a whip, the child.

I give a great and put-upon sigh as if no one has ever carried such a burden. 'For my sins, I shall be at the cathedral, talking to Bishop Walter.'

98

* * *

However, when I arrive at the cathedral, I find several things I did not expect:

Firstly, a whispering weeping crowd that starts halfway down the street leading to the house of worship and becomes a semi-circle in the plaza in front of it.

Secondly, the Constable and two of his offsiders already on the steps leading to the portico, and they are staring, open-mouthed.

And, thirdly and most awfully, Bishop Walter pinned to the door of his cathedral by a series of knives hefty enough to hold up his weight.

They'll discover, later, another house in the poor canton, at the other end of the docks, another murdered family, evidence of two or three other assassins – and a dead man bearing the Anchorhold's mark, a brown cloak and scarf around his head, and a dagger in his back; the man who attacked me the day of the funeral. The assassins were clever enough to stay in separate locations, in case one group should be found or caught or killed by an heiress they didn't know was trained at least as well as they in the art of slaughter.

Freddie – who, having missed the Constable in his office, arrived not far behind me – will be beside herself at having missed the second group of killers, and as cold-blooded as I sometimes think her, she'll be genuinely upset as if the second family's deaths were somehow her fault. I'll tell her that it wasn't in her power to prevent them – the murders were committed before she met the man and woman, before they began asking about me. That any good assassin establishes a base first, and does their best not to draw attention. That they would have been in St Sinwin's for some while before they approached her, and that by the time they had spoken to her, both of those families were already days dead.

And a note will be found stuffed in Walter's mouth, a warning to me: *Stay away, do not go north!* as if having failed to murder me, a stern warning might do the trick.

But that's hours in her future and mine.

In this rich, red, regretful moment there is only the fact of St Sinwin's bishop pinned to his church. One of my father's oldest and dearest friends, a man I'd known more than half my life, whether I liked him much or not. Such a loss shakes your foundations, the world shifts against your will, and you discover that you perhaps cared more than you ever thought.

My face is wet and I can't see properly, and I don't understand why. Then I blink and it clears, then blurs again. The heels of my hands on my cheeks, my eyes. Crying. Like an idiot. Like a child. And making a terrible noise.

And I'm honest enough to admit that while a fair chunk of this shocked grief is for Walter – *Bishop* Walter – there's also a good wodge for myself. The girl who thought she'd get to have her own life. Who thought she might just escape and enjoy herself, not be condemned to following another's fantastical beliefs. Who thought she might be free.

I watch as the Constable allows the brethren to take their bishop's body down, tenderly laying him on a stretcher covered with his purple high holyday cloak, with its ermine collar and lining. His eyes are closed so I've hopes they killed him before they displayed him. I hope he was at least spared that agony. The god-hounds carry him towards their infirmary, the hospice.

Before the Constable follows them I ask politely that he learn what he can – I think of Walter coming to Zennor House last night without his escort, then returning alone after the Constable let him leave. I wonder when they found him, caught him; I wonder if he told them anything before he died. And I tell the Constable about the other hovel with its deathly inhabitants; that I'm going home and will speak with him there later today when he has gathered whatever information he can. I tell him Freddie will show his men where the first site is and that she's under my protection, working for me, that she's to be treated with respect. He looks as if he wants to protest, but wisely keeps his mouth shut.

I turn and am walking down the stone steps into the piazza when I sense someone shift into my path. Tensing, I look up, expecting another black-clad cold-faced assassin. But no.

It's a tall woman, head-turningly beautiful, with green eyes, porcelain skin and unbound red hair. Her outfit is expensive, well-made, a redingote of deep purple over black velvet breeches and knee-high leather riding boots. A satchel is slung across her back. Her smile's tentative.

'Miss Zennor? My apologies, I know this is a very bad time – the worst – but my name is Asher Todd, and I really must speak with you.'

11

I'm reluctant to take this Asher Todd to my home – what with visitors not being great successes the last few days – and I'd like to remain in a public space should she prove more harmful than she's assured me she is. In her favour is the fact she's not tried to stab me – yet. Miss Madisson's Coffeehouse seems the best location for such discussion. There are padded booths for privacy and the clientele will be genteel. Besides, we're both too well-dressed for any of the less salubrious inns; here no one will take note of us. It's light and bright, large windows, different shades of blue, crystal chandeliers, the display cabinets filled with all manner of treats, and the competing scents of hot beverages and freshly baked cakes.

Miss Madisson herself leads us to one of the booths at the very back, then takes my order of 'Whatever you think we'll enjoy,' glowing as she retreats at being trusted to choose. The place is busy; most conversations as we passed other customers seemed to revolve around Bishop Walter's awful demise, who might have been responsible and whatever will happen to a town without a bishop; as ever bad news travels faster than good. I've taken the seat facing the door. Asher Todd looks a little uncomfortable, adjusts the satchel still slung across her back; I suspect she's used to being the one keeping watch. I grin.

'Don't worry. I've an eye out. Unless you've got specific enemies you're concerned with? Any particular identifying marks I should look for?'

She grins, wicked and sharp all at once, the studied air of being reasonable and approachable dropping. 'Not today, but I cannot vouch for tomorrow.'

'Noted.'

There's a brief interruption as two platters – one with a variety of cakes and pastries, the other with neatly sliced bread, ham and cheese – float onto the table from the hands of one of the servers, a lad of maybe seventeen with long lashes who sneaks glances at my companion. She doesn't notice or doesn't bother to – refreshing that such beauty doesn't need the reassurance of any and all gazes. The lad departs, thanked but a little crestfallen, and is replaced by a girl with a silver tray laden with porcelain cups and saucers, a silver pot, milk jug and sugar bowl, and two delicately etched glasses holding measures of tokay. It's a huge amount of food, but we both reach for it immediately. I didn't eat breakfast – I'm exhausted from a lack of sleep – and despite the number of corpses I've seen today I'm suddenly starving. Asher eats as though she's been deprived for some days.

Several pieces of cake later, I ask: 'So tell me, Asher Todd, who are you and what do you want with me?'

'Straight to the point, Violet Zennor. An admirable trait.' She leans back, runs her long fingers through her hair, takes a breath as if wondering where to start. 'I received a letter, three months ago from your father – or rather, from one of his representatives, a Mr Titus Pendergast, Esq.'

Three months ago, Hedrek was at the beginning of his final illness. His hands shook – whether from the illness or the alcohol, I cannot say – and he was generally no longer able to pen such missives as he wished. It was either Mrs M or I who dealt with his everyday writing requirements, but visits by Titus and Walter were regular and behind closed doors as they made decisions about my fate.

'Are you a researcher?'

She snorts. 'In my own way, but not on anyone else's behalf. I have… access to a very large library. Some very few people know this and it's more than their life's worth to speak about it openly. Those who do know are the sort who are willing and able to pay for the, shall we say, liberation of certain books. Also, if they've time to wait, a perfect facsimile can be made.' She shrugs. 'But if someone comes to me, they're most likely in a hurry.'

'And what was my father looking for?'

'He was very specific about the title. He said it was his last-ditch attempt to locate said tome. That it was critical. The fate of the world depended on it.'

'Well, my father did like his portentous pronouncements. What was it called?'

'It was a journal, by a scribe called Murcianus.'

I still.

She notices. 'Which is a book that doesn't exist.' Then raises a finger as if I might interrupt. 'But I knew something your father did not.'

104

'Which was?'

'That Murcianus never existed, but *Murciana* did. All those libraries across the world, and all those collections of books with a golden "M" on the spine. But there was never a man, Violet, to write them all.'

I blink. This is something *new*. Something requiring a reset of all the things I thought I knew. But it makes sense – that a woman's voice would be taken from her in such a monumental way. That she would be written out, all her works, her achievements, her documenting and witnessing would be stolen and credit given to a man and an imaginary one at that. 'How do you know?'

'I've spent much of my life in libraries.' She smiles. 'I've read many, many, many things. You'll find all the secrets in the world if you just read enough – of course, one also requires eternal life for that.' She shrugs. 'Murciana was one of the Little Sisters of St Florian at the Citadel at Cwen's Reach, centuries ago.'

'Cwen's Reach is a ruin.' Once, on a rare trip with my father, we sailed past the great promontory upon which that citadel had sat. There were only broken structures remaining, silhouetted against the sky, and I must admit my attention had been more taken by the sailing ship that was embedded in the cliff-face below it.

'Yes. Destroyed in one night so it's said, and its volumes dispersed and hidden, some burned or abandoned in the Citadel. The Little Sisters fled, carrying what they could of that precious library. Many of their descendants don't even know themselves nowadays, their stories have withered and become dust. But not all. Not all of us are lost.' She looks terribly proud. 'My grandmother told me that – that one of the Sisters married into our family.'

'But Murciana—'

'She came to the Citadel as a child and became the first of the Blessed Wanderers – a cadre of Little Sisters especially trained to gather knowledge and stories and lore, copy great books and small, and write them or steal them, if need be.'

Thief, I think. *Yet not a thief.* Or not entirely. Her clothes are so fine, her speech and manners likewise. What she does is as much, I think, for her own amusement as for profit; as much part of a family tradition. 'Still, so many books by one person?'

'I think,' she leans forward, 'they aren't all hers. I *think* she began it, but what if those volumes were collated from the work done by all the Blessed Wanderers. Don't mistake me, I believe she was terribly prolific, and there were original editions under her name, but when the Citadel was destroyed, when the Church got hold of whatever tomes they could, they annexed them under another name.'

I try to bring us back on track. 'My father sent my stepmother to find the very same book. She spent over two years looking for it – albeit under the wrong name but…' I tell her the places Tempe travelled.

Asher Todd shakes her head. 'There's never been, to my knowledge, any record of it being in that collection. Or being sent from this continent. I've found in various places notes that say it was stolen many years after Murciana's death, yet well before the Fall of the Citadel. Different Sisters are named and for different reasons, but the only one that seemed likely to me was a Sister Benedicte, who was also meant to have taken a grimoire known as *The Bitterwood Bible*.' She gives a sigh. 'What wouldn't I give to find that…'

'But why did my father want it?' I'm asking myself more than her.

She clears her throat. 'I don't know for certain. I always ask why someone wants me to find a book. They don't always answer. Sometimes I find it and I tell them I didn't because I don't think they should have it.'

'You read them before you hand them over?'

'I read everything, Violet Zennor. And this journal, I read it too. Your father didn't tell me why he wanted it, but some of its contents are telling. I think he believed it contained information about the origins of the Leech Lords…'

And I don't feel confident enough to tell her anything. That she's right. I keep thinking about Temperance being sent on a fool's errand; why Hedrek sent her and why she went. So I just ask, 'And does it?'

'It does.'

'Did Hedrek owe you money? I'll settle any debts he left.' *Or rather I'll send you to Titus to pay your bill since I'm not allowed to access any funds.*

She shakes her head, reaching for a pastry. 'Master Pendergast arranged a sizeable bank draft simply for my reading the letter, and finding the book was easy enough.'

I give her a disbelieving look.

'I found it by accident years ago. Read it, had it copied.'

'Why bring it here yourself? Surely you've got flunkeys?'

'I brought it because I think you might need it – and I don't trust anyone as much as I trust myself.'

'And where did you find it?'

Only a small hesitation. 'Whitebarrow.'

'The university town.' I laugh, delighted at the audacity. 'And its famous library, the most *secure* in all the land. Nary a book stolen from there in hundreds of years.'

'Not that they know of and not that they'd admit.' She leans forward again, a little manic. 'There's a labyrinth of shelves half of the librarians can't navigate, locked restricted sections that only one *man* has the key to, in a huge building with more secrets than they can imagine. And beneath—' She catches herself. 'Well, beneath is somewhere else to explore. One day.'

I can't help but snort; I think Asher Todd and I might get on very well in other circumstances. 'So: this book?'

'A series of journal fragments written by Murciana herself. Hard to believe, I know, so long ago, but I'm persuaded of its authenticity by several factors. It was in the restricted section, but it was in a bundle of books that appeared to have been tied together for ease of transportation but never undone. They've not been listed in the indexes, so clearly no one knew that they were in possession of *The Compendium of Contaminants*, *The Last Book of Lost Verse*, *The Ways Between and Beneath* or *The Herbal of Adlisa the Bloodless with Annotations by Sister Rikke of the Citadel* – among others. More than one source records that these books were held in the Citadel until its fall. Somehow, they've been forgotten, perhaps thrown on a shelf by some god-hound who put no value on the words women keep. Or maybe hidden there by someone else who was unable to come back for them.' She shakes her head, gives a frustrated breath. 'Not knowing will haunt me. All these possible stories… But I digress. The journal: disparate pages bound together mentioning her parents when her origins have never been known or recorded before – or were concealed for good reason.' She leans forward. 'Murciana came from the north. She came from the Darklands, before the Leech Lords appeared. *Just* before.'

'Oh.' I sit back in my chair, hold my breath. I think about the Anchorhold – the most northerly north. About Walter's tale of an unknown power to which even Leech Lords bowed. I wonder about the prophecy and my brother, about the huge thing I'm meant to accomplish, both destruction and salvation. I nod towards the satchel she's put on the table between us. 'Do you have it *here*?'

'Yes, but it's not really coffeehouse reading…'

'Where are you staying?'

'I literally arrived in St Sinwin's on this morning's coach and sought you out, only to be told by your excellent and terrifying housekeeper that your father had died, you weren't home and I should speak with the bishop. I don't think she wanted to let me across the threshold. A bit insulting, this is a very expensive coat.'

'The last few days have been challenging.' I grin, thinking I will explain later about last night's visitors. 'We have guestrooms aplenty, if you promise you're not an assassin.'

'An assassin, no.' A brief smile. 'And thank you. Just one night and then I'll return home. I have obligations.'

'Books to steal?' I drain the little glass of tokay. She guffaws, unladylike.

Outside, the afternoon shadows are lengthening. I direct her to an alleyway, a shortcut, a gentle slope. As soon as we set foot in its shadows, there's movement ahead of us and I curse myself for letting my guard down.

I assume it's Asher, that she's brought compatriots with her, that on her chest there's a scar in the shape of the Anchorhold's sigil and everything she's told me is a long and elaborate lie.

But as I hit the release on my dagger, feel it slip into my palm, Asher Todd simply raises a hand and the skin turns bright orange.

Flames leap from her fingertips, as malignant as dragon's breath, showing clearly the two men dressed in elegant black, swords raised, before lighting them up like harvest festival effigies.

They burn fast and intensely, so fast they don't even utter a cry. The heat drives us back several steps, leaving two mounds of ash and charred bone, and a meaty stink in the air.

Asher's apologetic when she says, 'Did I overreact?'

'I don't know anymore.' I scan the alley: no onlookers and no one coming to investigate the screams. Not yet anyway. 'Let's get home. Keep an eye out.' We move quickly because I don't want to have to explain to the Constable why I was at the scene of yet another gruesome death. And why I'm in the company of a witch.

12

How many more of them remain in the city, breastpins and brands hidden?

How many more houses did they infest?

How many more unfortunate families are rotting, undiscovered?

We make it to the gate of Zennor House without further incident. Once inside the stone wall, I drop the heavy wooden bar into place. Anyone who wants to enter will need to ring the brass bell; of course, assassins aren't known for sending a warning, but it's the best I can manage. Asher notices what I've done.

'Whatever your father wanted you to do – I don't think it's going to go away. My experience is that terrible obligations just don't.'

I blurt out, forgetting that Asher doesn't know who Freddie is: 'But what happens if I'm not here to protect them? Mrs M, Temperance, Freddie?'

She looks pitying. 'I'm not trying to be cruel, Violet. I think if you're not here, no one will be coming for them. They're after you and if you're in St Sinwin's, they'll try to use your family as leverage. If you're not here? They'll go after you. No one's interested in them if you're not around.'

I rub at my face with both hands, blocking out the sight of everything for a few precious moments. 'Gods, I hope no one saw you burn those bastards. You can't stay in the town more than one night – plenty of places to hide in the house, don't worry, but the longer you're here, the more dangerous it'll be, especially if someone *did* see. St Sinwin's is marginally more tolerant than some places, but that probably stops right at the point where you're powerful enough to set someone aflame.'

'I'm not a witch.' But her voice trails off. 'Well, I'm not much of a one. The fire just comes to my call.'

'I'm not blaming you. I just don't need your death on my conscience as well.' I touch her elbow, direct her along the garden path. She can clearly look after herself and there's a ruthlessness in what she did that I admire. But she's also so beautiful; she'll be noticed and noted, and someone will recall she was in my company. I'll delay the Constable's visit, stall until tomorrow when Asher's safely away from St Sinwin's. I can't be responsible for another death.

* * *

Seated at the kitchen table are my stepmother, Mrs Medway and Titus Pendergast (in a far less professional setting than he's used to, I'm sure). The solicitor looks decidedly greyer and older than before; I remind myself he's lost two close friends in less than a week. There's a black leather bag at his feet. There's no teapot steeping on the tabletop, but a bottle of very good imported winter-plum brandy (worth a fortune, the very bottle laced with gold and silver designs of mermaids and ships) has been opened and considerable inroads made into its contents. They're drinking from teacups, however– a sign of Mrs M's discombobulation.

'Hello, Titus. I take it you've heard.' The flippant tone is given lie by a tremor in my voice; I blink so the suddenly sharp image of Walter fades away. The solicitor nods and takes another slug of his drink. Tempe has tear tracks on her cheeks, and she looks terrified. All her hard-won daring has been eaten up by these past days. Mrs M's stoic as ever, the only sign of her nerves being the cost of the liquor she chose to break out. I take two more teacups from the crockery hutch and pour a measure for myself and Asher. It's warm as it travels down but there's no relaxation with it. That probably says more about my state than its actual quality.

'Asher, this is my stepmother Temperance Zennor, Master Titus Pendergast in the flesh, and you've already met Mrs Penelope Medway. Everyone, this is Asher Todd, who has brought me a gift of sorts from Hedrek.'

And I want to scream, that from beyond the grave my father's hand is still shifting and shuffling my life across the board of fate.

'*The* Asher Todd?' asks Titus.

'Hello, Master Pendergast.' Asher smiles and it's a striking thing, like sunshine, entirely disarming to Titus Pendergast who, after years around me and his dour daughter, is not used to young women being charming. 'I'm delighted to put a face to that elegant script of your letter.'

'Miss Todd? Why are you— Did you find—?'

'Just Asher, please.' She smiles. 'And yes, I did. But it's a fragmentary document, and I'm unsure that Violet will find what she needs, but we won't know until she reads it.'

'What is it?' Tempe's tone is sharp and her fingers knot and unknot. Mrs M's hand flutters out to cover my stepmother's.

'I think,' I say carefully, 'it's the book you were sent to look for.'

'Where?' In her face I can almost see the map of her journey, the better part of two years on horses, in carriages, on foot and by sea. The exhaustion of having agreed to do this for Hedrek, when all she wanted to do was leave him. And leaving him didn't require her taking to the road; she could have simply moved back into the tiny apartment above her bookstore.

'It waited in Whitebarrow,' I say, and my stepmother cries out, almost collapsing from her chair. Mrs Medway is quickly at her side, holding her up, forcing her to sip from the teacup, speaking so low I can't make out what she says. But Tempe's voice is clear as she repeats, 'Two years two years two years,' and rocks back and forth for a time. Eventually she calms and Mrs M helps her up.

'I'll take Mrs Zennor to her room,' says Mrs Medway as I hug Tempe tightly.

'Thank you. Tempe, I'm so sorry.' Because we both now know that Hedrek sent her off on a wild goose chase. That although he'd heard of the journal, he'd no idea where it was until recently. When he sent Tempe after it, it was out of spite. All because she wanted to leave him. But why did she agree? What leverage did he have? I'll ask later when we're alone.

Asher and I take the recently vacated seats, and she puts the satchel on the tabletop. Unbuckling it, she withdraws a slender tome, the cover a barely treated piece of gross-grained leather, undyed, no gold or silver foil. No name – neither title nor author – just a small insignia stamped into the bottom right corner: a St Florian's cross overlaid by a quill, its nib tilting down, the feathered end becoming a flame. The fire of knowledge, the words of light the Little Sisters of St Florian tried to etch upon the world, to keep safe. To preserve.

Asher pushes it towards me and I stare at it as if it might move, do tricks. Bite. When I finally pick it up, I let it fall open. The pages are aged and foxed, shading from yellow to cream to a coffee-stain brown. Some are paper, some pieces of reused parchment, some vellum. Disparate folios of varied quality bound together, handsewn I think, and I turn it over and find in the bottom left-hand corner of the cover an "M" faintly embossed; roughly done, 'prentice work. A composite of scraps, maybe stolen and hoarded, crafted into something precious to its creator because it was the very *first* thing they ever owned. Ever took or made for themselves – something which, perhaps for the very *first* time in their life, they felt would not be taken away from them. All those beautiful volumes scattered across the world, with their gold-lettered spines? This is where it all started.

This book, then, was an act of someone's hard-won faith.

The very *first* page, the oldest, wears a script blocky and childish: *My name is Murciana.*

And that makes my eyes heat. Who has seen this in centuries, besides Asher? Who has known her voice, seen her own words written for herself rather than all those great tomes of knowledge? Who has seen this initial place where she put her hand before her identity was stolen, her great work colonised and claimed purely because a non-existent man was more acceptable to the Church? So they remade her, re-sexed her, renamed her so she no longer belonged to herself.

I think the girl's hand shook as she wrote, claimed this book, claimed her own name. I flick quickly through other pages, see the script change, become more confident, smaller, more tightly controlled, beautifully formed. A collection of memories as she grew. I swallow. A collection of scraps pulled together like a desperate determined quilt, this little *history*, this journal, shows her claiming of herself.

Then Titus pipes up: 'Violet. You need to read this. Before there are more bodies nailed to your front door.'

Possibly the worst thing he could say, as if Walter's death is my fault. I swallow, consider banging his head onto the table, restrain myself, and notice there's a bulky-looking envelope in front of him, its fat purple seal looks sloppily applied. 'Are you delivering mail now? A new string to your bow, Titus?'

'It's from the bishop. For you. One of his acolytes delivered it to me early this morning, before the… I believe Walter wrote it last night after—' He gestures to me, the kitchen, the *everythingness* of this house. 'In case anything should happen to him.'

I stare at the old man, at the letter in his hands. At the journal in my own hands. I sigh.

'Titus, I'm going to need enough money to travel north. Can you arrange that, seeing as how you've cunningly removed my independent means of support?'

He has the good grace to look embarrassed, then kicks the black leather bag at his feet. 'There's more than enough here to see you through. Food, clothing, accommodations, fresh mounts, bribes—'

'Well, it's not a holiday and I can't carry a giant black bag of coin, but thank you. I'll take what I need.' I press at my temples. 'You must do two things for me.'

He nods, waiting.

'First, have one of your clerks put a notice in tomorrow's *Courier* saying that Miss Violet Zennor is taking a trip to the port-city of Bellsholm to recover from her recent bereavement and examine some business opportunities.'

'It's hardly the time—'

'Any assassins left within St Sinwin's walls will either read about it or hear about it from town chatter. Their intelligence gathering seems rather good. It might be enough to send them off on the wrong path for a day or several, giving me a head-start.'

'Oh.'

'Clever,' says Asher.

'And second, arrange for two horses – nothing fancy, nothing remarkable – to be ready and waiting tomorrow at four a.m. at the stables of the Birds of Passage Inn outside the city gate. Again, have one of your clerks attend to it, they're unlikely to attract attention.'

'So, you're going,' he says with a certain satisfaction, a certain disbelief.

'And, Titus?'

'Yes?'

'Go home and stay there. Don't open the door to anyone. Be careful.'

He nods and rises, slow like an old, old man before saying *Oh* and reaching into his coat pocket. 'Young Seven-Gates was hovering outside when I arrived. He asked me to give you this.'

'Thank you.' *Another* letter. I open it automatically even though I'd like to throw it in the fire and not think about it at all. Jack's sprawling handwriting takes up most of the expensive parchment page even though his message is brief.

Dear Violet,
I apologise for my behaviour. I've thought upon it and have
come to the conclusion that I was at fault. It was too soon after
your father's death, too precipitous an action on my part in a

public place. I hope that you will give me another chance. That
we might be free to pursue a partnership both romantic and
commercial — and do not dismiss the advantage of combining our
respective fortunes! — in the months to come. I am aware there
will be others vying for your hand, but I would like to think that
perhaps I might be the preferred candidate.

    Yours,
    Jack Seven-Gates

As an apology, it lacks a lot. As a proposal, it lacks even more. I
sigh again, refold the letter, stuff it into my dress pocket and see
Titus out.

13

After a silent dinner is had and everyone disperses to their respective rooms, I retreat to my own bedchamber and slump into the armchair by the window, stare out at the sky as it fades, watch the stars become visible, tiny sparks of light. I might stay forever if I thought it would freeze time, that my not moving from this seat would stop the future in its trajectory. Eventually, though, I rouse myself and light the lanterns, put a match to the fire laid ready and waiting in the hearth.

By the door is the black leather bag Titus delivered. It's ridiculously weighty; I'm not sure why the solicitor thought it a good idea to bring a queen's ransom. I think about the gold coin in there, the promissory notes. I think about making a last-minute bid for freedom, taking the bag and scampering down to the harbour, buying passage on whatever ship will sail on the morning tide. Leaving, and no one the wiser until someone comes to look for me. Yet in truth, there's a reason or several why I've not done it before now. Despite a lack of funds, I could have gone sooner, the moment I thought about it as an option. Could have borrowed a little money from Talwyn, left my jewellery with her as surety. Could have found a moneylender or the worst of the pawners down in the lower part of the town, those with not a scruple to call their own.

I could have gone, but I have not.

I take up Walter's letter, which feels heavy and its contents clink as I break the purple seal and upend the envelope. Out fall two breastpins, one gold and one copper – the former is the Anchorhold's sigil and he must have palmed it last night before he left, before the Constable's men could cart away the bodies; the latter a simple circle – and a piece of silver, ovoid in shape, twice the size of a large thumbnail, iridescent and bold, like no piece of silver I've ever seen before. It's cold to the touch, and far heavier than it should be for its size. I set it aside and begin to read…

Violet,

I have just returned from your home and I write in haste. Perhaps this letter will not be required and I am simply an old man prey to his fancies. Perhaps not. The rectory is locked, there are guards posted in the grounds of the cathedral, yet I cannot help but feel a sense of foreboding. In the morning I may well laugh at myself and burn this before you arrive, speak its contents face-to-face. I know there are other confidences your father would have told you, had he survived, but this is what I know.

These are the things you must do, and there are items you need to acquire. Those enclosed herein will help you. The Anchorhold's emblem may be useful when you pass into the Darklands – use the gold Assassins' pin should you need to pass as one of them. The copper pin is for merchants to ensure they are unmolested when they cross the border. Your father acquired it some years ago. It may be an effective disguise to keep you hidden for some while. Of course, it may not. These are, however, the best tools I can pass on for your use. Travel incognito, travel alone, do nothing to draw attention to yourself. They will be looking for you on the roads, so you must be wary. They will assume you are on your way.

We tried to keep you hidden, Violet, but your father's sending of Temperance to find the book somehow alerted those whose attention we've tried to avoid.

The third item is the only one we were ever able to acquire: a piece of O'Malley silver.

While there are items in the world that claim to be made of such substance, there's no guarantee of their purity, so you must find enough of these "coins" to forge a weapon. I know you're fond of daggers, they're easy to conceal, to manoeuvre, to throw. While ordinary Leeches can be destroyed by a hawthorn stake, or poisoned by garlic, we believe whatever you will face will be something greater than that, and silver of the everyday sort does them no harm. Indeed, the city of Caulder is built beside a silver mine, the vein still to run out. Its silversmiths and merchants have long prospered there. Ordinary silver has no effect on them; however, there is a tale, little known, of a weapon made with O'Malley silver that was used to assassinate the head of the Leech Lords'

Council some two hundred years ago. The priest was a member of a delegation (the last to ever be tolerated) to beg churches be opened once more in the Darklands, and when the request was refused, he... well, he did not survive but nor did the Leech Lord. His colleagues brought the tale home. It's said that O'Malley silver, unlike any other sort, never tarnished. Not ever.

That is the first thing you need, but the supply dried up several years ago. Once, it was delivered, I have it on good authority, to St Sinwin's by two men, Rab and Armel Cornish, from an estate called Blackwater. The thing is that no one knew precisely where that estate was. The men remained tight-lipped, but once I caught a whisper of a name: Isolde. But I never heard another detail ever – that was the sole slip – that might be the person in charge. Might not be, but it's all I have for you. Some while ago I sent two of my cleverest god-brothers – not the usual clodhopping sort – to follow the Cornishes home. I'd have put money on their not being detected, but near the last crossroads before the mountains, the Cornishes simply disappeared from sight. I enclose a map, with the exact spot drawn where they were lost – I'm convinced the Blackwater Estate is nearby and you will need to find it yourself. You cannot be without O'Malley silver.

Secondly, as you've already observed, the Leeches tolerate neither priests nor witches on their ground, and this is something I've long pondered. Priests, it's understandable when we fight for people's souls, and the idea of monsters coming back from the dead to rule the living is quite unacceptable. Priests in the Darklands would preach against the Leech Lords, urge folk to revolt, to not accept lives under the rule of the revenants even when they seem comfortable. Sin is always comfortable, Violet.

Now, witches. Also anathema to the Leeches – but why? Wouldn't you think two wicked things would co-exist quite happily? The great Archbishop Narcissus Marsh, he of blessed memory and saintly name, discovered that witches could hold the border with their spells. He reached an agreement with a family to the north, the Briars of Silverton, and in return for living their lives freely (or mostly, under the supervision of a god-brother, of course) they were charged with watching over the way into and out of the Darklands. After the Church had hunted down the remaining Leeches in the rest of the continent, when they'd driven the remnants back into their own place, the Briar Witches were given their obligation.

But, Violet, I am not entirely convinced about the nature of this protection – that it is entirely based upon spells. I have no proof, yet all my research has shown that Leeches have <u>never</u> dwelt where a witch lives, so what if it's something about the very witches themselves? You must speak with them, gain their trust. Find out what it is they do or have or are. Then beg, borrow or steal whatever it is and take it with you when you go into the Darklands.

*The Anchorhold, I fear, is different. I fear it is the
origin. Dormant for a very long time, but making its move
<u>now</u>. I'm sorry, Violet, that I cannot tell you exactly what
you will face. A Leech Lord, no doubt. But something very
different to those that currently exist. Something that can
open the borders and allow its kind through. Something
that will be as locusts upon the land. A dark tide against
which none can stand. You must destroy it, Violet, no
matter that it may be your brother. You must destroy it.*

Yours in God.
Bishop Walter
St Sinwin's

A scratching on the sash window pulls me back into the room. I
stare at the night-darkened glass. A face, pale and thin, presses
close. For a moment, I'm terrified until I recognise it.

'Freddie!' I open the window, lift her in like a sack. 'We have
a door. We have lots of them.'

She dusts herself off and shrugs. 'Your front gate's locked.'

'Yes, it is. Have you eaten?' I ask and she shakes her head.
'C'mon, then.'

I make plenty of noise on the way to the kitchen to forewarn
the beekie should he be attending to matters there and, finding the
room empty, I put slices of cold roast beef and bread with Mrs
Medway's excellent cranberried pickles onto a plate for Freddie,
and put a saucepan of milk to warm on the stove. In the little
laundry room in one corner is the pallet bed Mrs M leaves set up,
just in case the girl one day chooses to sleep in the house instead

of the stables. I leave the door ajar so she can see it, know it's there if she wants it, but not feel anything's being forced upon her. The child's a cat, a stray cat in her attitudes – show the slightest sign that you want something and the opposite will occur.

When she's eating with too much gusto for someone who's supposedly getting enough food, I watch her. 'How old are you, Freddie? Precisely?'

'Don't know, precisely. Things… things have run together.'

'Roughly?'

'Maybe nine?'

Two years older than me when my life changed forever. At least when we were poor, we were happy. I think we were anyway.

'Cake?' I ask as she finishes the last of her meal. The milk on the stove is beginning to steam. I pour it into a mug, then find the tin. Cut her a large slice of Mrs M's honey and raspberry cake. It disappears quickly. Then I wrap more bread and meat in paper, slip them into a bag with some fruit, just in case. I put it on the table next to her; she'll take it or she won't. She'll sleep in the laundry or she won't.

'Freddie, I have to go away,' I say. 'For a while. There's something I need to do.'

'What your father wanted.'

I narrow my eyes, wonder how much she's worked out with her eavesdropping and snooping. I nod. 'So, I'd like to employ you to keep an eye on the house, on Mrs Medway and Mrs Zennor. Come and go as you please, Freddie. But watch for anything or anyone suspicious – any sign of the assassins remaining in St Sinwin's.'

She looks at me with suspicion. Her nose almost twitches, sniffing for any sense of pity or charity.

'It's a proper job, Freddie. If anything's amiss, run straight to the Constable. If anything's really amiss, go to Talwyn Enys and the Harbour Guard. Two gold coins a week for as long as I'm away, and food and board in the house, if you wish. Your choice entirely.'

Finally, she nods.

'Thank you,' I say, rising. Without thinking, I reach out, stroke her head, too late thinking she'll bolt. But to my surprise, she stretches up, into the curve of my palm, a cat permitting a pat. If I had a child of my own— Then just as quickly, she leans away. I push my chair in, put my hands in my pocket, and leave her to her own devices. 'Goodnight, Freddie.'

My pocket-watch tells me it's just gone 9 p.m., not late. I should talk to my stepmother – we hardly exchanged a word at dinner. She was pale and drawn, her eyes red from crying. I don't know what I can say, but I need to say something. Tempe always told me that Hedrek wasn't as bad as I painted him. I wonder if she thinks that now? If she's remembered all those times when she'd pat my head and tell me that my father really loved me and that he believed he was doing what was best for me, even when she didn't actually know what he was doing.

At Tempe's room – a suite she took over on her return, *not* the chamber she shared with my father – I raise my hand to knock, but some instinct stays me. Instead, I try the handle, find it unlocked, turn it and push the door open.

A tiny lantern sits on the bedside table, its flame turned low, a nightlight for my stepmother who's always hated the dark. On the four-poster bed with its royal blue hangings, two sleeping forms are twined about each other, desperation in the lines of their bodies even in slumber. An impression of "I will not let you go-ness". Of "I did once and will not again-ness".

Tempe and Mrs Medway.

I think of Tempe speaking of her journey, of the details she refused to share because another's secrets were involved. I've been wondering why she did my father's bidding that one last time when all she had to do was leave. I think about Mrs M and Tempe and their familiarity, the number of times I found them with their heads close together in discussion. How quiet Mrs Medway was in the weeks and months after Tempe left, how cold she became to my father. I think about Hedrek sending Tempe away to find a book that had never left the continent. I think about her going and I wonder what his threat was? Exposure wouldn't have worked. But a threat of violence? Violence was never far from my father's choices when he was angry or thwarted, as I well know. If he found Tempe and Mrs M as I've just found them? His pride, his rage at discovering himself a cuckold? And Tempe desperate to keep Mrs M safe would have agreed to anything. Hedrek's price, a punishment, an act of spite.

And Mrs Medway here, a patient Penelope, caring for me, remaining where she knew Tempe would find her. Mrs M and her pigeons, tiny messages tied to their legs. The days when one would arrive looking weather-worn and exhausted, but Mrs M would be happy, buoyed. Mrs M when Hedrek fell ill for the last time. I imagine her tying a missive to a bird, sending it out into the world, telling Tempe it was time to come home whether she'd found the damnable book or not...

I step back, closing the door carefully and quietly. They've suffered enough. If I want my family to be safe, I must leave. If I want Tempe and Mrs M to be happy together, I need to undertake my father's mad scheme. Hedrek gets his way once again.

In my own room, I pack a bag with a change of men's clothing, a fat coin purse and a roll of promissory notes. Brass knuckles, firestarter, another knife to go in my boot, compass. Murciana's journal. Walter's letter and map, the two breastpins; the single silver scale I slip into my pocket. I lay out my outfit for the morrow: trews, shirt, redingote, sturdy boots. I will collect some food before I leave.

When at last I'm done, I climb into bed, punch the pillow, then bury my head in its softness, trying to force a few hours' sleep upon myself before the clock on the mantel wakes me.

14

'I must say, I've never seen quite such nondescript horses in my entire life,' my companion says, and I can't say she's wrong. Her mount snorts seemingly in discontent, but that might just be a coincidence.

'Exceedingly brown. Titus certainly took his instructions very literally.'

When I went to Asher's room in the very early hours, the door opened before I could knock. She'd dressed in the equally unremarkable outfit I'd loaned her from my father's wardrobe and tucked her bright red hair up under a brown cap. It didn't make her beauty any less notable but there's not much that can be done about that. She might avoid notice for a while longer, if she were to keep her head down, brim low, perhaps with some dirt on her face. She didn't speak, just nodded and slipped the satchel over her head. Her own clothing was folded neatly on the end of the bed, abandoned; she was taking our sneaking seriously.

In the darkness we left via the kitchen door to the potager and out into the larger garden where we could pass beneath the trees and the undergrowth, hidden from any watchful eyes as we made our way to the spot on the wall where we climbed over into the abandoned Seven-Gates yard, across that overgrown garden and over the other wall, and on and on through another three estates. Then a zigzag up the last few streets and alleyways to the postern gate, known only to a few, small and hidden on both sides by a fall of vines, and then finally to the stable yard of the inn where these two thoroughly ordinary-looking beasts were waiting.

'Do you think we were seen? Followed?'

I shake my head. 'I don't think so. Don't know what else we could have done to sneak out.'

'I think if we had been, we'd know it by now.'

The sun's creeping up and the sky is pink; we've been on the road for almost an hour, encountering no other travellers thus far. We've passed the fens that surround the approach to St Sinwin's and are on the sparsely treed plain that will lead eventually to the wooded skirt of the hills that later become a mountain range. But not for a long while. 'Thank you for your company.'

'Well, I'm fond of not being burned or drowned, as witch or otherwise.' She laughs to take the edge off, then says more gently, 'You didn't think I'd let you leave home alone? It's a hard thing, the loneliest thing. I've done it more than once in my life. I'd not wish it on anyone. Did you leave them a note?'

'A brief one.'

'Did you tell them where you were going? What you're doing?'

'Not the details. It would only worry them. Just that I was doing something Father had asked me to do.'

'And so you're going north, very much north.'

'Yes.'

'Into the Darklands.'

'Yes.'

130

'And what are you going to do there?'

I'm silent for long moments. This is a secret I've kept for so many years that my throat constricts at the very thought of speaking it. But, oh gods, wouldn't it be a relief? To have a confidante that's not one of three controlling old men? So, I spill everything. Everything that's happened to me, to my family, the loss of my mother and brother, their unexpected bloodline, Hedrek and how he changed, what I've been trained for, the weapon I've been turned into, the Darklands and the Anchorhold, and the prophecy.

She listens without interruption, nodding in places. Finally, I'm done. 'I thought I'd be free after Hedrek died. I thought I'd never have to listen to his madness about Leech Lords and dark lands, and never be told what to do again. But it seems Hedrek wasn't mad or not entirely. These assassins at least believe I'm a threat to whatever waits in the north. So I need to go, and I'm still my father's pawn.'

'Chess is a terrible game, horribly boring, but remember: the queen can move anywhere. And you're no pawn, Violet Zennor. You've a mind and will of your own, a fortune of your own. You're a queen. Do this one thing, then freedom is yours.'

'Are you? A queen? Has your will ever been your own?'

Her expression is a strange thing, regret and sadness, pride and anger. She shakes her head. 'No. I was my mother's creature for the longest time. I thought it was love, so I made promises. In the end I fulfilled them because I believed I'd gain my liberty from her – but the cost was so very high.'

'What did you do?'

'Terrible things. I gave her a second chance at life, I gave her all the things that had been stolen from her. But she wasn't

131

satisfied – she never would have been, only it took me until too late to realise that. So, I put her back in the ground.'

'Are you free now?'

'Mostly. But I still dream of her, of how she was once, how she should have been.' Asher glances at the foliage by the side of the road, the bushes moving and shifting as if an animal low to the ground pushes through them. Foxes most likely. 'The thing is, whatever I did, when I made it right or as right as I could... the world didn't depend on it. Not the wider world, the greater world. What I did just made small lives better.' She shakes her head. 'But you...'

And I want to cry. I don't want to bear this weight I never asked for.

'I mean, you have a choice. You can go and try to do what you've been trained to do. Or you can run away. And you can run away, but there'll still be consequences.' She sighs. 'It all depends on what burden you can bear on your soul. I chose to live. I own what I did. I wanted a life that was my own. No one who died through my actions was good. I did not kill children nor slaughter the innocent. It's not much of a hierarchy, I know, but any blade of grass on a slippery slope.'

We grin at each other, broken things we are.

'You'll make your choices, Violet Zennor, and live with them. I think you're that sort of person.'

She reins in her horse and I follow suit. We've reached a crossroads, surrounded by trees, the sort of place where gallows are oft erected, where bodies are buried to make sure they cannot find their way home. The markers point in almost thirty different directions, cities and towns and villages.

'And this, I'm afraid, is where I leave you, Violet. I'm sorry to say goodbye, I think it would be an interesting thing to get to know you.'

'Are you sure, Asher Todd? About the farewelling, not the interesting part. Don't fancy a jaunt to the Darklands? Risking life and limb?'

'Even though that sounds like a merry jape, I've a home to return to and, if you don't succeed, plans to make. Because if you don't succeed, the world will become considerably more dangerous than it currently is – and that's saying something.'

'I'll do my best not to fail,' I say, feeling less than hopeful.

'One last thought: the thing with the fulfilment of prophecies is that they require certain conditions to be met. But the world moves constantly, so sometimes the conditions simply don't converge at the right place or time or for the right person. Prophecies are often merely possibilities. Sometimes all a prophecy needs to fail is interference.'

'That is vague and unhelpful, but thank you, Asher.'

We laugh and lean from our saddles to hug, then she's off, turning to the right while I continue straight on. When I'm almost out of sight, I look back one last time, mouth open to bid a final farewell – and see a large wolf slink out of the undergrowth. My cry is stuck in my throat and just before it releases, the wolf rises onto two legs. Asher Todd brings her horse to a standstill, and dismounts. Asher steps into the now-man's arms as if she belongs there, as if it's the safest place in the world.

Ah. She's a wolf's wife.

His presence explains her certainty that no one has followed us. I watch a few seconds longer, then look away so they don't catch me and know their secret's out, something she didn't choose to share. I focus my attention on the road in front of me, and I notice the softness of the dirt – some rain during the night – and the shapes imprinted there. Bare feet, but strange. Human but changed – a heel, the weight of it light. Then the ball of the foot and the toes seemingly deformed, the split between the second and third toes becoming deeper, the tops of the toes curving around.

Hind-girls?

I remember Mother telling me the tale, half-spoken, half-sung: *The hind-girls dance along the narrow forest courses, throwing their heads with such abandon that sometimes the antlers of one get caught in those of another. But their feet are sure on these paths of beaten earth for they know those ways of old. Once upon a time on the far side of yesterday, in a land that never was, in a time that could never be, there lived girls who chose their own fate...* I've never seen them myself but the idea of them is one I love, connected so clearly with a fond memory of Vesper. In my imagination there are antlers on heads, some nascent, some ancient and covered in brown velvet, some hung with moss and flowers, some with copper bells, some with tiny bones of hands and feet souvenired from who knows where.

The idea of girls who chose their own fate bolsters my conviction that I'm doing the right thing – whether I want to or not. I'm doing Hedrek's bidding in spite of myself, but there's hope, perhaps, that after this is done, I might choose my own path.

* * *

Some hours later, I stop for lunch, leading the horse into the trees so we can't be easily seen by anyone on the road. There've been no other travellers, not since Asher and I left St Sinwin's. I eat one of the apples I took from the kitchen this morning, and I pull Murciana's journal from my pack and begin to read.

My name is Murciana.

'Tis three months, almost, since I came to the Citadel of the Little Sisters of St Florian. My goal was to steal, yet the Mater offered me kindness and protection, knowledge and a future. So, here I remain – thief still, for I stole my master's great book of spells and magic, the thing the Magister from the lands to the north had been adding to for years. Yet I've not suffered a moment of remorse – I was his scribe since he stole me from my parents, and most of the words in that volume were put there by my hand. The book is mine now, even if it wasn't before. I add to it when I can, when I find new enchantments or hedge-speech in the great libraries of the Citadel.

Most of the Sisters are older than me, some few around twelve and thirteen, the same as me. Everyone takes the opportunity to teach me their specialist skills or subjects whenever they can, or simply to share knowledge harvested by hobby or happy accident. I have only to ask a question and someone will point me in the direction of the best volumes for an answer – because doing one's own research is prized above all things at the Citadel – and I have free access to everything here that the Sisters have collected and kept safe. So the knowledge, whether good or bad, might remain in the world.

They are uniformly kind, and I have known little enough of that. None. I cannot recall much of my parents – I assume they were kind before I was taken away. Perhaps they were not. But I think, some nights, I recall my mother's face and how she smiled at me with all the love in the world. I wonder when they gave up looking for me?

I have a bed in the dormitory with the youngest of the Sisters – my own bed, with a mattress and a frame, clean crisp sheets and thick eiderdowns. Nothing like sleeping in the ashes of the Magister's kitchen fireplace to try and stay warm. There are bathrooms for use whenever you need or wish, I have clean clothing that actually fits, and will have more as I get bigger. And there are meals three times a day, as much as I can eat, and if I sneak down to the kitchen in the middle of the night, Sister Mayda the Cook will always have left some pastries out for me.

Mater Adela tells me I am no longer an orphan, I'm a daughter of the Citadel, and the idea fills me with warmth and pride. I want them all to be proud of me. I want to do them honour.

15

If I'm following the right path, I should reach Blackwater in ten days.

If I'm on the right path.

If I don't get waylaid by bandits or Anchorhold assassins.

If I'm not attacked by whatever monstrous creatures might roam the forests, trolls or wolves or witches less pleasant than Asher Todd, malign dwarves or redcaps and hidden folk, goblins and kelpies and the like.

If I don't decide to sit down in the middle of the road and have a good cry.

A precipitous departure is unsettling. Hedrek didn't intend me to go like this, but death overtook him. Walter and Titus waited and waited for him to recover, held off sharing anything in hopes he'd be the one to tell me everything I needed to know, to make sure I was properly equipped. But in the end he made things difficult for them too, arrogantly assuming he'd be able to instruct me as needed, leaving only scraps and notes often lacking in coherence.

And more pragmatically, did I bring enough food? Is Walter's map accurate? What happens when I get to the spot where the

Cornish brothers did their disappearing act? What if I can't find a way in? What if there is no Blackwater? What if there's no O'Malley silver to be had? And even say I find the place, I get the silver, then safely make my way to Silverton – what then? What's to say the Briars will be interested in helping? In giving me what I'll ask for?

What if, what if, what if?

Violet Zennor, you'll put one foot – hoof – in front of the other and plod on towards each goal. Burn your bridges once you reach them, or something like that.

Instead of focusing on the what ifs, I turn my attention to the landscape. More marshlands as far as I can see. Reeds and sedges waving and whispering in the breeze, the croak and pip of frogs, the splash of mudskippers, buzz of insects. The road runs right through it, liquid lapping either side of the built-up byway. Leaving the path risks sinkholes and deep water, sucking mud to pull you under, corpsewights (creatures that were people once) that no longer know themselves, faerie lights to lead travellers astray, spectral voices to lure you away, hinkypunks, sudden choking mists and miasmas, wicked ginnies and jims looking for children to feast upon. But no assassins so far, or none that I can see, so everything else is tolerable.

Eventually, the marshland begins to slope upwards, draining into rich farmland. I pass farmhouses, large and small, but always in the distance; figures move around outbuildings, feed and lead animals, till fields, hang strikingly white washing on lines between trees. No one's close enough for me to make out their details or for them to make out mine; I'm an anonymous smudge in brown and black. Later still, villages dot the land, but I stay away from them. At some point I'll need to replenish my supplies, but for now I've enough for a week of meals. Easier and smarter if I don't leave more of a trail than I need to, so best if I stay away a few days from people who might be able to tell any pursuers about me. Let me get far enough along that they might have given up. Wishful thinking, but a girl can dream.

I notice more prints on the road – hind-girls again, coming from the forest to the right and dancing for almost a league before they headed off to the forest at the left. I wonder if I'll ever see them in the flesh. I wonder if joining them might be a valid life choice after I do what I must do. If I succeed. If I survive. Then again, I'm very fond of well-padded chairs and comfortable beds, of libraries warmed by hearth-fires, and expensive whiskeys to sip, and I most definitely like pretty clothes and shiny things – I doubt very sincerely whether life as a hind-girl requires or allows for any of those things.

Ten days to Blackwater, all things being well. How long to find the entrance? Then to beg, borrow or steal whatever O'Malley silver there might be? Then almost two weeks to Silverton – again, all being well and excepting death or injury, capture, kidnap or other incarceration. Then how long to convince the Briar Witches to help? To give up their secrets or other aid?

The horse startles beneath me as a bird flies out of the undergrowth and across our path. I have to rein him in, calm him down, and I realise I don't know his name. I pat his neck, groom his mane. 'You're going to need something to answer to, aren't you? Ned, springs to mind, because I don't have enough imagination for anything else. So, Ned it is.' He tosses his head in protest, dragging his hooves. I dig my heels into his flanks, not too insistently, just enough to get a slight increase in pace. 'We'll never get anywhere fast with that attitude. Ned.'

* * *

When night's not far from falling, I come across the ruin of a church.

I'd directed the horse off the road, looking for a clearing, and found a small building, made of grey stone, but part of the roof's fallen in over the altar and in the dim light I can see the marks of a fire on the remaining timbers and some of the cracked walls. There's no door, but there's enough roof remaining in the front half for cover should it rain. A couple of intact pews can be dragged together at a ninety-degree angle, and I break up some of the non-intact ones as kindling. There are enough tumbled bricks to construct a small firepit – the higher I've gone, the cooler it's become. I can toast some of the bread in my pack to have with the dried meat.

The horse refused to enter so I hobbled him and left him to graze in the little burial ground. I wonder how far the nearest village is – churches don't tend to be built in the middle of nowhere, they're usually attached to a town, like an anxious parent hovering around a needy child. Then again, perhaps the village is gone too, a wreck eaten by the thick forest around us. If I wander out into the night, might I stumble into fallen beams and tilted walls, unloved hovels?

There's a well too, still functional, the bucket and rope waiting. I draw water for tea.

Normally, I'd never be this tired, this early, but then I've seldom spent so very long in the saddle and my backside has a bone to pick with me. I'm dozing on the bench, my pack under my head when there's a noise outside, a horse neighing, then at

140

the door, footsteps. The dagger's in my palm and I'm on my feet, ready for a fight. How many might there be?

The figure that appears in the doorframe is small, dragging off its hat.

'Freddie! What are you doing here?'

'I brought food.' Freddie's eyes go to my sad little campsite.

'I asked you to stay and keep an eye out for Temperance and Mrs M.' *To keep you safe.*

'They've hired guards for the house and to walk them into town. They're safe enough.' She's holding a pack in front of her. It looks heavy; over her shoulder is a bedroll. 'Please don't make me go back. I don't feel safe there.'

'Oh, come in and put that down.'

She smiles and almost skips over the threshold. In the pack is a range of food, more bread, more fruit, some jars of homemade jam, an entire plum cake, half a wheel of cheddar, and all of it definitely stolen from the pantries at Zennor House, chosen without the greatest practicality. I make more toast and cover some with jam, some with cheese that will not do well outside the pantry, while she lays out her bedding on one of the benches.

'Can't eat like this every night,' I say.

She nods.

'Got to preserve some supplies,' I say.

She nods.

'In a few days we'll stop at a village and restock.'

She nods.

'Freddie, did you ride?'

Another nod.

'Where did you get a horse?'

A sullen stare. Stolen, like the food. Gods, I hope it was from our stable, heaven forfend she be tracked by one of the Constable's minions for horse theft. 'Who taught you to ride?'

Silence, then a tangent: 'Where's that red-haired woman?'

'Mistress Todd? Gone her own way.'

She nods again, then puts some more wood on the fire, building it up, making herself comfortable.

'Why didn't you feel safe at home, Freddie?' As if mine is hers.

She shrugs. 'Too many men about, with those guards there.'

That doesn't sound right – Freddie's more than willing to kick a man in the balls if he even looks sideways at her. I've seen it happen in the markets and down at the docks whenever she's getting into something she shouldn't. 'Do you know where we're going, Freddie?'

'North,' she says, matter-of-factly. 'To the bad place.'

I nod. 'What I have to do is dangerous. You can't come with me, not past the border.' Why am I not sending the child back right now? I only know that there's a need for company that I can't explain. A need to not be alone; as Asher said, leaving home is the loneliest thing and I'm not quite ready for it, the entirety of the aloneness. I know it's irresponsible to keep the child with me, but I can protect her, better than anyone can. 'You'll need to wait for me in Silverton. There are folk who'll look after you.'

Or so I hope. I hope the witches will be helpful and kind. And if I don't come back, that they'll keep Freddie as safe as can be expected. Use their secret to keep the Leeches away from her. Because if I fail, then the witches are the last hope for anyone. Freddie doesn't say anything, just purses her lips to show she's heard me, but doesn't necessarily agree.

Instead, she changes the subject: 'Did you see the prints? The hoof-prints? Feet-prints? Both-prints?'

'The hind-girls. Perhaps they're migrating again.'

'I think they're always doing that, Miss. They don't stop, or don't seem to, so my mother said. Did you see *them*?'

'No. Not today. Maybe tomorrow. Have *you* seen them? Did your mother?' But I sense from the way she purses her lips she thinks she's said too much and I've asked too much. So I get up and this time I barricade the doorway with broken benches and chunks of mortar. It won't necessarily stop anything or anyone, but they'll make a huge noise coming in, give me enough warning to wake. 'We've had a long trip, Freddie. Time for bed.'

'Night, Miss Violet.' She stretches along one of the pews, wraps the bedroll around her, uses her coat as a pillow.

'Night, Freddie.' And in spite of everything – especially the putting her so close to danger – I'm very glad for her company.

* * *

I'm dreaming.

I'm dreaming that I'm flying. Such magnificent freedom, no gravity to hold me down, no obligation, no one else's wishes or wants. Such a looseness to my limbs. Then I realise there's a constriction around my ankles – both of them. The pressure of blood rushing to my head.

I'm not dreaming.

I'm dangling upside down, a giant pair of hands wrapped around my feet as if they're handles, slung over a meaty shoulder, my head and torso swinging, my face slapping into a cloth-covered thigh, while something carries me into a deeper darkness.

16

Blackness, pure as night – unsurprisingly but not because it's night.

We're not outside, not in the fresh air, not beneath a starry sky. There's a vague echo of the thud of large bare feet, a trickle of gravel in some place where weight displaces it. Subterranean. I can also hear – or I think I can – someone breathing not far from me, the soft muted sound of someone's face rhythmically hitting the back of a cloth-covered thigh just as mine was until a few moments ago. Not that the back or front of any thigh would sound measurably different, I'm sure, only I'm certain that Freddie is in the same position as me, but less awake because she would probably be talking by now otherwise.

I try to wriggle, kick, but the grip around my ankles merely gets tighter and I feel my bones grate a little (a warning) and there's a strange, discontented huffing that tells me not to try someone or something's patience. If I start a fight in the darkness, I'll be sure to lose – whatever's got us must be able to see here. A creature of under-earth, perhaps one of those things that answer to the Erl-King who rules beneath, or perhaps just something that abhors the sun and likes the taste of human flesh. A troll? They tend to stick to the mountains and deep forests, when they're active and not in their hibernating years. Of course that doesn't mean one might not wander away, closer to the coast, looking for food before it goes back to sleep.

But we were in a *church* and if I recollect rightly, trolls shouldn't be able to enter such places or at least not without dire consequences, their strength being sapped by whatever magic is imbued in consecrated stones. But then, what if that church above, my ruined sanctuary, had been *de*consecrated? If the local churchman decided it wasn't worth the effort to reclaim the place and so lifted the blessings laid on its stones and beams, altar and font? Once, Walter had said that mostly it wasn't done simply because folk forgot, or the churchmen simply didn't like to give up even one square foot of god's earth, expecting to one day return and reuse such a building. But what if that little wreck of a structure had been unhallowed for whatever reason, and thus a troll *could* make its way easily into and out of the structure when it smelled a tasty snack sleeping there like lambs? Stupid, stupid lambs.

How did it overcome us? Or *me* at least – I've no memory of an attack. No sensation of aches or pains that would suggest a fight. Yet here we are, being taken to a larder, untenderised? Did it use some sort of sleeping enchantment or a smelling salt designed to render a deeper sleep? That suggests a smarter than average troll, given their usual method is to just bash skulls in against rocks or tree trunks, whatever is to hand.

When I gradually begin to make out shapes around us as we pass, rocks and plants, rubble, the giant feet padding along – a tunnel – hope flares. There's a glow coming from those plants, from algae on the walls and mushrooms, casting an unearthly blue-green light. Which means I can see, which means I can fight.

The dagger releases into my right hand. Whatever's got us is too tall for me to reach its Achilles tendon, so I go for clumsy destruction and stab the blade straight into the back of the thigh. The reaction is enthusiastic: there's a monstrous roar and I'm tossed aside to crash into a rocky wall, the dagger stays behind in the thigh and the thigh's owner takes off at a limping run down the tunnel with Freddie still slung over the other shoulder. Swearing, I force myself up and – also with a hint of limp – tear after them to finally skid into a cavern, puffing.

A well-lit larder. The lights – a myriad of lamps and candelabra, all ablaze and placed near mirrors to magnify the effect – are literally stunning and I lose my sense of direction, of equilibrium. I'm reaching for the spare knife in my boot, blinking, when I hear a scream. It's not Freddie, although it takes me long seconds to figure that out. A woman, in pain.

My vision comes back into focus and I see two things: the creature in front of me, cradling Freddie like a baby, and a woman in a gigantic bed, face wet with sweat and features distended as she screams again.

Not a troll, an ogre.

No problem with hallowed ground at all.

Half a person taller than me, perhaps eight feet in height, his stance angled to favour the stab wound. Pale, greyish skin – subterranean – black shaggy hair, a strangely neat goatee, thick neck, shoulders and chest knotted with muscles beneath a shirt of rough linen, powerful legs in dark blue trews, hands like hams. And a face only a mother could love: jut-jawed, overhanging brow, sloping forehead, skewed nose (broken and not properly set) and pouting lips. Dark, dark eyes. Not a winning feature in the entire ensemble – except his expression.

Distressed and pleading.

'Help me!' the woman yells before the words flow into another scream.

'Help,' pleads the ogre in a thick, deep voice. 'Please help.'

I approach the bed. The woman's human, as far as I can tell, very tall even lying down, and very beautiful. Platinum blonde hair flowing across the pillows behind her, green eyes, ruby lips, high cheekbones, pale from living underground. And an enormous, distended belly beneath the disarrayed sheets, the points of her knees making a mountain range of the linen. Eyes huge, gaze panicked.

'Oh, thank the gods,' she grunts, then her face contorts again. A contraction.

'How long?' I ask, trying to retrieve the minimal midwifery lessons Mrs M gave because she believed it was something every girl should know. I look at the ogre; he gently puts Freddie, who remains asleep, on a velvet chaise longue, and holds up a finger.

'One hour?' He shakes his head. 'One day?' A nod, a groan, echoed by the woman in the bed.

There's a bedside table with a silver bowl filled with water, a cloth floating in it. I wipe her face and neck. 'One day?'

She nods, confirming the ogre's reply. 'Something's not right.'

'Warm water and soap?' I say, and the ogre brings another bowl, a towel, and as I'm washing my hands, I say apologetically: 'Don't take that knife out. I'll get to you soon.' Don't want him bleeding to death while he waits.

My hands tremble as I dry them off. I think of watching my mother give birth to Tiberius, of her cries and groans and shrieks. Of seeing her soul exit from her lips, a white mist that even now

147

I suspect dances still over the roofs of St Sinwin's. I think of her hollowed out by her dead child, devoured month upon month. And thoughts of myself when— No. I shake my head violently as if to toss the dark notions aside. I concentrate on the things Mrs Medway taught me.

After a thorough examination of the woman, I'm confounded. Finally, I say, 'I don't know what's wrong. It's not a breech. You look more than full term.' I keep my gaze carefully away from the ogre so she can't see my thoughts on my face: that a child with this father may well be too big for her to bear in the usual way.

'My mother,' the woman says in between desperate breaths, 'always said fae births are too hard. She didn't mean him, but all strange creatures, I think.'

And I remember Mrs Medway telling me tales of human midwives summoned or carried away against their wills to attend on fae women. Not because their skill was inherently any greater, but because the touch of a human hand – ordinary, unmagical, mundane – could shock the child out, which could well be a bit insulting. I do look at the ogre this time; he's most definitely not fae, though eldritch certainly. But I've already touched her and that had no effect.

I lay my hand on the woman's belly again, feel the heat of it, the movements of whatever's inside her. Nothing happens.

The woman shouts, 'Say a prayer!' and it takes me a good few moments to remember one. When I do, it's a mumbling, stumbling affair but it has the desired effect and soon there's a perfectly normal-sized baby girl – with a ridiculous head of black and platinum hair – in my hands. I give the child a cursory wash, then put her on her exhausted mother's chest. After making sure the woman's unlikely to bleed to death, I see to the ogre's injury.

Not as deep as it could have been and only because he tossed me away so quickly. But still. I'm very attentive with the cleaning and disinfecting, the stitching and then a bandage over the top. I don't feel guilty enough to darn the hole in his trews, but it's a near thing. Only then do I check on Freddie, who snores gently on her velvety throne. Whatever he used to make us sleep has had a stronger effect on the child.

At last, when I've done all I can, I take a proper look around the chamber. It's not some troll's cavern heaped with treasure and filth, nor a wicked ginnie's damp cave piled with bones. A sort of grotto, a bright jewel of comfort in the depths of the earth. Rooms are marked out not by walls or dividers but simply by furniture. On the floor, deep soft moss, and silken carpets. Across the ceiling, more of those glowing mushrooms and algae, a pink shade to go with the blue-green. Several long couches in velvet scattered around, bookshelves at random and frequent intervals, overflowing with volumes. The bed is enormous and its linens and coverlets very fine, the pillows fat and soft. In a far corner a stream flows from a crevice in the wall like a shower, then into a hollowed crystalline bathtub big enough for a prize bull or a horse or indeed the ogre who's lying beside the woman and his child, both parents cooing at the little scrap as she feeds greedily.

I'd thought the woman in need of rescue, but it doesn't seem to be the case, the glances she gives him when she can tear herself away from the child are filled with love. I wash my hands again, then sit on one of the chaises to rest, thinking it will only be a few moments, that soon there'll be a conversation between us, and I'll learn their names, how they came to be here. How the woman chose this partner, how long they've lived beneath the earth. But

149

I close my eyes, just for a moment, a single moment, now that all adrenaline's drained away, all energy's devoured.

And drop off to sleep almost immediately.

*　*　*

When I wake in the morning – full sun shining through the empty windows and the broken roof – I'm no longer on a comfy velvet couch. I'm on a very hard wooden pew in the middle of a ruined church. Across from me, Freddie's snoring, a kittenish sound. I sit up, look around.

Nothing and nobody, no sign of the woman and her ogre, their little child and their sanctuary.

'Freddie?' I call, gently; then less so: 'Freddie, wake up!'

She startles and sits bolt upright, wide-eyed. 'Oh, Miss. I had such a dream. We were in a cave and… and… I can't remember. It's all blurry.'

But I remember very clearly, all that happened, all that I did. And something catches my eye as I scan the makeshift firepit and its broken bricks: a flash of deep blue. I lean down and snatch the thing up.

A sapphire, weighty, a sort of starry light in its depths.

A thank you gift.

Beautiful.

I put it in my pocket, wondering what to do with it.

17

Against all odds, our horses (Ned the Nondescript and a small black mare that thankfully does indeed come from the Zennor stable) are still outside the church, grazing, throwing us curious looks. We set off once more, with Freddie relentlessly questioning me for hours on end about what happened. She then spends the next two days circling back to the incident, asking 'What if' about the ogre and his wife. Her memories were only dreams of things she'd heard in her probably enchanted sleep but that didn't dampen her imagination. What if the woman was fae? A stolen princess? A goddess in disguise or a forest witch? What if the ogre was a handsome prince? What if he'd been cursed into the shape of an ogre? What if the woman was his reward and he her punishment? Yet they fell in love in spite of it all?

However, she avoids answering any of my questions about herself and her family, even when I ask how she comes to ride a horse so well. Not a lot of street urchins have much opportunity for learning such skills. She takes the opportunity to change the subject. 'Tell me a story, Miss.'

I give her a sideways glance, think about arguing then decide it's not worth it. At least she's unlikely to run away to avoid queries. I wrack my brain for a tale, think about where we're going, how the O'Malleys were once masters of the oceans, if not whatever dwelt in them; I pick at something my mother once told me when I was small – two stories, really, but she couldn't separate them, laughed in the telling.

'Once, twice and thrice upon a time, there was a pond or perhaps a lake. It was inhabited by a mari-morgan who'd grant wishes if asked, if bargained with. Or there were twelve girls who swam there, and as beautiful as the starry sky they were.

'One day a woman asked the mari-morgan for a favour, for a good husband – or rather, to make her current husband *good* – and the mari-morgan agreed in return for a dress that would not disappoint. Or, one day the twelve girls were approached by twelve princes, for word of the girls' beauty had spread far and wide, and surely they must be in need of husbands.

'One night, the woman – a seamstress – made her way to the pond and cut a dress from the water, stitched it with silvery moonlight and gave it to the mari-morgan. The dress was perfect, did not disappoint. Or the twelve girls – princesses, sisters, daughters of a great king, or simply pretty maids – having nothing better to do, agreed to the princes' proposals, and so the wedding date was set.

'The morning after the night before, the woman led her husband, by means of half-promises and true lies, to the pond. When the man peered into the water, the mari-morgan peered into him; he was a bad man through-and-through, the woman's bruises testified to that. So, the mari-morgan pulled him in, dragging him down to the bottom of that deep-deep pond and held him there until he was a'drowned.

'Or the princesses, on their wedding day, down by the lake as they'd insisted so their relatives could come, found themselves the subject of scrutiny. The god-hound brought to conduct the ceremony was troubled by the little things: webbing between fingers, faint gills in throats, pearls that grew in their hair, a green tinge to their skins. He called a halt to the proceedings, began to denounce the brides as unnatural things. Well, the girls having become bored, exchanged a look that said nothing on earth was worth having to listen to such droning, not even the handsome young men of whom they'd had their fill, and all twelve of them carried the shouting god-hound to the water's edge and bore him down, a'down, a'down into the depths from which none of them ever resurfaced again.'

I look at Freddie, her head tilted as she considers. A quick nod. Acceptable.

We continue on the road, and I think more about the O'Malleys and their silver, dredging up and picking over whatever I can remember, scraps that might mean nothing to someone raised elsewhere, but to one raised in St Sinwin's, in a port-town with a lively commerce in goods and gossip? It would be hard to avoid such legends. Even though we're far from Breakwater, from Hob's Head on its outskirts, news can sail far more swiftly on the sea than it travels on land. But all I can summon are half-recalled whispers and rumours.

The O'Malleys had been spoken of seemingly forever; their seat of Hob's Hallow was a huge, rambling mansion. Their fleets and fleets of ships brought wares and treasures for sale and trade. The family (their origins lost perhaps even to them) grew and grew and grew, but that tight core of true O'Malleys, those who bore the name, seldom married out but mated in and too closely related some said. And the silver – always the silver no one could ever discover the provenance of, with its uncommon purity, the ingots stamped with a Janus-faced two-tailed mermaid, and always, *always* sold for a premium. The O'Malleys supreme in their ascendancy… until.

Until the flow of their silver began to slow to a trickle, the family suddenly miserly with its stocks as if the source was drying up.

Until the old blood began to wither. The extended families prospered but the O'Malleys, the truest ones, diminished. The O'Malleys, of whom it was said their children never drowned unless they were meant to, began to be lost at sea. To strange and untreatable diseases. To infertility – even when in desperation those true O'Malleys married out, married *commoners* hoping to harvest the strength of rough and robust breeding, either no child eventuated or those that did were weak and did not last.

Others began to track their diminishing, the arc of their fall, in particular members of the clergy, whose power had been neutered by the O'Malleys for generations – men like Walter who'd once been a younger cleric in the port-city of Breakwater. They'd made a lot of enemies over a lot of years, the O'Malleys, and the vultures were circling by the end. Yet that family had not remained so long without being cunning and stubborn.

Rumour had it the ancient matriarch had a plan, had made a bargain with one of the distant cousins, to marry off her only grandchild, the last scion, Miren. One last-ditch effort at not becoming *extinct*, the girl would be bought and sold to her cousin, who would bankroll the O'Malleys' resurrection.

And then the old woman died.

And then the girl disappeared.

And then the cousin followed suit.

And none were ever heard from again.

The house out on the promontory, facing the sea, always the sea, had crumbled, its roof fallen in, its few remaining treasures looted. And one day the promontory on which Hob's Hallow rested broke away, and that great and terrible house tumbled to its drowning, into the depths and taking the last evidence of the O'Malleys with it. Sinking into the waters from which others sometimes whispered they'd once risen.

Yet somehow before that final fall a supply of the very same silver began to come into St Sinwin's, differently marked, but according to Walter of the same unmistakable, uncounterfeitable quality; Walter, a man of the cloth, a finder and keeper of information, sharing it only when it served him. Murmurs that it came from an estate no one's visited. This estate no one can swear even exists. This estate to which no one knows the entrance.

The days bleed into each other – a ten-day journey from St Sinwin's to where Blackwater *might* be. The first four days we encounter no other travellers from either direction, meet no one at any of the crossroads; the next five we hear the occasional hoofbeats behind us and make a point of disappearing into the trees and undergrowth, peering out to see who it might be. No one we know, and no one dressed in elegant and lethal blood. No sign of the Anchorhold's day-runners. I wonder how much grace the false notice in *The Courier* will buy us – are they even now infesting Bellsholm? Surely, we're at the outer edge of our luck?

My luck?

There are some small villages we pass by and others we stop at for food – the larger ones are those I choose as we're more likely to blend in to the flow of travellers, to not draw attention. But I do prefer the farms, set back from the general throughfare, less traffic and less likely for pursuers to ask there. I hope. Besides, anyone following me will be looking for a woman on her own, not a woman with a young child. Freddie looks nothing like me, of course, but that means nothing; not every child resembles a parent. Sometimes we steal fruit from orchards and eat it as we ride. I read a little of the journal, but knowing how likely I am to lose myself in it, I try to keep it for night. And I'm paranoid about being taken in my sleep again, and the riding is exhausting so I'm already in danger of a too-deep slumber. We make camp well off the road, find sheltered clearings, keep the campfire very small.

On day ten, at dusk, I discover that we shouldn't have worried about anyone sneaking up on us because as we're about to look for a campsite, we hear voices up ahead, around the next bend. Voices that are raised in anger. We rein in Ned the Nondescript and the mare whose true name Freddie's decided is Molly.

'Well, where the fuck is the bitch?'

In a perfect world, it wouldn't be me to whom they're referring, but some other bitch.

'Fucking Zennors. Thorns in the arse, I swear.'

So much for hoping.

They've gone past us at some point. Earlier in the journey than I'd have thought – *The Courier* announcement seems to have had no effect – perhaps even the night when the ogre took us. That kidnapping saved us from another kidnapping altogether. The assassins must have kept going, passed us in the darkness as we were being taken beneath the earth by the ogre. Had I made camp closer to the road, they'd have found us. I dismount and lead Ned into the trees, Freddie following suit. When I think we're well enough hidden, I leave her with the horses and creep towards where the voices are still arguing about where I might be, whether my parents were truly married, what they might do to me, and whose fault all of this might be. There's the crossroads Walter's letter mentioned, the place where the Brothers Cornish disappeared, and in the middle of said crossroads, are eight figures in stylish black – they may be murderous, and perhaps less than efficient, but they *are* well-dressed.

Looking past them, past the bristling signpost, over the intersecting roads, I see more trees, and undergrowth, but something else catches my attention. Between the trunks and branches, there appears to be a relatively uniform bit of foliage. Had I not been in this precise spot, I'd not have spotted it; had I been here later it would have been too dark to notice. But the forest *looks* different, flatter, like something's been intentionally planted, a hedge trained to be just wild enough not to draw attention. It might be nothing, it might be my desperate imagination, but for now I just need to figure out how to get between it and the Anchorhold's well-dressed idiots.

I don't want to take on eight assassins. I mean, I could try; I might even win. But there's also a chance I might not. That I'd end up bleeding out into the dust and dirt of this crossroads like so many criminals over the centuries, and that is very unappealing. We can try waiting for proper darkness, sneaking through the woods behind them; sneaking, with two horses, and all the possible holes in the ground and gnarled roots, and uncertain soil in a forest floor, not to mention trolls and gods know what else might lurk in there at night. As I'm returning to Freddie, another sound makes itself known, over the top of the shouting day-runners, from the direction we came.

Many feet, slapping hard on the packed earth, a rhythmic wild sort of march – no, nothing so disciplined or regimented. A dance. Individual steps known only to each dancer yet somehow in tune with the whole.

In the lowering light, a crowd – a herd – of hind-girls processing towards us. Old and young and in-between, some naked, some clad in scraps of old dresses, old lives, some in skins, some with fur beginning to cover their limbs. All of them with horns on their heads, some nascent, some gnarled, enveloped in brown velvet, their own hair draping like veils. Female deer don't grow antlers, or at least very seldom; the hind-girls do. Twelve, fourteen, sixteen points.

A herd of hind-girls of varying sizes and shapes, heights and weights. A lot of them. The wild rhythm spikes a wild plan in me. It's the sort of crowd two other girls might get lost in or find refuge in for a while – or be trampled by, but at this point, it's better than the alternative. 'Freddie?' I whisper, swiftly unlashing our packs. 'Leave the horses. Get ready. Sorry, horses.'

Poor horses. Sudden freedom. But better this than fighting our way through – by which I mean *me* fighting *our* way through, trying to protect a child no matter how quick she is. The hind-girls froth and flood across the road, spill into our part of the undergrowth, and I grab Freddie's hand, pull her in as they engulf us like a tide. Moving to the middle of the pack, trying to crouch without falling and being walked over by those hard-soled feet (a swift look down: gods, some are beginning to *encloven*). The hind-girls don't bat an eyelid, don't flutter a lash or utter a word, though they do seem to close ranks around us, the noise of their steps growing louder, and Freddie and I are shuffled along that swarming, dancing, whirling storm of horned women, over to the other side of the crossroads.

And it works.

It works and I hear more cursing from the assassins as they're driven off the beaten path and into the far ditch by the irresistible press of women and girls. I scan to the right, straining in the last of the dying light. There's the spot, that suspiciously well-trained hedge. I manoeuvre us out of the herd's embrace and head towards what might be salvation or a dead end.

And it works – or it would have *if* the horses, apparently not in love with the idea of freedom, hadn't chosen to follow us. It might have worked *if* it had been dark enough for the day-runners not to have seen them, *if* the horses hadn't decided to make their protest with loud neighs. But *if* your aunt had balls she'd be your uncle.

Now the Anchorhold's assassins are surging over the crossroads, seeking but not yet seeing as the tail-end of the hind-girls slows, whirls, stomps and obstructs. I pull hard on Freddie's hand to swing her ahead of me (which might hurt but is better than being dead) and land her just in front of the hedge. Up closer, it's even taller than I thought and clearly brambles.

'Where is she?'

'Where is she?'

'Fucking things!'

'Don't kill 'em, it's bad luck!'

'It'll be worse if we don't find her!'

'Where the fuck is she?'

I flick my wrist, feel the dagger slipping from its mooring, whisper to Freddie to climb a tree – then hear a rustling behind me, feel the pressure of hands on my shoulders, and am pulled backwards through the bramble barrier.

18

The next moments are a confusion: dropped on the ground with a *whump* and the breath leaves me, our packs rolling across the dirt; two faces brief blurs, expressions concerned but not aggressive; the quietest of rustles as the panels of the hedge-fence are magically returned to their place. I note multiple layers slotting in, cunningly cut and it appears as if the leaves and vines and brambles actually weave themselves back to make it all look seamless – but surely that's just a trick of the light? In fact, the distraction it causes might be the only reason I don't start slashing about with the knife. That and the fact that we've been saved from the assassins for the moment.

Who knows what the next five minutes will bring? From pan to fire?

Or: Blackwater?

Freddie rolls against me as I sit up and tuck the dagger back into my sleeve. One of the men – dark-haired, dark-eyed, neat-beard – turns to us, a finger to his lips. *Ssssh*. Outside the barrier, curses and shouts, much muffled. The man holds my gaze while his companion – red-haired and short, stocky – leans closer to the weaving brambles – they *are* moving! – listening. The sounds from the other side lessen as my pursuers eventually give up, stumble off. The tension in the lines of our rescuers' bodies eases but doesn't entirely dissipate.

I pull my attention away from the dark-haired man, scan our surroundings. We're sitting on a track, not far from a neatly tended garden and a tidy gatehouse of red-grey stone. Its sash windows are shuttered but I can see some few splashes of light, and the front door's open to show a table and benches inside. A curl of smoke smudges against the early evening sky. Fruit trees – heavily laden – border a path away from the house, disappearing into the woods.

'Hey.' A gruff voice.

The dark-haired man's offering his hand. Without thought I take it and am heaved upwards. He's a little taller than me, not much, but muscular and broad, his palm's rough and wide, fingers long. I find myself staring at his high cheekbones, square jaw, soft-looking lips, thick red sweater with holes in the shoulder. He releases me quickly and I feel vaguely insulted.

'Don't they hear you? Outside? Through the brambles?' I ask, looking up at the top of the hedge; it reaches so high that I can't see where it ends against the night sky, discouraging anyone who might climb it. No one would be able to see the roof of the gatehouse, its chimney or even the plume of smoke from the road outside, the crossroads.

He narrows his eyes, considers me, then grabs up both our packs; doesn't offer them to us. 'No. The Lady of Blackwater has her ways. We can hear them, they can't hear us.'

Another witch? Never met one in my life, not knowingly anyway, yet here's two in under a fortnight.

'Inside,' he says, and gestures towards the open door. The red-haired man doesn't follow but mutters to the dark-haired one, calls him 'Rab'.

'I'll go and get Herself, see what she wants done with this pair.' He takes off down the tree-lined path, not running but there's a healthy pace to his step. Rab waits politely for me to follow Freddie inside. The smell of soup is divine and rich. We stand awkwardly in a kitchen of plain pine, counters and chairs and a crockery hutch, as he puts our packs by the door. A stone sink, copper plumbing, pots hanging from a ladder on the ceiling, a heavy iron stove in an alcove. It looks a little too stark for somewhere a wife might be – then again, his wife might be a stark sort of woman. I shake myself; why would I care?

'Are you cold?' he asks.

'No.' I am, however, aware I've not bathed for days. At my best, I am not. I ask, stupidly it might be argued: 'This is Blackwater?'

'Sit.' He waves at the table and benches, and we obey as he goes to the stove and shifts the large copper kettle onto the heat, scoops tea leaves from a blue canister from the mantle above the stove into a white teapot, then lines up four cups (clean but old, the sort you use for family and friends) on the counter. He fills two bowls from the simmering pot on the stove – beef and vegetable soup – cuts thick hunks of bread from a fresh loaf, plates them, then places the meals in front of us.

'Spoons?' I ask. If we're prisoners we're not going to be starved to death, not yet anyway. Spoons appear. 'Thank you.'

He busies himself with the steeping tea while we eat, fast and with an amount of slurping that would set my stepmother's face aflame with embarrassment. Most unladylike. When we're done (at shameful speed), from the top of a narrow cupboard he produces a pottery jar and puts it in front of Freddie, who gives me glance. I nod. *Have at it.*

Eagerly she pulls out one biscuit, then two then three. If I were her mother, I'd say, *One is polite, two is rude*, but I'm not and those biscuits look delicious and she pushes the jar towards me. Oats and honey and cherries. I take another and another. The big white teapot clunks on the table in front of us, and I look up. Rab's wearing a slight grin; defiantly, I take another biscuit.

'Who are you?' he asks, setting the cups in a row, then sitting across from me. Leaves the head of the table free.

'You're Rab Cornish?' A guess, but it's a good chance – how many Rabs will be floating around Blackwater? And this *is* Blackwater – *The Lady of Blackwater has her ways* – how many hidden estates will be floating around a mountainous region?

He gives me a sharp glance, recovers quickly, states: 'You're from St Sinwin's. I've seen you sometimes when we've delivered goods to the harbour.'

My turn to give sharp glances, and I raise an eyebrow for good measure. Hadn't realised I was so noticeable.

'I'm Freddie,' pipes from beside me, which is the most information I've ever heard her volunteer swiftly; it took her six months to tell me when first we met. I feel vaguely peeved, even though I know it's irrational. But she's smiling at him like he's her new best friend. He gives a sort of truncated bow as if she's a princess.

'I need to speak with' – *Don't say whoever's in charge* – 'The Lady of Blackwater.'

'A polite person would offer their own name, first.'

'She's Miss Violet.' Freddie reaches for the jar once more.

'I'd put these away if I were you.' Firmly putting the lid back on, I move the cannister away from Freddie. 'Travelling incognito is a bit pointless if you just tell my name to the first person who feeds us.'

She shrugs.

I clear my throat, thinking about Walter's letter, his one hint, try my luck: 'As I said, I need to speak with the Lady Isolde.'

'Well, you're several years too late, I'm afraid. Dead and buried.'

I feel sick. If there's no one to talk to about the silver, the *theoretical* O'Malley silver, what am I going to do. 'Who—'

'What did you need to ask her?'

'Why? Can you resurrect her?' Frustration makes my tone mean. What to say? What to reveal? He's been kind, saved us from the Anchorhold's day-runners, fed us. But sweet might as easily turn sour. Before I can smooth things over there's the sound of hooves outside. Freddie and I watch the opening door while Rab puts a jar of honey and a jug of milk on the table.

The woman is very tall, mostly willowy, with very long dark hair, dark eyes – she and Rab might be related – and skin that glows like the moon resides beneath it. Her sage green dress is high-waisted to accommodate a very pregnant belly. At her throat, a silver necklace, a ship's bell. Eyebrows quizzical and the full mouth quirked in something that can't decide between irritation and amusement. I'm aware of how scruffy I look and what wouldn't I give to be elegantly clad and perfectly primped once more to meet this glorious woman?

165

'Strays, Rab?' she drawls, walking slowly to the head of the table, carefully lowers herself into it with a precision born of a changed centre of gravity.

'Can't help myself, Miss Miren.' He puts a cup of tea in front of her. 'Cats, dogs, deer, foals, girls from St Sinwin's who want to talk to your mother.'

Miss Miren? Miren O'Malley, the last scion of the great house of Hob's Hallow? The one who disappeared?

'A little late.' She takes a sip of tea, makes a face. 'Honey, Rab, honey.'

'Sorry.' He pushes the jar a little closer to her, gestures to us with a flourish. 'Misses Violet and Freddie.'

There's a sense of ease between them, friends, almost like siblings, though she's clearly the lady of the manor. She dribbles a coil of brilliant golden honey into her cup, stirs.

I start: 'I'm sorry about your mother—'

'Never met her myself,' she says blithely, but there's a discomfort, a pain even, moving in her eyes. Even more motherless than me, then.

'—perhaps I can speak to you?'

She nods, casual, but wary.

'My name is Violet Zennor. Bishop Walter of St Sinwin's sent me here. I'm to ask about O'Malley silver.'

Her eyes narrow. 'Why'd you let them in, Rab?'

'Not so much letting as dragging in,' I correct. My backside aches from being dropped.

'Remember those black-clad bastards from the north that passed by some weeks ago? Aerin overheard them, followed for a bit. They were travelling towards the coast, a largeish group.

166

Well, there was a smaller group outside the gate tonight making a ruckus, on their way back if I'm not badly mistaken, and looking for *them*.' He nods meaningfully at Freddie and me. 'Didn't seem fair to leave them outside, although Miss Violet has a dagger in her right sleeve.'

Sharp-eyed. Excellent maker of soup. A man of hidden talents.

Miss Miren looks at me with interest. 'And you're interested in O'Malley silver, you say?'

I nod.

'What do you need it for?'

And I struggle. Again, that habit of secrecy, the *stricture* of it. How much to tell? I shared with Asher Todd because she'd helped me, she'd figured things out, and gods know I needed a confidante. Freddie listens to everything and I can't send her away every time I need to talk about this. But this Miren O'Malley? What might she do with knowledge of my mission, my *duty*. Apparently, I pause for too long.

'Well, you're plum out of luck, Violet Zennor of St Sinwin's,' she says coolly, still stirring her tea, not looking at me, just watching the steam curl and circle above her cup. 'Our veins of silver ran out some time ago and we've shifted our productive efforts to things like carving and weaving, making brandies and whatever other fortified spirits my people can dream up. So, whatever your purpose—'

'I'm to go to the Darklands and destroy the House of the Anchorhold, and whatever resides there – which might be my brother.' She stills, staring into her tea. 'Those black-clad bastards from the north are its day-runners, and they infiltrated St Sinwin's, slaughtered people in their own homes and set themselves up like cuckoos in nests. They threatened my family. They tried to kill me three times. Four if you count this evening.'

'Either they're very poor at their job or you're very good at yours.' The teaspoon finally exits the cup, *tings* on the rim as she looks at me. 'Why you? What makes you so special?' The question's not mean. She just intends, *Yes, I can see you're special – but in what specific way?*

'What do you know about the Leech Lords?'

'Enough to never let my people trade in the Darklands.'

I explain, as succinctly as I can, about my father, my brother and his fathering, about his birth and death, and my mother's parentage and terrible end. I tell her about the cloaked man from the north, with the golden pin on his collar, his persuasive words and my father's weakness, about my brother's tiny corpse being borne away and my father thinking to enquire *why* far too late. About the fortune his decision brought, about his repentance, the triumvirate he forged with a bishop and a solicitor to atone. How that atonement took the form of turning me into a weapon. I don't tell her everything that was done to me, but I tell her enough that it feels as if worms are boiling up from the very burning belly of me like I'm a brazen idol. All that rage and outrage. I tell her about Walter and his letter, about the legend of O'Malley silver being the source of a Leech Lord's demise.

Finally, I stop.

She sits back. Rab releases a long breath as if he's been holding it the whole time. Freddie stares up at me with something like pity.

'Quite a story,' says Miss Miren. 'Quite a story indeed. Got anything to prove it?'

Retrieving my pack from by the door, I take out Walter's letter and map. I take out the Anchorhold's sigil. And I take out Murciana's journal, which I've been hoping to read here if we're granted some days of rest. From my pocket I take the silver scale acquired by Walter. I lay them all on the table and Miren picks up and examines each one. When she comes to the journal, her long pointer finger shakes a little at the cover, strokes the emblem of the Little Sisters on the front, then turns it over, discovers the wobbly "M".

'Murciana,' she says softly. 'Oh, we had so many of her books at Hob's Hallow!'

She opens the cover, sees the words *My name is Murciana*. Tears well in her eyes, and her voice trembles. 'Do you know what it's like to see this? To see the truth of her?'

I nod.

'May I read it, please?' Her request is so tentative that I smile.

'I'll deliver it to you when I return or leave it to you in my will when this is all over.'

We grin at each other, then she says, 'There might be some silver still. In the old house. But there's a problem.'

169

19

From the bottom gatehouse (the one we entered by; there are two), it's a shortish ride or longish walk to the Blackwater mansion, or what remains of it.

After a long conversation into the night, a blessedly welcome and much-needed bath, and an even more welcome sleep in an actual bed, the morning seemed brighter. Hopeful. Filled with possibility. Rab's brother, red-haired Armel, miraculously recovered Ned the Nondescript and Molly the Mare grazing idly by the crossroads beyond the hedge as if being abandoned there was the most natural thing in the world, and it was only a matter of time before we returned for them. After breakfast (porridge, coffee, toast, a range of jams) Armel and Rab also took a protesting Freddie to Miren's home in the village with promises of meeting other children and (a greater inducement) more biscuits. I confided that I couldn't guarantee the child wouldn't sneak away to find me, so Miren's husband Jedadiah should keep a close eye on her, but I stopped short of advising restraints (which put me far ahead of my father in general parenting stakes).

We passed – I on Ned, Miren on a heavy grey horse more like a sedate ship – more fruiting orchards, fields that were a sea of gold and green, then into the woods of oak and yew and ash. Miren told me how, when she'd arrived, everything had been barren, green but infertile because her mother had been dead for months and no one was tending to the small magics required to keep the land giving. She told me she herself isn't a proper witch, or not a serious one at least, just a woman with a skill for ritual and intent, which is what most magic is; pay the crimson tithe, say the words, do the ritual, will it to be so. Bigger magic, worse magic, requires more of all those things, and she's never had the ability or desire to work it. When I asked about her mother, she shrugged.

'I don't really know – only that she was definitely a proper witch. The limits of her power? The best and worst things she attempted? I really don't know. I *do* know she used some of what she could do to look after the people here, so I do whatever I can for them.'

That's when the woods broke apart and revealed a sprawl of what had once been perfectly landscaped grounds – but a long while ago. Everything was growing over-abundant and wild, unpruned topiaries and hedges looked like insane wigs, archways of living trees were covered in roses. Birdfeeders and copper bells hung from branches and tinkled pleasantly in the breeze. Feral rolling lawns ran down to the lakeshore, no doubt the blackwater of the name, but it wasn't especially dark, was quite clear in fact, and all manner of birdlife floated there, swans, ducks, grebes, godwits, moorhens; an otter or two peeking from the far bank.

But even the lake paled into insignificance before the enormous ruin of grey-red stone, crouched like a toad.

'What happened?' I stare at the wreckage of what appeared to have once been a multi-storeyed home, a wing at each side of the central structure. There's an overgrown turning circle, weeds almost covering the gravel. The only things that are clear of growth are eight wooden and metal benches for sitting and staring out at the lake.

'My parents built it, so it was relatively new.' She seems to struggle, searching for the right words. 'There was a fire in the wing that contained the nursery. A child died. My parents died. Others moved in. They died. The place had been a prison for years. I couldn't be there on my own, not just me and Ena, my little sister. We moved into Jedediah's cottage in the village for a while but outgrew it – children will do that – so we built a bigger one.'

She sighs. 'Almost as soon as this place was empty, it began to decay faster and faster. I think houses are like people, if left unloved they die by degrees. One night, lightning struck, a much bigger fire then, and no one close enough to do anything about it in time. Besides, I didn't really have the will to – I grew up in a mansion and it did me no good. I want my little ones to have better than a place that's so big you get lost in it and no one can find you. Can't even find yourself. The roof mostly fell in. I think some of the floor too, but into the lake, which is partially beneath. And, I'm sorry, but that's where you need to go.'

'Lovely.'

Miren points to the lake. 'In its defence, it's much clearer than when I arrived – you can actually see several feet down now, and it's not as salty as it used to be.' Miren shrugs. 'Perhaps my mother's magic fading, I've read that happens sometimes.'

'And I need to go into the cellar and find where the mer-queen was kept.'

'Yes.' She'd told me the tale, last night, of how the O'Malley family fortune, their luck, was tied up with the imprisonment of a huge and ancient mer-queen. That the silver came from her scales – it *was* her scales – and that the bargain Miren's ancestors had made with the sea creatures depended upon their holding the mer-queen, and devoting one child of each O'Malley to the waters. A child that was not ever meant to be named so it would be easier to let go of when the time came.

And she told me, that when the O'Malleys began to wither, her mother had stolen away the mer-queen, brought her here and set her to producing silver once more. Pretending, here, so far from the sea, that it was something to be *mined*. Blackwater was built as her parents' – her mother's – dream and masterplan. Isolde had brought folk to live on the estate, to work, she'd cared for them and they were loyal to her – but none of them knew the secret of the well in the cellar of the big house, of what lay within, moulting silver scales, filled with centuries' worth of rage, imprisoned and more than a little insane as a result. A man and a woman came, tricksters and killers, who'd wiped out Isolde and her husband, taken their home and fortune, let the estate run down – and then Miren had arrived. She'd dealt with the tricksters and put things to rights as well as she could. She'd made a new bargain with the mer-queen, released her for the first time in living memory. She hoped she'd set herself and her line free.

It occurred to me then, though I'd refrained from saying it, that she'd lived a fairy tale, albeit a very dark one. Then again, aren't they all very dark?

We dismount on a ragged lawn, just before a set of stone steps leading to a front door hanging off its hinges.

'I'd go in with you, but—' She gestures to her great belly. 'There are spots I just won't fit.'

'I'd not have you come with me at all.'

'And Jed would have kittens and I'd never hear the end of it,' she admits. 'Oh, there's Rab. Hope he got that rope.'

I follow the direction of her finger, see him ambling towards us on a tall bay horse; he'd had to go to the now-disused mine for a long enough coil. As he gets closer, I can see it slung over a shoulder. Miren hands me one of the intricate silver lanterns she brought, O'Malley silver. When I asked last night why it couldn't be melted down to what I needed, she replied that the metal doesn't like being repurposed. It's fickle and finnicky; once it has a use, a shape, it's impossible to remake. *Fussy fish scales.*

Turning back to survey the house, I ask, 'And you're sure the mer-queen's gone?'

'For years now,' she says, her fingers playing with the silver ship's bell necklace at her throat. After a moment's hesitation she unclasps it, puts it around my neck. 'A loan, for luck.'

I touch the cool metal – it should be warm from being against her flesh, but this strange substance holds the cold of the icy depths, of a mer's chill blood. 'Thank you.'

Rab reins in next to us and Miren says, 'Rab, you just stay out of the water.'

'Never fear, it's my plan.' He looks tired, having sat up with us last night, listening, and agreeing to accompany me.

'And,' I say, 'the other *problem*?'

Apparently after the house had been abandoned, something had moved in. Left alone, it's fine, but the few times adventurous children had gone to play in the old mansion, the something had not been happy. Said children, thoroughly terrified, had mentioned a glimpse of a red cap, items thrown at them with frightening and malicious accuracy, and a lot of swearing and threats.

'Any chance,' I say, 'it might not be a redcap? But a brownie or a beekie? Something less murderous?'

'There's always hope.' Miren O'Malley gives a lopsided grin. 'I mean, the children all got out alive. We leave little offerings once a week, meat and milk, and something sweet. And in its defence, it stays in there, doesn't roam about, no livestock casualties, no babies plucked from cradles. It leaves us alone and we return the favour.'

I bury my hands in the pockets of my trousers, sigh deeply, rocking back on my heels. As if considering. As if I have a choice. I give Rab a sideways look. 'Are you *sure* you want to do this?'

'I very much do *not* want to do this.' He nods towards Miren. 'But if I don't the Lady of Blackwater, she'll turn me into a frog or take my balls for earrings.'

'It's true,' she says. 'Well, not the bit about the frog.'

* * *

Our lanterns cut into the interior gloom, and almost as soon as we get inside the foyer we have to move rubble and smoke-stained beams, black and white marble tiles cracked and splintered, the staircase and roof both collapsed upon themselves. No access to the upper floors; luckily (or otherwise) that's not where we're going. It takes an awfully long time to get to the kitchen, where the door remains intact in spite of the efforts of the rest of the house to implode. Rab and I pause, lean forward to listen to whatever might be on the other side of said door.

Chattering and chittering and some swearing. Weirdly, also a sound that might be sweeping. Redcaps, like brownies or beekies and even hob-lads, are very territorial and prone to hissy fits if insulted. Unlike brownies or beekies and even hob-lads, they're bitey, thoroughly murderous and violent, dying their caps red by dipping them into victims' blood.

'I do hope you have a plan,' mutters Rab.

I don't answer, but tentatively push the door open. What I have is a vague idea, nothing that could be mistaken for a plan in the dimmest light. But Rab Cornish doesn't need to know that. Probably best if he doesn't in fact.

In the middle of what was once a very large kitchen, now strewn with debris, broken sticks of furniture, mouldy food and a sea of smashed porcelain, stands the wee man. Hardly over two feet tall, grey hair streaming from the brim of his pointed red cap, but his beard is neatly tended. His trews are green, his iron boots have a strange sheen, a black waistcoat sits over a surprisingly white shirt – this is all heartening because in the general way of things, redcaps don't tend towards pants, they're more in the way of dirty shirts, bare feet and those damp red caps. This chap is very well-dressed, all things considered. He's wielding a twig broom, moving dirt around rather than removing it. He spies us. His gaze could light a fire in our hair, and I wonder if I've got it wrong; that I've found the one fashionable redcap in all the land.

'Now would be the time for that plan,' Rab says between gritted teeth.

I clear my throat. 'Hello, sir.'

'Oh, we're going to die.'

'Sir,' I say again, more loudly, and the wee man pauses, tilts his head to listen. 'I know this is your home and we're here without permission. I offer my apologies and wish to give you something in return for your leave to enter the cellar.'

His interest is clearly piqued, and he says in a guttural tone: 'What'll it give in return?'

I pretend to consider. There's a formula for this transaction because I'm a stranger here, this isn't my home and I have none of the rights I do in Zennor House. From my shirt pocket I draw a piece of yarn, red, pulled from Rab's sweater last night despite his protest. I twirl it around as if it's a lure. 'This pretty red wool – surely you want this.'

His face wrinkles in disgust. 'Idiot. No trespassing!'

'Oh, wait.' From one trouser pocket: a daisy-chain that Freddie wove this morning. 'This! Surely this is a thing to behold.'

'No trespassing!' His face is going redder and redder; beside me Rab's making a noise like a heated kettle.

'One last chance, please, good sir. But—' I shake my head, despairing. 'I can't imagine you'd want a silly, ugly thing such as this.' From the opposite trouser pocket I bring the ogre's sapphire, an expensive token but I also hope to gain favour for all of Blackwater and it's not as if I need another trinket. 'It's a poor thing, not a fitting tribute—'

'Gimme!!! The shiny, gimme the shiny.' He's jigging in place, circling the broom as if it's a dance partner.

'This dull dishwater thing? Well, I suppose everyone's got different tastes. But let's be clear: this buys my friend and I the right to go down and search the cellar, remove the thing we seek, and to leave again – safe and unmolested.'

'Yes, yes, gimme the shiny!'

I cross the kitchen and hold out the gem. As he reaches for it, I pull back. 'What's your name, sir? I like to know who I'm dealing with. I'm Violet Zennor and this is Rab Cornish. If you need aid in future times, we will provide it as long as we are able.'

Up close, I can see it's a beekie, and he knows such a promise is something rather grand; something better than anything in a pocket. I doubt we'll ever have to make good, but he'll be delighted to think he's got two humans in his debt.

'Robin Green Trews.' Well, appropriate. 'Your terms are agreeable. Now. Give. Me. The. Shiny.'

So, I do.

He examines it, muttering, holding the gem up to the light, chitters and giggles, then disappears into thin air with a *pop*.

Rab comes to stand beside me, looking relieved. 'That went better than expected.'

'Indeed. Now, where did Miren say the entrance was?'

In the back of a small room that once functioned as a workroom where Miren's mother made her potions and ground her herbs and uttered her spells, there's a trapdoor, unlocked. Rab heaves it open and the smell of damp, salt and long-dead things hits almost like a physical blow.

'Are *you* sure you want to do this?' he asks.

'I am not sure at all, but I *have* to.' I lift my lantern, he mirrors me, and starts down the stairs first. Gallant.

'Be careful, these are a bit slippery.' At the bottom, there's a large door with three intricate silver locks, none of which are in use because the door is hanging open.

'Has the cellar flooded?'

He's quiet for a few moments, just keeps moving down until

the sound of his boot hitting stone changes to a splash. 'Oh yes. Not entirely, though.'

'Huzzah.'

I catch up and stand beside him. The combined light of our lanterns shows a broad space, a still pool of maybe a foot of water clear enough for me to see the bottom. In the centre of the space are the remains of a stone well, just as Miren described. Around the walls runs a series of torches. I step down into the knee-high water, slosh carefully to the nearest sconce and light it with a taper from the flame of my own lantern, then as many as haven't been buried by the collapsed part of the ceiling.

It's still gloomy as if the darkness is hardly kept at bay, would gleefully eat everything if it could, but it's the best I can do. Rab and I meet at the crumbled lip of the well, and we peer over, lanterns held high. The water's surprisingly clear and there's the glimmer of the silver grate Miren said would be there, a hole torn in it when the mer-queen was released. Off to one side, that little niche where the shed silver scales once gathered to be sluiced down into the mines. And *there* I can see some sizeable scales remain – perhaps a dozen handfuls, hopefully enough for my purpose. And just as Walter said, there's no trace of tarnish to them.

'Well,' says Rab.

'Well,' says I.

I strip off, handing him my coat and shirt, trews and boots, down to my knickers and corset, modesty be damned because waterlogged woollen garments will drag me to the bottom and all my swimming in St Sinwin's harbour while Hedrek timed me with his pocket-watch will be for nought. In return, Rab hands over a smallish burlap sack, which I stuff down the front of my corset. I touch the silver bell at my throat and shiver in the chill air as it gives a gentle warning plaint. I wait for Rab to ferry my clothes over to the steps, before I start to climb over the lip of the well.

'Wait!' he calls, rushing back, shaking the coil of rope. 'Wait.'

He ties one end around my waist, checks his knots twice, then passes the other end around his own waist. I pretend I'm not mostly naked and that he doesn't smell good.

Clambering over the stones, I let go and float for a few last moments – those few moments when I might still back out, might still flee up the stairs, shrieking as I go. Instead, I nod to Rab. He nods. 'Well, be careful, then.'

I take a deep breath and duck dive.

The salt stings my eyes a little, but I keep them open. Down, down, down, until I can hook my fingers around the fine mesh of the grate. Fighting against the flow of the water, which is surprisingly strong, it's impossible to hold open the sack with one hand and scoop the silver scales with the other without hanging onto something. In the end, I stand on the mesh, curl my toes around and through its grid to anchor myself in place, then crouch and gather the scales. I work as quickly as I can against the push and chill of the liquid, the strange heaviness of the scales, and the slow burning that builds in my lungs the longer I'm submerged.

When at last I think I've got them all, I kick against the grate to propel myself upwards – and my right foot goes through the mesh, cutting the flesh and making me cry out, losing precious air. I try to free my limb, but the metal claws hook into me and every motion shreds at my ankle and calf. The water's beginning to turn red. My lungs are beginning to burst. My movements are slowing and I feel the life beginning to leave me. Clouds well at the outer corners of my eyes and soon my vision turns grey then black.

20

My head's underwater, held there by a fist curled into my hair. Sound is muted and all I can really hear is the rush of bubbles from my mouth and nose. Crushed against something, there are hard lines of pain across my chest, breasts and ribs. But mostly, I'm seventeen, almost eighteen, and I'm drowning.

My belly, where a highly polished boot made more than one connection, aches worse than my monthly courses. And I'm drowning, I know I am, so the other problem is the least of my worries. Yet *this* problem, this drowning, solves several others.

And just as it seems all my difficulties are done, screaming reaches me, piercing the liquid of the rainwater barrel outside the kitchen door. Mrs Medway and Temperance, I think; she's still there then. My hair's released, its meaty tether disappears. Hands on my shoulders – smaller, urgent, gentle – drag at me and I flop onto the ground like a fish, coughing water and vomit, aware of the dampness between my legs as what was growing inside me – that tiny flame, so hopeful and brief – flees.

Later, when I'm in bed, half-in and half-out of consciousness, the physician (hastily summoned) tells my father that I almost died. That he's almost killed me. Dr Meyerhof is stern; he's one of Hedrek's friends, but he disapproves of what's been done. Even if I've been sluttish, a little whore. He tells Hedrek there are other ways to deal with a difficult daughter – convents for instance, corrective governesses (such things would interfere with Hedrek's plans of which Dr Meyerhof knows nothing). But the physician doesn't and will never tell what's been done to me, not to the Constable nor anyone else, because a daughter is property, after all.

How a man deals with his *property* is his business, but later still, when Walter and Titus come to visit, the three of them – crows of men – gather around my bed, when they think I'm still sleeping, Walter warns Hedrek that carelessness will have consequences beyond the loss of an asset. Yes, my behaviour was *debauched*; yes, I was a foolish girl. But he, Hedrek, should have kept a closer eye on me. That I'm worth too much to have risked in such a way.

Titus chimes that the other part of the equation had been taken care of and will no longer be a problem. Ever. That I will never have children – Hedrek will never see grandbabies – and perhaps I might be allowed a little more *freedom* since there is no longer a hazard attached to such "tension release". Titus, ever the pragmatist.

Hedrek is kinder after this, for a while. There are fresh flowers for my room every day, rare and expensive treats to tempt my appetite, beautifully wrapped boxes held closed with glorious gold and silver ribbons and containing dresses and hats and gloves and scarves, and velvet boxes from various jewellers all with glittering apologies inside.

Mrs Medway and Temperance do not speak of it again. They tend to me, help me heal, think less said is soonest mended. Only once does Mrs M ask, 'Why didn't you hit him? You could have hurt him. He's turned you into tempered steel. Why not turn on him?' And the honest truth is that it had not occurred to me. How often does a whipped dog bite its master?

I learn from this incident. I learn, at last, that my father cannot be trusted. I learn to stop loving him – the last dregs of affection for the man he'd been *before* drain away, leaving no trace. And I also learn about blitz attacks; they hone my instinct and alertness in the way my previous training had not – the actual experience of it is beyond anything Talwyn might try to teach me.

* * *

When I finally open my eyes, I'm disoriented. This bed is not my own. My lungs and throat hurt, there's still the taste of saltwater, but there's no pain in my belly. I'm twenty now, not seventeen, not almost eighteen. The pain in my ankle and calf is, however, intense – I've never felt the like, not in the fighting pit, nor in training with Talwyn. A woman's murmuring and putting something cool on the wounds, and the heat and pain begin to calm almost immediately. Sleep pulls me back into its arms.

The second time I wake, everything below the right knee is numb and I panic, thinking they've amputated – and how much more difficult it's going to make everything – but I move my left leg and it finds a heavily bandaged other limb, so I calm down. Another soothing voice, male this time, tells me to *Drink this*, and raises a glass to my lips. Whatever's in there returns me quickly to a dreamless slumber.

Later still, I wake again and am lost for long moments. Then I focus on the room around me: one of the neat guest chambers at the gatehouse, where I slept that first night. A few candles cast a

184

gentle light, and the night beyond the windowpane is as slick as the surface of the lake. My throat's dry and I cough.

'Oh, hello.' Miren O'Malley sits in a wide and very cushioned chair beside my bed, resting a familiar tome on the curve of her pregnant belly. She sets Murciana's journal aside on the bedside table, struggling a little to sit forward, and pours me a glass of water.

'No,' I say, 'no more sleep.'

'It's alright – nothing in here to knock you out, not anymore. But you needed to snooze a while to heal. How's it feel?'

I pause, wiggle the right foot tentatively. 'It's fine. Very little pain. How long did I sleep?'

'Almost six days.'

'It's not possible for anyone to heal in – oh.' Almost no pain, just a lot of stiffness.

'Should be able to walk on it soon. Told you I'm not much of a witch, but healing and growing things are my gifts. My old nursemaid Maura taught me her tricks.' She holds up her hands. 'No great magics. Nothing more than clever mixing of herbs.'

'Thank you. I'm very grateful.' And I am. 'Oh, where's Freddie? Is she alright?'

'She's fine, been sleeping in this chair whenever we'd let her. But she's relaxed a bit since you've showed no signs of choosing to die. Sent her back to my brood tonight, promised her I'd watch over you.' She grins, then tilts her head. 'Who is she? To you? Tight-lipped little bugger, will talk about you until the cows come home – did you know the sun shines out of your arse? – but my brood have extracted very little from her. She and my oldest, Emer, are about the same age, fast friends, but still…'

'To be honest, I know not much more than you. She lives on the streets, sometimes she stays in our stables – don't look at me like that, I've offered her a home more than once, but she's afraid of something or someone. Not in my home, but…' I shake my head. 'One day she'll tell me. Maybe.'

'So, you sort of adopted her?'

I shrug. 'I met her after… a difficult time. She made me laugh. She's smart and brave and loyal. I think she deserves a better life, but you can't force change on someone – if I could, she'd be my ward already, she'd have her own room in Zennor House, and she'd be going to school to learn something other than stealing oranges from merchants and breaking into houses. Not that those aren't useful skills.' I sigh. 'Speaking of creative acquisition: the silver?'

'Over there.' She nods towards a cherrywood chest of drawers in a corner where the sack she gave me sits, fat as a little man with no self-control; the neck of the bag gapes a little, a gleam catching the candlelight. 'Rab said you wouldn't let go of it, heavy as it was.'

'Rab?'

'Who do you think dived in after you and pulled you out?' She looks amused. 'Not a fan of swimming, that man, but he went. Been taking turns sitting by your bed.' A grin.

'Are you trying to sell him to me? Not sure I'm in the market for a manservant.'

'Do *not* let him hear you call him that. There will be a fracas.'

'I'm definitely grateful for the saving.' I smile. 'Did he tell you about your "redcap"?'

'That was an expensive bribe…'

'I don't need it, and it might buy some goodwill for you and yours.'

She nods. 'You know, my old home? Hob's Hallow? We never had one there. Old Maura would have told me, and it was the sort of ancient house that *should* have had one – you'd expect it! But I think it was too… unwelcoming. Even a sprite or a hobgoblin wouldn't set up shop in there.' Miren rubs her hands over her belly thoughtfully. 'How little cachet must my family have had with otherworldly creatures? I suppose we were too known for twisting them to our will. Maura *never* mentioned a beekie. I wonder now if she was ashamed of the fact that our grand house was too terrible to have even the lowest sort of hob-lad.'

'But not you. You released the mer-queen, set things to rights. You're not like them. We don't have to be like our families.'

'Maybe? I hope not?'

We're silent for a moment, musing, absorbing.

'Enough of gloomy things,' she says, and picks up the journal again. 'I've taken the liberty of reading while you've been napping, and I think I might have found what you're looking for? Or a bit of it.' She clears her throat, reads aloud:

I had believed, early in my life and well into my thirties, that my parents had deserted me. That they'd not cared enough to look for me. I was fortunate, I told myself, that Mater Adela and the sanctified Bea and the other Sisters had become my family – all the family I would ever need. When I reached my middle years, however, curiosity raised its head; perhaps I became less certain, less judgemental – perhaps the childish pain of abandonment had simply lessened.

187

Any road, I sent forth some of my Blessed Wanderers in the trains of merchants for safety, to the place from which I'd been stolen, to the Darklands, to see if any trace or trail of my parents might be found. And to my eternal chagrin, they returned with the tale of the Lord and Lady of Caulder, Edward and Marcella, who'd refused to give their only child, a daughter, to a mage who'd come to view their library, who called himself "Magister", met the girl and decided she would make an excellent scribe. Who believed the girl was to become something special, a recorder of all his magnificent deeds. And that when the mage had departed in anger at the refusal, he'd later returned, having cooked up a black and bloody curse, that he cast over the Lord and Lady, then took their child anyway.

What he'd cursed them with was thirst. Utter thirst for the greatest thing any person could have: their life. His curse sent them to their graves, then made them rise again, both more and less than they'd been. More in terms of their strength and speed, their longevity; less in terms of their kindness and tolerance and sanity. The Lady Marcella mourned her child to such a degree she went a little mad, or perhaps a lot, and began "adopting" day-daughters from the city. None of them lasted because eventually the Lady realised this was not her child, when the illusion was broken, so the child must be.

So, even had my parents hunted for me, found me, what then? What life might I have had beside two blood-drinkers, soul-taker Leech Lords?

They were the first of their kind, but they did not remain so. They made others, sometimes for power, sometimes for company. From their blood came the Leeches who rule the Darklands today.

Their kind passed freely into other lands, other nations, enough to be an irritation, but never a plague – but who knew how long that would last? In all the years I've known the Church hunted such things, I did not know how closely connected to me it all was. When the Church built the gate at the pass to hold the creatures in, it began hunting those that had already crossed over into other lands. The Leeches died or retreated. The Church remained vigilant.

That was what became of my parents.

They live thus still, ruling from their manor house on the outskirts of Caulder, a series of loyal stewards to manage their daylight affairs, keeping a stable of fat, well-fed "winepresses", men and women from whom they feed regularly without killing because wastefulness is abhorrent to them. And the folk of Caulder live in this state for they are cared for, and all it costs them is a little blood, the occasional child.

I have some answers now, and there are days when I wish I did not.

Ignorance? I did not know how sweet it was.

Miren and I exchange a glance: neither of us had ideal parents. She didn't know hers, only her ruthless grandmother, and mine? Well, mine. But somehow Murciana's tale seems far worse. I clear my throat. 'So that's how they began. Not a natural thing. A curse – a spell, really.'

'Spiteful little mage.' Miren frowns. 'But there's a tale I read as a child, a single page in my grandmother's library, torn from some larger tome or perhaps a personal notebook, I think – when money was plentiful the O'Malleys would buy any scrap that interested them, that might have come from the Citadel. The story of the Leech Lord Adlisa the Bloodless who slaughtered the Lord and Lady of Caulder, then took their place.'

A thought occurs. 'Asher Todd mentioned a book in that lost bundle, *The Herbal of Adlisa the Bloodless with Annotations by Sister Rikke of the Citadel*. The same Adlisa, do you think?' I ask.

'The very same. The tale's been told over and over, copied and copied, but this was its original scribing, I believe. In some versions she's ruthless and ambitious, but the Little Sisters of St Florian always collected more than one rendition. And in this version, this scrap, there's the idea that she was just a girl seeking revenge for her family. And whose notebook should it be torn from? Who should have signed the page?'

'Was it Sister Rikke who annotated the aforementioned *Herbal*?'

'Precisely! A Blessed Wanderer who'd gone into the Darklands, well after Murciana's time. Her tale was that Adlisa was clever and cunning, poisoned the Lady with garlic bulbs fed to her winepress girls, then slit the Lord's throat with a hawthorn dagger, him also weakened by the bulb.'

'Long after Murciana's death, so she'd never have known that her parents died or how.'

'No.' She looks at me. 'Does it help you? Knowing any of this?'

'I don't know.'

21

The next morning, the door's flung open and a small whirlwind flies in. I'm grateful that she's careful where she sits, perching on the edge of the mattress. I don't think I've ever seen her so clean or in a dress – a loan from Miren's Emer, I imagine, bright apple green. Her hair's been braided.

'Watch out, Freddie, someone might mistake you for a civilised child.'

She grins, leaning in for a hug. 'How are you feeling, Miss Violet?'

'Very well indeed. I should be able to ride again in a few days.' That might be optimistic. But I notice Freddie's grin slip. 'You like it here, don't you?'

'I do. No one's after me.'

I assume she means the Constable's men when they're clearing the streets, angry stallholders who don't like their fruit being stolen, older urchins looking to take what little she has and, let's face it, assassins on the road who won't care if they kill her when they get me. I imagine both of us staying, hiding here while the Leech Lords breach their prison, pass us all by here in Blackwater with its magical hedge of brambles. As if we wouldn't be found, as if they'd not sniff out the blood hidden here and sweep over the barrier like a giant wave over a ship.

Here, Freddie has clean clothes, pretty clothes, she can bathe, she's not starving and her face has already started to fill out with regular meals, her wrists and arms too. She looks healthy and happy. I feel a stab of guilt that's not mine – *she* isn't mine – but I can't help it.

'Freddie, you can stay here, you know. When I leave, you can stay with Miren and her family. There's no need for you to come with me – best you stay here which we know to be a good place rather than going to Silverton which I know nothing about. Here, we have friends. I'll visit on my way back, I promise.'

She purses her lips and stares at me, too smart. We both know that my chances of returning are slim.

* * *

After Freddie leaves to return to Miren's house, to her friends, I read more of the journal, sinking into the life of the author. There are the everyday notations, things not of great importance to the world or its functioning but, at the same time, of the greatest importance to the diarist.

Tales of her first days, of meeting the other Sisters, initial joys softening to the gentle contempt of familiarity as time goes by. Friendships established and nurtured, others allowed to die on the vine, yet others slaughtered at a whim, on a misunderstanding, a loss of patience.

Daily schedules of meals, lessons and assigned tasks. Shifts in the libraries, retrieving books at researchers' requests, and returning them; scribing and art lessons for the creation of marginalia both beautiful and sly; cleaning and cooking, gardening and building maintenance, laundry and daily contemplative walks around the great court with its fountain mapped out as a labyrinth, perambulations for clarity of mind and strength of body. A never-ending rotation that marked the hours of a Sister's day from morning to night, from joining the Order to leaving it, from childhood to death.

The roster of the Citadel and its workings were their fulcrum. A comfort as well as a boredom. No prayers, for the books were their worship.

Rising through the Order, learning every aspect of its functioning. Being given more responsibility, more power and, at last, offered the greatest of positions, of obligations: Mater of the Order itself. Directing the Citadel; negotiating with other sects, institutions, collectors, archivists and librarians for permission to either acquire or copy their rarest books; daily consultations with the oracle Beatrix. And in the end refusing – because the call of the road, of the stories of the world, were stronger. Remaining a Blessed Wanderer, selecting those to join her, mothering them, instructing. Watching their triumphs and tragedies, faults and failings and recoveries.

Crushes that develop, become something more. Lovers who come and go as hearts wane. The enmities of loss softening over time to give way, once again, to friendships deeper and more valued. And those that remained, forever, a source of rage and pain.

What begins as a child's diary becomes a woman's life.

I'm acutely aware that time is passing, my brother's birthday drawing nearer, but this is a tiny bubble of time I'll steal while I can. Walking is still too much, though the wounds have healed, the muscles remain tight and stiff, and I'm unsure of my balance when I try hobbling from bed to bathroom and back again. I have, I tell myself, a little while yet. I wonder if the Anchorhold's assassins have given up and gone home, tails between legs, to report their failure. Or if they're still lurking somewhere on the main thoroughfare, hoping for sight of me. Or if they've deserted the Anchorhold's cause because the consequences of such failure are just too awful to contemplate.

* * *

At dusk, Rab pokes his head around the door. 'Dinner? Outside?'

'Fresh air?' I almost sing. 'Yes, please.'

'Then it shall be done.' He steps into the room, holding up a dressing gown in bright blues, heavy with floral embroidery and glittering beads, even fancier than anything I own. I blink. Rab clarifies, 'Not mine. Miren's. Or rather, her mother's.'

He shakes it – the silken ribbons wave sinuously and there are bells sewn into rosettes of lace; they jingle. 'Well, you're not likely to lose me.'

'Not even if I wanted to.' He helps me from the bed, wraps the robe over the top of my nightgown, ties it in a neat bow at the front. 'Would you like to walk or shall I carry you? Again?'

'Walk,' I reply shortly, even though he's muscular and he still smells good.

* * *

In the orchard, he's set up a table, two chairs, one padded footstool. Rab helps me sit, gently lifts my injured foot onto the stool.

'No picnic?'

'I didn't think sitting on the ground would be ideal at this point.'

'Thank you, that's so kind.' I'm glad it's dark, lit only by the lanterns he's hung on the low branches of the nearest trees, so the

194

blush in my cheeks won't show. 'And thank you for rescuing me, for going with me in the first place, for not letting me drown.'

'I wouldn't be much of a host if I had.' He pours red wine into a goblet and hands it over. On the table is a platter of meat and roasted vegetables, a loaf of bread, another platter of cheese and fruit. Under a glass cover is what appears to be a plum cake to rival one of Mrs M's. He must notice me staring. 'That's dessert, it comes last. Rules.'

'Boring.'

'Without rules, the world falls apart.'

'With rules, the world becomes constricted.'

He grins, serves me a plate of roast lamb, potatoes, carrots, turnips and greens.

'It's so good!'

'Don't sound so surprised.'

'Apologies. May I please have more meat?'

He obliges, looks gratified. Dinner table conversation dies a natural death until I clean my plate. I've been eating soup the last six days – most often while barely conscious – and this solid food is magnificent. I've never felt so hungry or satisfied in my life. I will, of course, never tell Mrs M this.

'More?' he asks.

'In five minutes, yes. But for now, I need a rest.'

'I'm normally cooking for just me, so it's nice to be appreciated.'

No sweetheart then, I think, and am immediately irked at myself. 'Your brother doesn't come for dinner?'

He nods. 'Oh, yes. Family meal once a week, and I go to Armel's place, and Elouen's – my other brother – and their families. Most nights, though, it's just me – my job's to be the southern watchman, after all. The gatehouse is here for a purpose, so am I.'

'Aha. The watchman.'

'Southern.'

'I stand corrected. The *southern* watchman of Blackwater. Sounds portentous. What does it involve?'

'Apart from rescuing wanderers from assassins outside the boundary? Accompanying them into ruined houses and watching them negotiate with creepy little hobgoblins? Then stopping them from drowning?'

'Full-time job, clearly. But apart from that.'

'Well, mostly watching the gate, being alert to threats. When it's harvest season, I help in the fields, sometimes I help at the forge – Elouen's the blacksmith now. I'm good with the horses, so I take my turn at the stables. When it's time to deliver shipments of goods and produce for sale to St Sinwin's, I go with Armel. Whatever Miren tells me to do, really.'

I nod. It seems like a worthwhile existence, that everything you do feeds back into your living, your community, the benefit of people you care about. 'Actually, may I please have some cake now?'

'Only in return for a story. The worst thing that's ever happened to you.'

'That's oddly particular. Not the best? The strangest? The funniest?'

'The worst. It tells you more about someone.'

'Worse than almost drowning?'

'Worse.'

'It'd better be the best cake I've ever had.'

'I feel confident.' He cuts a very large slice and that's enough to endear him to me. It might not be the best cake, but it's a close second. I don't tell him that, but I also don't give him my worst story. I give him maybe the third or fourth or fifth worst. I have too many to choose from, and he's heard me speak to Miren about some of those. I don't know why I choose this one – maybe it's the wine or too much cake. Maybe it's just to sound a warning.

'When I was thirteen, my father took me to the port-city of Breakwater for my first fight – *proper* fight. Once a Queen of Thieves ruled it, but she's long gone, and others have tried to take her place, pissant robber barons fighting over a canton or a street or a marketplace. The assassins' market remains well-patronised, and the fighting pits.' His eyes are pinned on my face. 'My father didn't place a bet on me even though he'd have made a fortune, all those punters watching a short teenage girl drop into a pit – there was no way they were going to risk their coin on me. The first of my opponents thought I'd be easy meat – they were dragged out with broken bones. The next round was much the same, then the third, fourth, fifth and sixth. All those killers and thieves were paying attention by then. I was exhausted, but that's when my father chose to tell me that I didn't get to leave until an opponent was dead.'

I shift in my chair, stretch the injured limb, then take a deep breath before going on. 'I'd been trained to fight since I was seven, but I'd never killed anyone. I knew how to do it, but hadn't ever... I also knew that if I didn't do what I was told, I'd only leave that pit as a corpse. And all those men they'd sent against me? All those big brave gentlemen? Killers and thieves and rapists and drunkards.'

'What happened?'

'I left the way my father wanted.' My hand shakes as I pick up the wine again. 'In the carriage on the way home he told me that what I'd done was important. That it was something I *needed* to do before I could be what he *needed* me to be.' I drink deeply. 'How does that rank on your scale of worst stories?'

'Normally, people just tell me about the day their dog died.'

'Well, I don't have any dead pet stories because I was never allowed a pet. What about you, Rab Cornish? What's your worst story?' I challenge.

He pauses, considers. 'I'm not a Cornish.'

'Then what are you?'

'I don't really know. Armel and Elouen found me wandering on the road, mostly starved. They brought me to Blackwater, took me in. Their parents became mine, they've never treated me as anything else. Which I suppose is my best and worst story: that I became a Cornish, but I don't know who I was before.'

'How old were you?'

'Seven, maybe? Armel says that's how old I looked.'

'Don't remember a name or a family?'

He shakes his head. 'Do you know why I'm called "Rab"?'

'Nope.'

'Because it was all I'd say when they asked me my name. Rab-rab-rabbit.' He grins, and it's sad and funny and hopeful and heartbreaking all at once.

'Something bad happened.'

He nods, turns away. 'I think I lost everything. Everyone.' He blinks, smiles. 'But I don't remember it. The lads found me, though. Gave me a new everything. A new everyone.'

And I think, suddenly, of Jack Seven-Gates, someone I'd known most of my life, a friend. And I realise I feel something for Rab that I never have for Jack in all that time: desire. And for the second time in my life, I don't think about consequences or whether an idea is good or bad.

And soon I'm hobbling around the table while he laughs gently, and I lean down to kiss his mouth, and soon I'm in his lap and soon he's carrying me inside to that kitchen table (which I like to think is being treated in a fashion entirely new to it) and soon he's in me. Then a bit later he carries me up the stairs to his bedroom (neat, masculine, smelling of sage and orange), and we do it all over again.

22

For a while – such a short while, such a long while – it's an idyll.

Freddie and I settle into Blackwater, seep into its life like rainwater carried in clouds from elsewhere. I've never known the child to take to any house, but she flits daily between Rab's where I sleep and Miren's (where she does) as if she's always had a roof over her head. I wonder, as ever, where she was before I first saw her; homeless then, but perhaps before that there was a home and parents. Then *something* happened. Something so terrible she never talks about it. But here, she's made friends, here she plays like the child she should be allowed to be.

Miren brings me books every day from her library and I can pretend I'm reading them as if they're just words on a page, not something my life might depend on. She lets me have that little illusion, even as she spends ages scouring her own bookshelves for things that might be relevant to my cause. The people of Blackwater, those who came here to work for her parents – for Isolde, really, and her intense charm – have taken Miren to their hearts. She treats them like the family she didn't have; and they've been kind and welcoming to Freddie and me. With her own children, she's determined to give them a life of knowing they're loved, and that their choices when they grow will be their own.

If I didn't have Mrs M and Temperance to return to, I might consider throwing myself on her mercy, begging for one of the pretty little cottages that currently sit empty, awaiting the newly coupled.

And there's Rab, who's like no one I've ever known. He's open and honest, and he's kind. His brothers treat him no differently to each other – even adopted, he's one of them and they never act as if there's a divide of blood between them. At night, pressed against him, I stare out the tall windows at the stars, letting myself believe this is my life now, that it will remain so. That I don't need to leave this place, this estate, this house, this bed; that there isn't a task waiting for me. Some nights it almost works.

Almost.

Because the reading, ultimately, reminds me of what I must do.

This, from *The Observations of Frater Egbert of Miriam-on-the-Wold* with copious reference to *The Recollections of Father Larcwide of St Simeon-in-the-Grove* – a different view to some sources that claim the Leech Lords weren't ubiquitous, were a relatively *small* trouble:

In the time before the Church erected the barrier around the Darklands to contain the heinous threat of the Leech Lords, the creatures wreaked havoc, decimating cities, wiping out entire villages. Those that remained in the north seemed to be those with a taste for order of some kind; those who roamed were lawless in all ways.

Those in the north are careful of how they reproduce – or rather, how many they make of themselves. They do so only on purpose, by the exchange of blood. Victims do not accidentally turn, they do not *become* without imbibing the blood of a true Leech. Nonetheless, the recommendation for dealing with victims' corpses is burning.

Of those Leeches who roamed, the wise ones who wished to remain safe would insinuate themselves with the rich and the influential, offering those mortals life eternal in return for the protection of their wealth and power. For some that would be enough, but the truly ruthless – hard to distinguish those degrees – would bide their time, embedding themselves in their patron's world, feeding off them to create a lien, a link, an obedience, all the while having business interests and properties transferred to themselves. When all they'd desired was theirs, the patron would be disposed of. Yet others simply thought in very immediate terms: feed, steal, flee, leaving behind a trail of dead.

There is even the tale, seldom spoken of, mostly suppressed but I will write it here, of the Leech who embedded himself in the household of the Archbishop of the ancient city of —burgh, eventually replacing him and turning the entire city into a feasting ground. The great cathedral was awash with blood, a place of decay and denigration – the Leech Lord and those he'd turned made it their feeding trough. This was the flashpoint when the Church began its crusade in earnest. Indeed, it's how the cathedral city of Lodellan rose to prominence –

on the bleeding ruin of —burgh. The battle abbeys (with the notable exception of St Catherine's of the Wheel) answered the call of Archbishop Athhelm, and the legions of the Church militant marched across the lands, seeking the daytime nests, cutting off their heads with weapons rubbed with raw garlic, and burning the remains.

Any that evaded this fate fled north once more. A great gate was built – some claim by the Leech Lords to keep the forces of the Church out; some claim by the Church to keep the Leech Lords in. Truces were made. Many years later, another Archbishop of Lodellan – Narcissus Marsh – sealed an agreement with the Briar Witches of Silverton: that they would guard the boundary, hold the gate with their spells and wards. And in return they would be free to live…

Silverton, my next destination.

And when I'm not consuming the books Miren brings, I take the time to lose myself fully in Murciana's journal each day.

On Leech Lords:

It wasn't that there'd never been a creature that thirsted for blood, but those were animals. There were the wolves that were sometimes men and sometimes lupine; there were trolls who adored babies as treats; kelpies who feasted on travellers; redcaps and the tiniest of fairies who bit deep when one crossed certain marshlands. But before that there'd not been anything that looked human yet wanted to drink one's blood and life with it.

It's strange the tricks the mind plays: the whole time I was with the mage, I would dream that my parents sought me, that soon they would find me and bring me home. The worst days, I would take refuge in my brief night's sleep to make myself believe I was safe. That my dreams were real.

But when I finally left the mage behind, I ceased to think upon my parents. I trained myself out of the habit. As the weeks became months and years at the Citadel, I began to resent my parents. I thought of them less and less, and only then with anger. The more I settled in with the Little Sisters – all my replacement mothers and aunts and siblings – the more I forgot where I'd come from. I could convince myself I'd always been there, always belonged.

As an adult, I roamed as a Blessed Wanderer, documenting the world around me, continued to do so as long as I could.

And as I grew older, when thoughts of my parents returned unbidden, and I'd sought and received news of what they'd become, they transformed into a haunting.

At last, I turned my steps to the north and went to find them.

* * *

One morning when I wake, Rab's still in bed. Usually, he's gone by the time I rouse, chores to do. Today, he's snoring, just a little, and I prop myself up on one elbow all the better to stare at him. Soon enough, the corner of his mouth lifts, and he says, 'Staring's terribly rude.'

'Then you shouldn't be so terribly attractive.'

He rolls me beneath him and before long we're a mess of sweaty limbs, gasps and tangled sheets. When we're done, I rest a hand on his chest, one of his hands stroking my belly.

'What are you thinking?' he asks.

'That I don't want to get up. That I don't want to go anywhere.' But I know that my injury is healed, that the muscles have their strength back, everything sped along by Miren's potions.

'You don't have to.' Then he adds, 'Not today.'

'Not today,' I echo.

'When you…' He swallows. 'When you do what you need to, would you consider coming back here? We could have time to… make plans for a future?'

'I—' The shy sincerity in his voice makes me ache and I'm keenly aware of his fingers on my belly, on the scar faded by a cunning cream Tempe brought me, where something once grew – but never will again. And I think he's seeing a future that I can't have, even if I survive this journey; if I don't survive it, no one will be able to have it, not the way people dream about. But I don't know how to tell him this. Not yet. Maybe not ever. Lamely, I say, 'Freddie does like it here.'

He smiles, a little sadly, kisses my forehead and rolls out of bed. He tells me he's needed at the sawmill, so Armel will be filling in at the gatehouse today. He leaves without another kiss and I know I've hurt him.

I've hurt *me*.

If I stay any longer, it will only be harder to leave. If I stay any longer, I'll feel worse about Freddie coming with me, being at risk. If I stay any longer, I'll have to tell Rab Cornish that I'm damaged beyond repair and can never give him what he wants. The longer I stay, the shorter the days to my brother's birthday.

I pack quickly – it's not hard, my few clothes are clean and mended by some of Blackwater's beldams, and I've been living in borrowed nightgowns and dresses. The sack of O'Malley silver

I put firmly in the bottom of the bag; I still carry the piece from Walter's letter in my pocket, a talisman, a luck charm. I strap the knife sheath onto my forearm for the first time in days – the longest time in my recent life that I've been free of it. It feels strange; normally, I'm unaware of it, because it just feels like part of me. I restock with food from the pantry, all the tasty things Rab has made, then heft my bag, and sneak out of the house.

Armel is in the little wooden guard's shed closest to where the gate can be opened. He's reading a book, not looking in my direction – why would he, there's no threat from inside. I make my way to the stable behind the gatehouse, saddle Ned the Nondescript and tell Molly she's to be a good girl for Freddie.

Then I mount and set off through the woods.

* * *

I'm standing in the tree line not far from the northern gatehouse. There's a matching little guard's hut by the hedge, and now I'm trying to work out whether I can simply walk up to the woman sitting in it and ask to be let out. How long before she tells someone? What if she refuses?

'You know you can't get out without help, yes?' Miren's voice is soft, amused and behind me.

'Good thing you're here, then.' I turn, for a moment find her difficult to distinguish in the shade. 'You really shouldn't sneak up on people like that.'

'I was checking on Arabella – her first duty – and who should I see lurking in the shadows?' She rubs her belly. 'You know, I started off with such energy, walking seemed like such a good idea.'

'Not now?'

'Oh, I'll be alright after a rest.' She draws beside me. 'So, what *are* you doing? This is a precipitous departure. Something we said? Did?'

'I need to get on my way. Get this thing done.'

'And Freddie? Rab?' I'm grateful there's no accusation in her tone. Just an enquiry, as if I know my own mind and she's merely curious.

'Freddie will be safer with you. She loves it here. She'll fit in, the way Rab did – it'll be like she's always been at Blackwater.' I blink. 'On the road… where I'm going… what I need to do… she'll be safe with you.'

'And Rab? What do I tell him.'

'Rab is wonderful but… I can't be what he wants me to be. I can't have…' I blink hard to keep the tears at bay. 'I need to do this on my own and I can't risk anyone else. Thank you for your help and your friendship, Miren, but it's time for me to go.'

Miren O'Malley puts her arms around me, an awkward hug with her great belly between us. She smells like lavender. Pulling away, she says, 'I'll tell them both you love them. C'mon, I'll let you out. Take the right when you leave, it'll keep you on course for Silverton. Watch for the day-runners, they might still be roaming the roads after you disappeared.'

'Thank you.' I watch as she greets Arabella, who eyes me curiously, then Miren raises her hands and the panels of the hedge-fence unclasp each other, shifting to the side, just wide enough for me and Ned the Nondescript, whose coat's developed quite the handsome shine in his days of grazing, to a trot.

'And, Violet? Beware of the Briars, they're like no witches you've ever known.'

I cry for the first hour after leaving Blackwater, silent tears, no sobs, just saltwater trickling down my cheeks, drippling onto my coat and collar. Eventually, I begin reciting rhymes to take my mind off thoughts of what I've left behind. I determinedly do not think about Rab in that bed, of all the things we did there. I ignore the heat that rises in me, keep reciting rhymes.

Around midday, there's the clatter of hooves from somewhere behind me and I urge Ned off the road, into the thickness of the forest where the trees' branches entwine with each other and the undergrowth climbs between trunks to weave blinds of leaves and flowers. I dismount and tuck us behind a leafy screen, petting the horse's velvety nose to keep him calm. I hope he'll not whiny when he sees the approaching horses; I hope he has a sense of danger and it will help to keep us hidden. I could push us in further, but I want to see who's following me.

The clatter becomes a thunder and a pack of black-clad riders flashes by. The uniforms of the Anchorhold. Perhaps the last of those lying in wait in St Sinwin's, or those searching these past twelve days? Perhaps others still?

I can't know. The only thing I'm certain of is that the best thing I can do is stay in the forest for now, moving parallel to the road, out of sight. I lead the horse deeper into the trees. It'll do me good to walk for a while, to work the stiffness out of my ankle, just for a little while.

23

I'm lost.

Of course, I'm lost. I kept going through the forest, longer than I should, thinking it safer, assuming I'd be able to rejoin the road easily at my leisure. That taking a little extra time would mean the assassins would get well ahead of me once again. But I got lost instead. Of course, I did.

The compass I packed back in St Sinwin's for just such an occasion was, I discover now, crushed and broken in my pack – no doubt from the first night at Blackwater, when Rab and Armel dragged us in and I dropped both bags as I fell. I will, presumably, be able to find my way in the morning when there's more light than there currently is. It's dark beneath the trees, they grow so thickly as to form a canopy and the sun spears through here and there, but in no great quantity, except for the occasional clearing. Again, this part of the forest is thick and old, not welcoming to those trying to pass through it. And I admit I was not paying attention to where I was going because I was too busy being miserable.

It's a relief, then, when I find the cottage, a red-roofed well out in the tiny front garden marked out by a black picket fence.

The dark bulk of a shingle-clad barn looms behind, but I hear no livestock. Ned nickers softly as we approach, and I dismount.

It's a surprise, the little place, pretty, yellow stone foundation and white-plastered withy walls.

In the garden is a woman, tall and straight, her face tilted to take in the last of the sunlight, standing in a sunbeam. Her long dress is a dun colour, her apron a brilliant red to match her lips. Black hair streaming past her waist reminds me of my mother's, but she's otherwise nothing like Vesper. An unusual amalgam, round face but high cheekbones, hollowed out beneath, wide-set eyes, emphatic brows, a chin that's little more than a suggestion but she's still quite lovely. There seems – and I cannot say why I think so, for she's motionless – to be a certain weightlessness to her. An air of ethereal lightness.

I'm reluctant to interrupt this moment when she looks so much at peace, a part of the woods itself, growing from the forest floor. Natural and inevitable, yet fragile. So, I wait until that pale liquid yellow dips into lavender dusk. Then she moves, breaks the stretching lines of her own body – the yearning towards the light – and relaxes, becoming smaller. Ordinary.

'Hello?' My voice sounds and I'm surprised at how loud it is here, how it almost echoes. The woman startles, gives a little leap, gaze searching the shadows. I step in closer, make myself easier to see, smile to show I mean no harm. Ned snorts. 'Hello. I'm sorry to frighten you. I'm lost. I was wondering if I could sleep in your barn for the night? And get directions to the road north?'

She stares at me for what seems a long time, as if she's not seen another person in some while. Blinks rapidly as if to make sure I'm really there. This place is isolated, clearly hidden.

'My husband will return soon,' she says and there's a studied neutrality to her tone. Does she think me a threat? That I'll be deterred from hurting her by this piece of knowledge?

'I'm sorry to be a bother. I really am lost.'

She hesitates, opens her mouth, her upper body leans forward, a foot shifts, the beginnings of a motion towards me—

'Good evening, traveller.'

Another voice, friendly and low. Both the woman and I turn.

A man steps around the corner of the cottage, as if he's come from the barn. Long white hair, taller than his wife by half a head, slender, wiry-looking. Black trews, a white shirt and green vest. An old-young face – older than his wife but it's hard to tell by how much. As he approaches, shifting from shadow to last light to shadow and back, there's the illusion of ageing and rejuvenation. I shake my head, blink to focus. Sixty, perhaps; closer to Walter's age; deceptively youthful, but up close there are lines and age spots, the hair that looked so abundant is actually thin and dry-looking, the dark eyes a little rheumy – I want to examine his wife more closely, see if her face is as tricksy as his, but I keep my gaze firmly on him. His hands are thin, elongated, sleeves rolled up mid-forearm, the veins standing out as if carved in marble.

'Good evening' – dusk is sinking around us, its bruised hue shifting to grey – 'as I was just telling your wife, I've managed to lose my way. I was hoping for directions and perhaps permission to sleep in your barn tonight?'

'My name is Kyril and this is Ixara. Directions are no problem – but the barn isn't for you, young lady. We have a small room that was once our son's, you're welcome to it.' He turns to

211

Ixara, gestures. Her back is very narrow, very straight as she goes inside. He takes the reins from me.

'Let our home be yours for this night. I will settle your mount in the barn.' Kyril leads the beastie away, the latter snorting with displeasure.

I thank him and take a deep breath, glad of the knife in my sleeve even though I'm not sure how much good it'll do me. I consider making my excuses, running, but doubt I'll make it far. However, this is a chance I've never had before, rare though dangerous. I'd be a fool to pass it up, as much a fool to take it. I cross the threshold, a thin line of ice beginning at the base of my spine and creeping upwards.

Such creatures as the Leeches are difficult to recognise because they appear, at first, like any other mortal. Despite rumours to the contrary, they are not especially tall, nor naturally slender. They begin as humans and whatever form they had in life, so they retain in death. Admittedly, upon dying, some of the body mass may be lost due to a change in diet. But a fat man or woman will become a fat Leech; a slender one, perhaps an even more so Leech. No great beauty attaches to a Leech Lord by their transformation no matter what one might like to believe; beauty in life will transfer to death, but an ugly mortal will not become aesthetically pleasing with death and resurrection.

They will be pale for they must avoid the sun. It will burn them to a crisp, although there are rumours that some have survived such conflagrations, taking centuries to recover themselves. I have yet to read a documented resurrection but the tale recurs frequently enough that I'm unwilling to discount it entirely.

Their teeth elongate only when they are about to feed. I believe this is a learned habit – or rather the keeping of them sheathed – in order to lull the victim into a false sense of security. Some can spin illusions like a lure, but few can maintain them for any great length of time. Leeches are terribly swift, they travel fast, they are inhumanly strong, they are…

FROM MRS DANILLA VERDIGRIS' *BY FANG AND FOE*
[UNFINISHED MONOGRAPH]

I'm careful not to eat, stirring my spoon through the soup, raising it to my mouth, but returning it to the bowl to ask and answer questions. I lift the fine glass goblet, pretend to drink. It's a shame because the soup smells delicious, thick and meaty, chunks of potato and leeks floating in it and with the strong scent of red wine as part of its make-up. I wonder where the meat came from. And the wine in the goblet is a beautiful crimson, deep and dark as blood. I cannot get past the sense that I should have made my excuses and kept on my way. That this "learning opportunity" might be my last. Yet I also can't help but think that I wouldn't have made it very far with Kyril aware of my presence in the forest.

Ixara eats, Kyril does not; he doesn't even make the pretence I do, the contents of the bowl in front of him slowly going cold.

He and I chat about places he has travelled. I make up a history for myself, as if I were born to the docks, apprenticed to the Harbour Mistress, brought up scrapping in the gutters. That I put to sea before I was thirteen, working my passage as a cabin-girl, that I saw wonderful and exotic distant lands, but my heart drew me back to this continent. That I travel north to see an aunt, the only family I've left in the world. Kyril observes what a colourful life I've led. He tells tales of cities and towns with names I don't recognise – presumably because he's so old they've died and disappeared while he's continued on, stealing lives. Ixara offers desultory yes and no answers when asked anything; her husband says she was born in Angharad's Breach, which at least is a name I recognise. She doesn't look at me, not directly, or only once that I notice. Her expression's mostly inscrutable, but sometimes I catch her unguarded and it's sad, regretful, resigned.

The longer the dinner lasts, the more I notice things changing. Nothing is as it at first seemed. Perhaps he's having trouble holding the illusion together because the neat, pretty cottage with its comfortable furniture, colourful curtains and hangings, coloured vases filled with flowers, now appears to have two layers, one on top of the other. The one that's clearest, sharpest is the most pleasing. The one beneath it, like a palimpsest shadow shows a decay, a greying and an ageing, a layer of dust, cobwebs spun between furnishings.

Eventually Kyril gives up all pretence; a change comes over his features, which become leaner, hungrier, the cheekbones higher, the teeth sharper, the lips thinner. I wonder how much energy he's consumed with spinning illusions for me. Foolishly playing with his food.

'When did you know?' he asks.

I glance at Ixara – no change in her. She's nothing more than she looks: an exhausted woman. I noticed, as she served the meal, the fine scars on her wrists, the cuffs of her sleeves riding up with her movements, and those on her neck as her hair shifted this way and that. A winepress, unwilling or not. How long has she been here?

'Almost as soon as you came close,' I reply. 'And you didn't ask who I am – presumably because one doesn't call food by a name.'

I've never seen one of them before, although Hedrek occasionally brought men to dinner who'd claimed to have done so. He'd have them tell me tales of their adventures as part of my education. Yet I knew what Kyril was so quickly – not quickly enough to escape, obviously. Strange he should be here, but then even though the Church had done its best to eradicate those who'd strayed beyond the Darklands before the border was made, there was no guarantee they'd find them all. This one had hidden far better than expected. And in a place like this? So isolated? Who would look here?

'Some instinct, then.' He sounds too eager. 'Do you have any blood of ours? In your veins?'

'I don't know.' But I do; I think of my mother, the daughter of a Leech Lord, of my brother, about Tiberius's conception and birth, about what it did to Vesper. But this thing doesn't need to know any of that.

'There's always a strain of human in the Darklands that holds the hint of us. Breeding's rarely successful, but sometimes...' He reaches for his wife, runs fingers now tipped with glass-like nails up and down her neck. She closes her eyes – perhaps so she doesn't have to look at him. So, he can't see her fear, her loathing. But I'm sure he already knows what's there.

'How are you here?' I ask.

'Got out before they set the gate in place, before those whore witches arrived and locked us all in.' He sneers, falters. 'I tried to return, once, when the god-hounds were hunting us down – seemed a good idea – but the witches and their spells... I couldn't get past them.' Then he laughs. 'Mind you, I'd rather be here with my bountiful winepress than fighting for a place in a court.' He shakes his head. 'No grace for those without power, without others to do your bidding. You're a lord or you're one of their retainers, or one of their night-runners.'

'Night-runners?'

'Assassins. Leeches can only move at night. In the sun's hours, there are the mortals, the day-runners. Or there were, in my day.' He shrugs.

'Who made you? When?'

'A Lady with a taste for peasants, longer ago than I care to recall.' He sits back, gestures to himself proudly. 'In my youth, I was beautiful though low-born. Enough to enamour a Lady of a great Leech house. She turned me, believing the obsession would last forever, that we'd be entwined for all eternity.'

'And?'

'Interest wanes when one's immortal.' He shrugs, looks away.

'And how do you exist now?'

'Frugally.' He laughs, his fingers tightening on Ixara's hair, pulling it cruelly so she cries out and jerks towards him. 'Except tonight, when a meal wanders so thoughtfully into reach.' He smiles and he's all teeth, white and shining with saliva.

'Do you know anything about the Anchorhold?'

He lets his wife go, his eyes skittering around the room.

'No one's spoken that word beyond the Darklands. Not ever.'

'Well,' I say, 'it's making itself known. Its day-runners roam the roads, speaking its name. It has plans.' Casually, I slip a hand into my pocket, praying this experiment isn't so stupid it'll get me killed, and repeat: 'Do you know anything about it?'

'Nothing good. If it's sent its assassins out, then… but that won't matter to you. I've still got time to—' He lunges at me, across the table.

As I'm throwing myself backward off the bench, I pull my hand out of my pocket, the single mer-queen scale from Walter I'd kept as a talisman tight in my fingers. Gods, he's fast, a pure predator, the teeth and fangs growing before my eyes and I'm only just fast enough to get my hand up and press the silvery scale against the flesh beneath his chin, all the while thinking this is an idiotic way to die.

Almost immediately on contact it begins to burn. It's so fast I can feel my fingers wrapped at the edge of the scale pushing through the flesh that now smells of burning, searing. I pull my hand away, but the scale stays embedded where it is, the effect continues, swiftly and brutally. Skin and flesh, tendons and muscles, all peel back and dissolve, as if acid has been poured on Kyril. The very bones of him disintegrate like chalk. I know he intended me for a meal, but I'm not sure I'd have sentenced anyone to this. His screams seem to sound long after he's a pile of damp white dust, and the silver scale of the mer-queen sits atop it, triumphant.

24

'How long?' I ask as we stare at the remains of Kyril. Part of my mind is occupied with the effect of the silver on his flesh, the speed of his demise. A smaller part – and perhaps I should be ashamed of this – is sorrowing for the woman beside me. 'Ixara?'

'He took me from my home when I was sixteen. Dragged me behind him wherever he led. Whenever I tried to flee he punished me, so in the end I stopped trying. I watched over him in the daylight hours, kept him safe. At night, he fed off me if there was nothing – no one – else available. Kept me alive because he said a beaten-down thrall was the best sort and not easy to come by. Not easy to create – that too many retained some spirit. He said I wasn't one of those.' She shakes her head carefully, as if her skull might topple from its perch. As if she's unstrung by his death, but not distressed. 'I've lost track of time. I stopped counting after forty. It feels forever. I did like it *here*, though, as much as I've been able to like anywhere.' She looks at me, wide-eyed and whispers: 'So *many* years.'

'*Was* he your husband?'

She nods, tears spilling at last. 'He thought it was funny. Said it was his promise to me of *forever* – wasn't that what women wanted? Had some priest-turned-Leech perform the ceremony in some tiny village we passed through. An amusement for the Leech who was lording it over that place, Feodor's Tor.'

I don't recognise the name. A place disappeared ago? She doesn't look young but nor does she look old – is the effect of being fed on long-term to also extend the life of the winepress? 'I'm so sorry. Will you stay? Here?'

'I don't know. I don't know if I can, without *him*.' She catches my expression, explains: 'He would hunt for deer in the woods. Made sure I was fed.'

Of course. No point in allowing his winepress to expire. Deer. At a pinch squirrels and rabbits, even foxes and badgers. Bears and wolves – no challenge for a Leech. 'What was in my food?'

She laughs. 'Nothing. Whenever a traveller wandered in, he never drugged them. It would have affected the taste, affected *him*. A little red wine was the only thing he would allow.'

'I'm hungry,' I say, which feels wrong. But I am.

She nods, goes to the hearth, and ladles a fresh bowl of soup for me, then gives herself another serving. I sit with a groan; more bruising on my backside. I've spent my life training and fighting, but I've seldom felt so battered.

As we eat, I question her about her Leech husband, trying to pick up any information that might be of use. 'He never tried to turn you?'

She shakes her head. 'No. Never – two mouths to feed, needing to share whatever meagre mortals he might find in the forest?' A harsh laugh, the first sound of mirth from her. Her voice grows quiet as she goes on, 'But I've changed over the years, as he's fed on me. I never tasted his blood, though he took mine, but I'm stronger than I look. Full daylight, though I seek it, has become uncomfortable – only dawn light and dusk feel safe.'

That bite, the long teeth, the transfer of saliva that's unavoidable in such a feeding. I wonder about prolonged exposure to such a substance. What might it do to a mortal? What about a mortal that's born of a Leech-human union? What might they become, with time?

When it becomes clear there's nothing more she can tell me about the creature she's been living with, I ask about her, about her existence before the abduction. It takes time, but as she speaks, she remembers, and stories tumble out. A simple life, a family's manor, country gentry, comfortable but not excessively rich. A lad she loved, a troubadour with a sweet voice, he came and went but always returned to her. Siblings and a rough and tumble life until her mother said it was time to behave like a lady. Then the evening when darkness brought a guest, a handsome man who looked well-to-do, a tale of separation from his companions, a request for shelter for a single eve. Kyril at her family's door, charming her parents, amusing her and her siblings, the recitation of his adventures, his travels, late into the night.

And in the morning no one lived in the manor house but she and the thing that did not breathe.

'You've had no children?' I ask gently.

'Just one. He did not survive,' she says shortly. I think about the mention of a son's small bedroom, wonder how long he lasted.

'You're fortunate,' I say, but don't share the details of Vesper and my baby brother.

We talk through much of the night, with me asking questions and her recalling her history as if it's a miraculously unwinding

220

tapestry, rolled up tight for too long. She talks and talks, about big things and small, about ideas and thoughts she's been unable to share in who-knows-how-long, and I think she's trying to make up for decades (centuries?) of silence. Briefly, we sleep, perhaps an hour or two, but wake to the thin light of dawn trickling from behind the thick curtains, making them glow.

'I'm sorry,' she says, 'I talked too much. I should have let you sleep more. I owed you that at least, since you freed me.'

'Not to worry. I've been well-rested.' I smile, recalling all those recent days in Rab's bed, sleeping and not. The thought of Rab sobers me. I ask again, 'What will you do now? Stay or find a new place without memories?'

She shakes her head. 'I don't know. I feel... I cannot explain it, but I feel *finished*. Done.'

I open my mouth to respond but we're interrupted by the stomping of hooves outside, a bridle jingling, snorts and general protests – and Ned the Nondescript neighing loudly from the barn lest anyone fail to hear him. My heart contracts.

The day-runners have backtracked. They've found me.

Except I hear Freddie's voice, calling for me.

'Miss Violet! Miss Violet, are you here?'

Ixara looks afraid. I rise, hold a calming hand out to her. 'Don't worry, it's my friend.'

That child, I think with exasperation. Determined not to let me go on my own. Tracking me like a little wolfhound. I open the door and step out.

Not just Freddie, but another horse beside hers. A tall bay bearing Rab Cornish, his expression a mix of relief, hurt and irritation. What looks like the handle of a battleaxe is peeking over his shoulder.

I walk into the garden, towards where they wait outside the low picket fence. There's a gasp from behind me. Looking back, I notice all the cottage's pretty charm is gone. The walls are crumbling, the thatched roof holed, the windows dirty and cracked – the illusion broken by Kyril's death and daylight.

Ixara's in the doorway, clutching a hand to her chest. Uncertainly, she descends into the garden, totters towards roughly the spot she stood yesterday for the final ray of sunshine. Hesitant as she wasn't last night, unbalanced in her gait, as if sudden freedom is a burden. There's a full circle of morning sun streaming down through a break in the tree canopy, and she steps into that circle. Ixara lifts her head, face bathing in the glow.

And she begins to disappear.

In seconds the woman is a collection of dust motes in the air as if the touch of the light was a physical blow, the puff of breath on a dandelion head. Then she's gone.

So. Human, but not. So many years fed upon by the Leech that she was changed somehow. Not into whatever he was, but some sort of an eidolon. Little more than a ghost.

'Miss Violet!' shouts Freddie. 'How could you leave us?!'

* * *

We ride on.

Silently.

We'd left the crumbling cottage quickly – I didn't want to stay any longer – as soon as I'd offered Freddie an apology of sorts. An apology for the desertion, but also a scolding for not staying safe. Didn't she understand, that I'd left her with friends, in comfort because I didn't want to risk her life any more than I already had? She told me, in no uncertain terms, that she wouldn't

222

be left behind – that Miren and her family were all very nice, but they weren't *her* family.

I don't say anything to Rab except: 'Hello.'

Hours drift by. We pass small villages, large houses of varying degrees of elegance. We take bridges over rivers and streams, careful to watch for trolls beneath and kelpies in the waters. There are some churches, smaller and fewer in number, as if the norther one goes the less the god-hounds care about being here. Or perhaps they're less tolerated away from the larger cities. We stick to the roadways, always keeping an ear out for the sound of hoofbeats, coming from behind or in front of us, but we encounter no one.

I wonder how many others like Kyril endure? Living in hiding, knowing their survival depends entirely upon concealment, on not reproducing, on taking only what they can get away with, only what they need. Knowing that massacres will lead to their own end.

Late in the afternoon, we find a clearing not too far off the side of the road and set up camp. Rab goes hunting, taking a bow and arrow, and returns with two plump rabbits. I light a fire and Freddie tends to the horses, talking to them in a low voice, fussing over Ned as if it's been weeks since she saw him, not a day and a half. Rab skins the rabbits, while I open Murciana's journal, thinking to catch up on my reading.

'I set a line of bells on a string around the camp, in case anyone should approach in the night. So be careful if you need to relieve yourself after dark.'

'Lest anyone know I tinkle?'

He laughs, a little unwillingly.

'How did you find me?' I ask.

223

'Violet, I've been hunting game most of my life and you leave quite the trail.'

I shrug. 'Fair.'

'Why did you leave?' he asks quietly, but I can hear his hurt. He's not looking at me, but at the bloody rabbits in his hands. *Rab rab rabbit.*

I pause, searching for an answer that will suffice, and realise only the truth will do. 'My world has been turned upside down in the past few weeks. My father had a plan for me, yet I thought myself free of it. I thought I had a choice about how I would live. Since then I've been attacked, my family threatened, and I'm hunted still. None of this ends unless I do what my father wanted. Or I die trying. And then, suddenly, there was you. A man who saved me from drowning, who's fed and cared for me for no other reason than he's kind.' I shake my head. 'And for a tiny moment I can see a life that might be mine – or I could pretend it was – with you, in Blackwater or St Sinwin's or anywhere we might choose. Then you mentioned a future, which means a family and I remember I'm not what you want me to be, I can't be who you need, I can't give you children.' I swallow down a sob. 'And I didn't want to tell you that. It was easier to leave you and you could think of me as an enjoyable encounter rather than a malformed... And it was safer to leave Freddie behind where she was making friends, making a home, where she finally seemed to relax. As long as I've known her she's been wary, hyper alert. She's just a child but whatever happened—'

'You don't know what happened to her?' he asks.

I shake my head. 'She's never told me and I learned early that if she's asked too many questions she'll disappear for a while.

224

Same if you insist she come to live in your home and be taken care of. She'd rather remain a street urchin.' I pause, think how easily Freddie settled in *Rab's* home, in Miren's. 'Wait. Did she tell *you* anything?'

'No. But… there's something, someone she's afraid of.'

'I mean, she's living on the streets – it could be anyone.'

'But she won't live in *your* house…'

It's something I've considered. 'She comes to visit. She sleeps in the stables. Since my father died, there's only myself, Mrs M and my stepmother.' Hedrek was hardly aware of Freddie's existence except as occasional annoyances; she was of no use to him. She only ever set foot in the kitchen, and Hedrek never went there, nor any of his regular guests. Temperance spent her time there, choosing menus, discussing the running of the house with Penelope Medway and presumably falling in love. I shrug. 'She'll tell me when she's ready.'

'And, Violet?'

'Yes?'

'I don't care about having children. I care about you. I care about Freddie. I found my family in the Cornishes, with Miren, the other Blackwater folk – why wouldn't I want to find another with you? With Freddie?' His voice breaks a little. 'Wouldn't you think better of me than that?'

225

25

The rabbit is tasty. We speak normally over dinner as if nothing's happened, although Freddie doesn't sit next to me so I'm not forgiven yet. I tell them, at last, about Kyril and Ixara, what I discovered and that the O'Malley silver worked, that the rumour recounted in Walter's letter was true, at least as far as its efficacy against Leech Lords is concerned. I tell them how little I got from Kyril about the Anchorhold but that he was clearly nervous at its mention.

'How many are there, do you think, like him?' asks Rab. 'Cut off from his own kind, existing on scraps?'

'Can't be too many. They wouldn't last if they drew attention. And their habits are very hard to hide, they'd be noticed if they slaughtered whole towns or turned any into nests or feeding places.' I shrug. 'If there were any more close by, I think Kyril would have mentioned them – he struck me as the boastful type. And Ixara said he'd never turned her because it would mean competition for blood – Kyril wouldn't have wanted to be where other Leeches were. I think he found the cottage, killed the original owners and has been guarding his territory ever since.'

Freddie wraps herself in her bedroll on the other side of the fire; soon she's snoring. Rab's doing the same not long after. I've had so little sleep, but Hedrek made sure I could function with not much at all. I throw a few more branches on the fire to build it up, then I retrieve Murciana's journal once again.

Before I left for the Darklands, I sought out Sister Constance.

Living with so many women for so many years – some leave us, the Blessed Wanderers such as myself come and go, but most remain – one learns the Sisters' stories, or a part of them. Some keep their histories to themselves but most, I think, reach a point where they wish to be known fully, and they write themselves into the Books of Little Lives. To let others understand who they had been before. Even me, writing these scraps down for no one but myself – I discovered long ago that writing gives one something to hold onto, helps to make things real. When I was dragged behind the Magister, writing was my anchor. And being here, in the Citadel, surrounded by all these books and tales and recountings and knowledge... how can one not want to contribute?

Sister Constance had arrived years before me, fleeing her home and persecution. She was perhaps eighteen then, older than I. She'd begun as a terrified maiden, a witch accused of crimes against god-hounds and the Church. She'd found refuge with the Little Sisters and, like most of us, became utterly loyal to Mater Adela who'd given us sanctuary, a home and a family. It was years after my first stumbling night in the Citadel that I learned she'd been despatched to deal with the Magister.

Even then, she was powerful and not afraid to use her magic; indeed, she'd been encouraged by Mater Adela to spend her days in the many wings of the Citadel libraries, reading and learning, writing new spells and practising them as she went. She's risen through the ranks, has outlived Mater Adela, and two other maters, Greta and Femeka. She is now our infirmarian. She was offered the Matership but refused – I think she felt that duty would have distracted her from her preferred activities.

Like me, she's been granted the privilege of not having her decisions or actions questioned, because the maters and Beatrix saw value to allowing us to reach beyond our grasp. She was allowed to refuse the highest position in the Citadel and I was allowed to continue as one of the Blessed Wanderers when I might have taken on a position more sedate and safe.

She's not so old, not yet, but is curmudgeonly with those she considers idiots. But she's ever been kind to me, has always kept an eye on my progress since I was new. I asked her about that night when she went to where the mage waited in that little cave on the beach. The spot where he'd pushed me through a mere crack in the rock wall – a space so small only an underfed child could fit – that fed into the tunnels honeycombing the cliffs beneath the Citadel and led upwards.

I asked what she had done.

'Why, child?' She called me that as if there was more than a decade between us.

I hesitated, pondered. 'My parents. I've been thinking about them lately. And myself. How I was taken. How they never came after me. Never found me. Some of my Blessed Wanderers have brought me tales of them, of what they became.' I did not tell her that I sent those Wanderers forth with instructions, but I think from her expression that she'd figured that out.

228

She pursed her lips. 'He didn't take me seriously. Laughed when he saw I was female. Told me **Run away, little girl**. So, I cursed him.'

'With what?'

'I cursed him with the worst thing he'd ever done.'

'What was that?' I swallowed.

'I'd thought it would be what he'd done to you, how he'd treated you. But now I believe it was what he did to your parents. The moment the spell left my lips, my fingers, he shrivelled before my eyes, turned into a snarling creature, grew teeth and nails. He saw the blood dripping from my hand where I'd paid the red price – such a small cut! – and he came for me. I ran, back out into the dawning light of the new day and he followed. Next I knew, he was screaming, a terrible sound, and burning in the weak early sun. He fled into the cave, trailing the scent of burned meat behind him.'

She shook her head. 'I was afraid – the first time in a long time. My magic, my power had protected me when my family would not. I admit I had not always been circumspect about its use. But seeing the effect on the Magister – I had not expected that. I cast the spell without real thought, a lot of spite, just wanted to make him suffer for the insult he'd given me. I... I couldn't imagine that the worst thing he'd done was to turn someone into... that.'

She shook her head again. 'Reports of the Leech Lords had begun to arrive a year or two before you came to us. I think... he did that to your parents. After he ran, I returned to the Citadel, called Sister Osterhild and her wardens but when we went back to the cave he was gone. He must have burned.'

'Or run further?'

'The next day... the next day, I searched the cave again and found a ditch, dug rough in a far corner, away from the light. I *can't help but think perhaps he hid there? That we did not search well enough.'*

I thanked her and went to my chamber to think.

I recalled that when the mage had sent me to steal knowledge from the Little Sisters, one of his questions was: 'How to live beyond one's time.' An aching irony.

A day later, I left for the north, to Caulder where my parents lived, where I had lived for such a short while before the Magister came. To Caulder, from whence rumours came of the Lord and Lady who fed on their folk like cattle. To Caulder, where I'd been born and stolen. If my parents had not come to find me, I would go to find them.

I dream of a time before the Leech Lords, of their beginning, but I did not know how to dream of their ending. While I dream, the faces of the people I read about are clear: I can see Murciana and Mater Adela, Sister Constance and Beatrix who's no more than a head floating on a pond of fire, the Lord and Lady of Caulder, and the mage who called himself Magister. But when I wake to the smell of bacon and coffee all I recall are blank ovals.

Rab crouches over the revived campfire, cooking. It's certainly the most luxurious travel breakfast on this entire journey. Noticing I've stirred, Rab gives a tentative smile. I sit up and take the tin plate he offers.

'An empty stomach is a bad start to the day. Means you can't concentrate, and we need our wits about us.'

'Aren't you worried someone will see the smoke?'

'As you said, the day-runners passed you by. If I were them, after myriad failures to catch you, I'd continue north, back where they came from. They know you're heading that way, and they'll plan to get you at the gate. It's what I'd do.'

'Well, that's cheerful.'

'Lost your trust in me?'

'Not yet. For the moment, I'll believe you're simply good at thinking like a villain without actually being one.' I shovel bacon into my mouth, and he turns away, plates up another meal for Freddie who appears from behind a tree.

'Anything?' Rab asks her.

She shakes her head. 'The bell line is intact – shall I bring it in?'

'After breakfast, just before we break camp.'

They're a little team; he trusts her and doesn't treat her like a child. Rab nods towards the journal, which lies on the ground next to me. I'd fallen asleep reading last night. He asks, 'Anything new?'

I tell them about the last entry, about Sister Constance and her curse.

'So that was the beginning? Or not quite, the Lord and Lady of Caulder were that, but this cursing of the Magister?' asks Rab when I'm done.

'Maybe? But what's he got to do with the Anchorhold? If anything?'

'What happened to him?' pipes Freddie.

'Maybe he died,' I say, shrugging. 'But maybe… maybe Sister Constance was right. With his skin burning in the dawn light, he dug himself a grave in the cold damp darkness of the cave, and he hid there until nightfall.'

'And then?'

'Then he dug himself out and ran. Or limped or crawled, depending on how badly injured he was. Then hungering and

231

injured, he found victims out in the countryside, trying to heal himself.'

'He'd have gotten far away from the Citadel and its witch as fast as he could, no matter how much he might want revenge,' Rab observes.

'You're right. That sort of burning – everything I've read about the Leech Lords' flesh says it remains mortally fragile though its powers of rejuvenation are manifold. But that must be fed with blood.'

'Shouldn't he have died quickly? So newly made?' Rab frowns.

I shrug. 'I don't know. He wasn't made like any other Leech, even the Lord and Lady. They were cursed, but he was doubly cursed by Constance, his own curse thrown back at him by a witch. I'm no expert.' I shrug. 'I read somewhere that magic changes its user too, the flesh and the mind. And it's some sort of magic that keeps the Leeches in the Darklands. That's why witches hold the border. Maybe the magic he'd done in his life had changed his flesh, enough so that it kept him alive in spite of his burning. Long enough to sleep beneath the earth, then to feed and help repair some of the damage. Maybe it made him hardier than an ordinary Leech?'

I've never seen, in all my reading, details as to how long it takes Leeches to repair and how much blood is required; I imagine it differs with age and injury, strength and resilience. 'I wonder about Murciana's parents, when they first woke from their cursing. Did they run out into the sun, looking for their daughter? Did they burn too? They were the first of their kind, everything they learned was by trial and error, even the effects of the sun, their thirst, their new natures. They could only have survived with the aid of faithful retainers.' I think of Sister Rikke's tale of their deaths hundreds of years after Murciana was dust. 'The fact her parents survived so long tells us that they *did* indeed have a very long line of faithful retainers.'

'Until Adlisa the Bloodless.'

'You paid attention. Until Adlisa.'

'How much more in the journal?' asks Freddie.

'Some,' I say. 'I'll read again tonight when we make camp. But I think we should set off now. Time's moving and we lost a good fortnight at Blackwater. It's still a long ride to Silverton, and we don't know what kind of reception we'll get, or how long it may take me to convince them to help.'

And how long it'll take me to convince them to keep you both there while I pass through the gate to the Darklands.

26

Despite mostly riding, my injured leg is aching and itching, the former distracting me, the latter driving me insane. When we come to a wooden bridge arching over a rushing stream, I decide I can bear it no longer and, pending the discovery of any trolls, I call a halt. Rab says he's going to scout ahead. Dismounting, I lead Ned down the gently sloping bank. With my trousers rolled up and my boots off, I ease both feet into the water, which is particularly icy – running as it does from the mountains where the last of the snows have yet to melt. Where they might not melt at all. Freddie plops beside me; still standoffish, this is closer than she's been in the last day, a sign of forgiveness perhaps.

'You should have trusted us, Miss Violet,' she says softly.

I nod. 'I know.'

'We're your friends.'

'Yes, Freddie. You are. But I wanted you to be safe. And you know, you haven't been entirely honest with me, either.' I keep my tone even, neutral. She looks away but I keep my eyes on her until she meets my gaze. 'You're afraid of someone – have been afraid of someone in St Sinwin's as long as I've known you. And you haven't trusted me about that.'

'No, Miss Violet.'

I'm concerned about her habit of disappearing when asked questions she doesn't want to answer. But we're not in St Sinwin's now and she's relaxed since leaving its environs – at Blackwater she was practically a normal child, hardly even a shadow of the nervous cat of an urchin I'd see slinking about the alleys. But I feel bad: she'd been able to forget for a while whatever bothered her, and here I am trying to reopen a wound that had closed. I say gently: 'You don't have to tell me, Freddie, whatever is bothering you, but I want to help. I want you to trust me, in your own time, because that's what friends do.'

The pause is so long I think I've failed, that she *will* disappear into the forest forever or simply stop talking to me altogether. But she clears her throat as if about to make an address, her little face spasming. 'It's my brother, Miss, half-brother, really. He's been hunting me ever since he found out about me.'

'Why?' I ask, but she shakes her head, shutting down already.

'I can't say anything else and I can't tell you his name, Miss Violet. Please don't ask.' She begins to pull her feet out of the water.

I touch her shoulder. She's trembling. 'I won't ask anymore, Freddie. If you ever want to tell me, I will listen. But I won't push you. I'm sorry. Just know that if you need my help, you have it.'

Beneath my hand she relaxes, her feet go back into the stream, and I take my hand away. We remain there until Rab returns from his recce. 'Too soon for lunch and we'd best keep going if we want to make good time.'

I grumble, but obey.

As we ride, I pick through my recollections of the small girl on her black horse. She appeared one day when I was down at the wharves, standing in for Hedrek whose illness had become more pronounced. It was my first spell outside of the house in three weeks, my first steps into the fresh air after what was done to me. I'd watched as she sidled around a shadowy corner and snatched two apples from a barrel left unattended after unloading from one of Hedrek's ships. She saw me watching and, bold as brass, stuffed said apples into her trouser pockets then took two more. I laughed as she scampered away, taking bites from the stolen fruit; I'm quite sure the theft made it all the sweeter. The child was like a ray of sunshine. Her mischief made me smile in spite of myself, made me laugh though it still hurt a little, below.

Later that week, I noticed her peeking around corners as I moved through the city on errands, going to meetings and classes with Walter and Titus, not yet returning to train with Talwyn but visiting her to talk, seeing to Hedrek's business interests, and some rare social visits with Tempe to the Wave Theatre, Miss Madisson's Coffeehouse and a few select restaurants where it was important to be seen by potential suitors if one's mother (or stepmother) thought you were going to be married at some point in the future.

One afternoon, Freddie was waiting outside the gate to Zennor House when I left and fell in step beside me, accompanied me to the bookstore, the modiste's, three shoemakers and the bank. She peppered me with questions about myself, from the cost of my purple silk walking suit with the flowers embroidered on the skirt, to how my hair had been styled, to the history of the town, and what I thought the rest of the world might be like. After that, she became a regular presence in my life, a child I could be kind to, be kinder to than my father had ever been to me. She'd sit in the kitchens with Mrs M and Tempe and me, helping to bake cakes and to eat them afterwards, hiding if anyone else – the tweenies, the butler, the gardener, the grooms, my father's valet – came in until they left once more, and she'd reappear like a sprite.

About six months in, she disappeared without a word. For months I sought her, even had the Harbour Guard on the lookout. But no one saw her. One night, when I'd given her up for lost, she fell into step beside me as I returned from the theatre, with neither fanfare nor explanation as to where she'd been. I'd missed her terribly – however, I'd grown used to how cagey she was with her secrets; knew that any insistence would scare her away, and I didn't want my little pet gone once more. She was skittish thereafter, wary, but would occasionally sleep in our stables, eat in the kitchens. But I never knew what had gone wrong in her life – or more so – and couldn't bear the idea of losing her again for she filled an emptiness for me, a hollowness that I did not create in myself.

I wonder now if that brother was the reason for her absence, I wonder what he did or tried to do and why. I wonder who he might be. I think about my own brother, that he's the reason I'm on this journey, risking my life, even though I never knew him. I think about how parents make older siblings look after younger, and what a burden they are to us. I think about how much I've resented Tiberius since his brief life and considerably longer death. I consider Freddie's brother, and what could she have possibly done to make him want to kill her? Was she lying? Exaggerating?

My experience of the child was that she's never given to either. Even if she is a thief, she's relentlessly honest.

* * *

We're another fortnight on the road, and the further north we go, the cooler the air, despite it being spring. The gradient gets steeper as we move further into the mountains. The nights are frigid, wintery; sometimes we find shelter in deserted farmhouses, others under rocky outcroppings where we huddle together for warmth, a fire built high. The landscape changes, the trees, the grasses, even the architecture of buildings we pass – more stone, less withy. There's no sign of the day-runners, though we remain cautious. I think Rab was right, that they've gone on ahead, figuring me too tricksy to catch now, but knowing that I can't avoid using the gate into the Darklands. My mind's been picking at that issue too, how I might make it past guards and assassins; thus far, no solution has presented itself.

We grow closer, the three of us, and I think this might be the little family I let myself imagine, curled in Rab's bed what feels like a lifetime ago. Hardly "normal", but one we made, one we chose. Though I still sleep across the fire from Rab and he's shown no sign of mending the break I made. I wonder if it's what I might have had as a child if Tiberius had not died and my mother with him, if my father hadn't been so weak and drunk and the sort of man who thought to sell one dead child for a fortune then turn the living child into a weapon to make up for his own sins.

Each night I eked out a little more of the journal, picking through the hints and scraps of her life, all the pieces she chose to pull together. The pieces she left behind of her own volition. I wonder how the journal made its way to the Whitebarrow

University Library. I wonder which of the Little Sisters of St Florian took it there. Someone knew of it, somewhere, sometime. My father found out about it – after sending Tempe off on a false trail, a punishment – and the miraculous Asher Todd managed to find it, hidden in the shelves of what's reputed to be one of the largest libraries ever built.

The last part of Murciana's tale is perhaps the hardest to read.

My travels in my younger days had been achieved mostly on foot. It was, I felt then, the best way to learn a place and its people. Touch the earth, feel its hum, it will tell you its secrets. A satchel for my notebooks and inks, my thick Wanderer's cloak and boots, an oaken staff for defence; I wandered the lands, I wrote their stories. And I went on this way well into my fifties, until the aches of ageing became more consistent and insistent. As resentful as I was of the necessity, I came to enjoy riding horses. A pursuit which brought its own aches and pains, but I covered distances more quickly, was able to get back sooner to the Citadel with my filled notebooks, then return to the world, seeking fresh stories to inscribe, fresh books of knowledge to copy for our library. Fresh knowledge good and bad to preserve.

The first of the Blessed Wanderers was I, and wander I did, back then. But the trip for which I now prepared might be one-way. Might have an abrupt end. Terrible news was told of the churches of the north being deconsecrated and turned into sleeping places for the Leeches. Of ecclesiastics fed upon as a delicacy until there were no more left in the environs and none who were brave enough to go

239

and replace them. They held no power over the Leech Lords. But there was a possibility for me, because merchants were considered sacred, or at least safe, ensuring trade remained active and the Leech Lords, for the most part, knew enough that it was essential if they were to keep their cattle fed and contented with any bargain they might make with the overlords. Folk might accept any sort of bargain, if the incentive is strong enough.

So.

I set off from Cwen's Reach, bidding the Citadel farewell in wary hope of return. I travelled for days and weeks and months. Finally I came to a narrow defile between two mountains and wracked my memory for a sense of familiarity and found it. Found the recollection of the Magister dragging me from my home, slung across his saddle, half-drugged, half-dead with thirst as he made haste to put distance between us and what he'd done to my parents. I closed my eyes, wiped the memory away, regretting that I'd summoned it.

I joined a long caravan train of traders – safety in numbers – and accompanied them to the city of Caulder. Found accommodation in an inn, not too fine, not too shabby; one where my incessant scribblings would not be noticed, or if they were noticed, then not commented upon unfavourably. Asked general questions of the girl who brought me to my room, and she told me that the Lord and Lady might be spoken to in one of their nightly sessions of hearing their folk's complaints. Or sometimes they wandered the night-markets (their armed and armoured retained close by), examining crafts, buying them and preserved fruits and cordials as if they still consumed those, and sometimes negotiating for new winepresses – young women and sometimes men who would be fed upon one night each month, living in the manor house, feasting on rich foods and wines to build them up for their next appearance at the Lord and Lady's table. A life of good food and indolence if one didn't mind being the main course over and over again.

That night, I looked from the window of my high room, saw that the church tower remained intact – of course, they would sleep in their private chapel in the manor house at the far end of the valley, would not destroy the holy place when it wasn't necessary. I stared across the roofs, dug into myself for a sense of this having been, once, home. But there was nothing. I'd been taken too young, travelled too far away, lived an entirely different life – and amongst the Little Sisters I had been **happy**. So happy. I'd never know if I might have felt the same had the Magister never taken me.

As I pondered, there was a stirring below.

Two rows of blue-and-gold-coated men-at-arms, pikes bristling. In between, two tall figures that made my heart stop.

They had neither aged nor changed, my parents. My father's ruddy hair, my mother's particular shade of gold – the same shade I'd had as a child, but which darkened as I grew until by the time I crawled up the innards of the Citadel I was muddy and mousey. They dressed with a special magnificence I didn't recall from childhood, but I knew enough as an adult to recognise it as all part of a **show**. A performance by the rulers for their people. They did not go out of their way to appear frightening, but magnificent.

241

Worthy of adoration. Of worship. Of replacing the princes of the Church they'd no doubt fed upon in their early years after being transformed.

They and their escort moved through the crowd like a gentle blade, not cutting, but with the potential to do so clear to all. The commoners around them bowed and curtsied, murmured blessings that omitted, very clearly, any mention of the god who'd once reigned in the now-empty churches of the Darklands. As they passed, I leaned further and further out the window until I felt my balance waver. I gasped. My mother looked up though my father took no notice. Instinctively, I threw myself back into the room.

There'd been only the briefest flash and flare of her eyes – those glacial blue eyes! – yet with a spark of red in their depths. I huddled at the foot of the bed, resisting the urge to peek out because I knew – **knew** – she would still be there, beneath the moon, and she would see me, those eyes would know me for who and what I was and I was certain that neither of us would survive that. I an old woman and she who'd born me no older than the day I'd been stolen away.

Whatever I'd hoped to achieve was wiped from my mind.

I left the very next day with another caravan, barely rested until I set foot back in the courtyard of the Citadel. I did not leave my room for days. Weeks.

<u>But I ask, my Sisters who might read this, should any of you go to the Darklands, document what you find there. Send your writings back to the Citadel, so we might gather as much knowledge as possible about these creatures. Someday, I feel, it will be needed.</u>

And here is something I've not seen before in the journal: underlining. That entire last paragraph, as if it has made an impression, as if someone has taken it to heart. And written underneath a simple notation in a perfect script:

Volo.
Sr Rikke

"I am willing.
Sister Rikke."

An acceptance across time, one hand extended, another grasping it. Sister Rikke, separated from Murciana by centuries, but taking up her request. She must have found the journal, well before the Citadel's fall, before the dispersal of all those tomes, and reading it galvanised her to journey into danger. To witness and write of the end of the Lord and Lady of Caulder, and to document whatever was growing slowly in the Darklands.

27

The signpost at the crossroads – fewer arrows pointing north, many more south, as if a warning in itself – tells us that Silverton is half a day's ride.

Almost there, then, almost at my terrible goal. I feel like I should be dragging my feet rather than rushing onwards, as if I can't wait to meet my fate. But the weather is beautiful, the horses are fair prancing, my companions are chattering and laughing and singing (as I might if I were not about to do what I'm about to do); in the face of such joy, it's hard to remain sombre even if I'm going towards my death. And Tiberius's birthday approaches, that terrible day when something will happen, when the gates will open and the blood-drinking dead will pour forth, if I don't stop them first.

We stop for lunch, finishing the last of the extra supplies Rab brought. We even light a fire – something usually reserved for evening camps – to make coffee and toast the very stale bread and render it palatable, and frizzle the remains of the smoked bacon. We've eaten well, I must say, which is better than ending up half-starved by the time you finish your journey – and of all the awful things my father prepared me for, starvation was not one of them.

Just as the pot boils, there's the sound of wheels trundling along from the way we've come. Rab and I exchange glances, then I notice Freddie tensing. I whisper, 'Into the trees, Freddie' – she'll be fast enough and small enough not to be noticed. She's gone with eldritch speed. Rab and I turn to face the ominous rumbling. I flick my wrist, loosen the knife; Rab hefts the battleaxe he's been carting about for weeks now, with many occasions for me to tease him about its concealability.

Under the rumbling comes something unexpected: the merry tinkle of bells.

What rounds the bend is a wagon painted forest green and faded gold – tones muted by age – two large red horses with feathered feet, glossy coats, alert ears, questioning stares. *Who are you and what are you doing here?* Copper bells, and iron, hang in clusters at the corners of the roof, cheerfully letting other folk know you're coming, and a warding against those of the deep earth, wayward waters and the fickle air who might propose mischief. A simple, sweet sound that says you're no threat. But easily removed if stealth is required.

The man on the bench seat squints, gives us much the same glance as his horses did. A gentleman-merchant – I've been around enough of such men to know they prefer that to the term "tinker" whereas the women are mostly content with "trader" – weathered skin, iron-grey hair, moustache and goatee, all neatly trimmed and brushed if I'm not mistaken, even though he's out on the road, far from anywhere. Brown doeskin trews, scuffed but polished brown boots, a green linen shirt and an embroidered blue silk waistcoat. Dandified. Definitely a gentleman-merchant.

He reins in the horses, who stop obligingly.

'Good day,' he calls.

'Good day,' we reply.

'Rare to see someone else out here. Yet there's been a lot of activity on the roads lately.' His gaze is assessing.

'Indeed?' I wonder if I'm going to have to use the knife. He's a sitting target, I can hit him from here with ease.

'Indeed. Men and women in some uniform or other, running their mounts ragged. Demanding to know if a body's seen a young woman, travelling with a scrappy child.' He shakes his head while I stiffen. 'Never trusted anyone dressed all in black, myself. Villainous, every time. And rude with it.'

There's something in his tone that makes my shoulders relax, just a little. Perhaps I'm foolish. Perhaps he's simply very good at this. Handy ability for a salesman, to put people at ease against their will. But I notice the same shift in Rab's stance too.

'As you can see, I'm a young woman with a young man. No child at all,' I say, all innocent and empty-headed, as if I might be mistaken for an idiot girl, a fashion plate wandering far from home. Then I remember I'm wearing patched trews and a washed-out linen shirt, my hair's in an untidy bun, I've not worn a skerrick of cosmetics for weeks and my boots are suitable for kicking in heads. I've never been so far from looking like an heiress, a simple marriageable Miss.

'Except the one in that tree. Quite scrappy-looking, I might add.' Then he laughs, almost a giggle, utterly disarming. 'You might buy my silence for a cup of that coffee, which I could smell halfway down the path.'

'Cheap,' replies Rab with a grin, and goes about filling cups. 'Hope you've got your own mug?'

Indeed he does and soon Edgar, gentleman-merchant, is sitting by our fire, sharing a fallen tree trunk with Freddie who's taking the opportunity to stare at him thoughtfully. Edgar had also contributed a tin of chocolates and one of glacé fruit to our meal, and if there's one thing I do know about Freddie is that, unless someone's an utter villain, she can be won over by sweets.

'You travel these ways frequently?' I ask, handing him a plate of bacon and toasted bread.

He nods. 'Most of my life. Inherited the business from my ma. Wouldn't know what to do, staying in one place.'

'Do you know Silverton? The Briars?' I ask as casually as I can.

'Aye, Silverton. Know it well. And the Briars. Have done for a very long time.'

'Are they… approachable?'

His laugh's so loud it's almost a shout.

'Sometimes. Ellie's reasonable. She's the Briar Witch now, has been about a year – different to those who came before. Bit more considered, I'd say. Very clever. She's settled in well, keeps the town safe, well-organised and running smoothly. Her man's a good 'un; talks a lot. No harm in him, always ready to help. They're a fine team, impressive. Yes, Ellie's approachable. One of the cousins, not so much, the other could go either way.' He leans back on the fallen tree trunk he's using as a seat, stretching. 'Mind you, it depends entirely on what you're asking for?' I don't rise to the bait of the question and clearly Edgar notices my reticence. 'But that's your business, Violet, and I'm not a man to pry.'

I suspect he is, in the right circumstances, but he's also smart enough to know that these are *not* those, and Rab's cunning and charming enough to distract from any discomfort by asking him about the horses drawing his wagon, their breed, hardiness, lineage and the like. Edgar falls into the conversation. He seems affable, though I'm willing to bet he doesn't suffer fools easily; I'm also willing to bet a lot of folk buy things from him that they don't actually need.

While they talk about all matters horse-related, I think about what I'm going to ask the Briars for. *How* I'm going to ask. *Do you have a deep dark secret, the why and wherefor of witches keeping Leech Lords at bay? Is it really just your spells?* I wonder if that will get us killed? I think about how I've nothing worth trading for that knowledge. That all I've got are warnings, and all I can do is beg and plead and I've never been good at either of those things. Beating and stabbing, yes. Begging and pleading, not so much.

* * *

A little later, Rab and I are riding ahead of Edgar's wagon. Freddie, possibly in hope of more chocolate, is perched on the bench seat beside him, shooting a steady stream of questions at the tinker. He answers equably. Once, when the chattering dims, I look back to see her disappearing into the wagon.

'Don't touch anything!' I shout, feeling Mrs Medway's voice fly all the way from St Sinwin's and out my mouth.

The tousled head reappears, an expression of outrage writ across the pixie-like features, and the reply, 'I don't steal from friends!'

Molly the Mare, tethered to the back end of the wagon, also gives a protesting neigh. Rab makes a noise that's clearly the swallowing of a snort. But he can't help himself. 'Very parental.'

That stabs at me and he sees it. 'Violet, I'm sorry. I didn't mean—'

248

I swallow and it's hard to do so, with words crowding my throat, the entire truth fighting to come out. I let them. 'When I was just gone seventeen, there was a boy. A man. A sailor, handsome and charming. I met him one day on the street. I'd been kept away, mostly, from boys – apart from my friend Jack. When my stepmother arrived, I was allowed a little more freedom, was taken to dances and the theatre. My stepmother didn't know my father's plans for me. She just saw a young woman without social grace, a young woman she believed would want to marry one day, and she convinced my father that I needed to be able to pass in society. Temperance was better born than us and it was important to her that we be accepted for more than our money. As more than gold-rich parvenus. I think my father decided it would keep my stepmother occupied, and it was also another way of honing me into a weapon. Social skills were still skills, after all. And I think Hedrek, like so many people who have mountains of money but no breeding, had a terrible fear of being looked down upon. No matter what other plans he had for me, I also had to be perfect in this: this acceptability to high society.'

'Violet—'

'Rab, this is hard enough to say, just let me get it out. Please.' I take another deep breath, feel my heart beating as if I've run up a hill. 'So, in between learning how to fight and maim and kill, I learned how to dance and sing, to play the harp – badly, I might add. I learned how to manage a household even though Temperance and Mrs Medway did all that. I learned how to be fashionable, witty and amusing – a sought-after addition to any dinner party. Even though my father had no intention of letting me marry, he wanted me to *appear* marriageable. Something he could

249

dangle in front of his business partners either for themselves or their sons or daughters.

'Something that he, peasant-born, had – and they did not and could not.'

I cough to clear my throat and the choking tale.

'But at seventeen, a girl wants things. At seventeen, a girl decides to take things for herself. And I wanted this man and I took him. I'd killed by then but was entirely innocent in other ways, the most dangerous of ways because no one had told me what might come of such congress. A few days, no more, of sneaking out, of passion, then he was gone, back on a ship and off to distant lands. The pleasure had been wonderful, but I no more missed him than one would an old breath; I did not mistake it for love. After a while, however, I began to feel *odd*, and when it became obvious to my family I wasn't quite *alone* anymore…'

'Vi, you don't need to—'

'Yes, I do. You need to understand. It's not just a sad story. First, my father beat me. He beat me so badly – tried to drown me too, as if I was some sort of a witch – that I lost the child. When the doctor was finally called, Hedrek told him to make sure it never happened again. That I would never get pregnant again. And the doctor was paid an enormous amount of money to ensure word was never shared of what had happened, what I'd done, how I'd *ruined* myself.'

'Violet.'

'And so, Rab, that's why I can't have children. I think you'd be a good father. But I can't be a mother.' I hold up a hand to forestall any comment. 'And I think I'd like to not talk anymore for a while.'

28

I ride ahead for the rest of the journey, close enough to hear them but far enough away that it's an effort for anyone to make conversation. Rab talks with Edgar about his travels, how far and wide he roams. Rab asks about the Darklands, and the tinker replies he's not set foot there for six months, but he's happy to answer any questions we have about the lie of the land and the great Leech Lord households. That he's heard from other travellers there are changes afoot there, and not for the better. Though I know I should join in the conversation, I simply don't have the will to do so; I listen half-heartedly, figuring I can always ask more later.

I've told Rab something I've told no one else. The only other folk who knew were my stepmother and Mrs Medway, Dr Meyerhof, and of course Walter and Titus because Hedrek never kept any detail about me from them. All three of them invested in my potential for cleaning up my father's mess.

Have I told Rab out of necessity, rather than trust? Told him so he doesn't make any more *plans* for me and my non-existent womb. So he doesn't expect a future I can't give. Have I told him because I feared-hoped it would push him away, and now he's out of reach as surely as the sailor-boy who put that child in me those few years ago. Everything that stirred in me when he was kind to me – a separate thing from what stirred when first I saw him and wanted him – now feels cold as a dead ember. I will not want what I cannot have. But will I destroy what I want because in wanting one makes chains? Promises are tethers, and my entire life has been a tether though the promises were not mine. Promises made for me by Hedrek; aided and enforced by Walter and Titus.

This journey, this quest, is a promise I'm keeping unwillingly – only the enormity of the consequences of not doing so keeps me on the path. I can't quite free myself of the care for others – of what might happen to Freddie and Rab, Tempe and Mrs Medway, Miren and all her folk – if I don't do what I must. I can't bear the idea of hiding myself away in a forest fastness, in a tiny cottage like the one where Kyril kept Ixara, hoping to never be found, waiting for the roof to fall in, while everyone else becomes food for the Leech Lords, freed from their borders and covering the lands. I can guarantee no future, especially when I don't know if I'll even survive.

The promise Hedrek made for me, therefore, is the only one I'm willing to keep.

These thoughts, running around my head like a weasel in a barrel, only stop mid-afternoon when I come to a stone bridge curving over a rushing river of spring melt. The horses' hooves, the rumble of the wagon's wheels interrupts the birdsong around us. I pause to take it all in.

To our right and down lies a large green common by a lake into which the river flows; then back and up is a sprawling sort of town of stone and wood, houses of various vintages and prosperity, glimpses of wide, well-ordered streets, a bustling market square, what looks like the bell tower of a church, and then the slightly shorter tower with a clockface inset, shop signs swinging in the breeze, and a very large house surrounded by a hedge-fence similar to that around Blackwater, its gabled roofs visible over the top.

The wagon and Rab rein in beside me.

'Well, that's new,' says Edgar.

And I believe what he's referring to is the stone wall being built around Silverton.

* * *

Silverton's been hard at work and the only way to get into town is via a tapering corridor, just wide enough so that only one wagon can fit; steep banks build up on either side, leading towards what will eventually be a portcullis set between two guard towers (for the moment, still a work-in-progress). What might be termed by the military-minded as "a narrow defile perfect for defence against attack".

'I didn't realise,' I say to Edgar, 'that Silverton was quite so fortified, or in the process of becoming so.'

'Nor me. Famously unfortified for three centuries, give or take. By order of the Church as I recall. This will set witchy cats firmly amongst ecclesiastical pigeons.' He narrows his eyes, shakes his head, muttering, 'Ellie Briar, what have you done?'

'Something to do with the Darklands, perhaps?' suggests Rab.

'Well, we won't know until we're close enough to ask,' I say, and nudge Ned the Nondescript into action. The others follow in my wake.

I watch the construction as we approach: men and women digging holes, others filling said holes with mortar, yet others laying what look like perfectly cut large stones in a line, checking with spirit levels. They're working precisely but quickly, each face mirroring the same determination, a singlemindedness of purpose. It's impressive to see.

'You!' A voice, loud and demanding. Female. In front of me, a rather tall redhead in dirty overalls, and large boots. Muscular arms, and if I look closely I can make out a random assemblage of tiny raised scars all the way up them – cut for the red price. A witch. Hair barely contained in a bun, suspicion in her glare, belly only a little distended, but clearly she's fruiting. As if everyone I meet can do what I cannot. 'Who are you and what do you want?'

'I'm here to speak with Ellie Briar. Are you—'

'Your name?' Her jaw juts aggressively in my direction.

I don't think when I should. I'm so eager to speak to the Briar Witch, yet I've still not figured how to say what I must. So I blurt, 'Violet Zennor—'

The words are barely out of my mouth when she shouts, 'It's her!' and a bolt of energy bright as the noonday sun shoots from her raised hands and hits me in the chest as surely as a rock. I'm knocked out of the saddle, all of the air leaves my lungs, and my head bounces against the ground to make stars swim in front of my eyes. Then there's more yelling, some shrieking, and I'm surrounded by all those labourers repurposing themselves as guards to lift me up and pull me to and fro. I think I hear Rab and Freddie protesting very loudly and with much profanity.

And Edgar saying very calmly, but also rather angrily, 'Nia Briar, if you hurt them, I swear I'll…'

But that's when I go to sleep.

* * *

254

When I wake, all I can smell is clean, fresh straw. Beneath me is the thin canvas of a pallet bed; above, a ceiling of oaken beams and plaster. Someone's talking quietly not so far away. I turn my head when I'm certain it won't part ways with my neck and take in the scenery. Metal bars. Cells. The neatest and tidiest of cells, I'm sure, but cells nonetheless, and no windows.

When I move to sit up, I realise that my chest hurts like I've been kicked by a particularly ill-tempered horse. 'Shit.'

'Miss Violet! Are you alright?'

I consider throwing up. Decide not to. Wait for the room to stop spinning. I put a hand to where my head connected with the ground and am surprised to find nothing more than a small tender egg. But my right forearm feels suspiciously light and a quick check confirms that the knife that belongs there and the back-up in my boot are both missing. And no sign of our packs – no sign of my hard-won O'Malley silver, of Murciana's journal, of all the things I need. A quick glance shows no sign of Rab's axe in his cell to my left. Freddie, to my right, has a chain around her ankle.

'What—'

'She's so small she can slip through the bars. In fact she did slip through the bars, so a helpful blacksmith came and fitted *that* to her.' Rab scratches at his head. There's a cut on one cheek, a bruise under one eye, but neither of them as bad as they could be. 'Another of the witches tended to us after the beating. Eira, I think.'

'How kind,' I mutter.

'Miss Violet?' Freddie's voice is very small.

'I'm fine, little one. Just grumpy and a bit dizzy.' I look around. 'No Edgar?'

'No Edgar. Last I saw him he was yelling at that redheaded one – Nia, I believe – and reciting everything she'd ever done wrong since she was three.'

An unexpected flare of sympathy for Nia blooms. 'So, we have one ally at least outside. Did anything else happen? Did you see anyone else besides this Nia? That Eira?'

Rab shakes his head. 'No sign of any of the day-runners, if that's what you mean. We were brought straight here, after you started napping, and that Eira arrived not long after.'

'Right.' I consider lying down again and going back to sleep, but there's the noise of keys jangling, a lock turning. The door opens on a young man not much older than me, with short red hair and clear green eyes, wearing the brown robe of a god-hound. He doesn't really look much like a priest, more like someone playing dress-up. But he's got a ready smile, which is apologetic.

'Hello,' he says, making a beeline for my cell. The door is unlocked in a trice. 'Sorry about this. Things are a bit, err, tense around here at the moment. And sorry about the accommodations. Clean though.'

'Very,' I agree, but I don't get up.

'Nia will be pleased to hear you approve.' He laughs and when I notice Rab doing the same I glare at him. 'I'm Huw. Ellie would like to speak with you now, if that's convenient?'

'I do believe a spot has opened up on my dance-card. What about—' I gesture at Rab and Freddie. He shakes his head, rueful.

'Just you for the moment. But meals will be brought down soon, so there's that.' He opens my cell door. 'And if you could avoid hitting me, I'd really appreciate it.'

'It's the furthest thing from my mind,' I lie. I'm honestly thinking about hitting as many people as I can.

'Besides, there's not really anywhere for you to go and we're assuming you came here for a reason. And you probably don't want to leave your companions behind. And Edgar's vouched for you.' Huw leads the way. Up the stairs, through a rabbit warren of small rooms and corridors, past offices and into a large communal hall, then finally out the heavy front door and past the four waiting guardsmen who fall in line behind us. If I thought they were all there for me – and my fearsome reputation – I might feel flattered. But I suspect it's for something bigger and badder and far worse than me.

It's a brief walk through the market square – still bustling in the late afternoon – and down a few lanes to reach the big house I spotted earlier, crouching behind the hedge-fence. The guards remain outside when Huw ushers me in the gate.

Up the front stairs to a long, wide verandah, then through the heavy carved ebony wood door, into an entry hall with coat and hatstands, benches for sitting on to apply shoes or take them off, then along a portrait-lined corridor and into a book-filled room. A fire crackles, there's a long sofa, a thick rug in front of it, and over the mantelpiece are a black obsidian mirror, a woodcut and a framed document with print too small for me to read without almost pressing my nose against it.

Behind a heavy polished ebony desk is a matching chair – almost a throne, with roses and apples carved across its arched top – and in the chair is a woman. Right now, her face is held in her hands (one finger bears a pigeon's egg ruby), but as soon as she hears us, she looks up – neither hurried, nor embarrassed, merely resigned. She pushes back, the chair scraping a little as she rises, and her steps are light as she crosses to us. Her hair's tawny and tumbling, her dress an olive gingham; she's very pretty, very pale, dark green eyes with shadows under them. She smiles kindly at me, then the smile brightens considerably when she turns it on Huw.

He kisses her soundly. 'Ellie, this is Violet Zennor.'

'Thank you, love, I worked that out.' They grin at each other.

'I'll leave you to it, then,' he says. 'And, Ellie, in her favour, she did not hit me.'

'Well, that speaks to her restraint because gods know I struggle not to.'

The door closes behind him, and we sit on the couch. Her smile turns apologetic. 'Sorry. Sorry about Nia. Things are—'

'Tense?'

'And strange and awful and dangerous – and I say that as someone from a family of witches.'

'You're building walls.'

'Yes.'

'You hold the border to the Darklands.'

'Yes. But I'm not sure how long that's going to last.'

29

'But where are my manners?' Ellie Briar rises and pours two glasses of winter-plum brandy, the same expensive sort that Hedrek always ordered, that I last drank with Walter after Assassination Attempt the Second, and before the bishop's gruesome murder. She hands me one of the heavy crystal tumblers and settles back down beside me. 'Now, how can I help you, Violet Zennor?'

I open my mouth, searching for a story I've told far too many times these past weeks. I reach for a version I've been constructing – or trying to – since I left Blackwater, the best possible version to get what I need from the Briar Witch, but in the end... in the end there would be no prizes for my storytelling. The Little Sisters of St Florian would never let me into their number. What flows out of me is a series of 'and then and then and then' of tragedy and horror and trauma, of the awful things done to me and by me, a rolling out of my life of blood and sweat and violence, of eldritch learning. Of a life devoted by someone else to one purpose, to stopping a child of prophecy when I was nothing at all. No one. There are tears and curses; there's begging and pleading for help.

I tell her about Miren, the Lady of Blackwater, and that I think they'd get on famously. I tell her what I've learned about the Leech Lords from Murciana's journal, and how Asher Todd delivered it to me. I tell her about the Anchorhold and its assassins, about its plan to break down the barrier she and her family have held for so long. I tell her everything I know and can't help but feel it's not anywhere near enough. I tell her that I've been charged with stopping it with only the vaguest idea of how. I tell her I need the Briars' secret of how to keep Leeches at bay. I draw on the desk blotter a shaky rendition of the Anchorhold's sigil, telling her that if I can only have my pack returned to me, I'll show her the very thing, and Walter's letter and the journal and all that shiny, lethal O'Malley silver. And I tell her I don't know what to do. I cry again and more, and she hands me a clean handkerchief.

Ellie Briar considers me for what seems a long time, tapping the tips of her fingers together as they steeple. When I manage to collect myself, she says, 'I think there's something you need to see.'

* * *

We walk through the woods, clad in dark cloaks (mine borrowed), that I'm told are enspelled to hide us from casual gazes. It's getting dark but the path is no trouble for Ellie Briar whose paces are swift and sure and graceful as dance steps; this is her home, she knows it. I think of myself running up and down the steep streets of St Sinwin's with ease; yet this isn't St Sinwin's and I stumble more than once. Behind us, the four guardsmen, all armed with swords and bows and full quivers. I note that my knives are yet to be returned to me and wonder when I'll see them again. I must look nervous because Ellie jabs a thumb back at the guards and says, 'It's alright, the vigilants will take care of us.'

'Aren't you a witch?'

She shakes her head. 'Not like the others. I don't have their magic or power. I'm good at hitting people with batons, though, if that helps.'

'Well, I was wondering how dark it gets here and how early and when the bitey things might come out.'

'No Leeches this side of the border, Violet Zennor.'

'It'd be nice to think that, Ellie Briar, wouldn't it?' And I realise that in all my rambling the one thing I'd forgotten to tell her was about Kyril and Ixara. So, I do that now, in a low voice so our escort can't hear because I'm smart enough to figure out that it's exactly the sort of thing that might make people panic. When I'm done, there's a frown on the brow of the Briar Witch and she says emphatically, 'Shit.'

'Shit indeed.'

The forest around us grows denser, the trees closer together, and Ellie bids me not to speak until she tells me otherwise. I become aware soon after that we're moving parallel with a road, and quickly I realise there are glimpses to be had of a huge gate, tall and heavy, made of wood and banded with rusted iron, hinged into the rocks of a mountain pass, and a press of black-clad bodies mills about at its foot. We keep on going until we're almost past the gate, then Ellie gestures to her vigilants and they stop, take up position to keep watch on the woods. She and I continue on until we're out of their sight and reach a spot where the trees appear even more tightly interwoven. Ellie takes my hand and steps into an impossibly narrow space.

As we move, the tree trunks seem to shift, allowing passage, then closing up behind us when I glance over my shoulder.

Eventually, we're spit out into a clearing circled by cypress and larch, yew and oak and pine; here there's a stone altar at the centre of fourteen enormous standing stones.

'Now,' says Ellie Briar, 'very few people have been allowed the privilege of coming to this place, so don't make me regret it.'

'I promise.' By which I mean I'll do my best. 'But we can't see the gate from here, and I'm assuming that's what you wanted to show me.'

'How are you at climbing trees?'

'I've a good working knowledge of the climbing arts.'

We shinny our way up an ancient yew, finding relatively comfortable perches on branches either side of the trunk. 'This clearing can't be found by anyone who's not a Briar. Even another witch would be turned around and tossed back out into the forest. The only reason you're in here is because I led you. If I leave you behind, you'll be stuck. Understand?'

'You mean not to push you out of the tree and betray you or I'm done for?'

'Correct.'

'You have my word.'

Ellie directs my attention to where the gate lies and the black-clad henchfolk looking like ants at its foot. 'And they can't see us, so don't worry.'

'Worry suspended.'

'Six months ago, maybe a little more, rumours started filtering out from the Darklands with the merchants and travellers. Tinkers and the like went to small towns and estates they'd traded with for years, and found them empty.' She takes a deep breath. 'The Leeches and their humans, all gone. And then some of the larger towns and cities? Their Leech Lords, long-term rulers generally, who respected the balance between Leech and mortal, knew that their economy of blood was a delicate balance? They were deposed or simply disappeared.'

'Something's changing.'

She nods. 'And that lot of idiots, all dressed in black?'

'Day-runners.'

'Idiots by day or night. Day-idiots. They began to appear with increasing frequency going in and out of the Darklands. Now, while merchants go in and out, sometimes Darklanders themselves who want to leave so they scrape together the price of exit, day-runners have never come out like this. Not in three hundred years.'

'They've been looking for me.'

'But so many of them? I don't think so. I think they're leaving in order to go and wait somewhere. For someone. But we don't know. We don't know and can't find out because most of the merchants have stopped going in due to the sheer number of their colleagues who've failed to come out again. Usually I can rely on Edgar but even he's baulking at the idea of a quick jaunt.' She shakes her head. 'Not that I blame him.'

'Can't you go in? Isn't your magic proof against Leeches?'

She looks uncomfortable. 'Not exactly. We could go in, but it would look like an act of aggression and I've no doubt we'd have to make a mess. And *witches* can repel Leeches, but as I said, I'm no witch so I'm just another snack on the hoof. Besides, how many Leeches can one witch handle? How many might overwhelm one of us? And, for the first time ever, the gate is guarded by day-runners instead of just the usual customs agents. Turning people away.'

'And you started building a wall?'

'Two months ago, we received an unfriendly visit from a pack of day-runners, bullying their way through the market square. I think they were testing us. Nia did to them what she did to you, only worse – sorry again – and I think it made them wary. A dozen armed soldiers laid low by one witch – a lot of injuries, one died in the street, the others fled and left his body behind. Then just last week a delegation presented itself, marginally politer, demanding that a – *the* – Violet Zennor be handed over to the Anchorhold as soon as she appeared on our doorstep.'

'I can see why Nia was nervous.' I rub my chest where the aching still sits.

'Not the first time we'd heard the term "The Anchorhold", but definitely the first time we'd heard *from* it. Briars have held the border for almost three centuries. The Leeches can't come out, and it seems they've had no inclination to do so, not since Gilly and her daughters set their wards, and the Church hunted down the last – or most of the last apparently – of those that had strayed from beyond the Darklands, and their fledglings. Locked in there, the Leeches set up their own little kingdom, have run it happily for all intents and purposes. The sensible ones know that in order to keep the balance, their lordship must ensure the lives of their humans are worth living. There's no senseless slaughter – or mostly not – none of the hunting parties that used to take place, scouring villages and towns in a single night. Blood *is* a currency. The ones with no interest in such restraint… well, they don't last long. Their council has its own order and it enforces it.'

Ellie Briar points, draws my attention again to the gate. 'But in all that time, no one's sent anyone to guard the *outside* of that gate. Edgar tells me there's a small building just inside, a sort of customs office where merchants declare their goods, pay their duties to the Council's representatives, renew their traders' licence and move on. No barracks. Gentleman-merchants are, in general, safe. Their breastpins mark them, and having trade with the outside world is a critical part of keeping the human economy running smoothly – upset that, you upset the Council and its applecart.

'All those idiots in black? Humans making demands on behalf of the Anchorhold, something about which we've heard very little in all that time. Whispers and rumours, nothing substantial. Yet here are its underlings, making demands as if the rest of the Leech Lords and Ladies no longer matter, or exist. What do you think that means, Violet Zennor?'

'I think it means the Anchorhold is making its move. Feeling secure in itself, secure enough to start taking over. I think my brother's birth-and-death day is approaching.'

'It's repositioning itself, removing anyone in there that might be a threat. Remaking itself as an overlord.' Ellie shakes her head. 'Things are out of balance.'

Perhaps I have even less time than I thought.

'Edgar said something about you *not* being allowed to build a wall.'

'We're not. Part of our agreement with the Church, because what could be more terrifying than a bunch of witches with a walled town? I wrote to Huw's father – the Archbishop of Lodellan. Or rather, we both did. Warning him that something was happening. What we heard back was that we were being ridiculous. That the Briar witches were up to something and under no circumstances we were to build any defensible walls.'

'So you began construction immediately?'

'We'd begun before we wrote the letters. If there's a reason why the Leech Lords – or rather whatever rules the Anchorhold – think they can start making demands beyond their borders? If they think they'll be in a position to back up those demands? I'm not leaving my people unprotected.'

'How do you hold the borders? What's your secret?'

There's a long pause.

'Only Briars have ever known this and if you tell anyone I'll kill you with my bare hands. Our bones. Our very bodies and bones repel them. My Great-Aunt Maud had a theory that the Leeches were a product of magic, and somehow we as controllers of magic were repellent to them.'

I think of the revelations in Murciana's journal, of Sister Constance. 'Your Great-Aunt Maud might be on to something.'

Ellie points to the menhirs below. 'The bodies of Briar Witches. All forming a barrier, sending a signal, a repulsion. And, I cannot emphasise this enough, if you tell anyone I'll kill you.'

'I'll take the secret to my grave. Do you think I want the Church marching in there, witches used as shields?'

'Funny, I said something quite similar once.' She grins. 'And you have…'

'O'Malley silver. Bishop Walter believed it might be enough to destroy whatever is waiting there, whatever purchased my brother for its purposes. I saw what just one scale did to a Leech, an ordinary Leech. For the Anchorhold, I think I need something different again, something *more*. Witch bones and O'Malley silver.'

'You want the bones of my ancestors?'

'Ellie Briar, if the Anchorhold comes through those gates, I don't think it'll matter how high you build your walls. We'll all be nothing more than bones.'

30

In the library of the Briar House, we gather when night's properly fallen. Rab and Freddie released and our packs returned to us. Edgar there to consult on matters of directions and geography. And Ellie, Nia and Eira Briar on matters pertaining to witchcraft and weapons. I show them the letter, the breastpins, the journal and the O'Malley silver. After much discussion and reference to *Murcianus' Magical Weapons* (located on the shelves with impressive speed) we settle on a dagger.

'A sword is too large, too obvious.'

'A sword cane is also suspect and takes too long to make.'

'A mace or morning star or axe needs more silver than we've got. As does the sword, I suspect.'

So, a dagger.

It's the easier weapon to conceal, it can be fitted to my forearm sheath, it's light and easy to handle, while my old knife goes into my pack, another backup. But, and this is a big *but*, it's also a weapon that requires, unless one's an expert at throwing such things with accuracy (which I am), proximity. A throw might go off-course, might be intercepted or deflected. A blow with a dagger might be delivered up close with the gentleness of a kiss. Yet getting near enough to use it, to disguise a gesture, puts one in greater danger, increases the possibility of being rendered helpless or dead before the deed is done.

The argument only starts when it comes to the matter of the bones. Or rather, whose bones should be used. As words begin to heat between Ellie and Nia and Eira, the Briar Witch looks at us and says, 'This is a family discussion.'

So, we retreat to the kitchen, where Rab makes himself at home and goes through the pantry, begins to cook. Freddie trails him around until he gives her tasks, ingredients to find, things to mix, tins and pots to grease. Edgar and I sit at the table and I unroll Walter's letter with the map etched on the back and show it to the gentleman-merchant.

'Well, that's not right,' he says and takes a stub of a pencil from a waistcoat pocket and begins to correct the map. 'A league,' Edgar says. 'Once you're through the gate, go this way and fast, enter the river here and follow it for a single league. Leave the water at the split rock that looks like a cat – you'll know it when you see it, trust me – and head west. You'll meet the road again soon enough. There's a signpost. Take the direction of Caulder. Find shelter there at an inn called The Bloody Smile. Introduce yourself to Winnet behind the bar, mention my name. Don't be wandering the Darklands at night.'

He looks up. 'Freddie, see if you can find some red wine. Navigating's thirsty work.' When there's a wine glass filled as only a child's pouring can affect, he returns to the task. More directions, and more, more notations and scribbled arrows, improved geological features. Places where one might hide if being chased – all, he says, ones he's used. 'Now, when you get *here*, outside of Aegir's Hold' – he presses the pencil against the map so hard that the lead bends – 'and do *not* stay in Aegir's Hold, it's a ruin and things sleep there. Don't be there at night. Go past it, another league, and you'll find an abandoned manor. It's boarded up, but around back there's a hole behind a fall of vines. Gets you into the cellar. You'll be safe there. It's a good place to stop on your way ever more north.'

More notes, more corrections, more tiny drawings, more instructions. I'm not sure I'll remember them all, but I'm very grateful for all his care. 'Sure you don't want to come with me?'

'Not on your life.' He shakes his head. 'Now we eat and drink because the Briars might be arguing for hours.'

* * *

As it turns out, it's a mere hour before the witches join us and eat the food Rab left warming for them on the stove. Eira asks if I wouldn't mind leaving him with them, trading him for something. I laugh, don't reply. Freddie sits close to me, leaning like a cat, watching the witches as if they might grow horns or fly on brooms or cackle; it's not fear but fascination.

When they're done with their meal, we're led through the town (Edgar, however, sends himself to bed) to the smithy, where Nia begins to heat the furnace – blacksmithing isn't her usual employment, but she knows enough to do what must be done, and a true witch is required for the making of this thing. Eira in the meantime is whittling a piece of hawthorn wood, shaping it for a hilt. When Nia gives the order, I pour the O'Malley silver from its pouch, all those lovely strange scales, into the crucible. Ellie pulls three fingerbones from her pocket – I don't ask to whom they belong – and wraps them in a piece of waxed cloth then pounds them to dust with a hammer. She sprinkles the bone dust onto the liquid silver, then turns to me, offering a small sharp knife.

All of this, according to *Murcianus' Magical Weapons*, must be tempered with my blood. Six cuts made over an hour. I make the first incision, let the ichor drip into the crucible and I could swear that the silver gives off no heat even though it's melted down. That the icy cold of the mer-queen's veins refuses to change its temperature. Another cut and spill while the mixture is still over the fire, then Nia pours it into a mould. We wait for it to cool, to harden, before Nia plucks it from the mould and begins to hammer it into shape. Another bloodletting, then three times more as she works the silver blade, then the cross-guard. As we go, Eira cleans each wound and dabs it with an ointment that stings only a little.

Rab and Freddie look on, more concerned with each cut, each clean, as if worried about what else I might be giving up with that blood. I don't know myself. I only know that it binds the weapon to me and I to it. When the thing is cool enough – I watch as Nia mutters a spell then blows an icy breath across the metal, snow and rime rising, and Eira binds the hawthorn hilt in place.

And at last it's ready. Nia puts it in my hand. There's no warmth against my palm, and while it might be the weariness, I swear I can hear the bones murmuring from within. Eira says something but I don't quite make it out so she repeats: 'There's one more thing we might do. With all those cuts on your arm…'

When she makes her suggestion, both Rab and Freddie protest. I can't say I blame them. 'No,' I say and hold up the dagger. 'This is enough.'

* * *

I lie in the bed in one of the bedrooms of the Briar House – plenty of space, Ellie said, and the safest place to be – but I can't fall asleep. My pocket-watch tells me it's well past midnight. After the forging, I spent some time talking with Ellie in the library, discussing strategies for what to do if I fail, how best to protect Silverton, how quickly they might plant the town's perimeter with garlic and salt, and begging her to keep Rab and Freddie here. And planning for what resistance might come later.

Finally I asked (possibly too belatedly): 'With the witch bones – will the dagger simply repel the Leeches? Will I be able to get close enough? Or will it warn them?'

'Good question,' she'd replied. 'I did consider that, believe it or not, and discussed it with Nia. We don't think there's enough in the dagger itself to act as a repellent. It's more like poison on a blade – in the blade. Unseen and unsuspected. It might even dampen your presence near Leeches, give you an advantage.'

'The best I can hope for, I suppose.'

Now, the dagger waits on the nightstand and I swear it's singing to me. I'm so tired I must be hallucinating. In the end, I put it into my pack and slide that under the bed.

Then I go along the hall to Rab's room. I don't knock, don't say anything, don't do anything that might make me hesitate. I just crawl beneath the covers and cling to him. Without hesitation, he wraps himself around me, and finally I fall asleep.

At some point in the early hours, we wake and he says, even though we've already had this discussion, 'I'll go with you.'

'You can't. You know you can't. I have to move quickly, attract as little attention as possible. I need you to look after Freddie, keep

272

her in Silverton, and the only way she'll stay this side of that gate is if you're here, telling her I'll be back. She trusts you.' I prop myself up to look into his face. 'Don't make this any harder than it already is. We can't use a wagon, Ellie said they've been searching wagons. There's one plan and it will only work if I'm alone.'

He huffs out a long breath, irritation, frustration clear in it. 'What if you fail?'

'Well, you'll be one of the first to know about it,' I say snippily, and almost regret my tone. 'Do you want to spend what might be our last night together arguing?'

He does not.

* * *

I set off before dawn, dressed in the black uniform (which mostly fits) the Briars stripped off the day-runner who'd died under Nia's hand, the Anchorhold's breastpin bright on my lapel; my pack mostly empty, and a cloak rolled up like a bedroll on the back of Ned's saddle. All enspelled by Eira to help me pass beneath notice – it won't help me trying to get through the gate, but it may well prove useful in other situations. The dagger is cold against my forearm; tied to my belt is the purse of coins stamped with the Anchorhold's sigil, the ones Freddie lifted from one of the assassins so long ago in St Sinwin's. There's the burlap sack hanging over the horn of my saddle, a faint reek coming from it; a desperate gift from Ellie. Otherwise, I'm travelling light.

The Briars wave me off at the edge of Silverton, but Rab and Freddie (also in borrowed cloaks) insist on coming to the gate, or as close as possible. When we reach the path Ellie showed me the day before, we dismount and lead the horses, sticking to the darkness of the forest, listening carefully for any sounds that don't belong. We don't talk and I feel drawn in on myself, running over plans and plots, each next step I need to take. I'm already far from my companions though they're only an arm's length away; in my mind I'm through the gate, across the border, heading to the rotten core of the Darklands. The Anchorhold, where it all began, where it will all end.

When we're not far from my goal, but still hidden by the trees and the early morning darkness, I stop. This is where we must part. Multiple torches light the gate and the area in front of it. I take a deep breath, am about to turn to Rab and Freddie and say my final goodbyes, when there's a clang and a creak as the gate separates into two panels, opening inward.

A line of day-runners marches out – why would they guard the gate at night when the Leeches roam, because what sort of a fool would try to enter the Darklands then? – but I'm not prepared for the man who leads the group.

Jack Seven-Gates, bold as brass, bright red hair glowing in the torchlight. Dressed in his usual finery, but on his cloak, easy to see even at this distance and shining in the torchlight, is the sigil of the Anchorhold. A mark, a protection, an allegiance.

Before I can say anything, Freddie chokes off a cry. Her face is pinched and pale and she leans into my side. 'Freddie, what is it?'

And she raises her eyes to mine, their expression utterly desolate. As if she's just seen something she thought herself free of. And I think about Freddie's mysterious brother; about why she was so tentative about coming into my house, why she refused a permanent place there. Why she'd disappear at times. Why she seemingly couldn't trust me entirely – because I was friends with Jack Seven-Gates and he was so frequent a visitor.

I kneel in front of her. 'Is that your brother? Is he the reason for… everything?'

She nods. 'He found out about my mother and me, that our father had been keeping us… He was so angry…'

I hold her tight as if that might make up for everything, hold her so tight that my arm with its fresh cuts stings bitterly. And I watch the group of day-runners led by Jack Seven-Gates, expecting them to move off, take to the road, but they don't. There's not a horse amongst them. This isn't a departure, but a waiting. Waiting for someone to approach. Someone who's managed to avoid the day-runners for weeks.

I look at Rab; he doesn't know who Jack is, but he knows that Freddie's terrified and he's smart enough to connect the dots. His expression darkens; I hold up a hand to forestall a discussion. 'I can't get past him. He's not going anywhere. Maybe I can wait until tonight, hope they open the gate again? Try to sneak in then?'

Then Freddie, sweet Freddie, darling loyal Freddie, says, 'I can make him move.'

And she darts away from my hands, faster than thought, carefully cutting her way through the trees so no one might see where she began, then she bounces out onto the road, directly across from Jack Seven-Gates, the brother who's been trying to kill her. My gaze moves between them, watching his face as he realises who she is, and the wash of rage over his features is terrifying, transforming my self-centred friend and lukewarm suitor into a monster. He screams at the men around him, and charges at Freddie.

She's off at a hare's pace, leading him and his merry band away from the entrance. I start to follow her. Rab stops me. 'Don't waste this. I'll get her. I'll make sure she's safe.'

275

He kisses me quickly, and disappears before I can argue. *Rab-rab-rabbit.*

He's right.

I can't waste this moment. I have to trust him. I have to trust her and her speed and cunning. I mount my horse, head straight towards the gap as if I belong beyond it. The shouts of pursuit are growing fainter and I wonder how long I've got.

Only two men remain, the two customs agents by their attire, who opened the gate and now lean against it. They're not dressed in the Anchorhold's livery. Red and blue uniforms, another house, and not much impressed with the black-clad day-runners, if I'm not mistaken. They've clearly lost interest in the chase. Boldly, I ride up. One raises a hand.

I jerk my head in the direction of the pursuers, as if I came that way. 'A bit early for that?'

He shakes his head. 'Idiots.'

So, Jack Seven-Gates and his allies are not held in high regard. Interesting.

'What's your business?' asks the other.

I draw myself up in the saddle, point at the gold sigil of the Anchorhold on my very fine, very borrowed jacket. 'I've brought a gift.'

'Well?'

'Violet Zennor.'

'So? Who do you think that lot have been looking for?'

And, sighing, I take from the burlap sack tied to my saddle the item Ellie gave me just before we left. At the time, I'd protested, but she'd said, 'I personally wouldn't appear at the entrance to the Darklands and announce that I was Violet Zennor, and oh by the way, haven't you been looking for someone of that name?' She'd pointed at the bag and I felt queasy. 'That should do the trick.'

I twitch open the mouth of the sack, reach in, feel the greasy hair against my palm, steel myself against gagging, and pull out the head, hold it aloft like a trophy.

The hair's muddy blonde, the eyes open but covered with the white pall of death, the mouth hanging slack, the teeth perfect, the skin beginning to turn green, and smelling of a few weeks' worth of decay. *Natural causes*, Ellie had said, *no family, kept in Eira's infirmary for research. A fair sacrifice for this purpose.*

I've got limited time before Jack gives up chasing Freddie, before Rab hopefully rescues her. Then limited time after that before Jack Seven-Gates returns and hears that someone claiming to have the head of Violet Zennor just passed by.

'Do you really think the Anchorhold would entrust such a mission to just one group?' My voice drips with disdain. 'And *that* group in particular? And do you think he'll be happy to hear you delayed my return?'

Both men go a little green, mutter under their breath because a woman who appears to have beheaded another is not to be trifled with. They step away from the open gate, and I ride on.

Into the Darklands.

31

To my right is the modest red-brick customs house Edgar mentioned – a second storey to it, I think, for the excise agents to live. He was right, no sign of a barracks, but there's a row of tents, currently deserted, presumably where the Anchorhold's day-runners have been camped for the past weeks, waiting for me.

Concentrate, Violet.

I make a point of not staring at any one thing, nor of letting my head dart in every direction like a startled rabbit. I do my best to appear as if I belong here, as if I'm on my way to do something very important; as if I'm as arrogant as I need to be and then a little bit more. As if I fear no one. I do give the area a good scan, doing my best to make it casual: trees, trees and more trees. A woman stands in the doorway of the customs house, carving at her nails with a knife that's far too big for the task, giving me a dead-eyed stare while she does so. I merely nod, unimpressed – *Yes, how skilled you are, how unconcerned for your fingers* – and ride on.

It's still pre-dawn dark, but the light's not so far off. I'll be safe from Leeches at least for the rest of the day; from humans, not so much. I keep Ned the Nondescript at a steady pace, not hurrying even though every instinct urges me to urge him into a gallop. Get away as soon as possible. Two more customs men in red and blue amble towards me. I'm still holding my gory passe-partout like it's a prize, so I give them a nod and raise the head as if it's a tankard. Their eyes pass over me, catch on the gleam of the breastpin, look away with an oily fear. What's happened in this place? That the Anchorhold has enough sway here that these men of another house don't question its lackeys? Then again, the Council's agents also don't seem to be throwing their wholehearted support behind the Anchorhold's day-runners. It gives me some hope that I'm not too late.

With Edgar's map in my mind, I continue towards the narrow path between two dead trees, then along an avenue of ancient oaks, their mistletoe-wrapped branches reaching across to form a canopy, like the cover to a hollow road that only the dead pass through. Cheerful thought.

Am I too late?

No. If I was, no one would be attacking me in my own home, nor chasing me up and down the byways for nigh on six weeks. Nor then trying to keep me out by guarding the gate to this place.

Jack Seven-Gates.

How could he?

As children, he was quite literally my only friend. In my world, those who controlled me were men dedicated to one purpose. Mrs Medway loved me (as did Tempe when she came along) I have no doubt, but she was in Hedrek's employ and even though she knew not why, she ensured I was awake before dawn each day, dressed and ready to do whatever part of my regimen Hedrek decreed. Even when my stepmother began to introduce me to the world of high society, none of those girls and boys became my friends; all remained acquaintances. I'd been kept in isolation for too long, their cliques had formed almost since birth and there was no room for the daughter of a commoner no matter how rich he might be. One might marry me for my wealth, but be my friend? Never.

Only Jack, whose house was so close to mine he could clamber over the wall and come visiting – largely because he'd been forbidden to do so. I suppose that made it irresistible. And I... he was funny and clever and rebellious. Both our fathers were bullies, but a boy standing up to his father was expected, met with comments about how he was becoming a man. A girl doing the same thing to her father was asking for trouble. Jack became my friend and confidant in most things – my purpose, my sailor-boy and all the consequences excepted – and it was only after his father's fortunes began to fail that matters changed. Jack would not visit any longer, or not much and not for long. It hurt because I thought it was me that he didn't like. Mrs Medway explained that the Seven-Gateses' "circumstances had changed" – that one of the oldest, proudest and wealthiest families in St Sinwin's was no longer so wealthy or so proud.

The night of the fire, with all their servants let go, Jack's father had either had a heart attack or was fall-down drunk. At any rate, a lantern was knocked over, and the mansion that had been in the family for generations burned to the ground, Mr Seven-Gates inside. Jack and his mother Evelyn moved to a small, mean house in a poorer area, and he stopped coming over altogether. He avoided me, would not answer the door when I tried to visit. I thought the friendship dead and buried.

Then, one morning, perhaps six months later, Mrs Medway announced there was a guest in the blue parlour. An apologetic Jack, splendidly attired, come to beg my forgiveness and tell me about his miraculously restored fortunes, about a clever investment he'd made almost a year ago, that his ship had quite literally come in. How he wished his father had been here to see it. And I forgave him because I was just so pleased to have him back, even though he'd changed. Sometimes he seemed harder, sharper, meaner, his comments cutting, but then he would laugh, say he was only joking, and I shouldn't be so sensitive. He'd always been my friend, almost a sibling, and a habit of forgiveness ever attaches to such relationships.

I wonder now, as I stuff that poor unfortunate head back in the sack, about the nature of that "clever investment"; about the nature of his investor. I wonder at the timing – of many things. The Anchorhold had left me alone for so long, Walter claiming I was no one while my brother was a dark miracle. I'd thought Tempe's wandering steps, her guileless questing and questioning, looking for the journal, made at Hedrek's malicious behest had been the reason, had been what alerted the Anchorhold to my existence. But surely there'd been no reason to look for me? No reason to think I existed?

I clear those thoughts from my mind because I have a destination. I need to remain alert.

Into the hollow road and around the bend, away from the prying eyes of the agents whose gaze I can feel on my back only now. Counting the yards until Ned breaks out into open space, fields on either side, no sign of habitation, and to our left the glimmer of liquid through another copse of trees. A quick glance around to make sure I'm neither followed nor watched any longer, and I head for the river. It's shallow and wide, and according to Edgar the stony approach means hoof-prints will be hard to track. Then into the water where the contrastingly sandy bottom means the horse won't be likely to slip. We go upstream.

The itching cuts in my left forearm are beginning to ache; Eira said that might happen when I saw her very early this morning. When I slipped out of Rab's bed and tiptoed to meet the physicker witch in the kitchen. Another defence, she'd said. Reversible when I return, she'd said. It had better be. One to which I've consented for a change. I restrain myself from scratching.

A league, Edgar had said. *Follow the river a single league. Leave the water at the split rock that looks like a cat – you'll know it when you see it, trust me – and head west. You'll meet the road again soon enough. There's a signpost. Take the direction of Caulder. Find shelter there at night at an inn called The Bloody Smile. Introduce yourself to Winnet behind the bar, mention my name.*

There's birdsong as we trudge along, as if nothing could possibly be wrong with the world. Ned whinnies in protest just so I know he's not happy with the cold swift silver water about his hooves.

'We all have to do things we don't like,' I say, scratching his ears, and urging him on.

* * *

After a while, thoughts I've been avoiding become unavoidable.

I worry about Freddie and Rab, whether they got away safely, back to the sanctuary of Silverton. Back to where the Briars are building walls and warding the earth with salt and garlic and preparing for war of one sort or another. Either Leeches and their minions pouring through the great gate, or the Church in Lodellan mobilising as they've not done in centuries all because a family of witches dared to take steps to defend themselves and those in their charge. A rusty Church militant, marching against the Briars because they suddenly appear to present a threat greater than the one they guard against: women who do not listen to the demands of god-hounds.

Rab and Freddie.

Being caught.

Jack Seven-Gates finally getting his hands on his little sister – half-sister, yes? Who was her mother? A mistress Ambrose Seven-Gates was keeping? Who'd have thought? – and spending his rage on her. Rab with his axe trying to protect the child because he's a good man, but there were so many day-runners and only one Rab. Rab, an annoyance to Jack Seven-Gates if he steps between Jack and Freddie, and possibly worse if Jack figures out what Rab is to me.

I shake my head. Just because I'm in a bucolic setting doesn't mean there's no threat about. Bandits. Wolves and bears roam freely this far north. Day-runners of various houses looking for anyone who doesn't belong. And gods only know whether my Anchorhold sigil will keep me safe or get me into trouble sooner rather than later. The burlap sack bumping up and down on the pommel reminds me that others have it worse than I do.

I can't do anything about Rab and Freddie. I can only do what I'm here to do. I can only use the time and opportunity they gave me and pray the cost wasn't the sacrifice of themselves. Before I go any further, I find a spot with soft earth and dig a hole for the nameless head. I could hang onto it in case I need to repeat the same lie, but the reek is also making it likely that predators will be attracted. I pile rocks over the top to keep her safe from animal predations. I whisper thanks and an apology before I leave.

* * *

Caulder, from Edgar's descriptions (and Murciana's), was supposed to be a great city. The home of the first Leech Lords, Edward and Marcella, Murciana's parents. After them, ruled by the famed Adlisa the Bloodless, whose reign was kind by Rikke's account and others – she did not glory in bloodletting, only ever took what she needed, treated her winepresses with respect, ensured the mortals under her care were looked after. Then, perhaps two centuries later – the sources are unclear – she disappeared, either murdered or displaced or fled by her own will. No one knows or no one is saying. Her place was taken by a Lord Hannequin, decent enough for a Leech, but more given to corporal punishment when he felt it required, although not cruel enough to incite rebellion. The advantage of Leech-ruling trees is that its Lords are generally long-lived, there are fewer branches, less to remember. So, Hannequin should reign still.

However, when I reach the outskirts of the city the place is looking… downtrodden. Degraded. Decaying. There are folk about, moving swiftly in the last of the afternoon light, a haste to their steps as if eager to be at their destinations before nightfall. Who can blame them? But Edgar's tales were all of a safe city that thrived night and day; the human population divided between those who lived in the bright hours and those who became nocturnal to run the city for the Leech Lords when they went abroad by moonlight. Servants, merchants of night-markets, tailors and other makers of personal attire (wigs, jewellery), blacksmiths and armourers, horse trainers and traders, carriage makers, weavers and tapestry makers, artists and decorators, for the rulers and their ilk, the blood-drinking retainers, nobility and middle classes who'd bought, begged or lied their way into eternal life, all had the same requirements for beautiful, useful things as day-dwellers.

Yet this looks like no jewel to me.

No guards at the gate, no one to question me. I pass beneath the portcullis and take the cobbled main street. Far ahead, a straight shot to the end of the valley, is the manor house where Hannequin resides (where Adlisa once did, and Edward and Marcella), but all I can see in the lowering light is a ruin. Edgar hasn't been here for six months. So much change. Where is the Lord of Caulder now? Does he still sleep there? Beneath the ruins, in the crypt about which Sister Rikke wrote? Or is there no longer a Lord of Caulder? Or at least not the old one?

I look for street signs, find the one I seek and turn left. The Bloody Smile, according to Edgar, was a fine inn. A place frequented by a better sort of traveller.

But when I come to the spot where it should be, there's only a burnt-out husk, the singed remains of the shingle hanging by one rusty chain on a single smoke-blackened post. The buildings on either side have been badly damaged. The street is terribly quiet. I sit and stare as the night slithers in, the horse moving under me impatiently. My arm aches, I'm tired from a day in the saddle, the tension of constant alertness. All I wanted was somewhere to lie down; now I'm left wondering what to do next.

32

I dismount to get a closer look.

I shouldn't do it, it's stupid because the sun's set while I've been searching for this inn that no longer exists, and I realise just how stupid the moment my feet touch the cobbles, as if the danger is transmitted that way, up through the soles of my boots. There's barely a sound, the lightness of foot, no puff of breath from a thing that doesn't draw it. *It* is, however, foolish enough to snigger (madly), thinking me easy prey. I sway backwards to avoid the blow, those terrible glass-sheened talons, and let the reins go as Ned rears up. His hooves connect with the slender body of the Leech.

I hear the strikes to its chest – male or female I can't tell in the darkness – and a grunt, yet it doesn't seem to slow the thing much at all. Renewable flesh, so very hardy. But it turns its attention to my horse and as it leaps, I catch a glimpse of the face in the bright sliver of the risen moon: thin and starved, mad-eyed, lips drawn back over fanged teeth, spittle catching the moonbeam. Ragged clothing, a stench of old blood and death, so strong in my nostrils. The mouth is moving, the teeth slamming together, seeking something to bite. Utterly enraged. In the natural order of things, I'd say it would keep coming for me, but the interference of Ned the Nondescript has kindled its fury.

I leap, flicking my wrist to dislodge the new dagger, and the brand-new blade and its silver edge only just kisses the Leech's throat as it tries to throw itself out of harm's way. It almost succeeds. Almost.

The creature makes a terrible sound, rage and pain, as it drops in its tracks, hits the cobbles – except there's nothing to reach the stone street, or hardly anything. Before it even touches the ground the thing's body is gone. While there's the stink of burning flesh the corpse bursts into a shower of glowing embers and fiery dust motes that float briefly, then burn out leaving only after-impressions of flame against my eyes.

An even more volatile reaction than Kyril's to the single mer-queen scale.

I slide down the wall, gasping for breath and sobbing. The emergency over, fear and despair rush in to take the place of adrenaline. What hope do I have against whatever lurks in the Anchorhold? I may as well stay here and wait for another Leech to find me. Then: a snort and a whiny in my ear, a wet tongue on the side of my face as Ned lets me know that's not a solution. That I have to keep going. If I didn't know better, I'd say the horse was on Hedrek's payroll.

I return the dagger to its sheath, then push myself up. Something shiny on the cobbles catches my eye: it's a gold signet ring, chunky, on its face a stylised "C". I put it in my pocket, take the reins and lead Ned along the street, back to where there seem to be more streetlamps. On one corner, illuminated, is another inn: The Bride's Bounty. It will have to do.

The room is small, but neat, the bed comfortable enough; a long tin tub takes up one corner, and I start running a bath. There's a lock on the door, and the single window has night-shutters of iron secured to keep anything unwanted out – or at least the noise of tearing it open would hopefully wake one and let you get out of the room. Fresh air takes second place to safety. I wonder how many Leeches are crawling the city. I wonder at the one that attacked me; the more I think about it, the more it appeared to my inexperienced eye to be… rabid, reactive. Not a clever hunter stalking its prey. Attacking without thought, easily distracted by a horse.

I try to recall any such tales in my studies.

In *A Slim Volume of Leech Lore by Mr Adair Adagio Before His Untimely Death* there was a theory that sometimes the very ancient lost their reason and became nothing more than killing machines. A sort of dementia took hold of their minds and all caution or care for themselves or those they ruled was lost. Sometimes entire towns or villages fell this way, taken in a single night by the Lord or Lady who'd once protected them, but then became afflicted. I recollect Hedrek telling me this one:

Once there was a Leech, who became obsessed with mirrors. It's hard for them to see themselves in reflective surfaces especially as they age, all there is, is a blur, nothing sharp or defined. No truth in the image – or perhaps too much; either way it could be maddening. This Leech began to lose his mind. He tried to resolve the problem by a twisted logic – he turned his people into Leeches, one after another, that he might see himself in their faces, make them living mirrors.

Yes, I know, Violet. It doesn't make sense. That's the point. Now be quiet.

And the Leech kept doing this, trying to make mirrors of himself until his estate no longer had any humans to work it or to be fed upon, only a troupe of ravening Leeches that attacked his neighbours' holdings and fed on their *people. And on it went until the Council had to intervene. The entire estate was destroyed – by the Leech's vanity. So, mirrors, Violet, are wicked. Don't let me catch you staring at yourself again.*

Unhelpful.

A knock rattles the door, and a female voice says my dinner's here. Taut and ready to use the dagger, I creep the door open an inch. A woman in her forties with pale blue eyes and greying dark hair, wearing a lavender dress and a tired expression holds a wooden tray laden with bowls.

'Miss Cornish?' she asks, and I nod, letting her in. I'd blush at how easily I adopted Rab's surname if I didn't have bigger things to think about. The woman sets the tray on the small table under the window. The bathtub's almost full, and she takes it upon herself to turn off the taps.

'Thank you…'

'Winnet,' she says. 'Will there be anything else?'

'Oh. Winnet! Edgar told me I'd find you at The Bloody Smile,' I blurt, pleased to find her alive and not a victim of the fire or anything else.

She smiles brightly, but with a touch of weariness. 'Edgar, the gentleman-merchant?'

'The one and only.'

'I've not seen him in a long while, was a bit worried something had happened. Mind you, we're not seeing many of his sort nowadays.' Her expression darkens, and she rubs her hands on her crisp white apron.

'What happened to the other inn?' I ask, curiosity getting the better of me.

She frowns, glances at the still-open door, shifts to swiftly close it. 'A messenger came several months ago to our Lord, a day-runner dressed all in black, an emblem on his collar that was seldom seen. From the north, a demand for Lord Hannequin's allegiance. A place called the Anchorhold. It had been so quiet for so long – dormant – mostly it had been forgotten about. Hannequin refused.'

I'm glad I'd removed the Anchorhold's breastpin from my cloak before entering Caulder and replaced it with the copper Merchants' one. Instinct told me it was the wisest thing to do.

'My sister worked in the manor house – I have this information from her. A few weeks after he sent his reply, a coffer was delivered; the Lord took it for a gift, but it contained a curse, sent him into madness. He killed many servants in the manor house, before the guards drove him away into the night. But our Lord still haunts the streets, hunting us.'

'Oh.' I think about the creature I killed, about the signet ring that sits in my pocket – "C" for Caulder. Probably best not to mention that I killed their beloved Lord Hannequin, no matter his most recent position as predator of his own folk; either someone will want revenge on me or someone else will want to celebrate me. Both will bring unwanted attention. 'I'm so sorry. Has... has this happened to other cities or villages? Recently?'

She nods. 'Those that submit to the Anchorhold, go on as before. Those that do not, are made to fall. I hope your stay here is brief, Miss Cornish. It's a dangerous place, even more so now. No one rules here – no one cares. Twice someone's tried to organise, to lead, and twice the Anchorhold's day-runners have come and cut them down in the market square, always in front of witnesses, so we learn our lesson.'

That's how the Anchorhold wants those who don't bend the knee – rudderless, leaderless. Winnet leaves and I'm thinking how bad it must be when someone whose whole life has been spent living under the rule of a Leech Lord in the Darklands thinks her home has *become* dangerous.

* * *

Bathed and full of food, I prop myself up in bed with Murciana's journal. There's nothing left to read, so I don't know why I'm looking for answers in the feeble candlelight.

I skim the pages, remind myself of her journey from stolen girl to a woman looking for her past; trying to discover what her parents became, why she wasn't of abiding importance to them. A lost girl who found a new family, a woman who uncovered answers that ached. Then again, don't all answers? Even just a little? A woman who left a request for others to help gather information, a collection of knowledge in one place, all designed so that at some future date it might be used for good.

Examining the journal again, the physicality of it, that progression from cheap paper with the pencil marks mostly erased, to the vellum whose old existence was rubbed away with pumice, then the thicker sheets, whiter in colour, a uniform texture to its entirety, and the handwriting so perfect. The journal, like the girl, made of scraps and experiences and gathered secrets. No wonder she was so obsessed with writing things down, documenting everything she found, myths and truths, legends and lies, small lives and large.

There's a mark on the last page that looks too regular. I hold the folio up to the candlelight and make out what looks like a line drawing – an architectural sketch. I sit up, roll out of bed, perch on the edge of the mattress and then carefully run the paper as close as I can to the candle's flame without setting it alight; a trick Tempe taught me in the bookstore to show when a tome was more than it seemed. Another piece of vellum, there's just that slightly seared smell of something that was once more meaty than papery. The heat has the desired effect, though.

A map on the page, beneath the final notes of Murciana's life.

A map of a building that looks like… a convent, fortified, one of the church militant's battle abbeys. Beneath it is scribbled "St Catherine's of the Wheel". I scour my memory: so called, I think, because the warrior-nuns of that place would torment their foes' bodies on the breaking wheel, extracting confessions and screams in equal measure. Those days – gone now, most of the battle abbeys disbanded, their sister- and brotherhoods dispersed – long ago, the days when the church made its march across the lands, bringing religion and submission. St Catherine's had been one of those, their reputation is dusty but can be recalled, and I vaguely remember from *The Observations of Frater Egbert of Miriam-on-the-Wold* that it was also one of the abbeys that did not answer the call to crusade against the Leech Lords…

There are notations about gates and doors and locks and cellars and sewers and wells and ways in that no one except one of the

Sisters of St Catherine should know. But then, the Citadel collected all manner of information. Maps of places and of buildings, specialist tomes on the architecture of battle abbeys, ordinary convents and seminaries, small country churches and cathedrals, follies and labyrinths as well as variations in ecclesiastical attire, even in the differences in fabric weave. There's no reason why Murciana wouldn't be able to find such details at the Citadel.

There's something else scribbled beneath "St Catherine's of the Wheel":

Now, The Anchorhold.

33

I'm gone from the inn just after daybreak, with a hearty packed lunch from the hand of Winnet – last night's encounter with the ex-Lord Hannequin has made me even more leery of the darkness, even its remnants – and there are very few people around. Unusual for a city of this size, or even a smaller one, but a sure indication of the population's being cowed. Without a leader, the economy will suffer, employment will dwindle along with business, there'll be no reason to rise early – indeed, the inhabitants of this once safe city will be as wary of the dark hours as I. The remaining markets are small and mean, the produce wilted and too old to be sold, yet housewives and husbandmen buy them anyway. I can't avoid passing the place where Hannequin attacked, but there's no sign anything untoward happened there, merely the shiver that goes up my spine and the sweat breaking out immediately after.

At the crossroads outside the city gates I consult the signpost, choose the direction of Aegir's Hold, in accordance with Edgar's detailed instructions. Another long stretch of travel, and a destination that will find me no comfortable accommodation for the night, but at least closer to the Anchorhold. When I'm far enough away from Caulder, I reaffix the gold breastpin to my lapel.

The day passes without event, which probably should have made me suspicious. I eat in the saddle, only dismount to relieve myself, keep riding. Everything is perfect (well, all things considered) until an hour before sunset. The day birds have stopped singing and the night birds have yet to begin, so there's nothing to hear in that strange lacuna except a brief sharp whistling in the air, which ceases abruptly when I feel a punch in my upper back, left side, into the meaty muscle of the shoulder – half an inch higher it would have missed, half an inch lower it would have been more serious. The breath leaves me, shock coming before pain, and I slump over the horse's neck. There are shouts and cheers. I don't look behind because it doesn't matter who's done this, bandit or day-runner, I just need to get away. I stay low and kick Ned into a gallop.

Though every hoof thud against the ground throws an agonising vibration through me, I'm grateful for his speed. Though my mind's a jumble, I'm trying to calculate how far off they were when they took aim, how far off to ensure I didn't hear them. All the distance they have to cover to catch me. All the distance Ned the Nondescript can put between us. All the distance between ill-willed folk and the abandoned house well outside of Aegir's Hold (where things sleep).

The shouts seem to be diminished in volume by the time we approach a tumbledown building, an old stone manor, boards over doors and windows, brightly coloured shards where broken glass still lies in the grass. The ruin Edgar mentioned; *You'll be safe there*. I half-fall from the saddle, grab my pack and whisper, 'I'm so sorry,' to the poor twice-deserted horse, then slap his rump as hard as I can. He rears and takes off down the road. I can only hope they follow him, that he keeps going for leagues and leagues before boredom and weariness get the better of him.

I stumble towards the back of the building, seek and find the thick veil of vines, and dive beneath it, heedless of biting thorns or sharp twigs, and feel rather than see the slim opening low to the ground, a window to a cellar or basement kitchen, just as Edgar had said. I push myself through the narrow fissure, catch my hips and think I'm stuck, take a deep breath and wriggle. I tumble head first, making a softish landing into a dank, dark place that smells of mushrooms and something sharp. My head swims, my shoulder aches, my arm itches. I give up trying to move, roll myself into an agonised ball and pass out.

* * *

When I wake (so many wakings!), I'm not where I fell.

Or it doesn't feel that way.

I can still smell mushrooms, although more faintly, and less of the other whatever-it-is. Beneath me is a mattress that feels a little damp, but I'm not about to complain. On the other side of the room – and it is a proper room, not a cellar – there are candelabra in a line down the centre of a magnificent dining table, highly polished, designed to seat a dozen, and where an old woman sits. More candles burn on the mantelpiece over a hearth where a roaring fire crackles; it might be spring but we are north, norther, norther and it's chill in the sun, cold after it sets. However, the room is strangely purposed – table, bed, two chaises in worn velvet, several groaning bookshelves, tapestries (unicorns and bears and wolves dancing around beautiful boys in cloth-of-gold) hung on the walls and, I think, over windows because they move with a breeze that must sneak in past the boards and the last of the broken glass. And what looks like an alchemy station rests in one corner, beakers and glass tubes, vials, a mortar and pestle, a small oil burner, canisters, dried ingredients and things in glass jars that once were alive.

I take in the woman's lined face, silver-grey hair, the unnatural thinness of the wrists and forearms that stick out of the sleeves of her faded ochre dress as she works, dipping a quill into an inkpot and scratch-scratch-scratching at the large book in front. Her collarbones protrude from a yellowed lace collar. Her expression is serene yet there's something fierce about it. Perhaps it's the tips of the canines I can see denting her lower lip; as I recall Mrs Danilla Verdigris' *By Fang and Foe* said they only grow when about to feed, but perhaps Mrs Verdigris never saw a Leech of this age?

'I'm exactly what you think I am, girl. But don't worry, you're safe from me. From us.' The voice is rough, rusty as if from lack of use, but there's a long scar across her throat, healed fat and raised. Once upon a time, someone tried to garrotte or slice her – succeeded, in fact – cut deep, and despite her eldritch ability to heal, a mark still remains. 'Do you have a name?'

'Cornish,' I say. 'Susan Cornish.'

'Really, Susan Cornish?' She holds up my pocket-watch, that birthday gift from Tempe, engraved with my name, lets it swing almost hypnotically. 'And does Violet Zennor know you've stolen her treasure?' She chuckles at my expression. 'I told you, girl, you've nothing to fear from us.'

'I'm Violet Zennor,' I confess, trying to sit up and my wound reminds me what happened. I swear. The arrow, at least, is gone, and my shoulder is thoroughly bandaged, my shirt missing, but my arm and its precise cuts have been left untouched as if my nurse realised that limb was not to be trifled with or tended to. I smell herbs, perhaps some of the same that Miren put on my foot and calf seemingly so long ago. I manage to sit on the edge of the mattress, mostly upright, and contort myself to get my shirt back on, bloodstains, tears and all.

She grins, those sharp canines shiny and white. 'Long time since I've had to save a life. Bit out of practice.'

'Thank you for helping me.'

'Well, you caught our curiosity, tumbling into the cellar like that, disturbing our mushrooms and garlic.'

'Garlic?' *That* was the sharp odour! 'Aren't you—'

'We're very old, toughened. We've made an accommodation with it. It has its uses.' She grins again, a private joke. Then she holds up a familiar swathe of pages; she's been reading it, making notes into the larger book. Her voice trembles almost imperceptibly. 'Where did you get this?'

'A friend found it. Do you know it?'

Her eyebrows rise. 'I read it when I was much younger.'

'You're not… Murciana?' But even as I ask, I know that's not right, and she laughs, not unkindly.

'I was – am Sister Rikke, of the Citadel at Cwen's Reach, a Blessed Wanderer and a member of the Order of the Little Sisters of St Florian.'

I sound, I realise, a little worshipful when I say: 'And you read the journal, Murciana's request, and you wrote *Volo* on the page, and even though she'd been long dead you went into the Darklands.'

She nods. 'Where did your friend find it? I heard that the Citadel had fallen. They'd have sent the books away to be safe…'

'This was found in the library at Whitebarrow University, in a bundle with *The Compendium of Contaminants* and a herbal of Adlisa the Bloodless, among others.'

She laughs, shocked. 'The herbal was the first book I copied when I came here, sent back for the collections.'

I shake my head. 'I don't know how any of them got there. Accident perhaps.'

'Accident is the universe's sense of humour on display.'

'You're—' I raise my hand to my face, don't manage to shut my mouth soon enough.

'Old? Very.' She laughs without malice. 'No one's reckoned young and beautiful once they're changed after fifty, hen. You remain what you were when you turned. Even those who come to the night when they're young? Personally I think they're terrifying. Hardly seems worth all the trouble, does it?'

'How… Who…'

'Made me like this? You'll meet her soon.'

'Where is she?' I look around, staring hard into the dark corners as if "she" might be waiting, listening.

'*She's* outside. Hunting the last of the ones who shot you. Making sure none of them got away.' Rikke takes in my expression, raises her bony hand. 'Don't worry. They returned once your horse had run out of puff, stopped to eat grass, but it was a long pursuit. Didn't get back here until after dark.'

'Thank the gods they didn't get in here,' I say. 'Poor Ned.'

'Oh, he's happily ensconced in the barn.' *More lives than a cat, that horse.* 'And two of your attackers *did* get in. How do you think I came by my rosy glow this evening?' She touches her cheeks as if to show off a dab of rouge. I feel a little queasy, although in no way sympathetic that those who shot me were turned into this Leech's dinner. 'How do you think I knew about the horse? Always ask questions before dining.'

'Thank you. Who shot me? The Anchorhold's day-runners or general all-purpose bandits?'

She gives me a calculating look. 'Interesting you should ask when you wear the sigil of that place. Interesting when they happily loosed an arrow hoping to kill you.'

'What did your dinner tell you?'

'Just that you were an enemy of the Lord of the Anchorhold, which was enough to interest us.'

'Interested enough to save my life.' I gesture to the bandages.

'One does what one must. Death is so dull and permanent.'

'Clearly not so much for some.'

'Mind you, eternal life can also be dull and permanent.' She sniggers, then tilts her head to the side, listening. 'She's back. Wait here.'

And Rikke, once a Little Sister of St Florian, moves so quickly I can barely see her. It's like she leaves a blur on my vision, an impression of movement, silvery and smudged.

I force myself from the bed and limp over to the table. Everything aches. On the smooth shiny surface lie my possessions: pocket-watch, firestarter, Murciana's journal, tiny bottle of lavender tincture, and the dagger in its sheath, the spare from my boot. The dagger's been pushed to the far end of the table – between witch bones, O'Malley silver and the hawthorn hilt I'm amazed Rikke could be in the same room as it. Tough old bird. I can only hope whatever's in the Anchorhold isn't so tough.

I flip through the pages on the table, the large book – an old accounting ledger that she's using as a notebook. There are tales here, recipes for potions and poisons, notes on little lives and large, and many, many snippets of the life of Adlisa the Bloodless.

'Well, here she is – generally obedient to the instruction *stay here*.' Rikke's rasp comes from the doorway.

'You weren't specific about the exact location,' I point out, turning to take in her companion.

'Obnoxious with it,' the other woman says. She sounds young. Confident, commanding, but young – like a child who inherited a crown at birth and never learned to speak of childish things. And she looks perhaps sixteen – pale blonde hair, green eyes – but there's something so ancient about her, a strangeness as she moves across the room, like a butterfly, a bat, a spider, almost a cat – all of these things made of shadows and webs. There are moments – seconds, it's not long at all – I think I can see through her, to the death of her, to the ragged bones of her skeleton on which this fiction of a person is hung.

'Adlisa, this is Violet Zennor. Violet Zennor, this is the Lady of Caulder, Adlisa the Bloodless.'

An annoyed hiss. 'Gods, don't call me that, Rikke. Long time since I was lady of anything. Since I was anything but homeless old bones, mouldering here.'

Rikke, following her into the room, says confidentially, 'It's a self-pity day. Come now, m'dear, cheer up, you ate three people this evening.'

'Four.'

'I stand corrected. All the more reason for delight, your best meal in an age.'

'Pleased to meet you, Adlisa.' I resist the irrational urge to curtsey because it seems like something that might annoy her. 'Were any of those people especially well-dressed? I mean, spectacularly dapper?'

They both shake their heads – so Jack Seven-Gates hasn't become a snack – then Adlisa gestures. 'Sit. Rikke, do we have any food for our guest? People food?'

'Fortuitously scrounged from the packs of the extinct day-runners, yes.' Rikke sets about making me a meal of bread and cheese; there's also a mix of mushrooms and garlic, which is delicious, and a hip flask of spring-cherry whiskey. They wait politely while I eat my fill.

Then Adlisa leans forward, puts her elbows on the table and points towards where the silver dagger gleams like a threat.

'Now, tell us about *that* abomination.'

34

I tell them everything.

Perhaps I shouldn't be telling these ancient Leeches – creatures I've been trained to destroy – anything yet they could have killed me already while I was unconscious. Finding the dagger and the evidence of Eira's work upon me would be more than reason enough to wipe me from the face of the earth. But they didn't. They didn't hurt me, have fed me, done their best to heal me, saved me from my pursuers. Perhaps I feel, because I've known them from my reading, that they can be trusted. Perhaps, I'm an idiot. But perhaps not.

I recount my life – something I hope never to have to do again – and the sad tale of Hedrek and Vesper and Tiberius, of my upbringing, of Walter and Titus and their lessons, of Walter's demise, of Asher Todd and Miren O'Malley and the mer-queen's scales and of the Leech Kyril (Adlisa barks with surprised laughter at that), of Jack Seven-Gates and Rab and Freddie, of the Briar Witches and my weapon of choice. I tell them about my brother being a child of prophecy, Walter's talk of a dark miracle, and how I am nothing, unsuspected, and they exchange a glance, but remain silent.

I tell them how and why the dagger was made and I'm polite enough not to arm myself again. They keep a respectful distance from it, but don't seem afraid. *We're very old*, Adlisa said, *there's a toughening that occurs with such age*. I wonder if whatever waits in the Anchorhold will be as resistant. Gods, I hope not.

When I'm done, Adlisa sits back in her chair and steeples her fingers under her chin, contemplating. I don't think I imagine the dawning hope I see in her face. 'How did you get here? Not the Darklands, but *here*, our home such as it is.'

'A gentleman-merchant called Edgar, friend to the Briars. He gave me very specific directions.' Oh. Edgar.

'Blessed be the Edgars.' Rikke laughs as does Adlisa.

'You know him?'

'For a long time. He keeps our secret, brings us things we need – half of these books, as a matter of fact – takes messages where we need them. He's a good man, is Edgar, though he'd grumble to hear it, so let's say nice things behind his back.' Adlisa shakes her head.

'Yet he sent you to us,' Rikke says, gazing at me as if the universe has just shifted in their favour, just a little.

'So it would seem, though he didn't mention it to me, and I will be having a word with him in future, and such word might also include my boot applied to his arse.'

'Ah, these last months, he's been spooked and there's only so much we can ask him to risk.' The Lady of Caulder rises, pours herself and Rikke glasses of something red – it reeks but I'm too polite to say anything, and she doesn't offer me any. 'And it's critical that he tells no one about us.'

'You're in hiding?' I ask.

'Well, I hope you didn't think this décor was by choice.'

'But you were the Lady of Caulder. You weren't a peasant, easily disposed of…'

She laughs. 'I came of peasant stock, or mostly. My father was an overseer at the silver mines; he was a man of many, many wives which led to many, many children – and the Lady of Caulder back then—'

'—Murciana's mother—'

'—kept trying to replace her missing child with day-daughters. It was a financial boon to a family, to have a daughter chosen, to go and live in the manor, be treated as a princess.' Adlisa shakes her head. 'But the Lady Marcella was mad, driven so with grief, and eventually each day-daughter disappointed her until she would cry, 'Impostor!' and a corpse would be delivered back to a Caulder family. Now, my father? He sent three of his daughters to the Lady Marcella, one after the other. Two bodies were returned.'

I can't quite decide if Hedrek was better or worse than that. 'But not you.'

'I had no intention to replace them, the Lord and Lady. Only revenge was in my mind and I'd not thought beyond that. I killed Marcella, and then in killing Edward, he killed me – or tried to and I thought he'd succeeded.' She and Rikke glance at each other. 'And then I woke up. Rikke's was the first voice I heard in that new life.'

'I worked in the manor. I'd watched her make her plans, her moves, her strategies.'

'What happened, though? Everything I've read says Leeches are only made through an intent by both parties.' I feel myself frowning.

'I wish I could say "accident", but I've never heard of it happening to another. The gruesome detail is that my father-in-darkness, the Lord Edward, bled out while trying to kill me – I slashed his throat and the blood entered my mouth and the wounds he'd torn in my chest. I thought I was content to die with my vengeance complete – but perhaps I did not want death no matter that I'd sought it. The proof, I believe, is my survival.'

I can't fault her – how many times have I come close to death and though my existence is not perfect and there is so much grief, I've never willingly let go nor stopped fighting.

'Have you been there? To the Anchorhold? To the Battle Abbey of St Catherine's of the Wheel?'

'Both of us,' says Adlisa, 'although at different times.'

Rikke looks at me shrewdly. 'When I first came to the Darklands, I listened to everything, every whisper and history, rumour and lie, conflation and fairy tale. I wrote them all down as is the wont of a scribe. And one of the whispers I heard was of the Anchorhold – how none who went there ever returned, how the mere mention of it put fear into the hearts of the entire Council of Leech Lords.' She grins. 'And I was younger—'

'—not much—'

'—shut up. I still burned with the zeal of learning, of taking up Murciana's quest. I thought that one person on their own, one little mortal might pass beneath notice.' Rikke holds up the journal. 'The fact you know the name of St Catherine's, a name that's mostly passed from memory, tells me you found my map.'

'You took Murciana's journal when you left the Citadel,' I say.

She shrugs. 'A little kleptomaniac urge. And I took it with me when I sought the Anchorhold. I found the abbey, I found my way inside and no one stopped me, no one was there, no guards. I made my way in, mapped as I went, never encountered a soul but...' she clears her throat, takes a sip of her awful beverage, 'but gradually I gained a sense of being, if not watched, then at least that someone or something was aware of me. When that sensation became unbearable, I fled.'

'The journal...'

'I made my notes, my map, made them invisible except by fire – see, they're already fading once more. And then I sent the journal back to the Citadel because I knew I couldn't risk keeping it here.' She shakes her head. 'Something *knew* me and I feared it would recognise me if it ever saw me again – and I've never been so scared in my life.'

I look at Adlisa, who's staring into the fire. 'And when did you go there? What did you see?'

'I'd been ruling in Caulder for centuries when word came of disruptions in the north – villages and estates being emptied, no trace of them found. The Council sent troops – none of them returned.' She shapes her mouth as if to push out a deep breath, but there's no breath in her, so it's just a remembrance of being human, a leftover habit. 'When the Anchorhold sent its first threat, the Council agreed to leave well enough alone. But I couldn't.'

She doesn't look at Rikke. Rikke's lips purse.

'I didn't know, then, of Rikke's journey there when she was mortal; we'd never spoken of it. But I knew she wouldn't be happy to know I was defying the Council. Taking a risk. So, I travelled alone, in secret.' She looks at her friend. 'Lied to Rikke, said I was visiting The Spire to discuss a trade agreement.'

'Lied to my face.'

'Frankly, if you didn't know I was lying after all those years, it's your own fault.' Adlisa pokes out her tongue. 'But the Anchorhold, it knew I was coming. Or it sensed me when I arrived on the outskirts, when I took the tunnels through the sewers beneath, knew when I entered the battle abbey proper.'

'Did you see it? What it was?' I ask eagerly.

She shakes her head. 'Saw nothing. I don't know if it was even *watching* me, but as I moved through those halls, I felt *this*.' With the talons of one hand she draws back the bodice of her dress, exposing the right side of her torso. No breast, but a mass of blackened tissue – leech flesh that should have remade itself whole and perfect – but there's only the white of ribs and sinews peeking through the mangled meat. Rikke reaches out, touches Adlisa's shoulder, squeezes it as Adlisa says, 'I tried.'

She covers herself. 'I thought I was dying. I made it outside to my horse, fled until daybreak then found a place to sleep safely. Became so sick I couldn't move. Eventually, Rikke found me. Bless your suspicious little heart.'

'And you returned to Caulder?'

'Briefly. A letter arrived very quickly at the Council demanding my execution. We had enough time to flee. Hannequin took my place.' I do not mention what I did to Hannequin; they've not found the gold ring, obviously. 'And we've spent just over a century since running and hiding.'

'Didn't stop you from investigating, though?'

'No, just made me more circumspect.' Adlisa grins, unrepentant.

I turn to Rikke. 'And you. You chose this life?'

'Had you asked me even five minutes before my death if I'd make such a choice, I'd have sworn it would never happen.

Had never been something I'd even contemplated.' She licks her lips as if they're dry. 'But when the time came? When I could feel the last seconds of my existence ticking away? I couldn't go. Didn't want to. There was still too much to do – too much to write and to read, to learn and see and discover. I'd lived almost eighty years in the light by then – a little blood seemed a small price to pay for a new life by night.'

'Was it?' I ask. 'A small price?'

'No. Nor has it been a little blood – I've been the author of so much death.' She points to her friend. 'Although, the blood from her, ancient as she is, and given to her by the first of the Leeches? Undiluted by any other sires or dams? It means I can go for longer without feeding, be sustained by less. But over these centuries? What does it matter? One lake of blood or four? It's still a lake of blood.' She smiles sadly, fondly. 'And... and I had taken care of her for so long. Almost thirty years. "Old woman" she calls me, yet I was just on fifty when we met!'

'I was sixteen, Rikke – everyone seemed old to me.'

'She's the closest thing I had to a daughter and she gave up so much for Caulder and its people. She stayed when she could have walked into the sun that first morning or any morning after that. How could I leave her alone?'

'You'd read the journal,' I say, 'you know about the mage who called himself a Magister, who stole Murciana away, who cursed her parents with the thirst for blood, and was in his turn cursed.'

Rikke nods. 'And how he was burned and fled.'

'I think he came north – back to this place where he'd done his worst thing, travelling by night and feeding to try and repair his wounds, sleeping by day.'

Adlisa nods. 'We think he slept for a long time.'

'Recovering,' Rikke says.

'He should have been destroyed in the sun, but somehow it didn't do its work fully.' I scratch my arm, wince. 'Though the Lord and Lady of Caulder were the first Leeches, he was the source of the curse and when it was thrown back at him… he survived. He's stranger and stronger than the rest of you all.'

I shift in the chair; the pain of the arrow wound catches at me and I gasp. I look at Rikke, shaking my head, and say, 'I was forced into this by my father, but you came willingly all because of a journal…'

'Well,' she exchanges another look with Adlisa, 'in part. But not entirely true.'

I narrow my eyes.

Rikke turns to the back of the enormous accounting book in front of her, and fishes about in a pouch made by the endpapers. A piece of ancient parchment appears in her skeletally thin fingers and she hands it to me. 'In the Citadel there was Beatrix, of whom Murciana wrote. Our oracle, floating on a pond of fire – another victim of a mage, by all accounts. We scribes would take turns to sit with her because sometimes she would prophesy.'

I unfold the page and find myself familiar with the opening lines.

In the city of the saint by the waters
From the evening song will come the lad
With the lad will come the crossing place
Thirteen summers will pass,
For the blood will come the lord
To break the border, the lord be free

But the last part I've not seen.

In the breach
Stands one alone
A flower of faith, her life to atone.

Stupidly, I stare at Sister Rikke.

'I was with Beatrix when she said that – honestly, half the time she didn't remember what she'd predicted. Some of it was absolute nonsense, but other things came to pass – like the Fall of the Citadel, her prophecy was the reason there was a plan for the dispersal of the books. The violet represents faith.'

'But I've never seen this before. Never heard it – it certainly isn't what Walter told me.' My brain runs in circles. 'I'm nothing and no one.'

'I'd read Murciana's journal many times – the day I wrote *Volo* in it was the day after I'd heard the prophecy. I just… I just knew, somehow it was going to be important.' She scratches at the scar on her throat. 'And I knew that if the second part was known, someone would try to remove that "flower of faith".'

'So you hid it?'

'I kept what's in your hand, the original I wrote down from her mouth. The version I recorded in the official documents was just the first part. I thought… whoever came should be able to do so in shadow. Remain safe.'

'I—' I think of Hedrek's secrecy all my life, about what he was training me to do. How he made sure I'd never tell anyone why, or what I was meant to do. 'But—'

'Yes, it's a lot to take in and prophecies are odd things,'

Adlisa interrupts, echoing Asher Todd's words. 'But now, dawn is approaching, I can feel it. Go to sleep. Tonight, we will depart.'

'We?'

'You're certainly not going on your own, you clever curious girl, and you're hardly in a state to defend yourself. Travelling by night will be easier, fewer witnesses, a little more time for you to gather your strength, and no one is likely to try and stop *us*.'

I'd like to argue but I'm exhausted. Rikke helps me back over to the bed, and I'm glad to go. She holds a goblet to my lips; I don't know where it came from. It tastes of honey and milk and only a little like medicine. I'm dead to the world by the time I hit the pillow.

35

The carriage, hidden in the depths of the barn behind the manor, is magnificent, though covered in a thick layer of dust. Black and, where I run a finger over its surface, shiny. Outside, brass lanterns and hardware that shine in the glow of our lamps; inside, plush red leather seats, thick curtains and pull-down metal shutters to seal out any light should we be caught in the day. The interior is dust-filled and takes a while to wipe clean with damp cloths. Rikke mutters about good help being hard to find when one is in hiding, but finally we're ready to go. The last of the food from the deceased day-runners is in a picnic basket along with several bottles of the Leeches' homebrew. Then Adlisa leads in the horses.

The horses are terrifying.

Where there is hair, it's ebony; where there is none, I see muscle and tendons, the white of bones and the dim hollows of decay in legs and rumps and flanks. Six beasts, all enormous, wearing black funeral feathers and tack as if to draw a hearse, some with tails intact, others with only stubs that look like shaving brushes. They snort and snicker, kick at each other until Adlisa hisses. She gives me an apologetic glance. 'We're not good at taking care of living things. To be honest, you're lucky to still be alive.'

'Unfair. We're good with the plants.'

'Where did these come from?' I can't help but ask.

Rikke makes a face as they start hitching the beasts into their traces, while I tie Ned's reins onto the back of the carriage. 'You don't want to know.'

I suppose she's probably right.

Apart from occasional pauses, we travel through the night. Either I sit in the cabin and doze or swap places with whichever of the Leeches isn't driving and enjoy the fresh cold air. Mostly, however, I stay inside because they are enjoying themselves so much, not hiding in the old manor, not wandering its tumbledown halls and dank cellar, sleeping wherever they slept in there, immured in a wall I suspect. I hear them laughing as they whip up the horses and we tear along roads and occasional fields and plains. During the day, there are caves or other ruined houses and the older women disappear into the depths of one or the cellars of the other, into the safety of the darkness. When I ask how they knew about these places, they answer that Edgar has always scouted such locations for them in case the need arose, that they've had backup plans for years. The reply feels flippant and I suspect there's something larger at work but choose to bide my time; no point irking my travel companions, and given my recent history that realisation feels like a sort of personal growth. While they slumber, I sometimes explore but am wary of being spotted so mostly I stay in the comfort of the carriage and study Rikke's map of the Anchorhold, or nap, willing my shoulder to heal while the other wounds continue to... *develop*.

Two nights in a row, we stop at ancient inns which keep a cadre of winepresses "on tap" for travelling Leeches. I don't go in – as Rikke says, I'll be noticed there – but remain in the carriage. They wrap up heavily in hooded cloaks, and when they return both are more alert, perhaps even jittery, although Adlisa mutters in disgruntled fashion about "undiluted blood" and I wonder what she means. Rikke jollies her before I can ask, saying one night or two won't kill them. They laugh at that.

The third night, however, there's no inn on our route and they both return from hunting without having fed. They look even thinner, paler, eyes gleaming when they step from the darkness into the light of the fire I've kindled in the grate of the small abandoned cottage we've holed up in for the daylight hours. There's a cellar, deeply dug, where they can sleep. They've kept me fed with food from the inns. I don't wish to see them weaken – they're out here on account of me – so I offer, as willingly and bravely as I can, a little blood, if it will help.

Both are shaking their heads before the words are fully out.

Rikke says, 'That's kind, but we'll not take from you. You're still recovering and you cannot spare your lifeblood, Violet. Never fear, we won't starve one or two or even seven nights. Might get a little grumpy, though.'

'And,' adds Adlisa, 'I have an idea that something of what we are stays in the blood after we've fed, just as a mosquito or a midge leaves its saliva behind to itch and irritate the skin. Something endures.' She sits across from me, in one of the three intact chairs. 'I've been pondering your brother, his uses. Remember that Leeches haven't merely fed off humans, but have on occasion bred with them – your mother, a rare creature, and you also. Half-bloods always fall on the human side – I think it's because they favour what is *alive*. Then your brother, his mother with Leech blood in her veins, and his father a full-blooded Leech, that horrible combination – three-quarters *not* alive. And his kind are always born dead, taking the mother with them – but still something of the Leech will have remained in him. I suspect that's why the Anchorhold, be it mage or magister or something unknown, wanted him. All that potential.'

I can't say I'm not relieved at the refusal of my offer. I cannot shake the feeling that no matter how tightly they both cling to the portion of themselves that was mortal, the bit that's inhuman, that's fed for centuries on blood and darkness, has lasted so much longer, and may well be stronger on some nights. This refusal brings comfort, and Adlisa's brought together some of my musings into a more coherent fashion.

My brother, Tiberius.

Potential.

Spare parts.

* * *

Another night, our last, and the scenery has changed. No more riverlands or fens, nor rolling fields, but roads that go this way and that, rising on jagged hills with little or no vegetation, and snow lying in drifts even though it's spring. We are so far north that winter never flees, not entirely. Here, winter makes its last, eternal, stubborn stand, nipping through my coat and cloak. It doesn't seem to bother the Leeches.

And this night, I'm awake and alert. The soreness in my shoulder has lessened considerably and the tiny itching aching cuts in my arm aren't a constant signal of pain interrupting my thoughts. I'm filled, however, with tension, taut as a bowstring, worried about what I must do and whether I can do it. Rikke is driving and Adlisa is inside the carriage, sitting across from me. I'm dividing my attention between the landscape and her searching stare. Eventually she says, 'You've only killed a single Leech? That Kyril?'

I hesitate. Now's the time to come clean; I pull his signet ring from the pouch where it hid perfectly amongst all those Anchorhold coins. 'And Hannequin. I'm sorry if he was a friend and ally, but he attacked me in Caulder. A woman there said he'd refused to bow to the Anchorhold's demands, was cursed with madness. He'd been feeding on his own folk for months.'

'Ah.' I can't read her expression, but she takes the ring, slips it onto one of her thin fingers. 'Well. He wasn't the worst of them – us.'

'I'm sorry,' I repeat.

She waves a hand, dismissive. 'Apologies won't serve anyone, Violet. You can't be soft or weak. You're quick and clever or you wouldn't have survived one Leech, let alone two. Whatever else your father did, you can be grateful for the training because it's saved your life.'

'But I wouldn't have been in this position except for my father and his weakness. I'd never have needed saving, but for his mess.'

'True.' She shrugs. 'But you *are* alive, and that's a thing to celebrate, whether you think so now or not.'

'Did you celebrate? When you woke after you thought yourself dead, your goal fulfilled?' I ask meanly, irked at her defence of Hedrek.

'Not at the first taste of blood, not at the first piercing of a winepress. Not as I learned how to run a city with all that life in it that I'd made my responsibility because of my desire for revenge.

No. But… there was one night, the first when I didn't think about what I'd lost. I sat on the roof – we can't fly, no, but we're good climbers – and felt the wind in my face, the moonlight on my skin, my belly was full of warm blood willingly given, and I felt free for the first time in my life. That moment? I was grateful that true death hadn't claimed me. And grateful, I think, that I'd taken up the mantle of Caulder's Lady and looked after its people.'

'I'm sorry,' I say, then whisper, 'what if… what if I can't do this? Everything I need to do?'

'Perhaps you can't. Perhaps you'll fail. I won't feed you platitudes about destiny and inevitable victories.' She shrugs. 'But violets are symbolic of faith not just religious, but faith in things. In self. In a path. In what you're doing. Just a thought.'

The carriage comes to a sudden halt before I can reply. Rikke appears in the window-frame, upside down, her hair streaming in the night breeze. 'They started following us an hour ago.'

'Took their time,' grumbles Adlisa.

'Impressive that we went without notice for so long,' Rikke says, then flips to the ground, athletic. At moments these past few days, I've forgotten they're not human.

We scramble out, me gathering my pack – very light now, mostly empty – as I go.

Rikke's parked the carriage at the edge of a bank that drops down some six feet; a ditch with a film of ice on the bottom, a trail splitting left and right. The former disappears into a thick coverage of undergrowth at the foot of a mount that rises high above us. The latter leads to a bridge and a cobbled road towards the façade of one of the great battle abbeys, in this case, that of St Catherine's of the Wheel.

The Anchorhold.

Adlisa is pointing to the left (and her talons are growing longer and longer!) even as she asks Rikke, 'How many?'

'Twenty that I can hear – not light-footed. Not old ones. Young, newly made, insufficiently cautious, and spectacularly flammable.' The older woman pulls a copper flask from her pocket, opens it and takes a good long swig before handing it to Adlisa, who does the same thing. All I can smell this close is garlic – fermented – and old blood.

'What are you doing?' I hiss, looking around – I can't see anyone, but then I don't have the senses of a Leech Lord, do I? Rikke reaches up, unhooks one of the carriage lanterns and hands it to me; in its light, the Leeches look positively eerie, teeth having lengthened, eyes grown larger, all the better to see you with.

'What we've been doing for some time. If we were to be found? What do you think might happen if our blood were drunk by whatever, whoever waits in the Anchorhold? Or any of his underlings? My blood, direct from the font of the First's throat, and I never made a fledgling except Rikke. How powerful do you think that might make another Leech?' Adlisa gives me a look. 'So, in order to guard against that, we've been—'

'—slowly poisoning yourselves with garlic.' I think of their thinness, paleness, the half-starved look, the jokes about undiluted blood. The sharp smell of their homebrew. They've been making themselves unfit for consumption, with the sort of clever malice in which old women ill-used by the world excel.

'You're a quick study, Violet Zennor.' Adlisa gives me a grin, and pulls a wrapped bundle from beneath the carriage seat. 'Garlic and a little something extra.'

'How have you survived it?'

'I was feeding the Lord and Lady's winepresses a mix of garlic and belladonna, the blood I took from my father-in-darkness was already changed – so I developed a higher tolerance.'

'We've lived a long time, Violet. All those lakes of blood,' Rikke says, helping to pull the oil cloth from whatever Adlisa holds. Swords. Two swords, quite plain, heavy-looking, sharp edges. 'We have a lot to make up for. Let us do this.'

'Now, remember Rikke's map?' Adlisa asks. 'See that undergrowth there? Brambles – be careful. Behind it is an opening that will take you into the sewers – don't look like that, shouldn't be too much of a problem, Leeches aren't known for shitting – follow that. It should lead you up to the kitchens. From there, you can find your way to the Anchorhold – the actual, proper Anchorhold room, the place where both life and death exist. That will be where you find what you seek.'

'But you two—'

'Will buy you what time we can. Go.'

A brisk hug from one then the other, then Rikke tugs Ned the Nondescript's reins loose from the carriage rail and slaps his rump to set him running, perhaps in hope the other Leeches won't feed on him in the frenzy, but surely he's tired of this treatment by now. Adlisa pushes me over the edge of the bank so I slide down the slippery slope. I hit running, and keep going, along the culvert and up the slope on the other side, towards the brambles and vines that shouldn't be growing in this cold.

Closer, I can discern a path that's only slightly overgrown, not something used frequently, but a definite way through the thorns. I wrap the cloak tightly around me and step into the brush, feel the branches and thorns pluck at the fabric, but I forge forward. The opening to the sewer system is easy to see only when you're almost upon it. I stop, though, and turn to stare because I can't help myself.

I have to watch what's happening in the moonlight.

Those old women have stepped away from the carriage, standing side by side on open ground. Twenty figures, black and silent to my ears, run towards them from the trees, unbelievably fast, a night tide. On the flanks, one or two break away as if to leap down the bank and into the culvert. As if to follow me. But there's a flash of bright metal in the moonlight and I realise that Adlisa's slashed her wrist. Rikke does the same, and very quickly those outliers who might have pursued me are arcing back in towards the old women, drawn by the rich scent of their ancient and powerful blood.

It's less a battle than a ballet.

An elegant suicidal dance.

They both move as lethal leaves on the wind, talons slashing left and right, blood arcs in the air, limbs are severed, wounds opened in pale skin. Silks and long hair drift as they leap and spin, defy the pull of the earth. Neither Adlisa nor Rikke will go quietly. Indeed, they know well enough that were they to be too easy to catch, the fledglings would lose interest in a hunt with no chase. Older Leeches might have been suspicious, more cautious, but the young ones are easily feinted.

But there are so many of them, a legion, ravening and new, fresh-born Leeches with fangs and claws, bottomless hunger and the will of their master running through them. By sheer weight of numbers Adlisa and Rikke are dragged down.

And I'm frozen, witnessing their deaths, watching them become nothing more than drained skin, torn flesh and broken bones on the cold, barren ground. Then, the fledgeling night-runners turn in my direction.

Their eyes are glinting; I can see the dark blood around their mouths, dripping from whiter-than-white fangs, spatters of ichor on pale faces. Lips tilting hungrily, first fatal steps being taken, and then…

One by one they topple, falling like towers, curling into balls in the dirt, then jerking straight in agony, screaming. Bursting into flames, spot fires in the night. Poisoned blood, garlic and belladonna, faster acting on these young ones; what the old women had a resistance to is absolutely toxic to these *children*.

Screams and shouts cut short by a combustion that's swift and effective.

Soon all I can see are piles of embers being blown in the breeze.

I think about Adlisa's *a little something extra* – perhaps saltpetre? It preserves meat but is also used in creating explosives – and Leeches have their own finely tuned combustion mechanism. Adlisa and Rikke, all those years, reading and experimenting with their little alchemy lab. Rikke gloating *Young, newly made, insufficiently cautious, and spectacularly flammable.*

Once again, I've been bought time by another's sacrifice. I cannot waste it.

36

Outside, it's still night. Inside the tunnels – the sewers, I remind myself and step gingerly – it's as black as a goat's guts. But the carriage lantern throws its light ahead of me, and I hope I'll get sufficient warning if there's something in the darkness. I'm paranoid that one of the night-runners showed some restraint, didn't feast on the ancient ones with their curated blood. Perhaps an older one holding back? Is there a creature sneaking around outside, hunting me?

I shake myself. *Idiot*. Adlisa and Rikke would have known, would have sensed any older ones, would have made sure they died too, either by tooth and claw or those swords.

Ahead, several small pairs of red eyes flare – rats. Only rats that give me a stare before dispersing too slowly for animals that might be afraid of a human. The tunnel has rounded walls of dressed stone; the ground is dry, built-up dirt and dust, thankfully nothing wet or damp of uncertain origin. The smell is strange – as if the application of water would make it an entirely different thing altogether. It feels even colder in here and my breath fogs in front of me. The pain's returned to my left arm, and I can feel a fever burning through the flesh like an infection. If I ever make it back to Silverton, I'll be having strong words with Eira Briar about her clever ideas and handiwork.

I listen carefully, hear nothing. Glance back towards the round opening where the darkness is of a slightly lighter sort, leavened by moonlight; then face the utter black beyond the creeping reach of my lantern. I don't need to look at the map: the route is burned into my memory from studying it in the carriage, and Rikke testing me over and again as to which turn must be left, which right, when to continue on straight ahead, where to find the spiral stairs that lead upwards.

To the Anchorhold.

To where everything began.

To where everything must end.

No more sight nor sound of the rats. I suspect they're so unused to any presence but their own down here, that they'd rather not examine me at close quarters – unless I'm dead and ready to be made into bite-sized chunks. I come to a T-junction; take the left path, continue on until a fork. Turn right. Continue on. Trip on a small step, recover my balance. Keep going. Left, left, left – it's not lost on me that the path is mostly "sinister" – then right and right and right.

I stumbled into a large cavern, so large I can barely make out its edges even when I hold the lantern high and turn and turn and turn, letting the light and shadows flicker and dance. I notice something neither Rikke nor Adlisa had mentioned: coffins. Thirty in all, lids askew. Empty, I ascertain. The hackles at the back of my neck rise, until I recall that there were twenty new Leeches who partook of my friends and paid the price. I'm calm for a few moments until I consider that ten Leeches – if indeed only ten remain – are still more than I would choose to confront. That two of the oldest Leeches in the world died to dispose of twenty. And that doesn't even include the whatever or whoever waits in the Anchorhold that is even more ancient than Adlisa and Rikke were.

I rub at my right forearm, feel the familiar shape of the sheath and the silver dagger within and draw what comfort I can from it. My mouth's dry: I fight for some saliva, swallow, trying to moisten my lips, my throat, so it's not so parched that I begin to cough and make more noise than I need to. More noise than I should – which is precisely none at all. I pick my way across the stone floor of the room – crypt? Wine cellar? Root cellar? There's no sign of a subterranean well that might be used for water in times of siege – when the abbey was designed for battle, it would have needed such a thing. I reach a door, large and wooden, iron-banded, a pointed arch at the top. I think about Adlisa not mentioning this as a sleeping place – then realise that when she was here, tiptoeing through the gloom, there was likely no army of Leeches here then, no cadre of Anchorhold night-runners, or not of any notable size. At that time, whatever lay at the heart of the Anchorhold was still coming back to itself. Healing. Even then the Anchorhold could send a plague to wither the flesh on Adlisa's chest, as a warning. But what if it was indeed Murciana's magister, burned by the sun, spending literal centuries to heal... what if his actions, his warnings to the Council were no more than a front, a camouflage to make them think him more powerful than he was. What if... what if they'd all pushed then? Might the Council have beaten the magister, removed the threat of him? If only they'd acted with more decisiveness? What if it was all a huge, masterful bluff on his part?

Who can say?

But now is not then, and I won't be facing a wounded creature made vicious by pain and fear. I'll be facing a creature that's recovered – or mostly, surely? – that's choosing to be vicious in its search for power and blood. That seeks to walk beyond the gate of the Darklands.

Thirteen years ago, the Anchorhold had a man in its pay who found us, traced us – my mother Vesper, the "evening song" in the city of the saint by the waters – and resources so great that buying my brother's corpse for its own purposes rendered my father nose-bleedingly wealthy. Now, the Anchorhold has minions, legions of night- and day-runners to do its bidding. The Anchorhold can destroy cities by sending a curse in a box to their rulers.

Focus, Violet.

The door opens with a low creak, and I step into yet another corridor – no longer a sewer, part of the lower floors of the battle abbey. Habitable, or meant to be. There are doors hanging open – inside are the ruins of small cells, narrow beds broken, rotten blankets strewn about, chewed away, once a dormitory now a home for rats and mice. On the walls are rusted swords and shields waiting at the ready as if the nuns of St Catherine's might rise again at any moment. In corners, a prie-dieu for prayer, small desks for letter-writing and study, some intact, others no more than kindling. I wonder if the destruction occurred when the magister – if it is indeed him – came, chose this place as his fortress in the north, before the border was closed. His sanctuary to feed and sleep and recover for centuries, before he woke and began to plot and scheme.

I wonder about the Battle-Sisters of St Catherine's of the Wheel. Did they all die on the same day? Night? Or did he pick them off, one by one, night by night as he fed his recovery with their blood? Did he turn any of them? It seems unlikely he'd want competition for food. Did they realise, at last, what was happening? Did they fight back? Try to find him? Hunt through the foetid spaces below? How long before the last Sister was dead and drained like a discarded waterskin?

Up ahead, another set of stairs. I'm careful not to scrape my boots on the stones, not to make any noise as I go. I do need to find somewhere to hide – night will be done in a couple of hours according to my pocket-watch. What I must do will be best done in the daytime – easier to overcome day-runners and mortal retainers than the night-runners and any other Leech factotums who serve in the night.

The Anchorhold.

Before all this, an anchorhold was a space where an anchorite – a religious recluse – went to be neither living nor dead. To be in that strange *between* state, to be both things, in the limbo between earth and their god; further from one, closer to the other. A place to read and write and contemplate, to be of the world but not truly in it. A crossing place, a doorway, a liminal thing.

There were hints in some of the books Walter made me read, that the battle abbeys and their nuns worshipped differently, hid behind the façade of the Church to keep themselves safe from the zeal of the god-hounds, but that their true allegiance was to a different deity. A goddess with horns and cloven feet, who danced on the forest paths. Did the magister know this or suspect? Was that why he chose this place to make his own? And I think about the legendary coffers of the battle abbeys, the treasure rooms and bank vaults, filled with all that coin – enough money to buy a dead child from a grieving man, to pay spies, to hide for century upon century.

Because the between space here, between life and death, wasn't quite as hallowed as it was meant to be?

I reach the top of the short flight of stairs, find more doors, these ones intact unlike those below. A cursory glance shows one even has its lock still in working order, a key in the hole. There is a chair, whole, a mattress, rotting and piled high with rolled-up blankets, a functional desk. A candleholder with two tallow candles in it, covered in dust. As good a spot to wait for dawn as any.

I close the door, lock it. Light the candles then extinguish the lantern, which I'll need later. Drop my pack on the desk and sit, lean forward, rest my head against the wood – can't use my arms as a pillow, not at the moment. I'm exhausted – though the past few days have held a lot of sleep time, there's also been a lot of travel, tension and strain – I feel slumber's taffy fingers begin to wrap around me. If I close my eyes, I see Adlisa and Rikke in their final flight, whirlwinds of rage and determination and… and I think at least one of them was laughing. They'd lived so long, they were tired. They were trusting me to finish the watch they'd begun. Just a little rest first, just a tiny nap.

Except a creak comes from the corner. The silver dagger is in my hand and I swing around, bringing the blade up, and launch myself across the room.

My glance, clearly too cursory, didn't distinguish the form on the bed from the blankets piled over it. But now the gleaming point of my knife rests at the base of a dishevelled man's throat, his mouth caught in an open but soundless scream, a trickle of blood coming from the tiny cut made by my blade.

Jack Seven-Gates, no longer resplendent, stares up at me in abject terror.

37

'What are you doing here, you bastard?' I hiss, staring at the drop of darkest red welling in the hollow of his throat. Jack's fine clothes are torn and filthy; a week or so ago, when I last saw him at the gate to the Darklands – chasing after his little sister – he was still elegantly attired, seemingly untouched by the long journey from St Sinwin's. Now, he looks like a tramp, smells like one too – and given that I've not bathed in some days, that's saying something. There are scratches on his face, up his neck, but no sign of bites. Nothing's fed on him. Yet. I twitch the blade. 'Well?'

'Hiding,' he blurts out, eyes darting around the room, into the shadowy corners the candles are too weak to reach. 'Hiding from the monsters.'

There's a rage in me that wants to push the blade *in*. I think of poor Freddie, hounded from pillar to post by someone who should have protected her. How she was afraid of coming to me because of him, not trusting me because I was friends with him. And him *at the head of a troop of the Anchorhold's day-runners looking for me*. All the rage, the offence, all the questions come out of me as a roar of 'Why?!'

There's enough of the old Jack to make him say, 'Which part?' and I almost do stab the bastard.

'Why align yourself with the Anchorhold? Why pursue me? Why try to kill your sister? Why any of these things?' And a needy little squeak sneaks out and betrays me: 'I thought... I thought we were friends.'

He looks away. 'We were until...'

'What? What did I ever do to you?'

'It wasn't what you did, it was what you *had*. What you *kept*! It was what you *were*.'

'What?' I back away from him, resume my seat but keep the dagger at the ready. I know Jack Seven-Gates well enough: he's not going to attack me, he's never fought a day in his life, not even for the last macaron on a high tea plate at Micklethwaite's Pastry Emporium. He's sneaky though and if he thinks he can surprise me, he'll try.

'Money. Position. Power. Your father never earned his money – he sold a dead child!' He shakes his head, resentment overcoming fear. 'Bought his way into society, bought a place for you – do you think without that money you'd be anything but a street slut? And you still think you're too good for me?!' He must see something of that sting in my expression because he smiles, cruel, satisfied.

'That's what that kiss was about? Trying to show you could have me? Yet with all your breeding, all the Seven-Gates years of marrying with the best of St Sinwin's society – and foreign brides when your blood got too thin, your chins too weak – your father still couldn't keep his fortune intact,' I sneer.

'Foolish speculations and risky investments, con men and whores – like the one he kept when he was telling Mother and me

331

we couldn't spend anything! Had to tighten our belts. Economise!'
He screams the word as if he's never hated anything more.

But something's bothering me, pricking at the back of my
mind. A sudden burst of clarity. 'How did you know about my
brother? About my father selling him?'

The Zennors' greatest secret, the one that never went beyond
four people, beyond Hedrek and Titus, Walter and me. Not even
Mrs Medway or Tempe. A sacred trust, a painful binding, one
I've only broken in recent weeks to people I've trusted, the little
band that's gathered around me since I left St Sinwin's: Freddie
and Rab and Edgar, Asher and Miren and Ellie, Adlisa and Rikke.
None of whom would have told Jack Seven-Gates even if there'd
been an opportunity.

He grins again. 'Oh, Violet. Dirty little secrets have become
my stock in trade.'

'Jack…'

'When my father first lost his – *our* – fortune, he went to yours
for a loan, which he received and promptly threw at the gambling
tables. Father went back twice more – Hedrek was generous
whatever other complaints you have about him – but on the fourth
occasion, he refused. My father had to come home and confess
what he'd been doing. What he had done. And that some of his
wealth had gone to maintaining *a second family*.'

'Freddie,' I say.

'Father felt it would be best for all concerned if his whore and
bastard child moved in with us. Into the Seven-Gates mansion,
which had been built two hundred and fifty years ago by his
forebears. Built by the sweat of our brows and the fortune inherited
from the first Seven-Gates to arrive in St Sinwin's, one of the

founders of that fair city.' There's a little froth at the corner of Jack's mouth. 'He wanted me and my sainted mother to live with a prostitute and a bastard, so he could sell the house he'd bought for them as a stopgap measure to pay off some of his creditors.' He shakes his head. 'His daughter could even, and I quote "Ride her pony in the gardens". He'd bought her a fucking pony! But everything else was gone. It was just going to be a slow death, drip by drip of blood and money and reputation.'

'Jack—'

'I spoke to my father quite reasonably after he'd presented me with this proposition, expressed my concerns – Mother had gone to bed and, he said, such things weren't for her ears. It was up to the menfolk to decide the fate for all of us. It would be hard at first, he said, but we'd all come to terms with it. Grow used to being one big happy family.' Jack swings his legs out from under the pile of blankets, sits on the edge of the bed. 'And that was when I hit him.'

'Jack—'

'Violet, honestly, if you keep interrupting me we'll never get this story finished.' He shakes his head. 'Where was I? Oh, yes – and that was when I hit him. A lot. A large number of times. With a marble inkwell, made a terrible dent. Series thereof. We had no live-in servants by then and Mother's room was far from the parlour, so no one heard a thing. I was somewhat bewildered. Confuzzled. I thought that perhaps Hedrek might help me. We were friends, you and me, and he'd helped Father. Of course, he'd said no to Father's fourth request, but this would be my first. Irresistible, surely. So, I climbed the wall, as we've done all these years going to visit each other, and then I climbed in a window – it was late and I didn't want to disturb anyone, and I tiptoed along to your father's library. Except he wasn't alone.'

And I think about those weekly councils of war between my father and Walter and Titus, to which I was occasionally but not often invited. In the security of his own home, Hedrek and the others would have spoken freely.

I close my eyes briefly, open them quickly. 'And what did you do, Jack?'

'I listened, didn't I? That was far more interesting than begging for help. For a loan.' He waves a finger in the air. 'And thought, Jack, me lad, here it is. Your answer. I listened all night – couldn't they talk, those old crows of yours? – and when I heard them saying farewell, I left, straight back over the wall, into the parlour and poured every bottle of alcohol I could find over my father and set him alight with a taper. Ambrose flambé. I collected what few valuables remained to us while Father got a good burn on, rescued Mother, and watched the whole thing turn to ash. Mother kept asking why I hadn't summoned the firefighters, but she didn't say anything when the Constable arrived. I told her I would take care of her. And I did.'

'What did you do then, Jack?' I ask wearily.

'Remember how we moved into that terribly little house in that terrible little street? Remember how I stopped visiting? Well, I took a little holiday. To the north. To Caulder, and I asked around for the Anchorhold's representatives – how might I contact them, if you please? And no one would tell me, looked at me as if I was mad.' He shrugs in disbelief. 'And then one night, while sitting in a tavern, drowning my sorrows and wondering how I was going to pay for that drowning, a man in a black cloak sat in front of me and said he'd heard I'd been asking unwise questions.' He laughs but I recognise it as no more than bravado. 'He threatened me, but I told him I had information for the benefit of the Anchorhold. Information about the body bought and about the boy's sister – that it had been played false.'

'And in return?'

'My fortune made again, the same bargain as your father had received. Where he sold his son, I sold his daughter.' He laughs. 'And the Anchorhold's man was very interested indeed. And very, very generous.'

Nothing to do with Tempe and her search for the journal.

'I kept an eye on you, reported back. Housed some of the day-runners so they could watch and assess. I don't know why they didn't just kill you as soon as they knew about you. It was months and months before the word came. The Anchorhold took its own sweet time to decide you were a threat and had no use.'

They watched for a while, observed. *Then* decided I was a threat.

My father and his friends keeping secrets. Rikke hiding part of a prophecy so I could grow safely in shadow. And Jack Seven-Gates ruining it all.

'And Freddie? You could have just left her alone, forgotten her.'

'Because I wanted no trace of what my father had done left behind. The woman, his whore, her mother, was easy to find. Selling herself on the streets, all I had to do was present myself as a customer – without my father to pay her bills she'd gone back to the only work she was fit for – and strangle her in her brothel bed. The child' – his face twists – 'saw me and ran. Didn't report me, however.' He shrugs.

I think about Freddie and her distrust of authority – of men in general – no wonder she wouldn't have approached the Constable. 'And you just kept trying to hunt her down.'

'Child's like a rat, slips through cracks in the street, disappears like smoke.'

'And she gave you the slip again, just outside the border gate.' I say it firmly as if it's a fact, in the hope he won't contradict me. And he doesn't, just looks even angrier. 'Jack, when the Anchorhold does what it's going to do, it will walk out into the world and turn every human into cattle.'

'Not me, it promised to let me join the Leech Lords, become one of them – that I'd live forever.' His gaze is mad, his stare glassy.

'But you're hiding down here, Jack Seven-Gates, in the bowels of a disused abbey. Hiding from the monster. Neither friend nor ally to your cause.'

'It doesn't like failure. I failed to catch you or kill you.' He scratches at his neck. 'I'm lucky to be alive.'

'Have you seen it? The Lord of the Anchorhold?'

He shakes his head. 'Its steward, Viktor, speaks to it, for it, gives orders.'

'Why wouldn't you just flee, Jack? Why stay here?'

'Hope. Hope of advantage. That I might yet be made immortal.'

'But you won't be able to go back home. You won't be able to cross the border again, once you're a Leech. You can't walk in the sun again.'

He grins. 'When the Anchorhold brings down the barrier, we'll cross through into other lands and use them as grazing. I can go home to St Sinwin's, wealthy and eternal, bring the city to heel. Have my very own cornucopia! I've already started extending my influence to the docks, right under the nose of that idiot Harbour Mistress.'

'You. The smuggling…' I look at the candles, which have burned down, check my pocket-watch. Dawn will have broken. It's as safe as it's ever going to be here. For me to do what I need to do. I rise and relight my lantern, shoulder my pack, and switch my grip on the dagger. Jack Seven-Gates is no threat to me; I can snap his neck like it's a twig rather than dirty my blade on him.

'Where are you going?'

'To the Anchorhold, to do what it fears I'm here to do.' I put my hand on the key in the lock, turn it. 'And you, Jack Seven-Gates, are staying here. Maybe someone will find you, maybe no one will.'

I take the key from the lock, intending to shut him in from the outside. But when I open the door, I'm briefly blinded by the flare of someone else's lantern. I blink and blink until I can make out a slim silhouette. The expected attack doesn't come, only a soft voice.

'Violet. I've waited so long to meet you, sister.'

38

The figure in the corridor is slight and shorter than me, the voice light – a boy's, not yet broken – and that's all I can distinguish.

'Get that lantern out of my face,' I snarl. Immediately the light is lowered.

'Oh. I'm so sorry. I didn't think. It's because I'm shorter than you. I am sorry.'

'Step back.'

He does, but only a pace, nothing significant. 'A place has been prepared for you, Violet. A better one than this. Come along, please.'

I don't move.

'I'm asking nicely, sister. If you don't comply, I'm afraid these gentlemen will offer assistance, and they're not gentle *despite* what the title implies.'

It's only then I notice two other figures, stepping from the shadows where their black uniforms have hidden them. Day-runners. I wonder if they were part of Jack's cadre, throw a glance over my shoulder but catch only his expression of blank humiliation. Were they his troop taken by Rikke and Adlisa outside of Aegir's Hold – the thought *No* makes me smile. No one would have entrusted hardened fighters, experienced day-runners, to Jack Seven-Gates. My sight's returning to normal and I stare at the boy in front of me. His features begin to make sense, almost.

Black shiny hair, high hollow cheeks, large dark eyes, Cupid's bow lips, skin the colour of snow. My mother's face. Clear as the nose on my own face, those features are the same. Generally soft and sweet with only a slight masculinity to them; with that long hair he'd pass as a girl if he dressed in a gown. He's as beautiful as Vesper ever was, how she lives in my memory. Much prettier than me.

'Sister?' The pitch remains the same, but I sense a threat in it. Strange, the lack of modulation in his tone. He's dressed like a lad, in black trews, shirt and a waistcoat. No jacket, no breastpin. Presumably he doesn't need anything to make him stand out in this place.

'Don't call me that.' I step through the door.

'Your weapons, Violet, please.' Tiberius nods to the nearest day-runner who seizes my pack, while the other pats me down. He finds the knife in my boot and the sacred silver dagger up my sleeve. How I wish he were a Leech and careless with it, thinking it mere silver, and setting himself alight with an accidental touch. Tiberius asks, 'Anything else?'

I shrug, feel the ache in my left arm, shake my head, and say 'No' for good measure.

'Good girl.'

If I thought I could get away with it, I'd punch him in his pretty, pretty face, but it's best that I appear obedient for as long as I can. This, I think, is better; I'll be taken where I need to go rather than wandering around these halls, making sure I follow the map in my head. Or I hope I will.

I look at the child and all I can feel in the very core of me is hatred.

Having never met him before, not growing up with him, neither learning to love nor tolerate him, there's nothing but hatred. Hatred for a younger sibling, for a mewling needy creature that I had no say in, the responsibility for whom was imposed upon me – the same, I suppose, as if he had lived. If we had grown up in the same house. There's a natural resentment in all older children, given the burden of caring for those who come after us even though we're still children ourselves.

Tiberius Zennor, whose birth and death took both my parents from me – even though my father's body remained, he was not the man I'd known. He was not the father who'd loved me, told me stories, sang me songs, brought home tiny sweet treats for me whenever he could, who held me when I cried, washed scraped knees, climbed trees to retrieve abandoned kites so we could fly them on spring days while Vesper watched on.

He lost himself – a process that started, I suspect, when he realised that Tiberius was not his, was the product of a union, willing or otherwise, between his wife and a Leech. When he saw the hollowed-out mess Tiberius had made of his beloved Vesper. When the cloaked man appeared and offered to take the loathed newborn-newdead away, not only making it disappear, but paying a large fortune for it.

Then I think about Jack Seven-Gates, stalking his half-sister through the streets of St Sinwin's, hoping to murder her so all the shame of his father's acts might be washed away in a red tide.

Making it impossible for the little girl to sleep in one place for more than a night, keeping her alert every moment because the one person left in her life who shared her blood wanted to spill it. And I feel ashamed to think we're not entirely different, Jack and me. No less resentful, but ashamed.

'You,' Tiberius calls past me. 'You come too, Jack Seven-Gates, you've a charge to answer. Come along, Violet, my master wishes to meet you. He thinks, perhaps, it's better that he did not succeed in having you killed; that your friend has proved so useless as an executioner.'

And I think about how he knew Rikke was here in his home, and later even Adlisa, so old and clever and quiet. How could I think he'd not know I was here? Or that snivelling Jack Seven-Gates hid down in the bowels of this once-sanctified space? Tiberius tosses both of my daggers back into the room, they clatter on the bare floor, and we are invited to follow my brother.

* * *

Tiberius leads us along corridor after corridor, staircase after staircase and I'm amazed by the size of the place. I suppose I shouldn't be, having seen it from the outside, having studied the map, but it seems to take forever before we're at a level where windows puncture the walls and grey light comes through. The landscape beyond the glass looks no less frozen in the day. Down there, far below, is the black smudge of the carriage, one lantern missing. Neither Tiberius nor his escort flinch at the touch of the light; not Leeches, nor becoming them. So, is my brother as human as he ever was?

We pass through enormous kitchens, libraries, past more cells for contemplation, an apothecary's room, an infirmary wing, an internal herb garden – surprisingly green and abundant – a lavatorium, a dining room, warming room, more dormitories and I wonder just how many battle-nuns once lived here. There are some few day-runners, gathered idly at certain spots, in some spaces, watching as our procession passes. At last we step out of the abbey and into a courtyard. In the centre of this courtyard is a cathedral – bigger and more magnificent even than the one in Lodellan, which I once saw as a child. It lies at the heart of St Catherine's of the Wheel, of the Anchorhold.

The day-runners push the double doors open – carved ebony and embellished with gold – and we move inside, down the very long aisle, footsteps echoing on the mosaic floors and their inlaid gems; carved stone pillars reach to a ceiling lost in shadows, a sculptural forest. Tiberius looks neither left nor right, while my head is almost swivelling to take everything in, Jack's doing the same; Tiberius is presumably used to it all. The stained glass in the windows is mostly intact, but there are breaches where the design has been shattered, and almost all of the pale birch pews have been smashed to splinters. Ahead, there are two pulpits, carved in the shape of trees – we walk between them towards the altar, a pristine slab of white marble. The day-runners steer Jack and me to the left of the altar, towards a door so simple and unembellished that it looks out of place in all this grandeur. Tiberius matter-of-factly pulls a large brass key from his pocket and fits it into the lock.

'The Lord will be with us momentarily.'

The Lord. Not "my" lord.

'It's daylight,' I say.

'Quite so. And if he were anything other than what he is, if he were ordinary, that would be a problem. But the Lord is different and so is the space in which he resides. An anchorhold, you may be aware, is usually built so that an anchorite or anchoress who's chosen seclusion can watch the rituals of their brethren and sistren, partake of mass – although this one has no such access. It's built above the nave so that the one who lives here can watch over proceedings. The space is meant to be removed, although not entirely, from earthly things.' Tiberius turns the key, the lock clicks, the door pops open. 'Please, follow me.'

As if I have a choice.

The day-runners take up position by the door; Jack limps past me, past Tiberius, drops into a seat at the table.

The room into which we step is relatively small, perhaps sixteen feet by sixteen feet – although probably much larger than most other such spaces created for this purpose. The long, highly polished table has seating for ten. Light comes from sconces on the walls; there are no windows but there is a lightwell in the ceiling and pale sun pours down. There are sideboards, empty but for some bronze statuettes and busts, some vases of colourful blown glass and copper bowls – again, hardly the standard décor for a locus of seclusion. The floors are grey stone, no rugs to soften footfalls. At the far wall is another altar, also of marble, but smaller. One of the sidewalls has a large hearth in it, a fire blazing hot enough to make me sweat; I take off my cloak. No one comments on the blood on my left sleeve; no one cares. On the wall opposite the fireplace is hung the wheel of St Catherine and, although none of her daughters exist anymore to turn it, a man has been tied to it.

Strangely familiar, that handsome face, although he didn't look like this the last time I saw him. The cloaked man, the man who came to my father, offered him so much money he could buy another life, a better one for himself and his remaining child. The man who never saw me peeking down from my little loft room – perhaps if he had he'd not be in his current position. His eyes are slitted, his breathing is terribly shallow, he's naked but for a cloth draped over his loins, and in both ankles have been fitted brass spigots to funnel the blood for a fussy drinker. He's become a winepress, literally. An act of torture and frugality. How long has he been like that?

Tiberius must notice the intensity of my gaze, my curiosity and says, 'This is the price of incompetence.'

I drift over and touch the man's skin – dry and fevered – but avoid the spigots, and he groans, shifts. The ropes that hold him to the wheel creak as he struggles weakly, but they hold. His eyes open, he stares at me, groans.

'He was instructed to take the boy, whether he lived or otherwise, and find any other children, kill them lest something like this happen,' Tiberius states matter-of-factly, pointing at me when he says "this". 'But you didn't, did you? Viktor?'

There's a lift in my brother's voice, a spite and a bitterness that feels entirely too personal; strange to hear after his lack of tone every other time he's spoken.

'How long has he been like this?'

'Months, since your little friend told us of your existence.'

'Has Viktor tended to you? During your… life? Cared for you?'

Tiberius nods. Yet there's no sign of any old fondness nor gratitude nor sympathy for the suffering man.

'And tell me, Tiberius, how do you come to be *alive*?' I shift my attention from Viktor to my brother. 'I saw you in the emptiness of our mother. I know what you are. What you did to her without intent – I know it was your nature.'

'The Lord of the Anchorhold had a plan for me. He has powers you cannot even begin to imagine. He will bring a new age.'

'Ah.'

My brother tilts his head as if listening to something no one else can hear. 'He comes.'

There's a creak and a scrape and the top of the altar – a crypt, in fact – begins to move, cantilever sideways. An extended moment, painful, then a hand appears, white as bone, almost as thin, with glassy nails almost as long as the very fingers themselves.

39

A bald head follows, face almost featureless, the sort of strange smoothness that comes to healed skin after a great and deep burning. Eyes filled with night. A length of white fangs protrudes, hanging over the bottom lip, rather like Rikke and Adlisa, but his even longer; he, even older. Narrow shoulders, a plain black robe. It – he – the Lord of the Anchorhold – climbs from the tomb, lizard-like. I half-expect a forked tongue to appear, tasting the air, seeking prey. There's no athletic leap up and out; no floating, nor levitation like some holy resurrection. No. A creeping, a crawling, almost a slithering, over the edge of the stone box, robe flapping to show off knobbly knees, thin legs, hairless thighs, and thankfully nothing else.

Standing before me, it – he – is tall and thin. I notice two fingers missing on one hand and he walks with a limp. Leather sandals on splayed feet, a rope belt at the waist like it's holding together the neck of a sack. He gives me a passing glance, curious and irked, then looks at Tiberius, smiles fondly.

'Sit, my boy. You've done so well. Rest.' The voice is low and rasping, a hasp pulled along a piece of wood. Tiberius flops into one of the chairs at the table, as if exhausted by his endeavours. The Lord's attention turns to Jack, now sitting upright and terribly still, across from my brother. The Lord of the Anchorhold frowns. 'A disappointment.'

Jack's expression says, *Please, I can explain*, and his mouth follows suit. But the Leech Lord's taking no excuses. His gesture seems one of mere dismissal but it's something else, a signal the day-runners appear to know of old. They surge forward, one draws a knife, grabbing Jack's hair and pulling his head backwards; the other grabs a copper bowl from one of the sideboards. Before my childhood friend can utter a single word in his own defence, the knife is travelling across his throat, the room smells of iron, and the bowl is filling with Jack Seven-Gates's last gasp of life.

I don't know what to do but watch as Jack empties out. My funny, treacherous, venal friend.

I can only stare as a day-runner gingerly carries the brimming bowl to the Lord of the Anchorhold. Stare as the other tenderly pushes Jack forward in his chair until his forehead rests on the tabletop where the last of his blood pools then drips to the floor, seeping between the gaps in the flagstones. Stare as the Leech Lord takes the bowl and drinks greedily until there's nothing left but dribbles down his chin, droplets falling onto his robe and losing themselves in the darkness of the warp and weft. I wonder how much of the fabric is stiff with dried leavings. Tiberius hasn't moved since he sat; how many times has he witnessed this sort of thing? Facilitated it?

When he finally hands back the container, the Lord burps. I can smell the stench of it even from six feet away.

'You,' he says, taking the seat at the head of the table, 'have caused me no end of trouble and strife.'

'I'm sure my father would commiserate with you.' I remain standing. He gestures again to the day-runner closest to me, who forces me into a chair. But there's no knife, no bowl. Not yet.

'Your father. Oath-breaker. Bargain-shatterer.' He shakes his head. 'After all I did for him. The life I gave him. All that money from my coffers.'

'You mean the coffers of St Catherine's? Which you stole when you came here. Slaughtered them.' It's a guess but it hits the mark; he swipes aside the comment, though.

'Your father, the liar. Promising there was no other child. And yet there you were, a little fly in the ointment. Had I known about you – had I been able to trust my own people' – he gives Viktor a sour glance – 'I'd have had you slaughtered then.'

'But you didn't know. Didn't know about me.' I tap a finger on the tabletop. 'Yet you knew about my brother. How? You couldn't have fathered him – still too weak from your great burning.' I hazard a guess again, am rewarded.

'When I was mortal, I knew of this place and I knew of the library here – I had once been allowed access for my studies. A mage always looks for prophecies, we can use them to our own advantage. Such places, like the Citadel at Cwen's Reach, exchange copies of their tomes in return for ones they do not have. At some point, such an exchange happened between St Catherine's nuns and St Florian's Little Sisters; the prophecy of the evening song and the saint of the waters was in it, but I didn't find it until after. After the change, and the burning, after years in agonised sleep, neither dying nor living but always in pain, after the witches shut us in… I read it eventually.' He sighs wearily.

'And I did not take the battle-nuns all at once: there were so many I drew it out for years and years.' He reaches over to caress my brother's cheek; Tiberius doesn't react. 'But when I found that prophecy, I began to dream of something larger. Of leaving the Darklands when I was healed. I'm a mage, the greatest there's ever been – I knew what was needed was an in-between thing. There were experiments, failures, false starts, but I have had spies sewn into other noble houses for the longest time, though they did not know to whom they reported, who paid their gratuities.' He sniggers, waggles a finger at me. 'So, when I heard what the fine Lord Corentin did when your pretty mother was foolish enough to return to the Darklands to nurse her own mother.' He shrugs. 'I just knew. I *knew*.'

'And you waited until the time was near and sent Viktor to find us.'

'You weren't hard to find, your mother's family were more than happy to give an address when Viktor asked politely.' He laughs.

'Why the worry about there being another child?' While I now know of the rest of the prophecy, Rikke kept the only copy for herself.

The creature shrugs. 'To diminish chances of interference.' He points at me, the "interference". 'Not drawing attention has ever been my primary concern. I could have had Viktor slaughter your father and take the child. But that would have led to an investigation. We might simply have stolen the corpse, but steal such a thing and people will pursue it on a matter of principle. Buy that corpse? Make a parent a conspirator? Why, you can do almost whatever you want then. It silences them. Give them a fortune and they will drown themselves in excess and guilt.'

'Or the guilt will force them to confess and they'll spent the rest of their life trying to atone. Or forcing the remaining child to do so.'

'Poor little Violet,' he croons.

I change tack. 'It's day. How are you awake? How are you in the light?' He's avoided the direct glare from above, I've noticed that, but he's not flinching, doesn't seem fearful of it as a Leech should be.

The smile again, superior. *I know more than you. Will I share or won't I?*

But he likes too much to appear clever.

'As I told you, an anchorhold – an ordinary one – is a between place.' As he speaks, my mind catches on that *I*. Not him; Tiberius. 'A place where someone chooses to put themselves in limbo, a state being neither one thing nor the other. A religious person chooses to be neither alive nor dead – between earth and heaven. A conduit between two places or modes or existences.'

'Like the Leeches are dead in life. Like my brother is, an in-between thing, neither dead nor alive, but a little of both.'

'Smart girl. Because an anchorhold – my anchorhold, *The Anchorhold* – is neither one place nor the other, neither alive nor dead, it exists outside of day and night. Therefore, its light cannot hurt me.' He smiles again, wider, even more smug. 'You might live forever, Violet Zennor. Girls like you would do well to put your cleverness to better use, in the service of someone else.'

'Girls like Murciana?' His expression changes, as if slapped. She remains unforgotten by him, that defiant little escapee.

I continue: 'Her name is still sung, yet no one remembers the mage who tried to steal secrets from the Little Sisters of St Florian.'

'Dead and dust now, every one of those bitch Sisters.'

'Yet one of those bitch Sisters did this to you, turned your own spell on you. And their descendants live on, their work lives on, spread throughout the world like seeds on a breeze.' I lean forward. 'And here you are, the greatest mage that ever lived, trapped in a tiny room in a cathedral in the Darklands.'

'You're very mouthy for someone who's soon to die,' he sneers.

'Oh, no more offers of immortality? I'm crushed.' I glance at Tiberius once more. 'What did you do to him?'

'He was simple enough to resurrect once delivered by Viktor, and has provided raw matter over the years for experiments and spells. I've tested pieces of his flesh in homunculi dung heaps, seeing what grew. Even in the womb of a pig. Ultimately, though, the original was the superior artefact, properly aged and developed. Oh, don't worry – waste not, want not. The failures were fed to newer versions. And I must confess a few choice morsels found their way to my very own plate. I believe it will ultimately make the process go more smoothly.'

I don't look at the Leech, but I do stare at Tiberius, the thing of his flesh, the thing with his face. My brother hasn't said anything in quite some time, nor moved. Not since the magister climbed out of his box. I squint at the boy – the expression slack, eyes dull, one hand in his lap, the other hanging by his side. No animation at all. In fact, I can barely see his chest moving with breath.

'It was you,' I say softly. 'You all along, controlling the puppet. He's a husk. There's nothing of my brother there but the flesh.'

He grins. 'Said you were smart, didn't I.'

'Tiberius is a shell, a meat-puppet, and you're going to slip inside him. Transfer your mind into a functioning, new body that's never suffered damage – and never been a Leech, won't be affected by the wards and spells of the witches' border. You've never really fully recovered, have you? Centuries of sleep and hibernation, oceans of blood to feed your rejuvenation, yet here you are, still with a limp, still with fingers missing. That burning should have killed you.'

He's staring at me, eyes half-hooded, waiting to see where my mind goes.

'And you've made bargains with the Leeches who'll listen, just like you made bargains with an idiot like Jack, and if you couldn't do that, you destroyed them – displays of power to cow the others, bring them to heel. What have you promised? That you'll set them all free, break the boundary and let them feast to their heart's content on the lands beyond the gate.' I feel a grin start on my face, unwilling, instinctive, too horrible, like laughing at a funeral; but almost immediately there's a pain in my palm as something erupts through the flesh and skin. I make a fist, try not to let the agony show. 'But that's a lie. Only you'll be able to pass through the border in your new flesh – neither human nor Leech, neither alive nor dead, an in-between, a crossing place. Your own personal, ambulatory anchorhold. You'll be free of the curse of Leechdom, you'll make your way back out into the world, laughing, with all the magic you've learned, and you'll leave the great houses behind. You've promised them freedom and fat fresh pastures, but you'll forget them as soon as blinking. You've sent a legion or two of day-runners out to wait for you, a welcoming party. But it'll just be you feasting to your heart's content because I can't imagine you'd give up the blood while you conquer the world.'

'Too clever by half, but I've one last use for you,' he growls and rises, gesturing to the day-runners, who move in on me. I kick my chair back, falling with it, avoiding the grabbing hands, hit the ground and roll to my feet. The first day-runner I punch in the throat, leave him gasping while I pull the dagger from his belt, its blade still damp with Jack Seven-Gates's blood. I spin about, slash at the other day-runner, tear into his jugular, then pivot to stab the other man who's still struggling for breath. Then I face the Magister.

The Leech Lord laughs, begins to approach with measured steps. 'A silly little knife? Do you really think that will have much effect on me? Before I can drink you down and repair the damage? Your other little toy is so far away…'

'No,' I say. 'But prophecies are funny things and one needs to have faith.'

And he's rushing at me now, doesn't slow down, doesn't think me a threat as I bring my left arm up and hit him in the jaw. We both scream in pain.

Eira Briar suggested the cuts in my forearm from feeding the blade during its making might have another use. There was a risk, she warned, of infection – but I thought it worth it. Each cut was sewn with wild rose thorns. Each thorn tipped with the last of the molten O'Malley silver and ground up witch-bone dust.

A thing that would grow on and in me, a living weapon.

The thorns that have pressed through the linen of my shirt. The tears in the Magister's face are not healing as he windmills his arms and falls backwards. I follow him down, beating and punching him, raking the thorns across his throat, watching as his flesh is eaten away, disappearing before my eyes. A hand grabs my hair, reefs my head back. I stare up into Tiberius's face, the magister's eyes blinking in and out of the puppet as he tries to transfer himself for good. I bring the dagger up and plunge it into my brother's heart – silver or not, it has the desired effect on a body that's all too human.

The shadow of the Magister leaves Tiberius's eyes. The Leech's body on the floor in front of me writhes and writhes until, at last, I punch down hard into the chest that's become friable, break through the ribcage and wrap my thorn-clad palm around the heart that should have died a long time ago. I squeeze.

Then I'm kneeling in a pile of dust and rapidly cooling embers.

40

I found my way out of the Anchorhold, out of the place that was a threshold, neither one thing nor the other, the liminal place between life and death – surprised to find myself still alive. Or mostly. My arm was aching, though I'd heated water in a copper bowl over the fire and poured in the lavender disinfectant Eira Briar had given me and washed the tiny sharp wounds thoroughly. When I was done, I granted the man on the wheel's wish, and put him out of his misery. Part of me considered leaving him to suffer for his part in all this, but I knew that the cruelty would haunt me, and I supposed there'd be enough things to wake me up screaming for the rest of my life. I rolled his body and Tiberius's into the enormous hearth to burn but did not stay to watch. The day-runners and Jack Seven-Gates I left where they'd fallen.

As I made my way through the battle abbey, back down the way we'd come, I found no more day-runners, all strangely fled during my time in that tiny crossing space between life and death. In the little room where I'd waited the last hours before dawn, I collected the dagger of O'Malley silver because it was too rare and precious to throw away even though I'd not used it for its purpose. Besides, who knew what I might encounter on my way back to the gate?

And when I got to the great cavern with all those coffins? Where night-runners should have been sleeping? Empty but for piles of ash and dust which had not been there when I'd passed through the first time. The entire enormous edifice was deserted.

I found Ned the Nondescript had returned to the carriage, chewing on the meagre green pickings in discontent, but no sign of the beasts that Adlisa and Rikke reckoned coach horses. There wasn't even dust or crumbling bones – perhaps they'd died when the two women did, their summoners gone from the earth.

The picnic basket remained untouched in the carriage, and I fed my beastie one of the two apples remaining and ate the other myself. I had a week to traverse the Darklands, to return to the wide, wide world beyond them, surely I'd find someone to sell me food in that time. Perhaps medicine. I put my foot in the stirrup and mounted, setting off without a backward glance.

The first day on the road went well enough. Drinking cold clear water from streams, riding in bursts of an hour or two. That day, I saw no one. Camped in an old church, but only after a very careful recce. I woke with a fever, with my left arm barely willing to move in its socket, but I rode again for shorter periods (with greater struggles to re-mount each time).

And I began to notice things.

The land was in disarray, villages and estates when I encountered them at last, were filled with frightened folk. I spoke to a woman in the marketplace of a small town, one of those where Adlisa and Rikke had slaked their thirst on the inn's winepresses. Their Lord and his retainers were all gone. Turned to dust sometime during the previous day.

The further I rode, the more I heard the same story. Overlords, good and bad, gone without so much as a warning. The woman saw the sigil of the Anchorhold still on my ragged cloak and asked if I knew of anything – had I noticed anything similar *there*. I told a little lie, that the bastion had been empty when I arrived, that I'd searched it from top to bottom and found no sign of either master or servants, retainers or assassins. It was as much a mystery to me as to her. I took the breastpin off after that. When folk are scared it's never a good time to admit you were responsible for their lives falling apart. Not all of the Leech Lords were cruel and rapacious. Some, like Adlisa, had been kind, looked after their people, a fair exchange of blood for a living, protection. Many would not thank me for what I'd done.

I'd not thought that destroying the magister would destroy all the Leeches, but the more I considered it, the more sense it made. He had created the first of the kind: the Lord and Lady of Caulder. He, like they, had been made what he was by *magic*. It was not a naturally occurring thing in nature, not an evolution from one form into another, but an enchantment and not all magics last forever. The Leeches, then, were products of that magic, a red thread that linked them. I pondered Adlisa's words, the idea that some of what Leeches are might remain in our blood, those progeny of rare successful matings between the one and the other. I wonder if she's right, if the strain endures, and how strong it might be. I'm glad to have retrieved the dagger.

Eventually, the Darklands and its people would settle. New rulers would rise, probably from amongst the castellans and mayors who'd helped the Leech Lords keep order. Those who knew that life had to continue on, that there were people to feed, industries to run if an economy was to be maintained. That people needed to live. And, eventually, they would realise that their world had been made anew, and there was a freedom in losing everything that had held them in place for so many years.

That there would be choices.

Decisions to be made.

Consequences to be borne.

A fresh start to be had.

* * *

I keep riding though my fever's rising and rising, occasionally swapping the sweats out for shivering tremors. Delirious, I continue through the night, or most of it, somehow clinging to the saddle until we come to a dark shape that I seem to recognise.

Adlisa and Rikke's ruin of a home.

And I think that if I'm to die, this feels like the best place to do it. Where I was rescued and aided, where I met friends and allies who gave up everything they were to help me. The logic is fuzzy, I know, I cannot quite grasp hold of it, it's not a firm and certain substance, but then nor is my mind as I get sicker and sicker.

I half-fall off the horse, spark the carriage lamp (I decanted the remaining oil from the others before I left), find my way to the hole beneath the vines, and slither my way inside. The mushroom patch feels soft still, but I don't stay there. I force myself up and find the staircase, rising, rising, rising until I'm in the room where I woke to Rikke and her writing. The book is still on the table, open, but I can't make head nor tail of it, cannot get the letters to stand still long enough to read.

I kick off my boots, drag off my jacket, then my shirt and look at the mess of my arm in the light of the lantern. It's all I can do to kindle a very small fire in the hearth to fend off the worst of the chill. One of the bottles of tincture Rikke had given me for the arrow wound waits on the table. I swallow almost all of it, then stumble to the bed with its damp-feeling, damp-smelling linens – and nothing's ever seemed so welcoming – and I roll myself on the mattress, beneath the covers and promptly fall into sleep or death, I don't really care which.

* * *

I dream I'm on a ship, rocked to and fro by the waves, the sound of a wild wind clamouring in my ears. Then the storm gets worse and I'm being tossed hither and yon and the clamouring is getting louder and louder – until I wake up to find myself not in the bed I began in, but on a narrow bench bed, being shaken to consciousness. I cry out.

A voice from outside – Rab's, and with recognition comes a rush of warmth – says almost severely, 'Freddie, you didn't wake her, did you?'

'Nooooo. She was having a nightmare.' And a shame-faced Freddie is hovering over me. Behind her head I can see the bare ribs of a wagon's curved ceiling, see the hanging things that Edgar stocked his vehicle with, the stacks of shiny fabrics he'll use to tempt seamstresses and rich women, the glass bottles of spices and salts and powders for cooks and witches and poisoners.

'You little liar,' I whisper hoarsely. 'I was having a perfectly peaceful sleep.'

And there's a Freddie-shaped lump on top of me, and hot tears splashing on my neck where she's buried her face, and it's the most wonderful sensation in the world. 'He's gone,' I tell her, 'your brother's gone and he'll never bother you again. You're safe. You're safe with me.'

* * *

Later, a little later when Rab convinces Edgar to stop and I'm carried out, protesting but not very loudly, to sit in the sun while the grumbling gentleman-merchant kindles a fire and makes coffee, I hold onto Rab Cornish like he's my last hope. He tells me I'm lucky to still have my left arm, that Eira Briar sent them with every manner of potion and powder she could, knowing what might have happened after the spell she'd put in me. They'd spotted my horse as they followed the route Edgar had discussed with me back in Silverton.

They'd set off when word began to filter through of the disappearance of the Leech Lords. Edgar found his courage again and, curious as to the fate of Rikke and Adlisa, volunteered to help find me. They'd stayed in the ruined mansion for three days, watching me hover between life and death, in my own personal anchorhold. Debated whether or not to cut off my arm, but by the end of the second day the thorns and their roots had withered in my flesh and begun to fall out onto the sheets. The next morning my fever was gone, but I still didn't wake. Rab decided it was time to start home, to get me to the Briars as soon as possible.

I cry as he tells me this, and so does he. I tell him all I did – *all* of it, whether it makes him love me less or fear me, I don't care. I tell him that I killed my brother, or what had once been my brother; how I killed Viktor and the day-runners; how I pounded the heart of the Magister to dust. Essentially beating him to death.

How I slaughtered an entire species, for good or ill.

And he doesn't look away from me.

He tells me he loves me and I whisper *Rab-rab-rabbit* in his ear, and when Freddie dances over to us, a daisy-chain between her fingers, we pull her to us and enfold her in a family.

AUTHOR'S NOTE

I was determined for a very long time to never write a vampire story. Just as I was also determined to never write a Jack the Ripper story. Yet here we are, with a vampire novel and several vampire tales in my bibliography (not to mention a Jack the Ripper novella floating around).

The lesson is "Never say never".

My first vampire story in the Sourdough world was "The Night Stair" which appeared in *The Bitterwood Bible and Other Recountings* (and which will be reprinted by Titan in 2026). Having decided to write (at last) about vampires, I didn't actually want to call them "vampires", because while the Sourdough world is a reflection of ours, it's not the same. Plus, I am contrary.

So I picked at what I knew about vampire lore – which is a LOT because I've been reading about them since the beginning of forever – and worked out which bits I really liked, really didn't like, and what seemed to be indispensable. That's how I ended up with the Leech Lords who rule The Darklands – and then I left them alone for a long time (literally ten years).

When I was brainstorming for this book and Violet Zennor appeared to me, I knew I wanted to have a mix of gothic horror tale, a bit of a *Buffy* aesthetic, a bit of Eco's *The Name of the Rose*, and to dig deeper into my own version of the vampire. So, once again, I wrote a bunch of alternative lore to make my Leech Lords at once familiar but also different. I loved the idea of a land where the Leeches had generally reached an accommodation with the human population – because I'm also fascinated by how people tolerate bad situations for a very long time (so I guess *The Crimson Road* is also a bit of a study of cognitive dissonance as well as a warning tale!).

And while it might seem everything is over for the Leech Lords, remember: the vampire always rises again.

ACKNOWLEDGMENTS

With gratitude as ever to my parents Betty and Peter, siblings Michelle and Roderick, housedads Ron and Stephen, also to my agent Meg Davis, my editor Cath Trechman, publicists Katharine Carroll and Bahar Kutluk, and the whole team at Titan for bringing another lovely book into the world. A huge thanks to Natasha MacKenzie for the glorious cover. And thank you to Tartarus Press, who published the original mosaic collections set in the Sourdough world.

ABOUT THE AUTHOR

A.G. SLATTER has won a Shirley Jackson Award, a World Fantasy Award, a British Fantasy Award, a Ditmar, three Australian Shadows Awards and eight Aurealis Awards. Most recently, *All the Murmuring Bones* was shortlisted for the 2021 Queensland Premier's Literary Awards Book of the Year and the 2021 Shirley Jackson Award; *The Path of Thorns* won the 2022 Aurealis Award for Best Fantasy Novel and the 2022 Australian Shadows Award for Best Novel. She has an MA and a PhD in Creative Writing and is a graduate of Clarion South 2009 and the Tin House Summer Writers Workshop 2006. Angela's short stories have appeared in many Best Of anthologies, and her work has been translated into many languages. She lives in Brisbane, Australia with a superannuated beagle and two very patient housedads. Angela can be found at angelaslatter.com, on Facebook as *angelaslatterauthor*, on Instagram as *@angelaslatter*, and on the app formerly known as Twitter as *@AngelaSlatter*.

For more fantastic fiction, author events,
exclusive excerpts, competitions, limited editions and more

VISIT OUR WEBSITE
titanbooks.com

LIKE US ON FACEBOOK
facebook.com/titanbooks

FOLLOW US ON TWITTER AND INSTAGRAM
@TitanBooks

EMAIL US
readerfeedback@titanemail.com